STAR HORIZON

JAMES GREGORY CHAPMAN

Library of Congress number: 2056321458896

Library of Congress Cataloging in Publication Data

Names: Chapman, James, author

Title: Star Horizon / James Gregory Chapman

Description: First Edition

Series: Chronicles of the Cosmic Song Book 1

URL: jamesgregorychapman.com

ISBN hardcover: 979-8-9912887-1-2

ISBN eBook: 979-8-9912887-2-9

ISBN paperback: 979-8-9912887-0-5

ISBN audio: 979-8-9912887-3-6

Dedication

This book is dedicated to Anthony Pryor, my beloved husband and friend, who passed away in 2023. We spent hundreds of nights reading to each other, and his spirit inhabits these pages.

Epigraph

Through grief, we often find our bliss. Through the fall from grace, we often find our salvation. The process remains a mystery, but nonetheless, the truth of it shouts with tears of joy.

Life steals. As a defense, we surround ourselves with pretty things and lose ourselves to cluttered thoughts. But life continues to steal--to the last breath it steals--until all that's left is who we are.

Regard this life of illusion. Death begins at the moment of birth, as with every babe, so too with the universe. We exist as mirrors to this ultimate truth: we are not here to live but to die, and in the process in-between, find a way beyond reflections.

CHAPTER I

What does it mean to be human when trapped in a life of cold and silence? Emotion roiled Kor's thoughts in vivid color, for tonight, he hoped to catch at least the most fleeting glimpse of what life could be outside the cage—as the future ordained for him, and others like him, was the giving of death.

Beneath the streets, with sewers and night crawlers as neighbors, Kor clutched the hand of his close friend with an excited flutter. Shadowy figures milled about in the bare flicker of light in a rectangular, club-sized space that had no address or name. Other green-bloods—boys under twenty without combat experience—dashed in from narrow entrances that appeared in fleeting flashes of light almost too quick for the eye to catch. Sections of the wall slid sideways, up and down, as the way in shifted to avoid detection. None of them had ascended to manhood. Ascension was a terrible day of ritual and celebration when, forever after, duty and responsibility must govern the rest of their blood-soaked lives.

"We come to share in the dream, brothers," a resonant voice said. "We come here to discover our true selves, to celebrate a taste of freedom, to claim our equality with our masters who created us, if only in small measure—to strengthen our shields against the killing fields on foreign worlds we face by the orders of the Starry Empire. Zorn, our home, must become more than a world of subset human slaves."

A counter set at thirty minutes and surrounded by a green-lit globe hovered high. The globe's color changed, pulsing yellow and red, spreading and then retreating, leaving a solid, beautiful green. The counter activated, and the seconds melted away.

"Security scans sweep for our presence. Measures are in place to prevent our detection. Our time is short. Those on the way are being diverted back to safety."

"Are you sure about this?" Jude whispered into Kor's ear. "The priests want to crack down on anything they see as subversive. Standard punishments are no longer assured. It's like we're about to dance on a minefield."

"Green means we're safe. And no, I'm not sure. That's part of the fun." *And part of the risk*. Kor's father tolerated the registered clubs, but the underground pop-up events were about as unregistered as life got on Zorn. If enforcers caught Kor, it would mean another night of lashings at the dreaded Punisher whipping post where no man or boy dared to scream.

Jude nuzzled Kor's ear. "You're lucky I like you."

Out of the dark, a stage with a runway popped into existence. Poles of flashing bulbs lit up purple curtains. Wielding a dance baton, Annie Lennox strutted into view in holographic wonder. Big, blue eyes flashed to cage one's soul. Perfection. Pregnant and glorious in a glittering black outfit, she belted out soul-tinged pop lyrics from red-painted lips. Mesmerized, Kor reached out an arm, wanting to touch, wanting to see if she was real, though she had been dead for centuries.

He had never seen a real woman before. Few of his kind ever did until far-off rulers on a distant planet sent them off to places to fight and die. The natural-born, those not engineered and who remained the children of God, created his people for that purpose.

No longer deemed human, dubbed as militants, they served as soldiers as required but were left to themselves until needed, like a valuable commodity put into storage.

Propulsive electronic beats overtook Jude. He pulled Kor away from the stage and twirled him around. Others in showy bodysuits swung their arms and hips in happy celebration. Not to be outdone, Kor's white bodysuit sparkled with reddish-pink sequins, while Jude's matched his bronzed cream-brown skin tone. At first glance, his friend appeared to be naked and the envy of roving eyes.

The counter overhead ticked to twenty-seven. Once it hit zero, the pop-up party would end. Freedom must exist within boundaries. Too bad no one else in their posse had made it in.

The mood shifted, and a black-haired angel sang in a commanding, spacey voice. Slow and grinding, organic and electronic, mind-opening synths pulled Kor into darkness, into brightness. Kor and Jude held each other, rocking back and forth, as Karen O, in post-apocalyptic clothes, rode a car from after the Downfall.

Whatever Earth might have been back then, in parts, her many peoples must have shared a version of Zorn's misery of hanging cages, execution plazas, whipping posts, death matches, and ordeals. The counter neared twenty minutes. A smear of red spread around the green globe. But under the streets, new ways fought to be heard.

"We're spitting at the edge of the world," Kor whispered to Jude as they rubbed noses. Flashing lights overhead, waves of darkness and brightness, pulled them deeper into a moment where the universe went no further than the heat of their flesh.

Jude's dark eyes flashed, and the corners of his supple lips turned up in agreement. "We're dancing on the clouds."

"We're walking on the ocean." Kor drew him in; the illusion of their separation vanished as the beat of one heart vibrated into the other. Kor, with his fair skin, gray eyes, and black hair, the classic features of Clan Steel Rose, and Jude, his future lover, brown bronze, with seductive brown eyes and full luscious lips, heir to Iron Star; a most perfect union between old allies.

Space shrank. Dream and hope merged, and reality took form where no one was a slave, where there were no killing fields, no graveyards of the forgotten, and his kind chose to dance their lives to realms of pure desire where angels sang, and the darkness held no sway. Secret confessions that were never to be uttered, not even to Jude, not to anyone on Zorn, where the impulse for obedience saturated the blood.

Another glorious Earther, a Black woman, materialized in a transition of silence. Whoever developed the playlist shared his passion for the Earthers' music. The back wall showed images of a cylindrical space station as the singer sang "Goodbye" in sultry tones, every syllable easy and yet weighed with importance. Jude sang into Kor's ear, an echo to the singer, over and over. The dream became true, and the outside world faded into a passing nightmare.

"I love you, baby," Jude crooned.

Kor repeated the verse, and dancers drifting around did the same to each other, a moment of unbounded bliss. Imagination unmoored from the accepted way of thinking. His eyes watered, and a headache stabbed against his illicit efforts. The natural-born created his kind to fight, to be obedient without question, and to have no dreams beyond the Code, which decreed their life and their virtue. But the more Kor tasted freedom, the more he wanted.

Red pulses surged across the green globe. Lavender Wreckage, a late-era band featuring five purple-powdered Japanese women, blasted a drifting, bleak angst. *I'm grateful I no longer feel, for the dying world will no longer heal.* The band unleashed their introspective despair. Twelve minutes flashed on the counter in a flurry of mental disruption. The music stopped, and the holograms vanished. Waves of hollow energy drained Kor's bliss.

The resonant voice boomed an urgent alert. "Enforcer unit scans pinged our location. Evacuation begins at once."

The walls parted at four points. Dancers disappeared into well-lit tunnels. Time reshaped into ice-crystal form, frozen and beautiful, and Kor wanted to hold Jude forever.

Jude gave Kor a light shake. "We must leave," Jude said, his tone restrained yet bursting with urgency.

For a fraction, Kor delayed. Jude put on a don't-be-difficult face, and together, they headed to the nearest opening. The dance hall existed within a complex maze with a dozen ways in and out. Run into a dead end, retrace; pivot when the walls move to reveal new paths, don't think, keep moving, and relax into faith. Together, they bounded up a stairwell, confident that the way out had been found. At the top, a corridor led to a plain grayish door.

Kor shoulder-touched Jude in a playful bump, and they shared drops of their sweat. "That was sweet."

Jude grinned, shaking his head, probably unsure of what to think of his crazy boyfriend. He pushed the door open. A dozen white-helmeted enforcers pointed blasters at them. "You're under arrest," one of them said.

Kor moaned a frustrated curse.

"Your father will totally kill you for this," Jude said.

***

The ride home in a windowless black hover-van passed in pensive silence. What could Kor say to Jude? A promise of fun and adventure had turned into a disgrace. To make matters worse, no one else had been caught. Yet another blemish to Steel Rose's virtue.

The enforcers released Kor at the Steel Rose compound gate, high on Heroes Hill. Cruel mountain winds lashed blue-web whispering trees that flanked the boulevard. As far as infractions went, an illegal pop-up party was serious, but his father, the General, had a well-earned reputation for discipline and held standing among the High Clans of Zorn.

"Another of those, and I'll refer you to a Judge," said a white-helmet, his tone flat and sure.

The hover-van glided down the mountain, leaving Kor at the imposing compound gate, a relic from an earlier, bloody age when the Starry Empire had collapsed, and civilization retreated behind walls, shields, and hardened hearts. The General would be waiting for him in the courtyard of lessons. Outer walls, facades, and the central hold itself faded from his attention as he made his way through expansive rose gardens. Heady, uplifting aromas enveloped him and imbued him with faith that the days of pain would end. Underfoot, the crunch of his steps over gravel grounded him deeper into his faith until nothing else seemed to exist. The moments that came—the fall of the lash and the return to his long room—passed in a rose-enriched blur.

The enforcers would have been disappointed had they stayed to witness Kor's welcome home. He rotated his torso to get a better view of his back in one of the bathroom mirrors. Raised, wicked-red welts crisscrossed from his shoulders to his buttocks. One strike for the unregistered event, a minimum blow for disobedience, and five for getting caught—blows to remind him of the price of failure. Shackled to the Punisher, there was nowhere to run, nowhere to hide, and his father's determination to have an obedient son would be tempered but not forgotten. His father was as proper a Militant as anyone to have ever walked on Zorn.

The wounds would heal in a day, one of the genetic gifts of being a Militant. In an echo of Karen O's song, Kor spat in defiance. Fear sought him out from shadows and places where he could not command, trying to snuff out his hope and his faith. If he did as any sane person would do, he would not further test his father's anger . . . at least for a few days. With the fading of his wounds, so too would fade the impulse for radical defiance. Disobedience required his active resentment.

The General had activated a security lockdown. A safe path lay between the bathroom and his bed in the adjoining long room. Stray from the path and earn another round of the lash. The burn of the welts should have pushed wayward thoughts into compliance, but the burn had become common, and it fed his momentary lapse of reason. He had disobeyed too much, and yet, he had not disobeyed enough.

A locker acted as a headboard. From inside, Kor removed a pouch full of fine powder. At the foot of his bunk, he blew the limestone dust. Invisible beams glowed red in a tightly woven grid—one of the General's recent installments, but never before employed, to prevent his trips up the mountain to stargaze and dream without nightmares. As expected, the dense grid would thwart any manner of acrobatic contortion. Worse, the beams changed position at randomized intervals. Escaping by outsmarting the detection grid was impossible. Kor grinned—precisely why months ago, anticipating his father's move, he deposited a virus into the clan's network to go live whenever the General activated the laser grid.

At 2:50 a.m., the sensor grid vanished—a three-second hiccup—long enough for Kor to dash by a parallel row of bunk beds intended for brothers never born. The compound's data room was below grade with an elevated level of security, but as heir to Steel Rose, the biological scans allowed Kor to pass. His presence would be registered and erased, thanks to a stealthy semi-sentient algorithm that he had planted with the virus.

Floating blue-white displays embedded with commands, search tools, and files illuminated the data room. Frigid air circulated, scrubbed of aromas, and filtered of contaminants. Discovery being a constant threat, he danced along the cliff's edge. Stay at the edge, risk the fall, feel the wind, and relish the exuberance. Success at getting the codes was spotty. Silver lines from a new dream whispered encouragement.

A sequence of numbers pinged his armband. Success! The algorithm calculated that the next randomized change would be in five seconds. Jump, leap into the unknown, and change the fates through choice and action. In focused speed, he tapped at one of the floating displays. The panel flashed green. Kor beamed with the delight of pulling off a major heist. Links to the Mesh, where the Earther's Metaverse and the Starry Empire's Macrocosm comingled, became available. Kor's hands moved in a flurry to open an encrypted account within the Earther's dark web.

The seconds accumulated. Was his father watching? Was he waiting to see what diabolical subversion his son had concocted? None of the usual sites had what he wanted, but he grabbed thousands of titles, a hoard to explore. Switching to the riskier Metaverse, he searched for *human.* Preset filters tagged hundreds out of millions of hits. Scan, absorb, be fast, be quick, and make a choice. Something caught his attention—a song—he downloaded it into his account. The title and the group's name held promise.

In a rush, he temporarily deactivated the sensor grid and headed back to bed, the burns lancing his backside—a warning and a reminder of a life he didn't want. He couldn't wait for morning to share the song with Jude and the rest of their posse.

CHAPTER II

Kor burst with radiant energy such that the heads of the trainee-heavy crowd turned their way as he and his posse made their way to their favorite table at the Cliff Ledge Cafe. Purple reds spread across the dawn sky, ariel crowns to the snow-topped mountains dotted with solar sun trees ready to capture energy for the city. Monolithic temples, gyms, assembling halls, residences, compounds, training, and administrative constructions hungered for power. Plazas, parks, and boulevards shaped the city into a pleasing, ordered harmony.

The shrieks and clattering claps of brightly crowned feathered fliers declared their equal importance as they patrolled above. The awesomeness of earth and sky nurtured a faith that would not whither, no matter the pain that burdened his world.

Kor activated a privacy shield around himself and his most trusted friends so that they could share in his crime. The transparent cone canceled sound, an absolute must when breaking the law in a popular cafe full of obedient trainees on their way to the Academy. The Chorus, a triumvirate who ruled the Starry Empire with dystopian verve, had become over-the-top paranoid since Earther ships arrived full of human cousins with a bewildering spectrum of factions, beliefs, and opinions. Prohibited lists multiplied as the Chorus struggled to control the onslaught of outside influences.

An onyx pendant with the head of a hawk and the body of a dragon dangled on Kor's chest, a constant reminder of his belonging to the Steel Rose clan. Would his clan's acceptance withstand his deviant desires to break the rules? A mischievous grin spread across his face.

"I curated a mass download of Earther music." The thrill of sharing a secret infused Kor's voice. "Mostly contraband—guaranteed, if we're caught, to earn us a near-death experience at a whipping post."

Baps, Kor's best friend outside Jude, fidgeted. His golden-skin face tensed. "Hold on; I signed up for nothing worse than a few lashes. How good is this privacy shield?"

"Standard grade. Anything better would attract attention. Try not to look nervous."

Creo of Clan Crew Defiance and Alapaat of Ice Bore exchanged amused smiles. Nicknamed the Pearls, Creo, yin-black, and Alapaat, yang-white, were a tight pair. "Knowing you," Creo said, "we're in fear for our lives."

"But we love you, brother," Alapaat said. "Brotherhoods such as ours are more precious than the most precious stone."

Jude clapped his hands in approval. Dark, playful eyes brightened—the color of wood distilled into a fine bourbon. Jude's brother, Dex, darted his eyes to the other tables, sipping his coffee with his body primed for a fast exit.

"Relax," Kor said, leaning over the table to give Dex a playful arm punch. "We've been coming to this cafe every morning for the past year before training. Nothing strange is going on."

"Surveillance never sleeps," Dex said. "I'm all for a good time, within limits."

Jude gave Dex a light punch on his other arm. "Lighten up, brother. Trainees like us are all around in matching black bodysuits. We're practically clones—all part of the landscape."

Kor rubbed his hands together in sinister anticipation. "Exactly. What better way to start breaking a few rules than by blending in with a routine?"

Creo and Alapaat high-fived Dex, and the three of them relaxed into happy grins.

Baps frowned. "I'm getting a bad feeling. How much risk taints your surprise?"

"A lot." On his second cup, the coffee electrified Kor's excitement, and its fruity and nutty aromas brightened his mood into euphoria. "Human," by the Killers, dared to challenge blind compliance and asked, *Are we human?*"; a question with no acceptable answer, not in his world.

"First, an announcement." Jude shoulder-bumped Kor.

In sync, Kor tore off a piece of pre-cut fabric on his upper right arm, and Jude did the same to his left. Tattoos rippled on brawny muscle. Kor spelled Jude's name within the caress of a vibrant red rose vine while metallic iron stars showered Kor's name on Jude's arm.

Baps's eyes glazed, like the fading of a sunset sky, his emotion unreadable. "It's official then. You're betrothed."

Alapaat, Creo, and Dex whooped and hollered their approval.

Kor and Jude leaned into each other, touched foreheads, and shared their heated coffee breath. For his part, Kor would never have dared such reckless disobedience if not for Jude's encouragement. Though a clan-arranged union, Kor loved Jude and would have chosen no one else. Once anointed men, they exchanged the freedom of youth for servitude, a fate endurable if imbued with love.

"I have a special Earth song to share," Kor said. "Last chance if anyone wants to back out." The posse gathered around the table knew he and Jude had been arrested at the pop-up dance and that those not present avoided that humiliation by being late and missing the fun. Yet they still showed up, whatever their reservations, though they extracted return favors—bargains among friends.

Yellow-white lights in the center of each table transformed into a sea of stars where dreams came to life. Stars in the night sky retreated to their daytime abodes as dawn neared. A group of trainees left a nearby table, but others holding fresh, steaming coffees claimed the prime spot overlooking the grand city below, which was filled with bronze, marble, and granite praises to dead heroes. Spread over a vast caldera, the far side merged into the breastplate of snow-capped mountains stretching into the sky.

Creo grinned and tapped his nose. "Remember your part of the bargain."

"A cliff-dive off Suicide Ledge." Kor gave an amused shake of the head at the things he had sworn to in the name of friendship. But at least the ocean dive would be in almost warm water. Alapaat bargained for a joint plunge into his favorite ice hole. The mere thought of that brought on a shiver.

Jude slid his fingers along his sexy clipped beard, a trendy way to buck social norms. "If we ever get into trouble, I will take your place in a firing squad."

"Not a chance," Kor winked.

"You are a purveyor of miracles," Jude said. "No one in my clan has an uncensored link to the Metaverse. You've earned yourself a candlelight dinner."

Alapaat gave Creo a good-humored punch. "I expect the same, handsome." Creo clasped Alapaat's black-tattooed forearm, a sensuous swirl from his elbow toward his hand—a match to the white swirl on Creo's lustrous oil-black skin. Whenever they brought their mark of betrothal together, everyone knew they were in total agreement.

"You're dangerous and sneaky," Jude said, "and I love you, Mister Daring."

"Aye, I'm all in with you, my amazing, brave partner." Kor brushed a finger over a temporary tattoo on Jude's forehead. Seditious, on the edge of illegal, the slashed, hooked lines resembled the Marshal-priest brands. Wearing such a mark would be viewed as an insult if not profane.

Baps's agate blue eyes intensified with an exotic allure. "My twentieth birthday is next month." The words dropped with flat notes as though he had announced a terminal illness.

"Relish the days you have left," Dex said. Jude's one-year-younger brother was a virtual twin but without a clipped beard. "Duty and death come for us."

"Tomorrow we die! Let's kiss the sky!" Everyone except Baps sang the posse's slogan.

"Time for us to celebrate life while we can," Kor said.

The golden boy of Clan Gallant shook his head in disbelief. "We celebrate death. It is who we are."

"We are who we decide to be if we have the guts to stake our claim." Kor pointed at the sun trees; their petals unfurled to welcome the star rising over the snow-capped mountains. "The sun trees claim their power every day. We should do no less."

"The sun trees serve their function," Baps said, "as we must."

"Like the things we're supposed to be." Kor fought to keep his voice casual, but accusation laced every syllable. The high clans of Zorn ruled within the limits allowed by the Starry Empire, and that limited freedom depended upon obedient service.

Baps turned his gaze to the snowy peaks. "We're surrounded by comrades who would skin us alive if they knew what we're doing."

"Go ahead and leave," Creo said.

"No arm twisting here," Alapaat chimed in.

Kor put an arm around Baps's back. At the other tables, boys in the approved skin tones clustered together—pink-white, snow-white, brown, pale black, bronze, gold, yellow, red, olive, black, copper, vibrant in presentation—they smiled, they laughed, they would soon be killers on demand. The song Kor chose exhorted a different perspective in a lyrical, dramatic fashion from a voice of enchanting thickness and volume. A new day began, a new song was about to be played, and if mountains could move, a new way would be believed.

Seditious musical words filled their privacy dome, awe-inspiring and hopeful. *"Are we human? Could it be that we are? What would that mean? Dare we sing? Dare we listen? Dare we believe?"* Halfway through, Kor belted out the lyrics with gusto. Trainees from other tables glanced their way but no more than passing glances. Music wasn't illegal, and singing wasn't abnormal, as long as the songs were not on one of the banned lists. He squeezed Jude, who joined in and tightened the hold, and they branded their love into a shared memory to last them forever.

Dimples spread atop Jude's strong jawline. "And you say I'm the fearless one."

Liquid fire roiled Baps's eyes. "You'll have us bled dry on rusted hooks."

The Pearls clicked their coffee mugs. "I'm a dancer," Creo said.

Alapaat's voice warmed with glee. "I'm a prancer."

"It's like they wrote the song for us," Jude said.

"This isn't a shit-faced game." Resentment seared Baps's tone. "I have to be better than perfect."

Kor squeezed Baps's thigh. "What's up with you, party boy?"

"My party days are over. I won't be a boy much longer."

"We all have to live with that," Creo reminded.

"High Clan boys," Baps said with an unsettling dark tone, "get away with more than us Emergents." Anger bubbled into tremors along Baps's jawline. Inclusion in the posse honored Baps and his clan but operating outside one's class or status always created challenges throughout the Starry Empire.

"High Clan or not, we're no more alive than the sun trees if we obey without question," Kor said.

Dex leaned forward, ready to join the battle on the side of caution. A ring of red pulsed on Kor's armband, then Jude's and Creo's.

"What's going on?" Dex asked.

"New orders," Kor said.

Creo stood. "War game. We report to Glory."

Baps's, Dex's, and Alapaat's bands pulsed red. "Warden," they said.

Kor squeezed Jude's hand. "Different spaceports, different sides."

Dex slammed a fist on the table. "This can't be chance."

Kor deactivated the privacy shield. "You worry too much—just part of our training." False conviction rattled in the admonishment as his mind tumbled into misgiving. Trainees about to go to the Academy occupied several tables, but no one else had been called.

"The lack of notice isn't normal," Alapaat said. "I was scheduled for field survival skills."

"Underwater combat," Jude said.

"Light armaments," said Dex.

"Fighter piloting in the simulator," Kor said.

Creo put a hand on Alapaat's shoulder. "Tactical defense on a dreadnaught—also in a simulator. The Academy isn't behind this."

Kor agreed. Training in the holographic simulator chambers was coveted and not to be wasted by last-minute cancellations. Orders had to be followed. The posse exchanged quick hugs, passing their friendship and worry into a group nerve-heating tonic.

The orders required taking a tube train straight to their respective spaceports. Instructions were downloaded via their armbands, which fed the data to their higher-function command and control, a direct feed into their visual cortex. None of them spoke. Their faces froze in protective neutrality. Surprise war games did happen, but they were rare. Worse, instead of the local chain of command which typically worked with trainees, the Starry Empire's *natural-born* officers ran the exercise.

A logistics sub-commander met them at the spaceport station. Kor stiffened and gaped and lost track of Jude's and Creo's reactions. Launchpads, control towers, and the flow of people and hovercraft blurred into the unreal while their handler's blue uniform, gold insignia with an arrow pointed up, and brunette hair tucked under a service cap sharpened into mind-stopping, visual-overload high resolution.

"Never seen a woman in real life, huh?" the sub-commander asked.

Kor and his comrades straightened, hand-salute to the heart with fist closed. "No, ma'am!" they said in unison.

The sub-commander's expression remained brilliantly flaccid. "I don't bite . . . on most days."

She motioned for them to follow. Kor stared in unholy intensity, studying the swing of her legs, the swivel of her shoulders, her hips, the curves, the scents, the energy—an entire unknown universe paraded before his eyes. Holograms didn't do real-life justice. The natural-born declared his kind to be Militants, and Militants were created to be in service to civilization but were kept apart. Few of his kind encountered a flesh-and-blood woman until rotations in the Brigades took them out among the worlds of other subset humans and of the natural-born—those with unaltered DNA, the blessed, the lucky, the divine natural-born.

Green-bloods—trainees—packed the troop transport; a double row of seats facing each other had an occupant. Kor and his friends grabbed handholds dangling from the ceiling. A Starry Empire officer—a mature woman with a skin tone like Jude's—commanded the aisle.

"You're the Blue Team, and your enemy is White," the officer said. "The game begins at touchdown. You'll get a download with battlefield topography and standard-issue blasters. Strategy and organization are left up to the respective teams. You have twelve hours to capture the White's fortress of darkness; in this case, a circle of stones with a red, pulsing signal emitter smack in the middle. The winning team gets an honor tattoo on the right bicep. The losers are disgraced in a media blast across all open networks. Any questions?"

Hell-frozen eyes made clear she wished for none from the empire's subset human slaves. Losing wasn't an option. Losing meant no dancing, no music, no fun with friends for whatever period the General decreed, and he only had seven months before he was anointed a man.

"Glory to the heroes," Kor said; Jude and Creo echoed the sentiment.

The troop transport sped over the horizon into the night, across an icy ocean, and dropped through storm clouds to a smooth landing.

Jude's eyes glinted in a playful challenge. "A wager between the three of us—whoever takes White's emitter gets a four-handed full-body massage."

"You're on!" Kor and Creo said together. The three of them stacked their hands to seal the bet.

Data streamed to their armbands, which updated their higher function command and control. Kor and his platoonmates sprinted down the transport's ramp to a grassy hill.

Sleet fell from gray clouds, clattering against the mountain's stony face. A man-made gash cut across the green. Blue banners flapped over the base camp located within the trench. Jude shouted orders. The Company hopped into a steel-buttressed trench bathed in dim yellow light, grabbed their blasters, and fanned out into the dark in four seven-man squads. Jude, Kor, and Creo, as the only High Clan boys, took command of three.

Kor and his squad scouted ahead. Conifers clustered together throughout the slippery, rocky terrain in protective formation against a stiff, bitter wind sweeping down from the snow caps. Kor hand-signaled his squad to belly-crawl to one of the thickets. The Militant vision spectrum had been enhanced to include infrared. The trees would screen their advance. He focused on his grips, on his next handhold, where to put his feet, and where to move forward without hesitation. Icy cold penetrated his bones, a taste of war. In creature-fluid motion, he and his team reached the thicket's perimeter.

Aromas of smoky mint and sage wafted from the ground as his hands sunk into a carpet of moldy needles. Concerned that he and the team might be behind schedule, Kor signaled the others to stand. Using the trees for cover, they swept through the thicket, moving from trunk to trunk in quick bursts. No alerts sounded. Outside the thicket, Kor spotted a pair of White copper-toned sentries crouched behind boulders a few meters down the mountain. He flashed two fingers to his wingman, and the sentries crumpled to the ground in a burst of stun-level blaster fire; the thump of their bodies was mere background noise to the clamor of sleet on stone.

Fingers flashing wide, Kor gave the signal to charge. As he and his team sprinted from the top of the thicket's tree line, the other Blue squads converged. They swarmed the enemy trench in a volley of blaster shots. The White squads fell back in a disorganized retreat. Smoke grenades detonated by the retreating troops spread noxious clouds in the trench.

Visibility reduced to a few feet. The feeling of separation, a pang, an elusive sense of woundedness, invaded his mind, and it hurt. Momentum waned, it reversed, and his feet rooted in place. Where were Jude, Creo, and the other squad leaders? Kor's squad surrounded him, but Jude and the others were lost to the smoke.

Pain stabbed Kor's frontal lobe. His breath shortened as his lungs filled with panic instead of air. Steel-buttressed trench walls, smoke, and excited platoonmates in mud-smeared battle gear about to charge their demoralized opponents blurred into the substance of a mirage.

Swirling wind pushed smoke down the hill, enough for it to disperse into a breathable haze. Kor squinted. His blood pressure spiked, and his skin flushed with sweat. A comrade—Jude—came close, concern leaking into his eyes. Jude should be leading his squad. Blackness framed Jude's face. The world shrunk. Someone tried to control Kor's mind.

Telepaths—Psians—amplified their will through Kor's higher functions. Urges bent his desire; "Grab hold of the gun, shoot to kill." Skull and bone contorted with muscle and nerve. Better to kill himself. Better to die. *To live is to fight is to die!* Love poured from Jude's fear-draped eyes. His love exhorted Kor to resist, to win the moment for the rest of their lives.

"Medic! Medic!" Jude yelled. Desperation flushed his trembling face.

"What's wrong?" another man shouted; a voice familiar to Kor yet incomprehensible.

"No freakin' idea!" Jude said, screaming and sobbing. "Get a goddamn medic."

Others rushed to Kor's side. Shouts punctured through to his pain, strengthened his heart, and fortified him to rally and to survive.

"Hold on, big guy," Jude said in a tightened voice. "Candlelight dinners for a year if you stay with me."

Someone jabbed a needle into his arm.

Friendship and love waited for him on the other side of the mind-scalding pain. The pressure in his head escalated into unbearable weighty layers of extra gravity. Kor buckled. Hands grabbed hold, and boys with white badges shouted words he no longer understood. Blood leaked from his nose and ears; gargling noises—was that him or from others? Every neuron resisted the impulse to obey.

"What's wrong, medic?" Jude's voice shattered into discordant notes.

"Serotonin nears lethal levels. Neural activity is off the charts. Alpha brainwaves show extreme disassociation—indicators of resistance to a Psian."

"Why would a Psian be part of the wargame?" Jude's eyes widened at the onset of horror.

Reality inverted. Those in control forced Kor to stand tall. The weight of an ice sheet smothered his sense of self, and yet, the reality beyond filtered into his awareness. He was no longer himself but a mere puppet.

No more shaking, calm and composed, he shot the man straight ahead, his betrothed, whose face froze in shock and disbelief. Kor spun and fired in a hurried ballet. Boys fell to the muddy ground. Death surrounded him, a peaceful horror. As the Psians withdrew, his mind unlocked to emotion too intense for his heart to bear, and he wondered if it might burst. Pressure exploded, guttural cries fought for release, and reality decomposed into the surreal. No tears, no evidence of weakness manifested to betray a grief big enough to cover the world in darkness.

Alone, Kor collapsed in the mud, held his dead betrothed, and gave in to primal grief, to yells, to screams at tortured stars in a prayer for insanity to kill the agony. The clouds no longer wept, and no tears came to wash away the sin. Bodies burned, muddied, and bloodied lay everywhere. Voices cried out in the distance, coming closer, but none of them would bring a cure. Would his death satisfy them? How was his blaster not locked to a stun setting? How could he have allowed himself to be used?

His breath suffocated, and his heart fractured into pieces, into bits, into dust, into bloody mud, full of tragedy. One thought wailed in his mind in locked ravaged shatter: *Why?*

CHAPTER III

Kor meditated on the gun that Psians forced him to use to kill his betrothed and friends.

Six months had passed since that wretched day. Four months and four days ago, the psyche-wardens released him back into the world. Three months and two weeks ago, his father commanded the ritual as a reminder of the cost of Kor's failure. Nine and a half minutes to go before he finished his daily penance. Eternity devolved into seconds.

The gun was unremarkable, just a standard-issue blaster. Everyone on the planet, from high clans to second tier, to low tier, to priests, and workers alike—almost everyone in the Starry Empire who watched video content—had seen the gun and the carnage it had wrought. Jude was gone forever. Ten others were dead, including Creo, an understanding that scorched his mind.

The gun took center stage, mounted at the top of a ziggurat-style pyramid, his altar of worthiness, draped with a few medals from youth competitions and challenges. The long room's double row of bunks, unused except for his, faded into a peripheral indistinct blur as he gave the source of his disgrace undivided attention. Mud and bloodstains covered much of the blaster's light-absorbing synthetic frame. The General refused to let him clean it. The weapon would exist through time as a soiled memorial to his weakness.

One minute down.

If he were a mere Militant, then was he human? And if not human, was he worth anything more than a biological machine made to die for a natural-born cause he cared nothing about? The meditation stimulated such thoughts full of self-doubt, and the relentless quiet bled energy to his mind's darkest corners.

Soapy sea moss and bark odors, the barest hint, alerted Kor to another presence. A retinal display went into active mode; a sensor in his armband scanned for intruders and fed the data to his higher-function mental command and control landscape. Kor took a slow sniff. Lockers acted as an industrial-style headboard at the head of each bunk. The odor was strongest from the one to his left at forty-six degrees. He stepped in that direction when a small, wiry figure bounded into the open and threw a sheet over the mounted gun. Smiley faces spray painted in neon colors decorated the otherwise white sheet.

Wolf, twelve years old and ready to conquer the world, crossed his arms in a what-are-you-going-to-do-about-it challenge. The boy had the trademark Steel Rose gray eyes, black hair, and fair skin most of the other high clans found irresistible. Though for the moment, his sleek, second-skin bodysuit concealed everything but his eyes, nostrils, and lips.

Kor circled his younger cousin, looked him up and down in approval, whistled, and gave an affirming thump to the shoulder. "How did you get a stealth-grade bodysuit?"

"When Tracker went on a service rotation, I broke into his locker, stole one he hadn't used in a while and got one of the workers to re-tailor it. I call it creative buying." Wolf did a quick jig.

"Fancy work, cousin, stealing from your elder brother. You're quite the troublemaker."

"Following in your footsteps."

Kor flashed a thumbs up. "Awesome paint job. I take it you disapprove of the morning meditation."

"That gun killed eleven people, and it's trying to make you number twelve."

Kor winced. "Orders trump feelings."

"Nothing was said about adjusting the scenery."

Technically true, but not in the spirit of house rules. Three minutes down. Kor decided to let the sheet stay. Militant enhancements included rapid recovery to improve their utility. On top of that, he had developed a resolute pain tolerance from his frequent visits to the whipping post. Besides, who was he to discourage an artist?

A sly grin creased into Wolf's cheeks. "I challenge you to a game of *chase*, this room, five minutes, winner on time."

Before Kor had a chance to respond, Wolf tagged him. "You're it!"

Open doorways book-ended the long room. Wolf scampered toward the one to his back. The stealth suit blended in with the beige walls and beige stone floor, and he disappeared into the empty sameness of the room. But bodysuits breathed. The increasing heat of his younger cousin intensified a soapy odor trail. When Wolf doubled back behind the lockers, Kor pounced to catch and grab hold.

"You're it!" Kor gave a winning grin.

He bolted to the bathroom off the long room's middle and flipped the master switch for the group shower. Two dozen shower heads erupted at full blast. There was nowhere to escape, but Wolf hesitated at getting his fancy bodysuit soaked. A virtual waterfall engulfed Kor, and he grinned like he had won a coveted prize. "It's a little-known secret that those stealth suits malfunction with too much water."

Wolf's eyes glinted, likely debating whether Kor attempted a fast one. While his cousin worked it out in his head, Kor redirected a pair of shower heads toward his cousin. Drenched and spitting water, Wolf put a palm on Kor's chest. "It!"

A trail of water exposed Wolf's line of retreat. Instead of going for a quick tag, Kor used driers built into the bathroom's main area to dry off. His black-with-white-swirls bodysuit would drip dry in no time, but he stacked up violations by breaking the meditation, not removing the sheet, using the shower heads as part of a game, playing *chase* during a designated duty, and he hadn't made it through the first meal. Besides, he wanted his cousin to win; victory came in many shades, and his cousin's smile was one of them.

The water trail led under a bed. The time favored Wolf. Feet first, Kor dragged his cousin into the open and lifted him to the bed. "Winner!"

Wolf pulled back his skullcap, releasing his thick black hair, a freedom soon to be lost with age. "I call thirty seconds of tickling." He proceeded to flutter his fingers along Kor's rib cage. They broke into laughter, a gut-fulfilling, red-faced, tear-jerking outburst of built-up tension.

Wolf's face shifted to earnest. "You feel like your old self."

Old, as in before the day of slaughter. There was a saying, "An old Militant must be a coward." The words pursued his mind in a hungry devouring of self-love . . . many on Zorn said Kor had been a coward, and grievances smoldered, though the Militant Plebiscite's official account blamed the empire's Psians. The Starry Empire made no comment, which fueled speculation as to whether they acted with motive and intention. Casualties in war games did occur.

Wolf's eyes watered with the fleeting shimmer of a hidden pain. "I've missed you. We all have. You keep this place alive. Every one of my brothers thinks so."

Confusion rippled through his muscles and tendons. Opinions on the slaughter varied among the clans, but for Kor, it remained a disgrace forged into chains wrapped around his dreams. But in the playful banter with his favorite cousin, the chains crumbled into dust—if only for the most precious moment. Wolf and Kor held each other's hands.

"There's a lot of anger," Wolf said. "I feel it. People are really, really angry at the Chorus. Every time you push a rule—or break it—you give us hope."

Kor ruffled Wolf's hair in appreciation.

The time! He had for a moment lost track . . . nine minutes. . .

Earthy aromas alerted him to the General's entry behind his back. Even unseen, his muscular presence dominated the space. The boisterous fun died a quick death.

"I should be disappointed in you," the General's heavy baritone voice convicted. "But I haven't heard you laugh since the tragedy. The halls of our compound have been the lesser for it."

Kor rolled off the bed and surveyed his father like he had gone bonkers. Empathy wasn't part of his father's playbook. Without needing to be told, Wolf scrambled to the nearest exit.

"Does that mean the blaster goes?" Kor asked.

"I see a young man in search of his heart. We are Militants. We serve the natural-born. We fight and we die for them. They made us for that purpose. Forget you ever had a heart. When you forget, I'll destroy the blaster."

"How can our hearts be superior in design, and yet somehow we are less?"

The General engulfed Kor in a hug. Gray eyes to gray eyes, both in black training bodysuits—Kor's with swirls of white flare— fair skin and black hair, the father reflected in the son. Though his father was a battle-hardened warrior, and he was a young green blood, the haunting in Kor's eyes when he looked into a mirror was the same as his father's.

"I have been lenient with you these past months because no one should endure what you have endured. Coercive possession by telepaths is rape, and they added to their sin by forcing you to kill your platoon mates. The evil of their actions shall burden you to the end of your days."

Gravity pulled on Kor's resolve. The mention of telepaths left him rigid and unsure. Transgeneticists engineered most of the subset humans long ago, but not the mind-invaders. They predated the Starry Empire, and without question, had been modified to project consciousness in energetic forms and to exert force in the quantum universe of entangled states. How could any of them be sane with their minds never quite anchored?

"Thirty days, a drop of time, before you ascend to manhood," his father continued, "and the empire Conscriptors add your name to the draft register."

"Death pool."

Sharp energy pummeled a gap of silence. "When the Starry Empire calls you to serve, you must obey."

The General gave him an extra squeeze. "Time for you to return to the Academy."

Kor touched his armband and accessed an updated duty roster. It was as he feared. "You want me to go right now?"

"I arranged for Baps to join you for a walkthrough."

"I want the gun to go."

The General's face softened. What did he see in his son? Kor wasn't sure who he was anymore—a life no longer recognized, taken away in a few seconds of pure horror. The familiar world shifted beyond reach. What had he become? Did that show? Did his eyes betray his hidden truth?

"Tell me you no longer need to dance, listen to music, or walk in the woods to cope, and I will relent. You try to heal your broken heart, but it will never be unbroken. Harden it. Wrap it with steel and grit. It's the way slaves survive."

The suggestion chilled Kor's blood. "I planned on meeting up with some friends at the White Pearl for dancing tonight."

"No need to change your plans. Savor your last few days of freedom. We are leaders among our kind, and as heir to Steel Rose, I expect you to become the man of obedience and service required of us by the natural-born."

Kor crossed his arms in salute.

The General grabbed Kor's shoulders. "Don't do anything stupid."

***

After morning exercises and first meal—the usual pungent blackhole broth, a mixture of boiled meat, blood, salt, vinegar, greens, and winter rye—Kor detoured through the compound's rosariums on his way to the entrance gate. Dutiful workers tended the roses—prized throughout the Starry Empire and the origin of the clan's name. No acknowledgment passed between them.

The heady aromas seduced Kor into a slow sniff of white, burgundy, orange, and yellow blooms. Every inhalation deposited a residue of wonder. The universe was dark, but it was also light; it was pain but also roses.

An alert popped into his command-and-control functions. The next hover transport approached the compound. He hightailed it to Hero's Boulevard and pinged it to stop with seconds to spare.

The transport, a basic hovercraft with long benches separated by an aisle, sped down the mountain. The fortress estates of the high clans rolled by; a mix of allies and staunch enemies held in tenuous check by tradition and disciplined authority. A static wave in the topography divided them from the smaller domains of the second-tier Emergents, many of whom hungered for greater status. On the downside of the wave, Baps hopped on. Kor flashed the posse call sign, index and little finger up and thumb out, to the newly ascended man of Crew Gallant.

"Much gratitude that you survived your first tour of duty," Kor said, embracing his friend.

"The trainers prepare us to survive."

The transport's glide path smoothed as it entered Presidium, a city built to an overwhelming scale, with monumental buildings, plazas, and parks spread over a vast valley surrounded by snow-capped mountains. A larger-than-life capital of heroes remembered in monuments, shrines, and statues for their lifelong kill totals in battles and cleansings.

They hopped off at a Valiant Boulevard station near the Academy's main entrance. A steady flow of men and boys in bodysuits, groomed, athletic, and strong, cruised the linear park that split the avenue. The weak didn't last long on Zorn. Trainees wore the standard black bodysuits of the Academy, while other boys celebrated color in their attire. Men stuck with regulation uniforms. The holy X over the third eye branded the men as cattle. Kill-total tattoos, a mix of iron bars, skulls, and anatomical hearts, tallied their worth.

Kor glided his fingers over a death head tattoo within his friend's bodysuit cutout. "How many did you kill on your rotation?"

"I neutralized thirty-eight gentlefolk terrorists holed up in a bombed-out city. A total rush. I'd never felt so alive."

Baps gestured to his cross-bone skull, reveling, grinning, and receiving high-fives and thumb-ups from those passing by. Kor swallowed his guilt at being less than thrilled. His friend was older by a mere two hundred days, an afterthought in time, but the holy **X** forehead brand on Baps's golden skin christened him a man.

Kor wiped away a bead of sweat. "Let's get this done. As my father reminded me, thirty days to the death pool."

"Draft register. Our purpose, our honor, our faith, to serve as we are designed."

"Not long ago, you thought differently."

"I used to be a foolish boy who thought the twin moons granted wishes," Baps said.

"I still do." Kor headed to the Academy's multi-story gate. Steel giants, supporting worlds on broad shoulders, guarded the heroic passage, a reminder of his father's expectations.

Troubled determination propelled Kor into the Prime Training Academy's foyer, a soaring chamber of stark space. Embedded screens dominated each wall. On one, a sea of names brightened and dimmed for those in active service. For most of his kind, the purpose of life was to serve, to obey, and, if necessary, to die.

Unable to tolerate the view, he shifted his attention to another wall where the names of those killed while in service scrolled. Jude of Iron Star would be among them. Another shift of his gaze brought up an image of his flute, hand-carved over months with the help of YouTube videos procured through his backdoor access to the Earther's web.

Thirteen-year-olds and up mingled—others walked in and out of concourses, a purposeful flow of bodies focused on their mandate to train for service in the Brigades. *Prepare and survive*—a motto stamped into everyone's psyche. Until the tragedy, he questioned, but he believed. Now? He had no idea. Telepathic agents forced him to kill friends and comrades in a test for resistance to coercion. Who was guilty? The man who fired the gun? Those who forced him to? The ruling Chorus? Kor's resistance was exceptional. Why had he not turned the gun on himself to save others when he realized the attempted possession? Everyone had an opinion on which question mattered the most.

Kor's presence altered the foyer's flow of foot traffic. A group of teenage boys coalesced around him from Moon Sky, Crossed Dagger, and Crew Defiance, clans who remained loyal to Steel Rose. Back smacks, hugs, genuine smiles, and "happy to see you" followed in a friendly, mood-lifting back-and-forth exchange.

"Everyone ready to swing their hips at the White Pearl after duties?" Kor asked. Grief waves surged with the weight of oceans. Never again in the physical world would he get to share his joy with Jude. *Wish you were here*. The scar on his heart would never fade—he refused to let it fade—an ever-present reminder of loss, of futures forever lost. Emotion lanced the scar, but dancing brought Kor closer to Jude in a beautiful pain—in the movements, aromas, and sweat, an echo of his lost love came alive. "I got a hot new playlist of Earther music."

Their hands went up, except for Baps's, and his jaw set to combustion-ready. "You're unbelievable. Eleven dead, Jude and

Creo, and you still listen to that blasphemy? Do you ever think about what you did?"

"Every day." Kor's voice trembled despite a single-minded effort to keep it steady.

"You profane the memory of those who died in that trench when you play an Earth song. I deleted my music, everything with an Earther taint."

Alapaat joined the group. The teenager, about a year younger than Kor, showed off his snow-white skin with a burgundy bodysuit, typical of Ice Bore but unusual for his clan when among outsiders. He wore no contacts, showing off his time-stopping eyes, the color of icebergs. He gave Kor a quick kiss and hug. "You're an idiot," he said to Baps. "The empire's telepaths were here. The song might've triggered the wargame's timing, but we had already been marked."

"None of you have learned your lesson." Baps's face flushed a darker gold. "None of you know the *why* of what happened."

Alapaat rushed forward and raised his oil-black tattooed forearm across Baps's eyes. Like Kor, the man of Ice Bore had lost his betrothed. "Never, *ever* pretend that you know my heart." The heat of his anger pierced every word.

Chastised, Baps receded behind an unreadable expression.

"Every time we dance, we remember our friends," Kor said, his voice subdued. "Tomorrow we die, let's kiss the sky. The music keeps me alive against a horror that consumes my soul. No one here expects you to come." The others grunted in agreement. Ascended men—the vast majority—devoted themselves to duty.

"What have you got on tap?" asked Nirga, a copper-toned, ultra-fit eighteen-year-old from Crossed Dagger.

"Madonna, Foo Fighters, Barnes Courtney, B-52s, 'How High' by The Record Company, Lady Gaga, and the Proton Vapors." The latter, part of the final wave of rock and roll bands, was a toe-tapping, arm-swinging exception to the dark, bitter, and angst-tormented songs, a.k.a. Lavender Wreckage, prominent of that era. Excited to share the PV groove, Kor did the posse's trademark vogue move—a fluid arm pinwheel around the body.

"Totally awesome," Nigra said. "Download the playlist to our group account. I want to get the rhythms down."

Kor tapped Baps on the shoulder. "What about you?"

"You're poetry in motion when you twist and shout. But I can't pretend anymore to be free. You'll get it when you're a man."

Within the periphery of his vision, others mouthed curses of "murderer," "killer," and "baby doll," bullets intended to maim.

"Ignore the fan club," said Alapaat, "Your ex's clan has a lot of people stirred up, but we've got your back. However, there is a problem."

As a group, they moved into one of the concourses and kept up an easy nothing-is-going-on banter. On either side, training rooms prepared trainees on survival skills, endurance, strength, and combat weapons, from hand-to-hand to Phase-Cannons on a dreadnaught using top-notch holographic simulators. There was nowhere to go without being monitored, but Alapaat led the group into an unused simulator to get out of the concourse. Formed up into a circle, they exchanged hugs.

Alapaat's ice-white-blue eyes shifted to a hard glower. "Iron Song forced a vote this morning among the Academy's Commandants on whether to allow you admittance. Several clans sympathetic to Steel Rose, including mine, were excluded from the voting quorum. They knew you were coming and organized in secret."

Everyone quieted. Expulsion from the Academy amounted to unqualified disgrace. The bronzed men of Iron Song, once long-standing allies, became blood enemies to Steel Rose on the tragic day when the stars wept hot tears.

Kor met Alapaat's purposeful stare. "I only found out myself this morning."

"Iron Star has been waiting for your return, and they were ready to pounce. Someone tipped off Iron Star. Someone betrayed you and your clan."

Lightheadedness hit Kor with the force of a DeathWatch brew, a local ale renowned for its full-bodied punch. "What's the result?"

Alapaat put a hand to the side of his head, a gesture to indicate he had received an update. "Academy deputies head our way."

"Not good," Kor said. "Evacuate?"

Everyone glanced at each other. "Evacuate!" they said in unison. They dashed out of the simulator and sprinted toward the exit. Trainees clogged the hall, slowing their speed. They burst into the foyer. From the other two concourses, a dozen deputies in dark blue bodysuits poured in to cut them off. On their chests, an emblazoned white sword pointed down marked their authority.

A deputy stepped forward. Clan affiliation often drove how confrontations played out. Based on the deputy's flaxen skin tone, high cheekbones, and mustard-colored eyes, he was Harvest Fire, low status, and someone who would be cautious.

"What's the meaning of this?" Kor asked.

"The Commandants doubt your readiness to return," the deputy said. "By their decree, you're barred from the premises unless you survive an ordeal."

"Why wasn't I notified of the potential sanction?"

The deputy glanced at his comrades. "A debate for those of higher rank."

A crowd gathered. Baps, Alapaat, and the others muttered their outrage, but nothing too audible.

Kor planted his feet, shoulders squared. "What kind of ordeal?"

"You will be left in a blind drop far into the White Desert without water or food. You must make it out in seven days or forfeit your worthiness. No aid shall be rendered. Prepare and survive. Your ordeal begins in three days."

A matter-of-fact tone matched the ominous words. The desert wasteland, a shifting sea of powdery gypsum in the driest part of the planet, had claimed many lives, adding bleached bones to its treasures. Kor's friends placed their hands on him in a show of support. The ordeal might kill him, but he must accept. No rightful heir to Steel Rose would refuse the test. Survive, and he might at last prove his worth to himself and to his father.

***

Kor headed back to the compound on the transport, quiet and lost—his friend Baps by his side, the person who, in all probability, tipped off Iron Star. Worse, Baps would be thinking the same thing and guessing at Kor's conclusion. The sensation of the press of their legs against each other magnified into a fear crawling up his spine.

Baps put an arm around Kor. Blue-agate eyes softened, a recognition of the bond from a friend Kor knew and loved and who had always been at his side. "It wasn't me."

Kor leaned into his friend. "Thank you. But you would have told your father."

"I've heard things . . . promises of high clan status if Steel Rose falls. But that doesn't mean Gallant betrayed you."

In the dulled light of their eyes, they exchanged their helplessness. Distrust would linger and swell with the blight of untreated disease.

Baps hopped off the transport. Through the window, Kor waved, wondering if they would ever meet again as friends. Would there be any choice? Mistrust was a pestilence that was difficult to contain once unleashed. Baps and his clan may have been blameless, but the General's outrage at what happened at the Academy would fan the pestilence to every corner of the world.

A priority communication confirmed Kor's worry. As soon as he exited the transport, he met his father in the compound's central hall. A wood-topped table constructed from a single tree harvested from the clan estate bisected the space. Steel leg arches supported the heavy wood. Ancient tapestries around the walls added a hint of reverent mustiness. The General, in an official Steel Rose bodysuit with colors of red and white, studied a holographic display showing a tactical view of the estate plus those bordering, which included Iron Star.

Opposite the General, Kor sat on a long bench and waited to be acknowledged. Mounted on the wall behind him, was the skull of an arvorg; a seventeen-hundred-pound long-snouted, big-headed carnivore with an unhinged jaw packed with slashing incisors and a pair of lethal canines. The General slayed the rugged four-legged beast with his bare hands, a testament to his strength and determination and a warning to others who would dare test his fortitude.

Details of the situation gathered into accelerating mental processing that his father wore the Steel Rose crown, a headset with an onyx dragon in the center, last worn during the Oath Breaker Rebellion. Stoic and hard, Strom showed no outward emotion. Worry got the best of Kor. "You're thinking of fighting them?"

The holographic display remained, but his father glanced through it, his eyes fearsome, fanatical, the power of stars burning through, beautiful and terrifying to behold. "If you die, Iron Star and their allies will pay. Jude has eleven brothers. You are my only son, and the Starry Empire bears the crime of what happened."

An alert pinged Kor that his duty roster had been updated.

"I've added combat training to your schedule. Those not serving in the Brigades are being recalled to the compound. Everyone, boys thirteen and older, must prepare for war."

The seriousness of the situation hollowed Kor's spirit. When Militants fought each other, there was no surrender. *To live is to fight is to die*, a truism encapsulating the whole of their lives.

"War will tear the planet apart."

"Which is why I challenged Iron Star to a valor-game match tomorrow. They accepted. If we win, Iron Star has agreed to withdraw the ordeal."

"If we lose?"

"Iron Star is content to celebrate our weakness. The thump of our boots if you die in the White Desert. One condition given and accepted—you must play."

Kor stiffened. The match would be nothing less than a blood feud, and Dex, the brother of Jude, would lead the charge; Dex, who had Jude's dark eyes, jet-black hair, and sculpted build, was the spitting image haunting Kor's mind—in another life, a good friend.

"Tonight, go and dance," his father said. "Be your most social self. If civil war comes, we need allies to survive. Watch for signs of betrayal."

They parted with a long hug. Strangely, Kor relished having to take on the ordeal to prove to himself that he belonged. The valor-ball match would be no less difficult. Iron Star fielded a much better team, the best of the best.

The day passed in target practice, simulators, swordplay, and hand-to-hand fighting with Steel Rose trainers. As others throughout Zorn heeded the recall to return, Kor greeted them with hugs, back slaps, and mock challenges to the death. Laughter and wild tales were traded between the extended family as they devoured sauce-drenched beef sticks smelling of nuts and fats. Life, for precious moments, felt normal.

After the last meal, he left for the White Pearl, and he carried the same heaviness as the friends he welcomed. War would involve everyone. Alapaat decked out in fluid, ultra-flexible couture glittering starlight, flashed the group call sign. Glittering black, Kor responded in kind. Sometimes, the smile had to be forced.

"Let's dance like there's no tomorrow!" Kor exclaimed.

Alapaat hooted. "Because we have no certain tomorrows!"

Ensconced in the surging tide of his dazzling friends, Kor moved to the dance floor, weaved into a crowd, and allowed his mind and body to go wild. The playlist worked its magic. "Vogue," "Learn to Fly," "Fire," "All-Star," "Love Shack," "How High," "Poker Face," "Heaven's High" by the *Photon Vapors*—tribal movement with friends in sweaty, gyrating bliss. A bubble formed within the club's liquid-colored psychedelic walls—an evanescent container of acceptance, fun, and euphoria, minus the grief, the blood-soaked fields, and the admonishing priests. Spin faster, rotate your shoulders, wave those hands, and jump to energize the world and to find one's dreams. The lyrics tore holes into the heart and soul, allowing forbidden energy into the light.

Somewhere in the ecstatic stretching of arms to the pearl-studded ceiling, dropping low to the slick floor, a part of him caged since inception broke free into life. Images of his flute incited his mind to dare a disobedience he had hesitated to risk. Tonight, despite the valor-ball match and the upcoming ordeal, he would, at last, play his flute in defiance of the prohibition against Earther instruments not native to Zorn, which meant most of them, outside of drums and horns. It would be an homage to Jude and their shared passion for Earth's music. The universe might never offer another chance.

Sweaty and happy, Kor hugged each of his friends with firm intention, with the knowledge that he might never dance with them again. Imbued with the electric warmth of their press, the aromas of musk and cologne, whispered reassurances for the challenge to come, he headed back to the compound with a buoyant gait.

In the lunar shadow of Steel Rose's fortress shield walls, Kor inhaled. Mellow and bitter scents of the estate's forests wafted with the earthy dampness of wet leaves from the prior day's rain, a tonic for nerves. The compound's gate, worthy of a dark lord from a dark fantasy, tempted his better judgment at going through with playing his flute, a forbidden act to match the energy unleashed at White Pearl.

The shield wall had been laid out in a rectangular grid over varied mountain topography. He hiked on a buffering meadow in the fortress's shadow; on the far side of the compound, a misty wooded trail wound upward to the tree line, into powdery snow, into the boundless sky. Cold wind lavished his face and hands, infusing excited expectation. An unmarked offshoot of uneven, rocky ground ended at the Painted Garden, a narrow gully at the edge of clan territory that formed a limestone shelter with spirit-tree bark streaked in greens, maroons, bright purples, blues, and pinks. In the Painted Garden, dreams come true if you believe hard enough and if you have earned enough cosmic favor.

Kor dropped to his knees, then murmured a prayer of gratitude for the place of living wonder that reforged hardened hopelessness into buoyant hope. The firm tangibility of rock and tree and soil cast a spell to lighten burdens. Prayers for peace, for acceptance, poured from his murmuring lips, earnest, hopeful, and unsure—his awakening yearned to break free.

A rustle among the trees, dark shadow in motion—potential intruder threat assessments snapped him into alert status. Kor lunged into the woods, tackled his target, and on the way down, realizing who he was about to slam to the forest floor, rotated his capture on top to block harm to his cousin. He landed butt-first with an audible thump. Muted laughter escaped into the open.

Wolf would not be spying unless ordered by Garrison, his eldest brother, and in spirit, Kor's as well. Wolf was the perfect spy-- old enough to be trusted but young enough to avoid strict surveillance.

Kor adjusted to a squat position and set his cousin on his feet. "Isn't it past your bedtime?"

"I know about the flute."

"Why, you little devil."

"You know who wants you to hold off until after the ordeal."

Assuming we lose the match, a worldwide consensus given the odds tallied against us.

A hundred reasons for returning to his bunk declared themselves to no avail. Retreating, crawling into bed, afraid of consequences, amounted to a slower way to die.

"Tell you-know-who that he has my love."

Tears welled in Wolf's eyes. "You know what doing something bad means. He'll take you to the Punisher post, chain you, and whip you. Our fathers' lessons get worse."

Wolf's quivering voice stretched Kor's resolve. He gave him another hug. Like every Militant, Wolf was designed to accept his fate. Kor would be no different if he had not shot his disbelieving comrades, friends, and betrothed from point-blank range, birthing a nightmare that would never end until his death.

Wolf tapped Kor's foot. "Your eyes glazed over again. Is the music you listen to messing up your mind? My father thinks so."

Kor laughed in part to cover the painful memory. "Like a crazy man addicted to fun. Besides, who else plays *chase* with you? You like me because I'm different."

"Just remember, you're my favorite cousin. I don't want you to die."

"Deal."

After Wolf left, Kor removed a rock jammed against one of the massive trunks, a low-tech hiding place to throw his father off, to retrieve a narrow case. Kor caressed the smooth lacquer finish of his hand-carved Earth-inspired flute; he kissed the bone mouthpiece. Hours upon hours of diligent nighttime practice and higher-function analysis where he blew over sticks in mimic videos featuring flutes would manifest into sound.

He put the flute to his lips and blew harmonic tones, a musical whispering new to his world. The hour passed in humming, sighing, clear and bright, silvery sadness and warm brightness; the fog of his breath shifted, and the tones moved in pitch, subtle perfection. He hugged himself for reassurance. The trees shivered a rustling melodic sympathy. He played, and he swayed, and he collected a few pieces of his heart. The tension of his world, restrained by grit and discipline, dispersed into the night sky.

A flash of red registered in his mental command and control landscape. In an abrupt shift, Kor bolted into the woods, grabbing Wolf by the arm before his cousin had the chance to react. But the damage had been done. Wolf had changed into his sensor-deflecting bodysuit and caught Kor red-handed.

"Sneaky son of a gun," Kor said.

"Amazing," Wolf said. "I hardly breathed or moved."

"My number-one fan. Am I going to hear a replay in the Macrocosm?"

"Your father will find out."

"I've accumulated inventories of secrets." Kor winked.

"He always finds out."

"You best get to bed. No use you getting into my trouble."

Kor tracked the boy's departure halfway to the compound. Satisfied, he returned to the fire. Another round of harmonics seduced. Between experimental notes, his armband blinked green in response to an incoming updated duty roster. He stiffened and braced for the worst. Commission Square hosted executions. Mandatory attendance—an exercise to remind him of what happened to those who refused to follow the rules.

The General toyed with him. In confirmation, a message dropped into an account restricted to his father: "Against my better judgment, I allowed you to create your flute. But you have succumbed to the forbidden. Destroy your flute by midnight tomorrow. Do it by hand; suffer your loss. You may play it once more before then—if we win the match." Kor's heart sank into a tar pit. Wolf was right. The General always found out. The shrills, twitters, whines, and whistles of the nighttime forest serenaded him on the way back to the compound. Back in his long room, his mood brightened. The smiley-face sheet remained over the soul-sucking gun. No matter what happened, no matter how harsh the General might be, he signaled his love. The lyrics of "How High" rode him into his first settled sleep since the tragedy, and not a single nightmare kept him company.

CHAPTER IV

After the usual meticulous morning hygiene and grooming routine, Kor headed to the compound's forbidding fortress gate. Faint hoarse screams, guttural croaks, gurgles, a soothing background buzz, a call from the restive morning forest, contested unsettling quiet. Nerves jingled as he leaped over stairs wide enough for giants to catch a hover transport about to pass by.

He jumped off at a station a block from Commission Square. The abodes of third- and fourth-tier clans dominated the street; iron, glass, and stone mid-rises jammed together behind a double row of spinning web trees interspersed with copper-gilt banners. White granite radiated; many had decorative crowns, intricate friezes, a show of minor power, a shield against disbandment, against predatory priests and enforcers seeking the fall of the weak and the weak-willed.

The Square's Blood Flag Gate had ten towering columns with reliefs of soldiers fighting and dying in glorious battles on faraway worlds. A court, a temple, and an administrative complex boxed the space with a market fronted by cafes, closed for the event. Witnesses filled the Square. No holographic screen matched the stench of death and the crazed, in-your-face fervor. A raised platform had five iron posts, one for each corner and another one in the center. Red-veiled Obedients, executioners of sinners, criminals, malcontents, and other assorted outcasts stood guard. *Cowards, thugs!* Kor flushed with the heat of contained fury.

A procession of priests entered in a river of virtuous white in veils. Once upon a time, the trendy people wore veils to tease and to entice, but no more, not since Earth ships arrived bringing new ways, causing dissension. The priests ringed the platform to give their blessing. Obedients chained a criminal to each post. A holographic spinning spoke wheel hovered. Kor put on his practiced stage face. Legs quivered. Thoughts flat-streamed. His breath shortened. Chants of *"purify!"* swelled into a nausea-inducing squall. Most of the condemned were workers who didn't produce or obey quickly enough.

The wheel caught fire and spun. The snap of the whip jolted—stirred repressed rage in a tar pit of kindred memories. Obedients struck blows in unison, a flow of poetry, a shock of thunder, a choreographed show to harden the spectators' moral fiber. Each stroke resulted in death; one moment, a prisoner breathed, and the next, he didn't. Morning cool gave way to sweaty blaze. Prisoners shuffled up the platform steps. Toxic leather smacked exposed skin. Jeers and taunts saluted the condemned. Fists raised and shook in approval. Kor resisted the urge to pretend his agreement. *I see them. To see is death.*

The whirling spoke wheel burned in a celebratory spectacle. A cleanup crew dumped lifeless bodies into a bulk container. There was no respect for the living or the dead. If you were disobedient, you were not even subhuman.

An Obedient shackled the last prisoner breathing, a low-tier clansman, to the center post. A data relay built into the platform broadcasted his crime—refusal to carry out a commander's order during a suppression action in a world inhabited by the nonviolent subset Organics. Tears shattered against the hard quartz. The man endured the inevitable; he would die alone and unloved, the worst of fates.

At the whip's crack, he slumped.

"Dead," the Obedient intoned, the one hundredth and one such incantation.

The lifeless man brightened; the platform diffused into the murk. The prisoner had been treated as if unreal. The Starry Empire scientists had treated Kor's dead comrades the same way: collateral damage in an experiment testing resistance to telepathic coercion. Everyone was disposable. Nobody was real. Organs squeezed against each other. Foreign sensations raged. Protective filters dissolved in the horror before him, forcing him to see.

A double-brick mason-wythe tattooed worker laser-cut a precise vertical slash in the stair to mark the clansman's cleansing. The cleanup crew scrubbed the quartz clean of tainted blood. Efficient, mechanical, and immediate; the grinding rhythm of Zorn.

"Move along," a voice said from behind. "Do not turn around. Walk away unconcerned. You're about to be noticed."

By security . . . unsaid but implied. Without looking back, wondering who his friend might be, Kor exited in a high-resolution replay video stream of the hopeless faces of men about to die. *Random streets, go anywhere, keep moving, and try not to think of the horror you witnessed.* Religious order dormitories flanked his path. The priests went about their earnest business on a walkway as wide as a street. Self-absorbed chants bounced from the residences with a soothing resonance. Watchmen of virtue, they ensured obedience; service and faith remained as one in Militant souls.

Kor plopped down on a bench in a courtyard park tucked between dormitories. Belts that cinched the priests' tunics, the badge of authority for those in the political wing, paraded by; green for novice, yellow for acolyte, high numbers for both, orange for apprentices, a sprinkling of blues for the upper order, the uncommon Advisor black, and the rare Marshal white. He counted until he lost count.

Spinning web trees provided shade against the hot afternoon sun. Medicated mind whispers urged him to be cleansed of his malcontent. Medicated whispers sapped his will to move on before getting noticed by the priests.

A green-belt emerged from a modest, flat-topped shrine set behind the park. "Do you hear the whispering trees?" he asked in a cracking voice, flipping between highs and lows.

"The executions wore me out." The words, slurred and mumbled, reached Kor's adjacent ears as a distant sound from the realms of dark energy.

"Your pupils are dilated. Your demeanor lacks vigor. You show the signs of an unbalanced mind in need of correction."

Kor nodded, and the mind whispers faded away. The boy headed to the shrine's paneled, blue-painted wooden door. Circles and curves formed secret symbols, but Kor's numb mind held no curiosity. The boy put him in a cell with wall-mounted handcuffs. "Prepare for lessons," the novice-grade said.

The boy's brown eyes watered. Kor hugged the boy, a break in protocol, but the novice grade didn't resist. Whether in the service clans or the religious orders, every boy understood the pain of lessons.

After the boy left, Kor stripped to his underwear and bound his wrists and ankles on the handcuff's sensor; steel locks netted the next victim. A blue-belt appeared in a full-head mesh purity mask that rendered him faceless—a self-blinded priest.

"What are you?" asked the blue-belt.

An easy question, but to answer would wound the soul. Silence thickened into a stalker of pride and fear. Burn weed thrashed into Kor's skin, a lesson in force from head to toe. Silence and pain formed an unholy union to break his resistance. *I am Militant*, a simple thing the priest wanted him to admit and to declare himself no more than an object to be used and discarded by those who belonged.

"I'm dreaming of a white Christmas!" Kor yelled in a surge of deviant glee.

The thrashing stopped, and the silence-stalker dispersed.

The blue-belt released the locks. "The spinning trees won't remain silent to your resistance. Report to a temple within three days for advanced lessons. Do not lose your worth."

Kor dressed in a hurry despite the stinging pain. The ordeal took precedence, and it was starting to look like the better option. The faceless priest escorted him outside the shrine. In the park, he lingered. The burn weed's acid imprint faded from his veins. By tomorrow, a blessing of his genetics, his skin would heal, but not soon enough for the next inspection. Kor needed to work on a full-proof story for the General to explain the lash marks. A veiled yellow-belt tapped him on the shoulder.

"I warned you in Commission Square," the priest said. "You're not like the others."

Kor used higher functions to scan the voice: artificial, a distorter in use, and difficult to procure. Maps flashed on Kor's retinal display. Escape routes were plotted. Prepare and survive. Kor suspected an enforcer's security trap. "I'm that obvious?"

"You didn't cheer or shout approval."

"Am I accused of something?"

"Dutiful and compliant, you submitted to correction."

"Not quite—I resisted the lesson."

"Next time, fake obedience. To gain our truth, we must live their lie."

The acolyte put a gloved hand over Kor's armband. "I uploaded a contact link. Activate it if you want a life outside the death pool. The link functions for two days. Take care and stay on guard against the whispering trees."

Questions cracked into wordless uncertainty. Heart racing, he realized that if he went through with a meeting, he would have to rely on faith. No one legitimate had the means to pull men from the death pool, and traitors didn't survive on Zorn by being chatty. Service in the Brigades amounted to a death sentence for body and spirit. Treason, betrayal to Steel Rose, to his father, had never been on the wish list. Either way, a terrible choice had to be made.

The veiled man blended into the flow of priests on the walkway. Ears ringing, Kor hurried to the tube station.

***

Co-ruler of a hundred and twenty worlds, ten types of troublesome subset humans with various classes, wife and mother, Sentinel demanded much from herself and those around her. In precise steps, she traversed a transparent bridge to a chamber's center within a globular metal shell housing one hundred concentric levels of seating. Unique and awe-provoking, the Oracular superstructure suspended in the interior of a pyramid awash in golden radiance. The Oracular invoked veneration among the natural-born as much as Sentinel's invoked fear. Co-rulership of the Starry Empire had its advantages if one had the stomach for brutality.

Elliptical-shaped sentry probes hovered in a protective formation. Three rings of blanched faces—Psians, seers of possible futures, a tool of last resort—tightened with the gravity of a criminal tribunal. *They will never be so lucky.* Unique among humans, they had been changed to perceive in quantum states, to tap into information flows written into time and space. The effort required suppression of self-survival instincts, and some would be lost, their energy spread too thin in the quantum universe, becoming as fragile as spun sugar. Simply put, humans were not meant to see beyond the present.

Whether they identified as male or female (or both or neither), they each wore midnight tunics, and they each had solid ash-coal eyes with the same half-dead stare. It was a miracle that such dispassionate creatures ever reproduced. Of course, Sentinel endured her husband's timid caresses long enough to produce two children.

Scattered throughout the sphere, rectangular segments lit up with a green bar metric for available poisonous gas by volume—a warning of the Oracular's capacity for a quick death if the sentry probes detected misbehavior. Killing the seers would be a tragic loss of resources, but more citizens would cheer their passing than weep. Still, Harmony, co-ruler and self-ruling, managed the subsets. Their reaction would be unforgiving if the communion went awry.

Sentinel weighed the possible outcomes of the communion versus doing nothing. The patterns identified by Intuitives, a sub-group among the Creators seeded throughout the known galaxy, hinted at existential danger. The Intuitives' heightened level of external sensing combined with their equally developed internalized thinking allowed them to perceive possibilities, patterns, and trends before anyone else; their recent reports were tantamount to alarm. Faults in the natural order of things stressed the continuity of civilization.

A balustrade rose to surround the central pedestal. She clasped the curved handrail. The dais rotated in slow, uniform increments. "You've seen the Intuitives' warnings. Focus on their truth. Focus on their lie. Show me the future. Show me what I must be aware of."

The telepaths tapped. Red and black brands on their bleach-white hands gave the illusion of traveling serpents. The rapid cadence evolved into a rhythmic, assertive dance. Sentinel wanted to throw out a command, but the Psians used her as a focal point. They required a calm lens. The verdict would not be hurried. Memories of simpler days filled the void: moments of idle conversation, cooking elaborate meals, sipping tea, and nibbling on homemade cupcakes—happier times, yet less satisfying to an unwavering need to matter more than anyone else.

The tapping trailed into stillness. Three of them slumped—acceptable casualties in the never-ending war to preserve civilization.

"What say you, Society of Truth and Gnosis, most farseeing of all the Psians?"

"Trouble comes your way," the Society said in overlapping waves. "Earth's foreign ideas take root among the peoples. The desire for self-determination infects, spreads, and corrupts."

"Tell me something I don't know."

"Subsets explore the boundaries of revolution. Militants, Organics, Data Angels, Creators, Meta-Mystics, Hypers, Workers, Cybers, Psians, Breeders, and Caretakers, none of us are immune."

"The Earthers exterminated their engineered humans. Must we do the same?"

"Much is hidden from us. Forces, influencers, actors, and players attempt to bend the future. Our clarity: Militants most threaten your continuity."

The balustrade lowered into the floor. She paced. The billow of her rich red gown against her ebony skin transfixed, pointing to the decision to be made. Militants kept the others, including the natural-born, in line. But if the soldier-slaves ran amok, the whole system would undeniably and irrevocably collapse. Civilization mattered, but as her mother often said, the game pieces did not. Whoever endangered the future would have to be adjusted or removed.

A final tap rolled through the Psians in a choppy wave. Wails, whimpers, and shudders followed in the wake.

She captured the seers with a brief inspection. "Tell me, Truth and Gnosis, what do you perceive?"

"A fall of stars, billions, burning, going dark, a warning of a future imperiled. The potential for your success runs high. But unintended consequences threaten the Starry Empire, the three human civilizations, and the cosmos itself."

"Sweeping grand warnings have the mettle of water."

"Unite us; let our brothers and sisters come to reveal what eludes our sight."

Every seer together, a full communion, was a never-before-done drastic move. But the times were indeed drastic. Fearless she might be . . . but there was no ignoring the deep-set shiver.

Sentinel departed in the confident gait of one who, in the end, always won. "I will summon your brothers and sisters. Do not disappoint."

***

The underground contact's offer swirled in Kor's thoughts in search of the right answer. He pressed his forehead against a hover transport window on approach to the Field of Crosses, a brown and pink granite memorial to athletic prowess built on a desolate tableland where Heroes Boulevard ended in the middle of larger-than-life-stunning-snow-capped-mountains nowhere. Pennants flew from the stadium's top-- the red and white of Steel Rose, and the aqua and orange of Iron Song. What if he knew the answer but could not bear the truth?

Kor's mouth went drier than the stone-laden tableland. The field existed before the city, an ancient relic predating the creation of Militants when Zorn was a normal world of natural-born people going about their normal lives.

The hover transport dropped him off at the Narrow Gate. He gave a gliding touch to the gate's columns, their painted art eroded by time, images from the mysterious afterlife, feeling the subtle rise of the paint's texture beneath his fingertips—a quiet testament to the layers of time and touch embedded within. The ancient Zornians venerated their art; perhaps that had been the mistake that led to their servitude. Long ago, Transgeneticists changed the peoples of whole worlds into subset slaves for a brave and better Starry Empire, but the reasoning behind the choices remained a mystery.

In perfect form, Kor sprinted across the golden field in a bio-steel bodysuit: top-grade, integrated protection, flexible, and ventilated. The burn of fresh whip welts punctuated each footfall, a continuous, ever-present reminder of the priest's lesson. Team Rose waved him over. Garrison, with dense gravity-compressed steel-grade muscle, ready-made to be a bronze statue someday, put an arm around Kor's shoulder, putting pressure on the lacerations. A reflexive micro-wince twitch betrayed his weakness, which he covered with a smile.

"Our ex-allies plan to target you, cousin." Garrison's face betrayed no expression.

"Better here," Kor said. "Let them have their war on the field."

Garrison pulled Kor close. "You're a pro at hiding pain, but I'm an expert at detecting it. Did the General take you to the Punisher?"

"The priests."

"Prigs," Garrison's tone darkened. "Take their power with your joy." Garrison kissed him on the cheek. The brotherhood closed ranks in a circle, hands to shoulders. Iron Song players wore black war paint, sharp contrasting lines on the face with stick man symbols on each cheek, joined together hand to hand with a line over the nose. They gave no concession that telepaths forced Kor to kill the favorite son of Iron Song. Kor spat in a surge of heated pressure: *Ghosts*, telepathic mind-possessing creatures who raped the minds of others, *Psians* in polite company.

"Iron Song wants to hurt our brother," Garrison said. "We will fight, and we will win."

"We are Steel Rose!" Kor and the brotherhood yelled their defiance. Win or lose, they would stand together.

They passed a kiss and geared for battle with throwing sticks, helmets, mouthpieces, and gloves. Fifty thousand gourd-banging clansmen packed the stands, their energy glorious and savage. Iron Song fielded the best team on the planet. The stakes were clear. An Iron Song victory would force their confrontation to escalate if Kor died in the White Desert, and it would diminish Steel Rose at the very time it needed allies. Fueled by the injustice of his life, Kor was ready to prove his worth no matter the resistance standing in his way.

The yellow-golden field stretched a hundred and eighty yards. Two electrolytic mirror-like silvery-gray iron rings, symbolic of

Zorn's two small moons, hovered thirty yards from the back line within a twenty-yard ring zone. Score the most points and win glory for the clan. The measure of one's worth wrought into balls, sticks, and the stamina to prevail over others.

Kor and Garrison took point in the face-off zone. Inches away, Dex's war paint glistened, and his teeth clenched. The brother of his lost love hardened into anger-lust. Battle and flight, grief and despair, ripped through Kor in a detonation of bottled-up energies pushing to be free. More than anything, Kor wanted to say goodbye to Jude and to hear him say, "I forgive you." But forgiveness had to be earned. Otherwise, any gesture would be vain conceit to drive out the guilt weighing the soul, except for interludes submerged into tunes, rhythms, and harmonies, the relief, the wonder of music.

The referee's jawline firmed. "This is war. The five-ounce purple ball cannot pass through the smaller ring. The two-pounder is orange. Scoring occurs from either side of the rings if shot from outside the ring zone. Points are lost if the orange goes through the larger ring. Prepare for face-off!"

Kor bandied sticks with Dex, who rolled off energetic, angry waves as he refused to make eye contact. Dex adored his brother, and he had put himself in the blame-Kor-for-his-weakness camp. A holographic timer hovering over the field ticked to twenty seconds.

The crowd rose. Yells dueled as a portent of war. Stadium horns blared a deep, industrial drone in a hair-raising call to battle. Adrenaline primed blood and muscle for action. The referee dropped the balls. With ease, Iron Song players scooped both, their strides and passing practiced and effortless, splitting Steel

Rose's defenders. The opposing team's attacks flowed in unstoppable waves, a concert of one-point scoring bells against the out-matched keeper defending the rings. The horn sounded, the rings rotated to a side-by-side position, and the clan's defense tightened into a scoreless battle.

Valor-ball permitted no rest or substitutions. War continued until defeat or victory. The third quarter started like the second. Frustrated, Kor hand-signaled the team to ignore the orange. With every man on purple, Kor streaked toward the enemy ring zone ahead of his advancing teammates. He snagged a long pass—and turned to take a shot. Defenders converged. He passed to Garrison, who ran through to the back end, making a scoring throw.

Iron Song battered the dash of hope with barrages of the heavy ball against the Steel Rose keeper. Two throws went in the wrong one, a six-point penalty. Reinforcements raced back to help, but a double-bell celebrated a ten-pointer. As expected, the opposing team dominated.

Kor and Dex faced off to start the final quarter. Dex didn't try for the scoop. Kor took the bait, sprinting with the orange back to the team's midline. Team Iron Song pursued in a dead-eyed craze of body slams to the ground, tackles, and pushes, leaving both sides muddied, bruised, and bloodied. With numbers, Garrison scored with the purple in successive attacks. Kor drew attackers in, who were eager to get their pound of flesh, absorbed body checks, showed his worth, and passed off when he had nowhere to run, a bludgeoned strategy to salvage the match.

At sixty seconds, a countdown started in a voice-synthesized babble to rattle courage. Kor slid between defenders and cut out the feet of the Iron Song player possessing the heavy ball, which rolled out of the stick's mesh to inside the ring zone. The keeper scooped and hurled the ball with a wicked spin—a direct nerve-scorching hit to his arm. The chance for glory fell dead at his feet. Fifteen seconds to defeat. He scooped. Spectators yelled the clan names in a dueling feud. A stick slammed across his back. The field wobbled into blurry wavelengths.

"Ejection player, Iron Song," the lead referee said.

Kor planted his driving leg. The keeper's eyes widened. Kor cranked back. The keeper scrambled in retreat to protect the ring. Kor threw. The orange sailed above the keeper's catcher stick in a flat arc to pierce the silvery-gray ring, a glorious double bell. Kor and his cousins screamed "Rose!" in unbridled ecstasy. In the pause of the shock, the purple ball soared through, a shot by Garrison. Unexpected defeat stunned much of the crowd into motionlessness; the rest erupted in wild jumps and arm pumps.

At face-off, Kor and Dex pushed against each other, a pair of ornery bulls. The ball dropped, and the final horn blared.

"Steel Rose wins," the lead referee announced.

Dex reached out his hand. Kor hesitated, unsure if he would be poisoned or sensor-tagged, but in a dream, Jude's passionate dark eyes invited, and their hands clasped tight before he once again saw his enemy. "Well-played match," Dex said. Dex offered his commendation with a hint of reluctance.

"Do I have your respect?"

"You reminded me of why my brother loved you."

Kor's eyes watered as he wrapped reinforced shields around his grieving heart. "Do I have your love?"

"You fight with your whole heart," Dex said, immune to Kor's plea for reconciliation.

"I loved your brother more than myself."

"Then why did you not take your life instead of his? Prove to me your soul-ravager regret."

"What proof can there be?"

"Figure it out."

Kor released Dex's grip. Random music blared in his head to ward off seismic emotions too much to digest. "I will get you your proof, for you, for Jude, and for me."

***

On the trip back home, the brotherhood screamed "Steel Rose" punctuated by "Glory to the Heroes" in splendid rapture. Kor yelled his throat raw on the transport, outside the compound walls, in the rosarium, through the central hall on the way to the dining hall's ring-shaped table where the other kin kick-started the celebration. Under ornate gilded beams, enclosed by walls with alcoves housing statues of ancient heroes, the victors sat at the long table with straight backs, proud in grass-stained valor-ball bodysuits. Mugs of ale banged together, and Team Rose talked over one another with alpha-wolf zeal, hand-slapped bumping elbows in a festive clamor, and showed off their game injuries with the relish of honor brands. Garrison's father, Bow, rose to give a toast.

"Savor your triumph," Bow said. "You fought as warriors. Others will be forced to reconsider their dismissal of us."

"We are Steel Rose." Spontaneous chants infected everyone.

Kor basked in the glow of ecstatic energy, enough to light suns and distant skies. The hard-bitten General grinned. Tankards clanged, food disappeared, and the valor-game match turned into proto-legend. The countdown to midnight chattered in the mental background. He grabbed a group hug before evacuating the victory party.

On the hike to the Painted Garden, he tallied the visible constellations. A spirit tree struck by lightning long ago regrew in an arc over the entrance. The base of the trunk withstood the sky's onslaught, and through its strength, it created a threshold between the dangerous world and a safe place. Kor glided fingers on the underside of the arc's peak to offer his gratitude.

He dug a pit and started a fire. Days were warm, the nights cold, and he had no need to hide. Arms held high, he lifted the flute to the blessings of the Twin Moons and kissed the V-shaped bone mouthpiece. Tentative notes mingled with the nighttime soundscape. The rich yellow wood sprang to life. With his hand, he created wonder from a stick of wood—*a vital act of life, a proof of soul and humanity*. Memories of Jude flowed, their times of dancing, listening to songs, drinking coffee, gazing at the stars, and wondering and musing, sometimes until the dawn sun pierced the mountain peaks.

To the crackle of the fire, he played, meandering, at first bright and careful, the lingering energy of triumph. But the tones turned dull and dry—his heart hollowed at what he must do. Bargains with the Fates rummaged in thoughts, offerings, and pleadings for alternative outcomes.

Firedarts emerged, an insect ballet of flashing citrine. The petite Twin Moons' eyes, bright equatorial bands with a brownish spot, showed with the accusatory glare of displeased temporal gods. He held the flute over the flames. A simple act of obedience, open the hand, and life returned to its expected flow.

He pulled back. The flute defied with unspoken power in the gleam of the fire. Back into the fire, closer to flame, to grief, he shared the instrument's pain. The pretense of being alive shriveled into a soul-darkening blot. What choice must he make, a sin to his soul or one to his heart?

The barren wail of the wind through the trees warned of his peril. He sprayed a fire suppressant to snuff out the flames. Pangs twisted into his mind, snaked down his throat and left an ache in his battered heart. Visions of the good, obedient son turned to ash. Flute in hand, the steps back home accumulated to five thousand victories. At the compound's entrance, his father brooded. In an angry hush, a hot simmer biding for flame, the General led Kor to the Rainbow Courtyard where he surrendered his wonder, his flute, to his father.

"Kneel," the General said.

Flagstones with the names of the worthy dead forged from iron dug into Kor's knees. The Twin Moons dipped in the starry sky. A hover light's beam illuminated his flute, perched on a stand beyond reach, proof of his weakness. In the courtyard's center, an obelisk soared within a column of light, its titanium alloy skin anodized into ribbons of bronze, silver, teal, rose, gold, blues, greens, and yellows, a work of divine-touched art. Every compound had a sacred whipping post, but none rivaled the Rainbow's magnificence. Forty-four horizontal coal-black slashes tallied its forgotten dead—the consequence of too much error.

Father circled, an engine of disapproval discharging waves of heaving bitterness, "What's your excuse this time, boy?"

Kor heaved a mental sigh. He loved music, listening, and playing, however imperfect. Music celebrated emotion, jingled the soul, and freed the energy flows—in lyrics, harmonies, melodies, and rhythms, proclaiming, *yes, you are human, you are real*. Music made him feel, and it connected him to Jude across the void of death. But no excuse.

The General ripped his shirt to shreds. A mosaic of anatomical heart tattoos covered his chest, a kill total numbering in the tens of thousands, worthy of an urn at death or a statue on the hallowed ground of the family shrine. Kor gave up a micro-flinch—the minimum show of respect.

"Stubborn, boy. We serve. We obey."

"We serve, we obey," he mimicked. "Our lives in four words."

Father placed the flute on a textured flagstone. He lifted a steel bashing bar, muscle flexing, jawline rippled, and in a metallic blur, splintered the wood into fragments, splintering Kor's already fragmented heart, grinding both into dust. The General loomed over his handiwork—a broken man held together by grit determined to force his son to reprise the father's choices. In a flash of quiet realization, Kor activated the priest's contact link.

The General pointed to the whipping post. After the briefest pause, Kor stood. Bare feet pressed into the raised cold iron of the remembered, into legacies and histories thousands of years old. He was Kor, and he was Steel Rose, and he was every one of the remembered. Gray writing in the Rainbow's colors emerged into view, the names of those who had administered a cleansing. Blood and death, the courtyard was sacred ground—once the General struck the first blow, there would be no stopping. A step away, he stumbled; in gray lettering etched on the post, *Strom*, his father.

The General locked Kor's wrists into thick, iron shackles. "To live is to fight is to die. You know enough if you know that."

Indigo, purple, and orange colored the horizon. The General brought the post's steel-tipped whip to Kor's eyes, but his gaze was entrapped by his father's name in gray. Silence stretched in a contest of wills. The letters spelling "Strom" hypnotized and conjured stories of what might have happened—a murder of family kept secret.

"Change your ways, boy. Next time, you won't be leaving this place."

The General was trapped in his ways, and Kor in his.

Strom released the shackles and walked away. "First meal is over. Duties start in ten minutes."

Dawn surged into the night sky. The stars faded, curiosity burned, and Kor's instinct for obedience clung with tenuous, frayed compulsion. His father had killed a man of Steel Rose at the Rainbow, a man erased from history, a warning that he would kill his son for continued disobedience. A scan of the duty roster confirmed a long day of routine duties. But he had reached into Pandora's box when he activated the contact's link.

The Rainbow blurred into a haunted memory as his legs plodded forward. The compound walls blended into one another in a blur of grey. Kor's thoughts looped endlessly in speculation as he entered the data room. Kor was the maestro of floating blue-white displays embedded with commands, search tools, and files. Frigid air circulated. In focused speed, his hands moved in rapid, spell-casting cadence—his breath the sound, his gestures the tempo, a refuge from the outside world. The clan's rosarium yields remained steady—income from hundreds of death pool contracts with the empire's Brigades stayed on budget. Forecast models were promising based on commander evaluations, rankings, service end dates, and survival and injury rates.

Behind schedule, he cleaned the bunk area at double-time speed until it was inspection-ready spotless, and then he groomed himself the same way. With the ordeal revoked, the war footing ratcheted down. The compound's normal rhythm returned. He ran the track at high noon, challenged the sky-whitening sun, showered, and inhaled a hearty second meal. Despite the pressing schedule and the risk of punishment for going roster-AWOL, the Painted Garden's natural splendor beckoned, and he heeded the call.

Spirit tree leaves glinted with silver sunlight reflection. Under the protective canopy, Kor meditated, shedding his disturbance of powerlessness. By the design of others, he would one day lead the clan, serve, and fight on faraway worlds, and rear sons to continue the preordained cycle. He kissed the barks, an offering to nature, life to life, an indulgence for cosmic favor.

Garrison showed up, shoulders back, his black outfit showing off every curve and angle, hero material with the requisite broad and thick chest. Garrison would go far, achieving the top rank of combat master if he survived.

"I thought I'd find you here," Garrison said.

"Does the entire family know I have a safe place?"

"The neighbors know."

"Not good. Came to shame me for disobeying the General?"

"Your father covered that base when he took you to the Rainbow." Garrison hugged Kor close, a loving embrace. "I hold you to a secret," Garrison said.

Kor gave a curt nod, as binding as any contract.

Garrison's breath caressed Kor's ear. "My secret fantasy is to play the guitar, acoustic with a bone saddle made from a sharp-toothed hell-hog. I admire you for being you, for daring what I never will. The Code runs too strong in my blood. Take care. Don't ruin the clan."

Kor pulled his cousin tight. Garrison, the textbook Militant who did his best to follow every rule, precept, and standard in the Militant Code, heard the call of his soul. An encoded file appeared in his message center from the contact: a meeting tomorrow at Club Emerald. Directions followed and the message self-deleted. Club Emerald . . . a registered dance bar but by invitation only, a big unknown, and a risk to go.

Garrison and Kor raced back to the compound, both behind schedule. After the last roster sign-off, Kor withdrew to his bunk and surveyed the other beds, perhaps once home to one or more nameless brothers slaughtered by the General. Other ways to live must be obtainable. Meeting the contact would be a start.

Eyes closed, the baleful crushed-gadget sheen of the Rainbow burrowed deep, pursued him into an adonized dream, into nightmares filled with salt knives, whips, and names written in letters of gray.

CHAPTER V

On most occasions, Sentinel preferred to arrive at events with everything made ready for her presence. Today wasn't like most occasions. The pressure of retaining control over a diverse and complex empire, on the surface stable but with undercurrents of discontent threatening to go wild, spiked into headaches and useless arguments with her overmatched husband.

Golden radiance awakened her senses as she stepped into the vast Oracular capable of housing several of the quaint Earther pyramids. Around the outer perimeter, she paced, up one leg, down the other, crossed to the center, drew in the energy of the Giza-dwarfing pyramid, and imagined Creation's fuel flowing into her life force. To keep civilization whole, she would gorge with a ravenous appetite.

Psians filed into the Oracular's globular metal structure at multiple levels with a weighty, soundless, sour presence. The Indeterminator, their most renowned, surveyed with a slight backward tilt of the head paired with a subtle arch of the brow. The lead telepath made her disapproval of the communion clear. Luckily for the Indeterminator, Sentinel appreciated a woman who stood her ground—within limits.

Showy armor boasted Sentinel's status. Gold bracelets spun into art pieces, and huge round earrings emblazoned with BOLD added pizzazz. Finishing off the haute couture jewelry was an heirloom necklace handed down for generations; it had a pink diamond big enough to corrupt the mind of a saint. The Indeterminator, however, was no saint. In some respects, she was a carbon copy of the other Psians, but her copper skin popped with an effervescent sheen, and her sharp yellow eyes glowed with the rile of unheeded warning.

Sentinel took her position on the central platform. Her co-rulers entered last. Harmony wore a fake smile with neon fuchsia lipstick; a novice might mistake them for being friendly. Nexus never bothered to fake fun or happiness; his heart pumped, his lungs expanded, but he existed to work. The telepaths' bleached white fingers, branded with red and black rings to reveal their talent and power, rested on rows of tables on multiple levels—dangerous, useful, and irreplaceable. The fate of billions was about to play out in an opera that mattered. Steel-coated nerves fluttered. Each moment delivered a satisfying rush Sentinel's husband only dreamed he could deliver.

Nexus shook Sentinel's hand, a gentleman at least. Harmony pounced on Sentinel with a space-violating hug. Sentinel went into rigid protective formation. "Like watching a viper hugging a razor-tooth spiny back," Nexus muttered in the background.

"Jealous?" Harmony asked, breaking off the embrace halfway to pull Nexus into a brief three-way handhold. Sentinel willed herself into calm. She was female, Nexus male, Harmony non-binary; she was dark, Nexus mixed, and Harmony pale; a perfect balance and the perfect blend to rule the Starry Empire. No love was lost between them, but they had been apart for too long. To save their civilization from chaos, they had to work together.

Harmony flashed an extra broad smile from an oversized opera singer's mouth. How likable, how endearing, how white-water treacherous the mind and emotions behind those model-worthy pearly teeth. "I do enjoy coming back home," Harmony said in a wistful tone. "Imperia is an amazing world that I appreciate more than ever. Let's do this more often. Catch-up. Share a bottle or two."

Harmony brushed a gentleman's cut fuchsia hair off their forehead. "By the way, how are the children? Your boy was quite the little alpha at adventure camp. Your daughter practically runs the Ursulla Heritage boarding school."

"I teach my children to take control," Sentinel said. "The alternative is to be controlled."

"Adult games are so boring, don't you think?" Harmony mused.

"Have the nerve to be a parent—then you might have a worthwhile comment."

Harmony's regard weaponized in shadow and glint, a warning and a promise of payback. "I would be such a disappointment. Come join me at the Improv. Humor your sense of humor." Harmony shifted to a lethal, charming crease of the lips. "Everyone needs playtime—helps us to pretend sanity."

"I never pretend. I do appreciate the efficiency with which you summoned Truth and Gnosis."

"We are a team," Harmony said, flashing their hallmark fake smile. "I enjoyed the first show."

She wasn't bothered that Harmony had listened in on the first communion, but the same couldn't be said about how they managed such a trick without detection. Spies were everywhere. Enemies, allies, threats, friends, the compliant and the restive required constant supervision.

Sentinel raised a privacy shield. Never before had the Chorus commissioned a full communion. Events forced their hand; unfamiliar words like resistance and defiance infested the Macrocosm. The Earthers' undisciplined ideas threatened their future. Taking the wrong action threatened everything. Exterminating the Militants would have unforeseen consequences.

Harmony gave a quick, sharp snap of judgment. "You want to end the Blue Compromise. We risk the people's faith."

"It is the one law that binds us," Nexus said.

Harmony and Nexus exchanged guarded disapproval.

"The plan to disrupt the Militant leadership has reached an advanced stage," Harmony said. "Why not let it play out? The clans and the priests will soon be at each other's throats."

Sentinel fingered her favorite bracelet, rich with lavish embellishments of ruby, amethyst, pearl, and jade set in intricate paneled friezes, a one-of-a-kind glittered gold-spun power extravagance. Harmony would never wear such a grandiose display of wealth despite an absurd lack of inhibitions and an abundant love of glitter. The Blue Compromise gave the subsets limited autonomy in exchange for their services, but no bargain lasted forever.

"The Blue Compromise served us," Sentinel said. "New times require new methods."

"You've always been fond of overkill," Harmony said. "Genocide cannot be undone, and cleaning up the aftermath will be tricky."

Sentinel took the hands of her co-rulers. Standing tall, she dropped the privacy shield. Both of them must be made to understand.

"We are ready," the Psians said.

"Show us," she and her co-rulers said together. "The future must not be left to chance."

***

The General despised liars, especially clever ones, but Kor had no honest way to meet with the contact. The Fire Baths hosted a celebration day event awash in food, frothy brews, steaming waterfalls, hot water pools pouring into cooler ones, and lots of sex—in short, good times all around. Upon arrival, Kor gave quick hellos and slipped out into the night. A mag train dropped him off near his true destination: a nondescript, low-slung warehouse of old stone wedged between lookalikes in a dark spot in an unnamed alley. No actual lies were spoken—nearly clever.

Lift the bunker lid fifteen feet to the right of the door, which has a white dot in the lower right corner. Sweat bubbled despite the sharp nighttime cold. *Security encryption enhances a privacy shield at the bottom of the stairs.* An inky curtain, undulated, a test of his courage. *Broadcast the password signal.* He scanned, feeding data to a command-and-control display linked to his visual cortex, searching for enforcer tech that would suggest a trap, getting nothing. Covert-grade curtain—the tech was too fancy for an underground club. *Enter within ten seconds.*

He reached for his charm, branding its notches into his palm. A quick flip. A hurried prayer. The charm spun. In a flash of fate, it landed notches up. The universe had spoken: gamble on hope.

"Peppermint Twist" serenaded his daring. With a swing of his hips, he passed through to the other side.

Men from across clan ranks wearing distortion masks mingled and danced, quite a few in flashy red high heels who somehow maintained balance in graceful flow as they rubbed against each other with no concern for proper hierarchies. A multi-hued photon rain fell from a liquid mirror ceiling, absorbed by bodysuits or scattered across a slick floor. Dancers spun, dipped, and growled with animal abandon. The energy—fast and slow, fluid motion, grace and youth—merged with sweat and cologne, a vibrant tonic. Every nerve rattled to be heard.

At the bar's upper level, everyone held a drink. Plenty of peekaboo masks revealed roving, eager eyes. *Take the last stool on the upper level. Remove an access chip bonded to the underside of the seat.* Frosted mugs by the dozens slid along a metal counter, snatched by quick-moving hands. He sashayed to the stool at the far end to "Twist's" fading lyrics. A survey of the patrons without masks tallied lots of beards, including the bartender's extended goatee—direct challenges to grooming protocols. In casual motion, he snagged the access chip and deposited it in an armband compartment.

"Your strongest stout," Kor yelled to the bartender, who, without missing a beat, slid him a dark red Deathwatch brew. The hard-bitter drink coated and relaxed his throat, and he pressed into his neck to activate a voice-com implant. "Are you here?" he said sub-vocally into the implant.

"Gravity-compressed, synth-metal mesh bodysuit?" a resonant bass voice said.

"Everyone gears up their fashion for a celebration day."

"Defiance both feeds and crushes hope. Are you ready? You dressed for an upper city exclusive. You call attention."

"My alibi is an upper city exclusive." He kept to the sub-vocals through the implant.

"What brings you to Emerald?"

Kor swept the club with scans to pin his contact, the upper level, the dance floor, the dim recesses, the bartender with his tattooed neck collar, unusual decoration for a worker, getting nothing. Whoever he spoke to, he would be close enough to avoid having their comm-signal detected. "The stars brought me here," Kor said, raising a finger for another brew.

"The stars speak to many of us. Those in Blood King have decided to listen. We will gather soon. Come, hear us out. In return, I'll secure you an Academy commission. No Brigades."

An Earth song throbbed, "Everybody Have Fun Tonight," a celebratory inoculation against the priests and their duty-and-death allies. The General would never permit his son to escape service in the Brigades.

The dancers heated to ignition point, which released an intoxicating bouquet of amber and leather to launch them into a heaven fit for artificial men. Notches on his stone charm dug trenches into his palm. The ocean-washed piece of black granite, once a symbol of love and hope for a happy future with Jude, became an object of fervent faith that the cosmos would re-balance from the day of horror when the stars wept. Yet the choices offered separated heart from family, soul from duty.

Safe living is a slow death . . . hop to the dance floor, weave, bump, press, find bliss, find drops of life. Grab a partner, spin him around, then pull him close for an exchange of breath. Move to the next partner, low tier clan, what did it matter, lock arms with a tattooed factory worker, seditious, let go, join the yells, scratch the scruff.

The contact repeated his offer. The dark red brew opened Kor's heart and loosened his muscles. Time for fun, time to live, time to forget the soul-sucking rules. Kor activated a mask of churning fluorescent cubes, threw down some dance steps, and shouted his throat raw.

A tiny probe buzzed. "I'm picking up security alerts."

Kor jumped and squeezed his charm. Higher function scans registered no threats; the contact must be using top-grade security-clearance tech.

"Enforcers coming," the warning, as loud as a shout, came from the probe.

"We're screwed," a patron said.

"Foolish boy," the voice said. "You attracted notice."

Kor swiped at the probe. Heat exploded through the network of his veins, moving in a thick wave. Patrons rushed to the exit, pushing and knocking over tables and chairs. Balance and space, he needed both in Deathwatch's blurry world. Fear and patrons packed the stairs, and with relief, he climbed to street level, running free into a boulevard saturated with security floods. A procession of monumental columns engraved with the Code's precepts led to the Office of Virtue, massive on the horizontal, flat roof, no fanciness, precise symmetry, bookmarking the boulevard's end like a pissed-off god unveiled.

"Your revolution needs High Clan men," Kor said.

The contact didn't respond. Emerald's patrons mixed in with startled Celebration Day throngs geared in colorful bodysuits. Air units popped up on long-range scans. He sprinted under the boulevard's spinning web trees, taking care to avoid their hypnotic weave. Higher function scans went dark from enforcer jamming. Escape routes fell off his retinal display.

A cluster firebomb detonated overhead; sonic blasts followed, knocking men flat. Flames engulfed the Office of Virtue's (OV) expansive length. Shouts, confusion, citizens stampeded in every direction, a full-blown riot. No one wanted to hang around without understanding the nature of the attack.

"I've been dying to blow up our edifice to moral servitude," the voice said. "You have your distraction. Show me you deserve another chance!"

Kor rubbed his charm. The Deathwatch blur dispersed. A leaf in a whitewater river, he ran away from the inferno along with the once festive throngs. Aerial drones blanketed the area with desaturated yellow scanning sweeps. Those pinged by the scans stopped in place. Holographic message display screens flanking the boulevard in half-block increments froze on **We Obey**. Audio looped in an earsplitting mantra: "Remember your training. Return to order." The confusing scene calmed.

Hover tanks, bristling with turrets and each with a badass cannon, arrived to subdue any resisters. Clusters of party-dressed clansmen milled around, with Kor among them, trying to blend in.

Some of them shouted orders. One group broke off to help fight the OV fire, while another launched a rescue operation. Those who remained organized themselves into small groups for efficient processing by the enforcers. The urge to join them burned through his nervous system, an unrelenting craving. Duty over life. So much for the revolution.

Kor deactivated his mask. The dancing wasn't illegal, not yet, but subversive, and he had lied to the General. Drones hovered over groups in cones of desaturated yellow. Kor inserted himself in the nearest one. Men in their prime brandished plenty of kill brands. Boys in wild mixes of primary and secondary neon bodysuits swaggered style. As he crossed the scan threshold, his link was pinged, and his presence registered.

The stars unveiled in the deepening night. The OV fire dimmed. A breeze whispered secrets. The weave of the blue-web trees sedated. Kor's eyes fluttered. The sway of the trees' delicate blue strands drained desire. *Accept your life; find peace in acceptance; right mind equals right thoughts.* Special unit black-helmets supported by regular security advanced up the boulevard, scanning links and checking for deviance. *Order is good. Order is virtue.*

A unit, one black-helmet, and three whites, fast-stepped in his direction. The men formed up into a line. The black-helmet checked the links. The others wielded blasters at the ready. Six men ahead, five, four . . . the black-helmet held a worker's link. Kor recognized the bartender's tattoo designed like a neck collar and his goatee; the worker's brown eyes accused, *your fault.* An enforcer pushed the bartender to the ground. Whoosh. Whoosh. Shot dead. The life left his eyes in an instant horror replay of Jude's death.

The blue-web trees murmured reassurance. *All is well*. The next man stepped up to be examined. Hardened feelings on the prowl drove Kor to inward escape.

Further up the boulevard, a Creator-class walked, *flowed*, up the street, owning it, wearing a cloak of hundreds of bejeweled acupuncture needles that dazzled in the security floodlights; locals and enforcers alike parted ways. The Creator locked gazes with Kor and headed his way. The non-binary human, with iridescent pearl-gray skin, glided into the scanning cone without a glance at the security unit. Kor bowed, unsure how to show the correct respect, but the natural-born loved to tally their bows, sip sparkling wine, and compare totals.

The Creator examined, drew energy in, and merged into Kor's bio-electric field. A protest fell apart. In a smooth motion, the Creator stuck three needles in each of Kor's hands, another smack between his eyes, and a pair in the ears.

"Hell, no!" Kor exclaimed. The web-trees' hypnotic whispering went silent in a burst of sudden clarity. The world's colors and sounds sharpened into the recognizable. The strange creature before him magnified connectivity a hundred times over.

"Come," the Creator ordered.

Kor followed. Obedience, he could handle.

"I am Demiurge-One."

Kor stumbled. The highest rank of the Creator class, and a minion of Harmony . . . the world spun into wobbling, bending wavelengths.

"Can't have you confused." They stuck him with another pair of needles.

A cool wave spread throughout his nervous system.

"Better," Demi said. "For the moment, I'm also your anchor. The needles help."

"You are way above my grade. How do you prefer to be addressed?"

"My feminine energy is ascendant. Address me with female pronouns."

"What happened to your perfect balance?"

"Life." Demi's energy amplified, pulling Kor's attention to no one and nothing else. "Imbalance drew me here. Your grief. Your lies. Your anger. Your conflict. Your dreams. Your fervent hopes for a hopeful future."

"All in a day's work." Kor marveled at his calm; the acupuncture really worked.

They moved up the boulevard toward the Gymnasia, a temple of fitness that rivaled the OV in girth and presence. No one challenged the Demiurge. The gym occupied the interior of a roundabout. Enforcers set up checkpoints in front of the roundabout entry points and formed a cordon in between. Kor's turn came; he surrendered his armband link to the enforcer, who downloaded and scanned the contents, which included the conversation at Emerald. The peace of the needles prevailed. The enforcer handed the link back without comment. Absent a challenge, he was in the clear.

The Demiurge flowed around the Gymnasia's glass and steel immensity to a grove garden separating adjacent boulevard cafes. The few men in the area sized up the Creator and moved on. "I like this place," Demi said. "Well-ordered and yet soft. Your people should do more of this."

"How did you alter the link?" Kor said.

"Attend your contact's meeting. Then we shall see the imbalance emerge into the light."

Demi's starry yellow eyes sized him up; to what purpose, he had no idea. The night had in no way gone as planned.

"What do you want from me?"

"I want us to play a game," Demi said.

"Based on your rep, I bet a tails-I-lose-heads-you-win game."

Demi twisted the needles and relocated others, showing serene acceptance while observing Kor with dazzling calculation.

CHAPTER VI

The return home was pulled off with the stealth of a thief. Unlike a thief, Kor struggled for sleep as though he faced off against an enemy combatant, tossing and turning in fits as he wrestled with guilt until the dawn. In the bathroom, finishing off his grooming hygiene, sea-gray eyes to the mirror, he decided guilt had lost.

Breath visible, Kor strolled through one of the compound's lower wards, long ago converted into one of the clan's rosariums. Operation Covert Meet-Up was underway.

Dawn would soon sweep away the dark and the stars. Screens unfolded overhead to filter the sunlight from the plants. Dutiful workers in nondescript gray uniforms watered the rows of bushes; others refilled tubes, dripped nourishment, or checked for pests. Murmurings passed between them—a basic language reduced to words necessary for their work.

Aromas of sweet and spice uplifted his senses, the roses were at their best in the cool snap of the night. The Emerald raid and OV fire upset the city's clockwork routine. The compound workers vibrated with unease. Going to the Blood King meeting was the worst idea. But "worst ideas" were his forte.

Father appeared with the stealth of a phantom, dead ahead, self-contained, showing off the bulges, curves, and striations of dense muscle with an ultra-tight mesh bodysuit emblazoned with Steel Rose's war symbol, the onyx dragon. Intricate patterns, meaningful only to the clan, wove into the bodysuit in plays of darkness and fiery light that hinted at secrets of pride and honor.

The General radiated a take-no-prisoners mood—a weapons depot restrained by flesh and bone, ready to ignite.

Slow the heart, steady your breath, and meditate on the exhalation fog cloud. Every encounter was a test, a challenge, an opportunity to disappoint.

"You're headed out early, son."

"A city run before duties," Kor said.

"Too busy to eat the first meal with your family?"

Kor's eyes drooped a micro. "Rough dreams."

"Where are you off to?"

"Gymnasia."

"Try the Red Beast workout level five. The pain cleanses the mind."

Kor nodded at the familiar direction. Lying became easier with practice.

"Stay alert. We haven't tracked the terrorists who bombed the OV."

"How is that possible?"

"The terrorists walk among us."

Father closed the gap. Some workers cast furtive glances. The resonant pitch of a gong signaled the shift's end, but the workers lingered to catch the inevitable drama.

“Trackers registered you near the OV after the bombing.”

The General grabbed Kor by the throat. “You lied to me. Where did you go?”

Kor’s throat went drier than desert sand. “I went to a club to dance.”

“Are you lying again? Lies travel in packs.”

Kor broke eye contact.

“Never look away, boy. Is it sanctioned or underground?”

“What does it matter?”

The General moved his chokehold to the nape and inched closer, close enough to hear Kor’s pounding heart. “Emerald, sir, private-registered.”

The General released his hold. “Terrorists and their enablers will be executed by starvation in a hanging cage outside the OV.”

Unsure if his voice would betray him, Kor let an uncomfortable silence stretch.

“Don’t make any mistakes, son,” his father said into his ear. “If you do, I can’t promise protection. Do you understand?”

The General’s warm breath remained steady. Kor locked gazes with a worker holding a basket of harvested roses. In a vertigo moment, Kor shared wordless pain at what he endured, and the worker returned the gesture. “Aye.” The answer was sure yet distant to his ears.

"Delete your cache of Earth music." The General leaned in; his lips space-violating close to his ear. "The priests' power grows. Keep to right thoughts."

He met his father's all-knowing gaze, then kissed him on the cheek. Right thoughts never brought anyone on Zorn peace or happiness.

"Duties begin at 0900," the General said, walking away.

Don't be late.

The worker approached in violation of protocol. A foreman made a move to intercept, but Kor waved him off. The worker handed Kor a flower, self-bounded in a tight bud, but it soon would unfurl in inviting fragrant curves to beckon one's mind into make-believe realms free of death and bondage. Their eyes met.

"You're a good man waiting to break free," the worker said.

Kor swirled the bud under his nose.

"Place this beauty in my locker. If anyone stops you, send them to me."

The worker smiled, as uplifting as the rose. Kor delighted in stunning lightness. He put a hand on the worker's chest. *You have my respect.* Workers no more broke protocol than a high clansman sneaking off to an illegal meeting. The Blue Compromise enslaved workers and militants alike, and both yearned for something more. They were, of a sort, brothers.

Beyond the compound's outer wall, Kor opted for a path that wound into Steel Rose's fog-cloaked dense woods with blue-green trees wailing their desire to venture forth. At the clan's boundary totem, abandoned watchtowers guarded against enemies long dead. An onyx dragon with the head of a hawk topped the rose-etched totem, pitiless black-diamond eyes forever on alert for the wretched days when his people fed the forest with their blood. Vines with glossy green leaves with reddish undertones, blister-inducing poison-leaf, reclaimed the towers.

Thick strands of light-catchers towered over the neutral ground; white nighttime glows dimmed to a dull blue. Double-winged horned flies swarmed the nectar burs of mighty knotted-copper needles. The flies scattered, singing in high pitch, an alert to the surround that dawn had arrived. Faster, his boots hammered buttery conviction into the mountain rock. Kor veered to a seldom-used offshoot covered in a blanket of moldy leaves, skipped over a tiny creek channeled by rocks and arboreal corpses coated in black algae, and leaped over lateral root growths reclaiming the land from human intrusion. He emerged from the misty woods at Heroes Boulevard near the fortress wall of Crew Defiance's compound.

A Defiance boy hopped a series of squares drawn on the boulevard's walkway, grinning—a reckless demonstration of happiness. An alert popped up on his retinal display. The boy played hopscotch. A training group charged up the hill in full battle gear.

Kor pulled the boy away and shoved him into a double hedge fronting the compound's wall, stirring up woody floral. "Go, fast!" Kor said.

The Defiance boy scrambled to the back of the hedge and made his way in a belly crawl to a worker passage gate. Kor swept his boot back and forth across the sandy blocks, scattering the offense. One of the trainers pinged him with a scan. In a quick-speed flash, he stood nose-to-nose with Kor, tactical goggles off. Sweaty musk overwhelmed the wood. Baps, the last person (after the General) he wanted to see, confronted Kor with a dead-eyed glare.

"Identify citizen," Baps said.

"Best friend?"

"You tell me, and it's *sir*."

Kor straightened to attention, eyes steady, chest out, arms to his sides.

Baps pointed to a streak of sand. "What is this?"

"A line, sir!"

"A lot of smeared chalk for a line. We've lashed several boys for playing Earth games. They've been daring each other to do it. Insubordinate runts."

Without missing a beat, Baps pointed to the hedge, directing one of his comrades to launch a search. "State your errors."

"Let's shortcut this by you telling me."

The talkback warranted a backhand. Instead, Baps pleaded with his eyes for cooperation. In truth, Kor was being an ass.

"On the ground, funny boy."

Kor dropped into a plank pose, palms against the pavement. Militants served, Militants obeyed, five reps, ten, he found his rhythm.

"Too fast," Baps barked. "No, yes, again no, control yourself."

Slow doesn't get me to the meeting on time.

Baps squatted to his haunches. "You'll be a man soon. Start acting like one or you'll be sent to the recycling tanks."

Kor locked his elbows on one last push and hopped to his feet. Vulnerability wasn't the Militant way. He stood at attention, waiting to be dismissed.

"I heard about the flute," Baps said. "What's next, a march for democracy?"

"I'm hurting on the inside," Kor said. "It's teeth and claws and energy suckers feasting on the wounds. I killed my love, and it has left me blind."

"On your face, blind boy baby doll. One hundred, or you're off to a cage until sunset."

Baps's comrade planted his feet and fondled his gun. Sapphire claimed the horizon. Antigrav transports glided up the boulevard to pick up trainees. Before the massacre, they had come for him. An escape run tempted; no offense if he eluded capture, but an extra-long stay in a hanging cage if he failed.

Worker drones tended the boulevard's parkway, topped the mulch beds of trees and gardens, added crushed granite to the walkway, and tested a sprinkler system shooting off streams and droplets at their targets with programmed precision. The workers wore pale gray shorts and short-sleeve shirts, showing off bracelet tattoos on their arms and bands around their calves, the designs simple, striped, solid, geometric—probably meaningful. No one paid them much attention. Kor had a keen sense that the opposite wasn't true.

Baps's comrade returned without the boy—a victory and a good portent for the day. With his friend distracted, Kor landed a right hook—the satisfying smack improved by the thump of Baps's ass hitting the pavement. As a bonus, the numbness faded. "That feel like a baby doll to you?"

The other trainer raised his gun. Baps waved him off and wiped the blood from his mouth. "You're lucky I like a man with balls."

Baps pointed at his gun-toting comrade to resume the training run. The trainees formed up and trekked up the hill. Baps grabbed Kor's bicep. "I know these streets. You shouldn't be here. After the OV bombing, everything and everyone out-of-place gets extra scrutiny." He kissed Kor on the cheek. "Stop with the Earther music obsession. Stay out of trouble."

His friend raced off to join his troop. Using his boots, Kor dispersed the smudged line, leaving no trace of a violation for anyone to ponder. The worker drones refocused on their tasks, becoming one with the landscape, but they had revealed themselves to be alive.

Calm lay in the count of his breath. Test walks to establish a routine would have been wise. In the boulevard's median, larger-than-life statuary challenged his morning mission. Kill-brands darkened the ancient man's leathery patina head to toe, a role model, a hero, the opposite of a self-seeking, music-loving, flute-playing sneak of a man.

Kaleidoscopes of tiny paintwings fluttered by in carefree whirls. Pretending the hopscotch board remained intact, he made a half move after the colorful insectivores. Real men didn't skip and hop. But why not? Jump long, then short, spread the feet, and do it again to invisible lines in an addictive replay.

The meeting time was getting tight. He rushed down the mountain to the nearest station. Onboard the tube train, away from others, he plopped onto a bench. The tube car sped down the mountain. Kor darkened the window, pretended to meditate, and after a twisting pause, deleted the Code from his link's active memory.

CHAPTER VII

"You've found someone, haven't you?"

Jeth ignored Sala's insistent question arriving on the drag of humid wind.

"Have you lost interest in me such that I no longer warrant acknowledgment?"

Meticulous and patient, Jeth continued to work on a visualization project, shaping soaring edifices topped with dramatic cones bathed in silvery, golden, copper, and amber lights, curving in easy grace, a painstaking replication of the view from his long-lost bedroom—Thalia, one of many lost cities of the first humans. Dramatic and poetic, Thalia developed into a vertical city of skyways, elevated parks, and balconies in the clouds.

Except for his research, Jeth had lived a small life. In that respect, not much had changed since his death.

Narrowing his focus, he adjusted the tint of a woven grass rug under his bed, adding yellow to the electric green. Was that right? Memories, dreams, and hopes blended until one became the other. Did he care? In far space, a nova burst in the starless night, a concentration of human destiny amplified by a cohort of telepathy-enhanced minds drew a part of his consciousness to a man destined to shape the future, a man who burned for his freedom, a man much like himself.

The continuum, the seventh dimension, the fundamental plane of true reality upon which all else floats, cannot lie. Humanity survived the Mass Exodus, and they are once again ready for great things.

"Answer the question, my juicy sweet."

"Never call me that, my pretty sunbeam," Jeth answered.

"Civilizations have no doubt come and gone while you spend endless hours on your viewscapes. Face the facts—you've lost your mind."

Unable to hold a human form any longer, Jeth changed into a rolling cloud. Bursts of black lightning framed in garish blue crackled throughout Jeth's being. Part of his form boiled and broke off, drifting away with the rotating rush of hurricane clouds.

"You're wrong, my pretty sunbeam. These creations keep me sane. I must not create anything new. I might forget; I might confuse what was real."

"Do you realize your precious rug started out as topaz?" Sala said.

"You're a spiteful figment of my imagination. You know nothing."

"I know you used to hate green." The temperature of Sala's voice dropped to an icy front. "You fancied yourself a god before Zaxa condemned your evaporating consciousness into this excruciating limbo."

Thunderous bolts erupted from Jeth's cloud form, an electric vomit of unchecked rage. Zaxa was pure evil in evil's wickedest manifestation—a name never to be uttered. Pieces of Jeth crystallized into dry ice. The shift to solid form hurt—preferable to Sala's smug satisfaction. He had failed to achieve his dream of using the Cosmic Song, his creation, his genius, to ascend into a god-form with his one true love. Trapped within the Cosmic Song's void, an expanse vast and yet nowhere, he was a god, albeit a caged one.

"You've found someone, haven't you? You've found someone who can set us free."

Jeth calmed himself to draw back his ebbing parts. "Yes, dear Sala."

Density concentrated. A woman with fierce, intelligent eyes set in elegant porcelain-doll cheeks emerged with the grace of a ballet dancer. Sala floated in her human form before she transformed into the monster Zaxa. Bold and young, she wore her favorite street clothes; electric red cropped leggings, low-heel shoes, and a graphic T-shirt of moths diffusing into flight. As always, she wore three matching bracelets, this time in cerulean blue to match the swirl in her hair. Sensuous lips beckoned for contact. Bits of Jeth fizzed into the emptiness.

"The seal upon this domain," Sala said, "is unbreakable."

"A crack," Jeth said, "enough for me to liberate a spark of my consciousness."

"Yet you waste time on your humdrum visual. Finding him was impossible, and that was the easy part. Your sanity slips. Your memories fade. Do you remember what it was like to be a real man?"

"A pox to your every molecule, dear Sala," Jeth said. "Why did I ever love you? Why did I try to save you?"

Sala dragged her fingers through Jeth's awareness, indwelling in him a perception of temperature, of liquid butterscotch warmth, a tender, mocking gesture. "Obviously, you like to cower in this prison. It's safe. It's boring. It's you."

Jeth concentrated his essence into the man he once was. Middle-aged, self-assured, with glasses to mitigate his high forehead. Over time, Sala studiously matched both her bracelets and a splash of hair color with his cerulean pocket square in his lab coat. Luta's snow-white blooms wafted in syrupy sweet bliss. If he surrendered a touch more, he would believe Sala nibbled his earlobe. The scent of her hair charged the void with electric possibility.

"I've connected to someone in the continuum," Jeth said. "Human."

"You're sure?"

"I feel his heartbeat. I hear his thoughts."

"Tell me his name."

"Kor of Steel Rose."

"Do you have the balls to do this right?"

"I will do whatever I must, my pretty sunbeam."

"You will have to bring him to this Cosmic Song to set us free."

"Done."

"You will have to conquer his spirit."

"Done."

"You will have to kill him," Sala said.

***

On the other side of the mountain range, 2,000 feet lower and far out of view from the central city, Kor hopped off the mag-tube at the Bottom's Up junction and stepped into an enveloping sea of workers, metal, and soot. The air stank of unregulated industry. Dust accumulated in the back of his throat and mixed with pungent cooking odors in competition with metallic fumes. Sex shops jammed against nightclubs, against branding parlors, against pothouses; a bewildering fusion of musty reds and yellows banked the flow of dutiful columns of gray heading to and from their labors, their processionals, grim to dull, peppered with lively talk, with hints of delight.

He glanced back at the tube station several times until he rounded a corner. It was his first time in a worker district.

More than a few locals sized him up. *I shouldn't be here. I know it. They know it.* No veils in this neighborhood. Tattoos curved around hooded eyes, swirled to cheekbones, around the workers' square forehead brand. One of them tracked his progress with laser focus. Kor stumbled into a street cafe steeped in doughy sweets with tables full of men demolishing their meals. Workers dipped chunks of pastry sugar into more sugar with amazing alacrity. *Quicken the pace. Move to safer ground.* The pipe-tattooed arm of a foreman grabbed him from behind.

"You stand out like sweet meat at a private bathhouse, pretty boy," the foreman said.

Heartbeats skidded into hiccups.

The foreman raised a finger to a pair of brawny comrades. "Hold him."

Kor shook them off and squared his shoulders. "Who do you think you are?"

"The one who makes sure no trouble happens in this district."

"I'm here to buy pruning shears for the estate's rose gardens."

"High Clan pretty boys don't play fetch."

The foreman's comrades re-established a firm hold. Higher functions streamed a virtual map of the area into his visual cortex. His handlers were outmatched in a fight. On the flip side, escaping would draw an enforcer action.

A middle-aged man sprinted past, barreling through the crowd.

"Runner!" A slew of men pointed at the fleeing worker, repeating the rebuke.

The runner grabbed a handful of foot bracelets from a kiosk and flung them at an oncoming white-clad Marshal whose holy mark bore three red hooks. Workers scrambled, pushing over food carts and each other to get out of the line of fire.

"Another piss-blooded Marshal," muttered the foreman.

An orange-belt appeared further up the street, zapping the runner with a red-lit control rod. Veiled priests, including the Marshal, dragged the code-breaker over to the foreman. Workers within eye-shot kept their heads down.

The foreman's burly comrades stepped back to kneel, releasing Kor. The Marshal's three-hooked **X** forehead brand required respect, but as an elder, a survivor who maintained a take-no-prisoners physique, he demanded more. Five ruby red eyes formed an arc over the holy mark; at least 50,000 cleansings, an impressive kill total to earn an honorary statue. Kor crossed his arms in an **X** and dipped his head to the Marshal, the correct protocol, and, as a bonus, avoided the priest's dissecting evaluation.

"I am Marshal Torz. Blessed are the men of Zorn who obey their superiors."

"I accept your authority," the foreman said.

"Surveillance detected this worker singing. Subsequent investigation found subversive music on his link."

"A minor violation. The lash should suffice."

"He pushed my apprentice. Degraded obedience conditioning won't be tolerated from a drone."

The foreman's shoulders sagged. His gaze brushed over the sprawled worker. "My top welder. I can't meet quotas when I keep losing my best men."

"A Judge confirmed my verdict."

"Take him then."

Marshal Torz turned to Kor. "What's your purpose here, High Clan boy?"

"Nothing for you to worry about, Marshal Torz."

"It's my job to worry."

You mean to meddle. Kor sensed Torz would see right through any "pruning shear" cover story. "I'm on a mission for the General."

Torz's eyes narrowed—likely debating whether Kor had the balls to dare such a lie. In the space of his hesitation, the Demiurge came into view, sparkling in a cloak of bejeweled needles. Was Demi tracking him? Torz's jaw clenched with displeasure. They inspected each other. Demi added a golden arc to the ears, rotated others, and poured serene energy against the Marshal's stone-faced resistance.

"A pleasure to see you, Marshal Torz," Demi said.

"Unexpected streets for you to grace."

"This young man agreed to give me a worker district tour before I left."

"Not according to protocol. This isn't your world. My home, my rules."

"Why, Marshal Torz, that had the ring of defiance."

"Push me too hard, and I'll bleed you dry with your own needles."

Demi's tunic shifted from purple to gray. Without a wince, the Creator placed a half dozen emerald tips in her hairless skull. "Coherence is in motion, Marshal Torz. Do take care that it doesn't crush you."

Torz motioned to his subordinate, and they dragged the welder away. Demi's eyes brightened. She removed a slew of needles—hinting at the beginning of a smirk. To the last man, the cafe cleared, leaving behind a mess of tumbled chairs, a few spilled drinks, and an assortment of eggs, breads, cheeses, and pastries from the never-touched to bits and scraps.

"Everyone thinks you're trouble," Kor said.

"Everyone has it backward. Opposites attract."

Demi's expression settled into a serene peace reminiscent of someone who had overdosed on happy pills. One hundred percent creepy and mesmerizing.

"Torz is no fool," the foreman said. "Go, before I think twice."

Demi's bejeweled needles twinkled with a bewitching shine. "You heard the man," Demi said, gesturing to Kor to move along.

Kor's command and control hologram popped into his visual mind, filling it in with real-world data within range. Heavy electronic surveillance stimulated a low-level headache. Between the kiosks and the foot traffic, they eked along in the sooty warren. Dutiful workers poured out of concrete-paneled cellblocks. A gaggle of short men in pink shrouds emerged from the crumbling entryway of a ten-story tenement, their faces hidden beneath coral veils. *The Cult of Husbands, caretakers of the breeders.* Pinprick sensations broke out across his chest, a cloak of thorns. *Never to be touched, to be acknowledged, or to be seen.*

The pink entourage headed his way. A cloaked Husband turned his way in a split of time; unusual for a Husband, he challenged with a hell-frozen, direct stare. Kor trembled, convinced of an impending curse. The world continued, or maybe the damned wouldn't know. Workers brushed past, smelling of metal and chemicals. They seethed in calm detachment. They avoided eye contact, yet their wayward attention betrayed their dissatisfaction that an outsider walked among them.

"You harbor wild faith, dangerous to play with," Demi said. "Beautiful and painful to experience. You must be rid of it."

In tow, he arrived at a grimy, four-story, gray brick tannery with a towering, decommissioned smokestack. A blade sign with a concave infinity symbol with wings in flight swung in a gentle creak, escaping, trying, frozen in rusted metal form. Under the swinging sign was a soot-covered name, Club Tanner.

"You are the spark," Demi said. "Something significant is about to catch fire."

"Will it hurt?" Kor said.

"Outcomes are undetermined. There is no avoiding a cost."

Demi relocated across the street in front of a gritty, open-air gym full of drenched, greasy men pumping iron, climbing ropes, running the perimeter, carrying weights in a farmer's walk, with nary an exercise machine in sight. The lot of them dosed themselves with determination. Grunts, heavy breathing, and final-rep yells from the workers' efforts intoxicated. Motionless, an otherworldly flower, Demi waited.

Kor opened a hidden compartment on his armband. Empty cavity . . . no access . . . no entry . . . a million credits that the General removed the access chip. A rash kick to the metal-plated door yielded meek head checks from passing low-tier workers.

Square windows started at the second level. Mold, soot, and dirt caked the clay bricks, a treacherous climb. Three minutes until lockout. A green-belt sporting a sheer veil advanced with hands clasped, reciting the Code. No worker warren grime sullied the white tunic. He trailed the novice-grade, rubbing his granite charm. Not long ago, the future priest spoke for Kor.

"We live the life of the brave," the green-belt said, "but not of the reckless. For the life of our people comes not from the mountains, the land, or the sea but from our blood that we sacrifice to the empire." In spans neither quick nor slow, the boy recited promulgations in rounds.

Kor absently crossed his arms in the **X**. Demi brought her hands together in a now-or-never signal. A worker headed into the club. In a burst of quick-speed, Kor zipped to the opening, hand on the worker's shoulder. They passed through an inky curtain into a no-thrills dance hall. Huge drums lined each side—hooks, naked of hides, studded the ceiling. Men slow-danced to "Moving in Stereo"—surreal, a buzz, driving thoughts to bend, to dip, to discover never-before connections.

In the dim light, bodies brushed him, swaying in languid ease. Musky aromas stacked with working-class perfumes dueled with tannery stench and stagnant chemical water. A man wearing a sleeveless vest, sexy and playful, took him by the hand, leading him in unhurried curves to the middle. The music shifted to an upbeat tempo. Kor put on vogue moves, stylized angular fluid grace, and invited his handler to do the same. Others formed a circle, shouting encouragement. Cheers and claps rippled in the group, escalating into joy as the men cut loose into a place without fear— a tribe bound in a shared spirit.

Leaders appeared on a stage in full bodysuits with faces blurred by mini-distorters; among them was a shrouded, veiled figure, shorter, smaller, unusual in stature. In a quick flash of change, the music stopped. The dancers became a rapt audience.

"Let us see!" someone shouted.

The onlookers stomped the stone floor faster and harder, the floor-quaking vibrations calling, "We are free, we are new"—a thundering march going nowhere. The sweat of men painted his body yet failed to quench the flames. One of the stage leaders, a Combat Master by his confident bearing, lifted the smaller man's veil. How could it be one of the most revered had become a traitor?

The smaller man's top half of his garment floated to the floor, revealing a supple figure unmarked by brands or other symbols. Braided hair entwined into an angel's crown atop a body lacking the musculature for carrying heavy guns.

"Recycle." The call repeated from scattered workers.

"Use your eyes," someone yelled. "She's female."

Kor started a stern rebuke. A tapering waist, rounding hips . . . he choked on the perfumed air. *No woman of the empire, not even the lowest servant, would allow herself to be on topless display to us sub-human barbarians. She can't be real.*

He took a hard turn to stillness. The breathing of hundreds of men became the new chorus. By the Red Beast, she was not a natural-born woman; he witnessed a real-life breeder. They had produced the Militant generations, but their existence was a sin that no one, not the natural-born nor his people, wanted to acknowledge. Motor controls resisted his frantic commands as he slumped over. *To see is death.*

Someone helped him up. "Look," the cultist said. "Fight the conditioning."

"Go away." Neck spasmed, nausea, noxious, sweat—his body shifted into full-scale revolt. *To see is death.*

The cultist held him fast. "Fight! Prevail! Exult!"

Kor yelled in return. Contortions wracked his legs. Fight for sanity. Avoid a direct gaze. Hold himself steady, a battle won. Many waged the same war.

The Combat Master took the breeder's hand. Kor stifled a condemning shout. In a burst of raw emotion, the shout stormed into the open. "Against the Code, against the rules, against the design of the Almighty Supreme!"

Stunned silence reverberated in the wake of Kor's judgment.

"Peace," said the Combat Master in a resonant voice enticing respect. "Welcome to Club Tanner, brothers, welcome to the Station. I hope you enjoyed the dance. We don't have much time. Surveillance never sleeps."

The commanding figure paused. "Few of us learn our true history, but hear this, my brothers. The Transgeneticists who created us to be the ultimate soldiers, separate from civilization yet in service to it, also created the breeders. They took away our mothers' intelligence, our sisters' passion . . . our daughters' feelings. They made them into farm animals to serve the machine."

Shouts of "free her" built into a raucous squall that shook Kor's atoms. The hairs on the back of his neck tingled. He must look away. He must obey. He must not see. *To see is death.*

"The Judges resist us. The Priests denounce us. Both need the Code to justify their control. The empire uses us against Psians, against Data Angels, against Workers, against Organics, to fight petty turf wars between the natural-born gentlefolk throughout the Starry Empire." He paused with dramatic effect. "They want us to do as we're told."

"No! We're free men!" the crowd growled. Infectious cries swelled, dooming them to the sin of disobedience.

"The crime against our mothers, our daughters, and our sisters belongs to others," the Master intoned, "but we will never be free as long as they suffer in bondage."

Kor pushed toward the exit; a brawny worker smelling of grease and pastry blocked the way.

"No one leaves until the Master finishes."

Kor's eyes burned. Abandonment of home and his clan sharpened into a desolate reality. Freedom called. Freedom screamed. But was that a selfish pursuit masked into something noble? He would bury his conscience, bury his feelings, surrender his needs, surrender his dream to be real. Better to honor his father's wishes. Better to live the life of a dead soul.

The lighting over the stage brightened as they walked in sync to the fore. He was hidden. She was revealed—a goddess of the Eclipse, smooth and black with shades of opalescent blues and compelling eyes highlighted in glittering gold makeup.

"I'm Tara. I'm here for you to witness. Mind. Body. Spirit. The Truth. Everything. Are you man enough to see?"

She has a name? She speaks? Kor's mind crackled. "It's a trick." The words rang loud and clear.

The breeder's bold gaze challenged the crowd. "You," she pointed straight at Kor. "Big talker. Ask me a question."

Feet shuffled. Conditioned air whirred. The room's heat spiked. A man coughed. Others wept. A beleaguered worker dry-heaved halfway to the afterlife. The light around the breeder tightened, wrapping her in a translucent cloak.

"Say something," someone growled.

Kor grasped at remembered fragments. "Name the service order ranks highest to lowest."

"Combat Master, General Superior, General, Strategist, Tactician, Commander, Major, Captain, First, Maris."

Breeders lacked intelligence, but she answered true. "You're a freak," Kor said, blurting the obvious.

"No more than you, big talker." Arms folded, she cast a potent spell to drain his strength. The Transgeneticists crafted the Code in perfect reflection of their Militant creations, writing the Code's truth into Militant DNA. Faith splintered . . . too much to un-believe and to believe in the same crack of time.

"Ask me the ratio of pi," the breeder said. "Give me a riddle to solve. Numbers to calculate. The priests taught me many things before I escaped the inner sanctum."

Kor bent over in a coughing fit next to a hacking worker who braced himself on the floor. Self-aware breeders in the holiest place. Impossible to conceive. What was true? What wasn't? Knowledge poisoned, he might as well flip his charm to decide the truth.

Colors went mad in his mind's debris. Strange feelings surged into the void of what he once knew to be true. The sensations bellowed for recognition. They came, they filled, they drove him to a compulsive craze of images to break his mind. *The Starry Empire engineered our forefathers to keep us apart from the natural humans created by the old gods. Yet I want to discover, to explore her for the simple wonder. I am infected with the desire, the need, to sin.*

Kor lashed his mind in frenzied haste—bit his tongue—no antidote to the unbridled wanting. Tara was more than a breeder, more than she was made to be, and so was he. The woman uncovered him in places the Transgeneticists had long ago failed to excise.

"What have you done to me?" Kor rasped.

"The Code, the book of our truth," the Combat Master said, "is a lie. If I sin, let the Red Beast gorge on my spirit when I die." He joined hands with the breeder. "Tara and I are one."

"You go too far."

"We love each other."

"Must you know anything else?" Tara said.

"I am also one with my clan partner," the Combat Master said. "Love manifests in ways as infinite as the universe. Listen to your heart and be amazed."

Tenderly, the resistance leader covered his wife with a shirt and escorted her off the dais.

No one spoke. How could he accuse others who followed their hearts? How could anyone? No one in the hall wanted to be what the Starry Empire decreed, what the Code dictated, what the priests commanded, what the clans required, whatever that meant and however that manifested. Everyone, freaks and all, was a true brother and sister.

In the lingering hush, the hall went dark.

Adrenalin flooded Kor's bloodstream. Shouts boomed. Fear spiked as men surged toward the entrance. *Bad move.* Metal from studded leather pressed into his skin with the force of branding. Command-and-control displays went inactive. *Outside interference. Very bad.* Spotlights flashed brightly—a room full of faces asked the same question—*how to survive?* The inky curtain vanished. Helmeted soldiers poured into the club. Screams of "save us" and "enforcers" blistered in a horror house of desperate howls.

The Master and his entourage disappeared. Workers dropped to their knees with arms crossed in the Holy **X**, bowing before the enforcers in a plea for mercy. Kor bulled his way toward the dais. Green targeting lights flooded the space. Red beams shot by. A kneeling man in beseeching prayer lurched, his ecstasy hardening into disjointed euphoria. Charred flesh blended with the spicy aromas and tannery stench. Enforcer fire multiplied in laser-lightening horror. Panic bound his stomach into choke points.

"Slaughterhouse," a worker cried in bewilderment. "Run!"

Together, they pushed through hapless, praying men.

The spotlights went dark. Vision switched to infrared. A lance of lava sliced into his outer thigh, and he fell on a fresh corpse. The worker reached out to help him up. In a flash, Kor dropped back to the floor. His newfound ally fell on top, scorched and dead.

An enforcer pulled the worker off Kor, blinding him with a beam. Was the enforcer a neighbor, a childhood playmate, a rival clansman? The enforcer moved on. Confused, Kor rolled over. Why wasn't he killed? Afterimages floated in his eyes, embers from a dying fire. The high-frequency laser shots ceased. Boot thuds fanned out across the room. Sickly thumps of piled flesh built into anonymous mounds to befit the less-than-human.

"Hang 'em on the hooks," one of the enforcers said. "Launch neighborhood tours."

On a rash impulse, Kor got to his knees and sang a buoyant Collective Soul tune he had played at the café before the tragedy. *Breathe…*

He lost track after the first verse, humming to the beat.

Enforcers formed a firing squad. Kor stood.

"He's the terrorist tagged by Marshal Torz," an enforcer said.

Green targeting dots lit up Kor's torso.

"Who should I piss on first?" Kor said.

The flash of blaster-fire lasted less than a moment.

CHAPTER VIII

"Om."

The number of free people totals no more than a chosen few. Handlers wait outside the womb for the rest to assign us to assorted prepackaged outcomes somewhere along the food chain of almost-human to fully dehumanized. By trick or by might, Charronna would rewrite her fate. Breathe, relax, listen to singing bowl enchantment, enjoy the respite from duty in her fortress of solitude, and repeat. No emergencies clamored for attention, no doomsday predictions stoked anxiety, a reprieve from playing the role of a valued Chorus lackey. In a universe committed to rationed happy endings, the best to be expected.

"Om." A hundred more of those, and she would survive another day.

Soothing deep-tone chimes interrupted. She didn't need her telepathic talents to ascertain that some trifling bureaucrat had arrived to request services for whatever the Chorus decreed as the urgent need of the hour. Sissy, her assistant, emerged from behind the Twin Helix altar. Expectant, she waited, exact as always with her presentation, tied up hair, no makeup except a bare hint of matte pink lipstick, wearing a spotless marine blue uniform, one hundred percent on duty, the ideal citizen.

"A savant calls," Sissy said.

"What color are his hands?"

"Jade, highest aspirant."

"I'll deal with the bothersome minion after my meditation."

"You dare keep an agent of the Chorus waiting?"

"This is my sanctuary from the Smiling Court. Trust me, I'm a much better minion after my downtime."

Sissy bit her lip. "The whisperers claim Sentinel brought seers to the Oracular."

A tingle spread from Charronna's neck around to her face-- a mind–body alert to beware. Standard protocol mandated her participation in any sort of welcoming committee for Psians. The Chorus relied upon her to keep the Smiling Court cleansed of their manipulation. Non-Psian telepaths like herself were rare. Fully informed? She should be eating and sleeping with the telepaths and eavesdropping to the fullest extent possible.

Water off my pretty ass. The well-worn mantra shield, reassurance that she could repel any threat to her position, calmed jingly nerves.

The mood shattered into amorphous scraps, she silenced the singing bowls and increased the luminosity from the hanging lattice lamps. The Chorus obsessed with worry ever since the no-idea-off-limits Earthers showed up with their showy, armed-to-the-death ultra-drive ships. A spa day would cool stressed neurons. Strolling through the Arcade, she could pretend she lived a normal life while dropping the credits in a carefree spending spree. Engage in normal conversations, eat fabulous food, wear the latest fashion, dabble in a back-and-forth on non-lethal hobbies over candlelight, opposite heart-stopping killer smiles from a stud of a man who understood how to be both hard and kind and at the right times.

Sissy reverted to her classic full-on observation mode, trying to decipher Charronna's mood. "I know I'm not the easiest gig," Charronna said. She motioned Sissy closer for a tight embrace and playfully nibbled her neck before moving to her succulent mouth.

Sissy giggled. "I would love a repeat of last night, but the savant. . ."

"Yes, yes, always ready to serve until insanity or death."

"We have no higher honor. Without our courage, the natural order falls."

Charronna kissed Sissy on the forehead. "Never lose your passion. See to my three o'clock at the Sweet Crave whorehouse."

"*Salon,* and you go too much. You're getting a certain reputation."

"Well-deserved. I can survive without love, but not without sex. See to your duty."

With Sissy dismissed, Charronna scrutinized the savant—likely male, though with savants, the lot of them asexual, such distinctions didn't matter. The intrusive peon waited at the hexagonal entrance, daydreaming of being a real human. Not that she would know—the Court's handlers earned doctorates on how to strip empathy, compassion, and love out of people.

Mirrored panels inset into the walls reflected feigned assurance. Black leather hugged her every delicious curve. Fishnet on the upper sleeve showcased taut, smooth, blemish-free, fair-as-fairytale skin. Killer green eyes—men lost their souls to those eyes. Gods, she was stunning.

The savant fidgeted. A petty triumph to put another at unease—the Court's favorite candy; payback for the insult names peddled throughout the Smiling Court behind her back. Red Witch, Red Dragon, Red Scourge, if Charronna adored her hair any less, she would dye it to confuse her detractors. The intruder raised a jade hand in a huffy demand for recognition, causing its striped gold and black sarong to swish. Charronna struck back with a time-tested, heart-chilling threat in the savant's subconscious: "*I know your worst fears.*" There was no reaction, not a twitch or a flinch from the ill-tempered underling, unusual for one of them to be so undaunted.

Charronna rattled a bottle of paradise pills, setting it back on a shelf unopened. "Enter."

The savant stepped in without a bow. Sprays of calming yellow-bell countered nascent anxiety. Receded chin, overhung flab on the belly—the self-assured savant pretended importance belonging to others.

"The farseeing Chorus has a vital matter for your attention," the savant said.

"Vital, you say? Well, I haven't heard that word used in a long time. Get to the point."

With a quick comb to the side of his thinning hair, the savant revealed a cybernetic device nestled within his skull. "I speak for Sentinel."

Unease punched holes into both lungs. Breathe in the yellow-bell, remember calm, sex, the morning workout, anything. "My apologies honored Sentinel. How may I serve?"

"A Militant of interest escaped capture on Zorn."

"You promised I would never have to go back."

"Promises remain valid in the conditions they are made. Conditions have changed. So, too, must the promise. Existential threat abides in the sphere of possibility. The Earthlings disrupt our stability—our empire quickens, evolves to revolution."

Revolution wasn't always bad. Best for Charronna not to say that out loud. The Earthers shared technology, including their ultra-drive, a boost to a civilization that kept technology at arm's length after the War against the AIs left billions of people dead. The Smiling Court had not yet deciphered the motives for Earth's ruling Magnates, who evolved from a complex merging of democratic, communist, and corporate institutions. But both sides benefited from the relationship. Information traded through the Grid expanded exponentially. In exchange for expansion rights in unclaimed space, they provided invaluable technical assistance to planetary engineering efforts in the Pleiades star cluster.

And the shoes, praise the gods, I love my heirloom Prada shoes.

Revolution, of a sort, was well underway.

"For the first time," the savant said, "Truth and Gnosis spread its awareness over the entire human web: our Starry Empire, the Earth Confederation, the Polarian League, the wild outlanders, and pirates beyond and between the three civilizations."

Charronna shuddered. Communions required loss of identity. The strongest Psian mind, stretched over parsecs, sometimes dissolved into solar winds, never to return.

"The Communion's focal point of instability vibrated a name."

"Which frightened you."

"We experienced fear. The Blue Compromise unravels."

Charronna froze. She had done more than her fair share of work to uphold the "compromise." The empire used her to ruin. Now, they wanted to level what remained.

Anger quarantined in internal lockdown escaped into her gaze, enough to melt the skin off the peasants. Twelve years ago, when she was barely a teenager, the Chorus ordered her to Zorn to crush the Oath-Breaker rebellion. Militants had no interest in women by design—no worries, the troops would rape or otherwise abuse the womenfolk. She might as well have been the devil. The godforsaken thoughts and images she fought through . . . six hundred and ten proud minds disintegrated under her inexperienced touch; one embittered survivor; two, if she confessed to the mental wreckage left behind by the interrogations.

"I was with them when they died. Please, don't make me go back."

"The matter is vital."

"Are you listening, you monster?"

The admonition leaped from her throat—satisfying and terrifying, a chilling loss of restraint to claim her power. An earsplitting pause ensued. Would Sentinel dispatch an executioner, the bloody ax held high to cut off another rebellious head?

"If you had said that outside your sanctuary, you would be executed despite our need and your privileged status." The savant raised a jade fist, a warning of impending punishment. "A tolerant society is a dead society. The people must be managed. Do not further push the limits of your favor."

Charronna repressed an errant sob.

"Militants captured your initial target, Kor of Steel Rose, at an illegal assembly. Discover his contacts. Root out the contagion before revolutionary impulses take hold. If you fail, we will declare a state of upheaval. The Communion revealed unacceptable losses, more than we expected. Marginal probabilities show us defeated. You are the key to better futures." The savant blinked without expression like the quasi-automaton it was.

No matter how much she sprayed the yellow-bell, high, low, in the four directions, a virtual downpour, the savant's revelation swirled in her mind with tormenting persistence. Charronna retreated to the Double Helix altar. The savant stood under one of the hanging lamps. Communions rarely called out actual names— groups, worlds, macro forces of many kinds, but not persons. *The future casts its ripples from clouded waters to what end? Who can tell? More often than not, it brings a harvest of cruel moments to test those trapped in the oncoming present.*

She slid a hand over a breast, transient and magnificent. How much longer would she be able to keep her youth? Longer than she deserved if she played it right. "I request a Psian to interrogate Militants, hardship compensation, and sovereign status. I want to see my parents."

"You want everything."

"As everything is at risk, a fair exchange," Charronna said in a cool and level tone that conveyed no hint of the retort the comeback implied.

"We agree to your first two requests. Nexus controls your fate, but I concede support for sovereign rights if you score a perfect performance review. As for your parents, a nonnegotiable prohibition."

The savant withdrew. Sentinel and her cohorts must be in panic mode to trust Truth and Gnosis with the integrity of their minds. Complaints would be futile and self-diminishing. Round two, Charronna versus Zorn, was inevitable. Bloody hell. In front of a floating mirror, she touched up her makeup, treated puffy and red eyes, and practiced a don't-mess-with-me glower until she saw no visible chinks of vulnerability.

Somehow, some way, she would see her parents, and on a bright sunny day, flowers in her hair, she would see the love in their eyes missing from hers.

Ready for the outside world, she stepped into a columned hall busy with Smiling Court minions. Styles of dress varied to an astonishing range, yet a strict code of etiquette governed fashion. Cleaners and other low-level workers wore white pants and shirts. Savants wore sarongs in bright and soft colors. Citizens lacking noble rank kept to simple tunics and linen shift dresses, stylish but simple. At the top of the food chain, aristocrats who wielded power that even the Chorus respected flaunted their status with extravagant hair and headpieces, custom-fitted high-end one-of-a-kind outfits that shimmered, flowed, shaped, and mesmerized. Artisans had applied elaborate makeup and tasteful jewelry for both the women and men to finish the looks.

The red inverted triangle com-badge on Charronna's chest encouraged all of them to keep their distance.

At three o'clock sharp, Charronna swept into the salon for a sex-tonic strong enough to outlast a mission to a planet of women-hating barbarians. She brushed off the manager's effusive greeting. A blond facilitator overly fond of bangles knew the drill.

"Your viewing room is ready," the facilitator said, intercepting Charronna in a smooth walk.

Charronna offered an approving look at the facilitator's intricate gold-spun hairnet. "New fashion trend?"

The young woman winked. "The more elaborate, the better."

Charronna followed her into a private room of pristine walls and concrete flooring—gallery sophistication—with three monitors that hung like paintings. A worker-drone brought her a bubbly pink-rose crawl. Men flashed in exotic backgrounds, varied poses, handsome, sexy to be sure; she had tried them all.

"I want something over the top," Charronna said with a dismissive wave.

The blond winked, tapping through a hand-held menu. "Excellent! I have just the thing. Gorgeous!" Her eyes fluttered with excitement. "A P-Hyper fresh from the lab in our new Tuscany line. Enhanced everything and upgraded prowess. There isn't anything he can't or won't do. Monitors don't do him justice."

The Hyper strutted in, wearing only a black strap stretched thin. Tall, muscular, and slick with oil, he reeked of super-saturated, musky manhood. With each step, muscles bulged and flexed in seductive tension. Bright blue-velvet eyes and luscious lips incited Charronna to take him for a rambunctious spin.

"Flawless," she said, leading him into a room of caramel walls with a silky-sheet bed roomy enough for a crowd. Lush pillows accented and an all-the-frills-and-thrills black stainless steel restraint system for anyone into bondage. Charronna didn't require any help.

"Be gentle," Charronna said. "Remember, I'm in control."

The man-toy flashed ultra-white teeth. Surely, if the gods existed, they must be jealous. Charronna purred, shoving the lab spawn onto the bed. For precious moments, she put aside her assigned role to save the empire, lavishing in the lab spawn's sweet, simple mind. *Water off my pretty sweet ass.*

***

A dream imprisoned Kor. Voice surrounded, light engulfed, thoughts dulled until the light and the voice merged. The clinical voice demanded answers. His blood, his DNA, his training, and repeated lessons drove that requirement into muscle, into neurons, into the sub-atomic particles housing his soul. The impulse to obey coiled into his brain and squeezed against his every resistance.

"Remember your training," the voice said. "You attended an unlawful assembly of Blood King terrorists. Yes or no?"

"Aye."

"How long have you been a member?"

"Does today count? If so, one."

"You served a stint in the Ninety-Fifth Trainee Battalion during a wargame exercise for green-bloods."

"You know the answer."

"Psian ghost-wizards coerced your mind. You withstood an entire telepathic company before succumbing."

Kor slammed his mind shut.

"After debriefing, the psych-wardens released you because of your exceptional resistance. How did the Psian tactic make you feel?"

Kor squeezed his hands into fists. "Wake me up, and I'll show you."

Where was he recruited? Who? How did the initial contact occur? What form of communication? What kind of probe was used? How tall was the leader? Mesomorph? Endomorph? Why did Kor attend? The questions pursued—a carnivorous pack hungry for answers.

"Do you love your father?"

The question dug into Kor. Without hesitation, he would die for the General. But did he love his father? Disagreement often divided them into warring camps. Mistrust separated them. But even in the dark places, he loved his father.

The ever-present light wavered. In a snap, he floated in a spacious sky, the weight of his treason dispersed in a weightless wonderland. The sensation, the sheer thrill of it, rivaled the first time his manhood revealed itself in full. Wings sprouted on his back. He hooted and laughed, doing double backflips into flurries of rainbow hearts. Lightning crackled above, ripping, shining blades that cut into the dream. Gloomy scars proliferated in the injured sky. A different voice reverberated, stiff and impatient.

"Tell us what we want to know, boy."

"Catch me if you can." Kor flipped over, flying, diving.

"You must obey or go off to lessons."

The booming demand hammered. Spittle flew from his mouth; his blood transmuted to unbreakable liquid iron. The bad guys could be defeated. The dreamscape below solidified, gained texture, and evolved into limestone, into weathered mesas and valleys that exuded the ancient, unyielding topography of Zorn. Kor dove—wings vanished the moment his feet touched the rough surface. Desperation erupted into a foot-stomping panic. The limestone remained intact. Light devoured a bleeding sky.

Think of anything—daydream, stargaze. For once, put those skills to productive use. Goldilocks pranced by in whiffs of warm cornflakes as she twirled a hand drill. On her heels, a handsome prince high-stepped while juggling self-playing flutes. A fairy princess sashayed around a digging fork, gliding in a greenish spectral fog. Further off, dwarves chased after a ravenous pack of chomping pruners. The General would absolutely disapprove.

"Does anyone have anything useful?"

Lilac, mauve, and rose stripes poured from the sky, a rainbow dropping to the mesa. From the liquid light, a mature woman in a poufy pink dress emerged holding a sledgehammer, its head polished to a wicked, red-slipper gleam. "Will this do?"

"Aye." Grinning, Kor bowed, took the tool, and heaved the striking face against the mesa. Blow after blow translated into bits of stubborn topography. Sparks flew. Drive amplified. Chunks of limestone dissolved from his furious onslaught. Boulders floated away in showers of electric arcs. He was Thor, the Hammer God, and nothing would stand against his might. This time, he would get away.

"Escape attempts are futile."

Within the torrent of flying stones, the devouring light swallowed him whole. "Show us the terrorist leader," the voice said.

Pictures formed of the Combat Master standing on the dais next to the mesmerizing beauty of Tara. The Master's distortion mask made him impossible to identify, but the use of such tech narrowed the suspects.

Growling, he slammed the sledgehammer into the limestone. Deep fissures snaked outward. He swung again into a haze of pulverized rock. He was no baby doll. The voice demanded obedience. With a battle cry, Kor swung the hammer one last time, drawing on the energy of his unprocessed anger. The meeting of rock and hammer shook the dream, and a gap appeared. Escape? A trap? *Gamble on hope*. Kor jumped through to the other side.

Peacefulness, a realm between galaxies, awaited him as the crack closed. In the midst of nothingness, a solid surface supported his feet. In the absence of light, somehow, he perceived into the depths. Direction was a meaningless construct. From behind, something grabbed ahold of him.

A double-winged creature, its scales half black and half white, its head half monstrous and half angelic, pulled him toward a swirling fog illuminated with heavenly brightness in an ocean of night. A blue pinpoint emerged from the fog, growing into a burning corona. Icy flames danced around the outer rim, striking out in volatile surges. The inscrutable eye penetrated his awareness. *The Red Beast preys upon weak souls, adding to its hunger with each consumption.*

A wave of weakness left Kor hollowed. The double-winged creature must be the emissary of the Red Beast; the creature's red eye burned while its green eye glistened. "One of the gods wishes to speak with you."

Oh, is that all?

In a sudden transition, the burning corona transformed into a disembodied face holding the flat boredom of existence sustained too long. A pale blue aura ringed the middle-aged visage with a supernatural vibe. The apparition drifted closer.

"I am Jeth-ka. You are my savior."

"*The* Jeth-ka? Get real. Not even gentlefolk kids believe in the old gods."

"Ignorance is timeless."

"Why does a god need saving?"

"I'm trapped in a void of shimmering sound."

"Sounds complicated."

"I offer a priceless treasure of one free wish."

Kor folded his arms. "You're no fairy godmother. What's your agenda?"

"Revenge," Jeth-ka said, "one of the few things able to sustain an imprisoned god through the bleaching of time."

"I'm no one's rag doll, and I'm not into revenge."

Color gushed from the pores of reality. White marbled floor spread under Kor's feet. An immense coffered dome rose from the expanding surface with a rib cage of crystal supporting panels of transparent rose and gold, a cathedral of light. The twelve pillars of life formed around Jeth. Vito-Chemical, water, heat, wind, electromagnetism, and matter floated in a half-circle. On the other side, in a matching sequence, love, blood, passion, breath, consciousness, and soul hovered. Above, vibration manifested as quivering strings that showered the pillars with streaming harmonics. In a greater circle, towering men and women shaped in granite, bronze, ice, wood, shadows, iron, and more observed in endless contemplation.

The Pantheon of Days . . . the splitting of God-the-Supreme into the forms of creation.

"The Observers represent what we once were and what we might be."

Kor passed a hand through Water, and his spirit sang. The urge to kneel cleaved into his bone, fired into the impulses of his inner, untrained child. If he permitted himself to relax, he would lose control. *Discipline.* The lessons had taught him that. He had failed to get away. The interrogator attempted to deceive.

"You will come to me," Jeth-ka said. "There is no time, no energy, to find another."

"Forget it."

"Our destinies are one."

CHAPTER IX

Three men glared at Kor—a Judge, a Ghost, and a Marshal. Kor cringed seeing the first, would kill the second if given the chance, and with fortune spit on the third. The ghost surveyed with inky, soul-feasting eyes. Few souls would escape his attention, but no one else had Strom as a father. The Judge, Broc of Crew Defiance, added bone-warping gravity through his formidable blue-black physique. Would his clan's historical ties to Crew Defiance help or hurt? Marshal Torz's rigid accusation completed the trio's damnation.

Kor confronted the gazes of interrogators with as much bravado as his shaky heart could muster, pushing off straitjacket bed covers in a huff. An energy curtain covered the windowless beige walls. A ceiling vent glowed with a lethal charge. Escape was impossible as if anywhere existed beyond the reach of the Starry Empire.

"Except for this dragon tattoo," the Judge said, brushing Kor's shoulder, "your skin is as clear and smooth as a babe's." Right in Kor's face, the Judge rotated his beefy flexed arms branded with clusters of bone-white skulls. "Where are your battle scars, your honor brands?"

"I removed them after the massacre."

The Judge motioned toward Kor's cock. "You might as well remove that."

"I don't need to prove my manhood to you or anyone else."

The Judge's lips parted in a faint grin.

"Enough," the Marshal said. He shook a hand scarred by burn weed. His red-eyed brands pulsed in three-dimensional fervor, a gateway for the entire Marshal priesthood to unload their withering contempt. "The interrogation failed. The people expect a public execution without delay, in the Crimson Circus, full spectacle."

The Judge doubled up his scrutiny to put Kor into a recognizable box to be sorted. Kor didn't flinch. The Ghost stirred; her pallid, ruddy skin flushed. With a simple projection of presence, a slight movement of the hands drew attention to dual rings of black and red on each finger, the highest rating, an improbability on the scale of the "improbability drive."

"No one has evaded one of my psychic probes without dying first," the Ghost said in a graveyard voice. "The exception warrants study."

"The Smiling Court issued orders for this one." The Judge wedged Kor's mouth open and grabbed his chin. "You're strong, lean, white teeth, healthy hair, a fine example of male genes. You could have gone far in the Brigades."

Torz's mention of the Crimson Circus gave Kor an idea—the worst ever—but facing his father would be unbearable humiliation. "I demand a blood duel."

The Judge's eyes flashed.

"The decrees of the Valiant Man guarantee the right to a blood duel for anyone who has killed on the battlefield," Kor said, his jaw muscles working against the Judge's hands. He relished each syllable.

Brawny arms sandwiched Kor's head. The Judge leaned in, his fierce gaze molten, raw, pissed-off, and feral.

"This traitor," Torz said, "murdered his platoon-mates during a training mission for children."

Memory burst from behind Kor's makeshift mental barriers. *I strike the first man, who slides down, hands on my chest, thighs, and calves, a bloody trail to mark my weakness. My soul flees into the lifeless eyes of my love before I shoot ten more. I shed no tears as I curse the forgotten gods. The psych-wardens reminded me a thousand times. "The boys who died were numbers," they said. "We are nothing more than numbers."*

"To the Psians belong the casualties," the Judge said. "Blood, however, soaks this young man's hands and his soul. I grant the test of honor in three days according to the old law."

"If he were my son, I'd whip him to a pulp."

"If I were your son," Kor quipped, "I'd never have made it to puberty."

The Judge's face softened from hard quartz to hard granite. "After your defeat, you will die the death of a traitor by the old ways—your corpse nailed to a yum-yum tree, your blood a feast to the ashen bark, your flesh ravaged by beasts and bugs, your bones left to be stripped by the wind and baked in the sun as a lesson to others."

Kor's pulse jumped. Ritual executions were reserved for men. The Judge set his jaw to conquest. "When you invoked the blood duel, you did so as a man of Steel Rose. Consider yourself ascended. After we leave, a medic will brand you with the holy **X**."

"Win," continued the Judge, "and your honor is restored. However, the Starry Empire put a claim upon you no one here can remove. Consider the merits of your death."

I'm to be judged as a man of Steel Rose. He pissed on the entire clan; his demand made his crime also Steel Rose's. The interrogators left in a snippy crossfire. Kor clasped his pendant, an onyx dragon with its proud birdlike feathered head. He was Kor, and he was Steel Rose, and the clan mustn't pay because he broke the rules, even if that meant the music would no longer play.

***

"Come to me at E'lan, the Dead Center," Jeth said.

He pushed intention into the words; the effort slipped into unconscious ease. If Kor had any attention to the present moment, he must hear. The unwavering message elicited no response. He shouted. He demanded. They had touched. They had communed. Frustrated, Jeth blasted elsewhere in Kor's awareness, full force into a heaving storm.

Someone had possessed the young man. Everywhere he resists, in the places he remembers, in the ones he forgets, in the ones he's never known. Nothing terrifies him more than losing control of his mind. Creation must give way to my pure desire to be forever with my beloved. This young blood must submit. Love such as mine must triumph.

Jeth shifted his attention into the void, leaving his spark dormant. Sala reclined on the bud of a stylized scarlet blossom, slow-eating a piece of juicy fruit. Unfamiliar presence filtered through a micro-leak in the prison, polluting a place impervious to external influence.

Done with the fruit, Sala sipped a cocktail. "Aliens probe the Cosmic Song. Curious beings, focused and ordered, dispassionate and purposeful. Definitely one of the Lords' many mistakes."

Jeth shaped into a thundercloud and crackled with repeated bursts. Lightning sprites sparkled around his form in a dance of peeved red glam. Sala never did approve of the old ways, creating intelligent species to amuse, an endless frontier of permutation to fuel the people's juvenile passion and the scientists' creativity. The continuum undergirding the universe rewarded creative force, whether divine or evil until mistakes were made; Jeth's had brought a full account of human hubris.

"We weren't ready to be gods," Jeth said.

"You think yourself divine material? We'll see about that."

"Don't be like the others."

"Like the women who laughed at your clumsy advances? The schools who mocked your Cosmic Song project? Or who fought against it? Your enemies are dead."

Not Zaxa.

Jeth immersed himself in thunderbolts to drown Sala's negativity in electric agony—a choice of pain to avoid another. *Once I'm a real god, she will love me. I will make her.*

Sala doubled over drifting rose petals. Jeth released the untamed energy and pulled tight to weather a buffet of roiling shocks. Phantoms drew close from the application of force external to the void. Always in command, Sala climbed to standing, eyes strained. Time flowed past, in minutes, in days; he had the patience of a god. Aliens put scanners, sensors, and monitors upon the Cosmic Song's alloyed skin—their intentions firmed, laced with danger and fear.

"Kimbrians," Jeth said. "Creators of anti-life weapons."

"They use us for some foul purpose," Sala said.

"Speculation."

"They seek the E'lani-human survivors."

"More speculation."

"You think those star-killers want to be friends? Please."

"Conjecture."

"It's over, my juicy sweet."

Jeth resisted the impulse to hide in a place devoid of hiding places; he might as well try digging a hole in the wind. Maybe he wanted the Kimbrians to destroy the artifact to end his everlasting excruciation—better that outcome than witnessing the triumph of the pitiless White Mother Zaxa. Created by Jeth as a self-renewing biological hive mind made up of millions of interconnected scarabs, White Mothers were a fallback plan for eternal life.

Vengeful and passionate, Zaxa would have found a way to survive despite the passage of millennia. Once she gained control of the Cosmic Song, in time, as she swallowed galaxies and spread into hyper and sub-space dimensions, she would remake this bubble of creation. His suffering would begin without delay. She needed to be no more than a small god for that.

****

Refreshed from her Sweet Crave diversion, Charronna headed to the Bureau of Facts and Circumstances via the Court's private tube system. Despite the rapturous sex, her nerves fluttered as she travelled through the tube leaving her mind muddled with anxiety.

The mere idea of going to Zorn left her adrift in places haunted by dreadful spirits. The Transgeneticists engineered Militants to resist telepathic coercion. No one wanted them under the influence of Psians, but neither be immune to control in case they rebelled. Every deep probe she had conducted on her Zorn mission escalated into a mind-scarring war. Vows never to return had been transmuted into gestures of powerlessness.

A seer, the Indeterminator no less, sat next to her in complete surprise. Few details escaped her sharp, penetrating yellow-brown eyes. "Feeling sorry for yourself?"

"You shouldn't be here without permission," Charronna said.

"I'm sensing hostility, dear one. I've never been your enemy."

"You act like one. I've lost count of the Psian plots I've dispersed."

"I've seen tens of thousands of futures. Whenever we try to take control, we end up as slaves, servants, in hiding, or dead. We never win. There are outcomes where we hold power. Still, we lose, no longer ourselves, mirrors to our worst impulses. We become the lie. There are nuances in our future, however, where we seek improvement."

"Sounds like my life. I'm sensing a punch line."

"I concealed part of the communion."

"You can do that? You are a sly one."

"The Chorus believes you're the key to stopping the Falling Star probability. The opposite is true. Whether for good or for bad, you and Kor are the key players to realization. Valuable as you are, they would, without hesitation, summon the executioners."

Charronna caught the Indeterminator's reflection in the tube window. Apparent sincerity was expressed in an open, relaxed face. But every aspect of the encounter could be a fabricated show to make her believe the unbelievable. "Revolution, seer mind games, or whining about my life are not on my agenda. I have a fantastic villa with a view of the ocean, a full staff, sex on demand, and loads of credits to buy whatever I want. Loyalty pays the bills. Why are you telling me this?"

"I'm fond of you. I enjoy our competitions. I enjoy them more when you think you've won."

Charronna turned to the seer with a faint smile. "Touché."

The seer's eyes expanded, fracturing mirrors brimming with possibilities.

"Survive the coming trials, and you will face the darkness alone. Elemental revelations await discovery, but monsters and night-foes guard the vaults of truth. Fall, and everyone falls."

"Exactly what did you see?"

The seer placed a hand on Charronna's forehead. "Hope and despair beyond measure. Call upon me when despair covers your hope, and I will come."

"Facing darkness isn't on the itinerary. I'll complete the mission and host a well-earned full-on glitz sovereign status soiree."

"Evade the future, hold back the wind, futile endeavors."

A soothing female voice announced the tube's arrival at the next stop. The Indeterminator kissed Charronna on the cheek and departed. The tube car accelerated further into the Smiling Court labyrinth. The sensation lingered, unexpected intimacy from someone who had always worked the other side. That the mission might not be as simple as expected competed with the kiss's afterglow. *Water off my pretty ass.*

"Bureau destination zone five," the female voice said.

After a retinal scan, she exited the tube and hurried through the network of corridors into her favorite place in the Bureau. Alabaster incense, perfumed of happy wildflowers, wafted in the Accumulation Room and blossomed in Charronna's lungs. The white smoke shrouded collection columns spewing raw metadata from telepathic, cyber, human, and AI agents throughout the empire. The heady fragrance saturated the bloodstream of Data Angles and enhanced their quiet focus. Statues of cloth in a whitewashed glow channeled the never-ending flood of data into something useful. Sift, evaluate, discard, or elevate, pirouette to additional information, a practice of meditative delight.

She directed a workstream to Zorn, a world under stress, thanks in part to Harmony's project to maneuver the religious orders to power by undermining the high clans, a dubious plan likely to be regrettable. Steel Rose battled marginalization, loss of status, and conflict brewed against traditional allies. Its survival was in doubt—the perfect breeding ground for revolution.

A query pinged her comm-link. A Smiling Court minion sought her attention. *Zorn and its sub-human barbarians await my disposal. The matter is vital.* The Accumulation Room was ensconced in the Bureau's lower levels, a layer of protection from interruptions. Irritating the upper powers had its many downsides, but she feasted on the game as much as she did Sweet Crave Hypers.

Eventually, a savant barged in, its brown-gold sarong in motion in waves of disturbance. "How dare you ignore our summons. The Arsh Shipyard released the War-Star Blue Serenity an hour ago."

A bit of data drew Charronna's attention. "Retrofitted with the Earth ultra-drives?"

"Of course."

The data point expanded into a file. The Militant Plebiscite granted her initial target a challenge fight. No custom, however ancient, excused their stubborn disregard for the law. Under a Court-tested placid smile, Charronna swore. Kor of Steel Rose had better remain in custody. She drilled into the data. Kor was the son of Strom, the barbarian she deep-probed in a war-star holding cell during the Oath Breaker Rebellion—the one who broke and who would never be whole again. She and Kor were connected in the communion, but their history together started in that holding cell.

A prickling sensation spread on her scalp, whispers, warnings, a panicked realization. The Indeterminator's yellow eyes, abnormal and compound, covered the mindscape with each photoreceptor playing a dark future. Black and bright mixed into a razzle-dazzle. An urgent need to stay home swelled. "The new engines will have us to Zorn in no time."

"Minutes count. On this, the probability is clear. Why do you delay?"

Because I don't want to go, nitwit, now more than ever. Does anyone pay me the slightest attention?

"Your silence says enough." The savant snapped his fingers as though summoning the help. "Come. I will be at your side as Sentinel's voice. She says, *do not screw it up.*"

Charronna sucked in a sharp breath. With Sentinel connected to the escort at her pleasure, every action would be scrutinized, weighed, and measured on a scale balanced between freedom and loss of privilege. She shut down the collection hub, unnecessary but satisfying, and brushed past the savant, leaving behind a misty domain of dormant data columns and dozens of sub-humans suddenly without purpose. How lucky for them.

The chinless, rounded savant maintained personal space-violating-closeness on the way to the spaceport, employing a steady stream of soft-spoken breathless chatter to move her along—a walking, talking bolt-stunner rammed into her back. Mental replays of her bon voyage Sweet Crave encounter distracted her building testiness. Fevered reruns of the Hyper derailed into nightmares, into the visage of Strom who babbled threats, revenge, and his promise to one day snap her neck. If the savant didn't beat Strom to the punch, he might, at last, have his chance.

***

Eager rumbles purred in Kor's stomach. A souped-up festival meal was spread out to the long table's four corners. Platters of spiced lowlander intestines, a supersized bowl of pickled vegetables drizzled with fragrant herb oils, hearty loaves of bread, each one filled with fruits, nuts, and seeds, jammed against an exciting array of seafood, deep water fish, shellfish, and mollusks. Paradise burst into his mouth with every bite. Kill twelve men to earn dessert. Iron bar tattoos would decorate his torso in no time. The General would be proud.

No longer hungry, he tracked down a medic to ask for a cosmetic adjustment to his forehead brand. The medic had to comply. A man about to enter the arena in life and death combat gained exalted standing. Stoic and proper, chest out and chin up, he presented himself at his assigned gate; the holy **X** on his forehead overlaid with "All Men Are Created Equal."

"The brand wasn't a smart choice," a voice said from behind, "but you're a sucker for doing the wrong thing."

Kor's heart skipped. A tall man with black hair carried a light torch in the stadium's darkened tunnel. Full eyelashes and thick eyebrows suggested seductive mystery, while plump, delicious lips promised passion, and warm, dark eyes showed kindness . . . a blood-rushing-to-ear moment—not Jude, but Dex, a living, breathing personification of heartache. Vertigo surged and faded—Jude's death, a horror that in Kor's mind had not happened, had occurred not long ago, and yet also from a forgotten eon. Time and timelessness ripped his spirit to shreds.

The brown-bronze son of Iron Song wore a uniform in his clan colors of aqua and orange—neither hostile nor friendly, a decided improvement from the Field of Crosses.

"Surprised you're here," Kor said, reordering his thoughts to the present.

"This fight involves more than you or Steel Rose. The priests are on the move. A few clans promised them fealty. Rumors of secret defections persist. Rumors of Starry Empire plots abound. I carry a message on behalf of the Plebiscite. Show the priests' weakness and our resolve. Do this, and you take a step toward earning Iron Star's forgiveness."

"How high is the mountain?"

"Into the clouds."

Kor clenched his stone as an anchor against grief tearing at his heart. For a brief flash, Dex relaxed, perhaps in compassion, into the friend he once was, into the beloved energy of Jude. In a glimpse, Kor gained hope for the redemption he believed impossible. He would win for Jude—for Steel Rose—for his broken heart. He saluted Dex, crossed his arms over his chest, and headed into the arena.

A signal flare streaked into the cloudless morning sky. Kor stalked into the packed Crimson Circus, bound in a daydream, a knight in shining armor girded to take on the forces of terror. Most in the crowd would understand the brand's meaning. Kor declared his independence from the priests, from the judges, and from the Starry Empire itself. If he couldn't live a free life, he would at least die a free man. Tens of thousands of men clad in wild couture heavy with the Steel Rose colors of red and white erupted to their feet, their initial rush to cheer falling apart in confusion. What they must be thinking . . . *Perhaps the priests are right. Perhaps this Kor is a terrorist-loving traitor.*

Thousands more brooded behind a sea of veils. A few years ago, trendy men wore veils to tease and entice, but no more. Earnest white-clad men and boys prayed for his death to prove they commanded the Supreme's favor. No pressure, stay alive, preserve Steel Rose's honor, and boost the prestige of the high clans, or let his world fall to the black-and-white sorrows of the priests.

In the adjacent field, a line of animal handlers pulled crazed yirgs toward a pen of outmatched howling Earth-wolves. The yirg packs swung spiked tails and stomped on stout legs, kicking up dust to shroud their advance. Thump. Howl. Pound. Wail. The Circus Guard raised crimson death banners for the grisly feast to come.

Kor fingered the onyx pendant as he marched across the field. Dead ahead, the General waited—an awe-conjuring, tattooed totem in a bodysuit designed to show off every brand. Anatomical hearts rippled along one arm, connected to a chest mosaic with skulls and iron bars color-blocking one of his legs—a living, breathing war clown showing off direct kills over dozens of battlefields. General Superior, a warrior, a survivor, a walking-talking fortress tower of flesh and bone topped with gray deadwood eyes—his youthful swagger devoured by a grim wrought fed by the fetid bitterness of Steel Rose's unspoken disgrace.

The General's folded, brawny arms invoked a manner of pestilent shaming. "I warned you about mistakes. You never listen."

"Good to see you too, Father."

The General backhanded Kor, knocking him to the ground. Blood pooled in the corner of his mouth.

"Don't get smart with me. Our lands will be seized, our homes razed, our shrines desecrated, your cousins, your uncles, stripped of honor—the inheritance you forced upon us with your betrayal."

"You speak of a future not yet certain. I haven't lost."

"Wake up. Blood duels are not meant to be won."

Kor's retinal display lit up with damage assessments. Scattered cheers broke out from the veiled spectators. He hopped to attention, shoulders back, chest out, ignoring the blood dripping off his chin.

The General's gaze drifted to a far-off place untouched by mercy. "I should have been harder on you."

"By using crowbars instead of whips?"

"Where did you get such a smart mouth?"

Strom wrapped a strong hand around Kor's neck, squeezing the blood flow to his jugular vein. "The priests would applaud your death by my hand."

"A fine strategy. Blood should never be wasted."

The General's grip tightened. A half-million spectators shouted and judged. The mountains surrounding the city transformed into the seats of vengeful gods. The crowd faded into a muffle. His eyes fluttered. His heart rate slowed to meditation speed. The battlefield slipped away. A tear welled. Three years and four months old, the last time he cried in front of his father; a sharp, shadowed memory engulfed in the strikes of a tireless retaliatory backhand. *Men . . . don't . . . cry.*

"I failed you as a father. Your shame is my shame. Steel Rose is greater than either of us. We come. We exist. We go. The important things are eternal: our clan, our world, our god. I wish twenty lashes cleansed your error. Some sins are never forgiven. Some errors in judgment are forever."

Strom released his hold. "Like the ill-considered brand on your forehead."

"I assume this means no birthday cake if I win."

"I would have forgiven if you hadn't been caught."

Much sin was forgiven if never uncovered—a corrosive practice, a toxin added to daily life until the lungs no longer expanded, and the heart no longer pumped. Militants walk the world dead to themselves, acting out in the programming handed down by the Transgeneticists, empty gestures for the greater good.

Handguns, Havoc Fire (HF) disruptors, vintage pulse rifles, sonic blasters, and mobile cannons gleamed in display on various mounts. The arena's hubbub pressed. A photon-grenade launcher, infamous for its havoc rating, tempted. Kor fired a handgun into the ground. The power readings dropped several thousand joules, leaving enough juice for three shots. The presiding judge took no chances that Kor might pull off a victory.

Strom ripped Kor's pendant from his chest and threw it to the ground. "I'm done with your deception. You crap on your birthright. You were never able to see past your pain. You fight alone."

"You disown me," Kor said, disbelieving. At the turn of a sentence, his mind detached, a drifting, burning fragment. Life outside the clan didn't exist. Thoughts spun into the crowd's sonic wake, unsure where to go, to be angry, ashamed, woeful, or self-righteous. Beneath a pole topped with the holy **X**, the divine symbol to protect against the Red Beast, his enemies united. Ten priests in white bodysuits, none showing rank, knelt in prayer, their hands held high, their necks arched back. Supporters broke into a chant. "We are Truth."

Kor started to form the **X**, stopping himself halfway. *Our service, in truth, is to be less than human, slaves to Naturals blessed with divine instead of engineered souls. The un-fit among us deride those of the religious orders as Tempters. Count me in.*

"Goodbye, son. Your name will never be spoken by the family or of the true." He plodded to the Steel Rose standard.

"There's nothing wrong with me. There's nothing wrong with any of us." Kor gulped breath in a ragged cadence and cinched spewing upheaval with armored resolve.

Cousins, uncles, and others in the greater clan gathered around his father by the Steel Rose totem. Garrison met Kor's gaze, mouthing, "I love you, brother." The twelve-and-under boys, a lot of whom loved to play *chase* with Kor as the chaser had their backs turned as part of the ritual rejection of shunning—brave Wolf the lone exception.

The priests formed the **X** to protect their souls from the world's evils. In this case, that would be him. *If I die as an outcast, I die free as well.* Kor bit into his tongue, trying to blot out his next thought. He would rather die loved than free. Victory in the blood duel would not cure his father's rejection.

Atop the north-end stage, the Master of the Circus carried the arena's ornate silver brass horn. His uniform, black with patterns of explosive white, added to the drama of his formalized processional. Energy waves shimmered around the field, stabilizing into a transparent barrier. The spectators rose to their feet. The friendly ones cheered or banged colored gourds with either hands or animal bones—the ancient anthem of the hunt. Ten masked Tempters unsheathed their guns. The Master blew the first call to battle.

Kor kicked one of the nearby guns—the most promising, an HF disruptor, felt too heavy, weighted by the consequence of what failure would mean to him, to his clan, and to his world.

"I'll trade you."

Kor blinked against the sun's glare. A tall buzz-cut figure, ultra-fit, his skin tinctured lustrous black, the epitome of a galactic marine, held a polished HF disruptor with the branded hands of a Combat Master, Broc of Crew Defiance, a man worthy of a statue.

"I pulled strings to be here," Broc said. "I want a fair fight."

Kor saluted.

"No need for protocol. In the Crimson Circus, we are brothers. In death, we are the same." He held out the havoc-grade weapon. Unsure what to say, Kor accepted the offering.

Broc wrapped a densely muscled arm around Kor, pulling him into an embrace. "You saved my son from the lash. For that mercy, thank you. Your father loves you."

"My father no longer counts me as a son."

Broc pulled back a bit, his jeweled green-diamond eyes in full reproach. "He's trapped. All of us are. How many times have you been the person forced upon you?"

Too many. Kor matched Broc's gaze forged from the shared hardness of their world. The love of a father to son might indeed survive in places where the General did not tread.

"The forehead brand is a ballsy touch," Broc said. "I respect a man who claims his crown . . . as long as he claims the consequences. No one standing alone has survived a blood-dual challenge. I want you to be the first. You have a strong heart linked to a careless mind. Redeem yourself. Hold victory in your heart. Be fierce, young man."

"Aye, sir."

"Win the day, and I will take you in."

Kor grabbed Broc into a bear hug. "I am most honored. I'll do the floors if I must."

The Master of the Circus used the horn a second time, the call to arms. The stadium's opposing factions erupted across the arena. A set of twenty pipes pierced the sky beyond the enemy standard. Broc withdrew to outside the shield. The cold metal of the gun fed energy to Kor's hands. He kissed its barrel.

"Death to the traitor," Tempter partisans shouted. Their discontent blistered in waves of hatred.

Hardcore supporters unleashed an explosive volley of colored globes that popped in mid-flight. The perfume balls released musky scents, leathery bouquets mingling with herbals and sugary florals, dispersing into the bright spring day.

Tempters formed up in front of their flag flapping proudly on a thin pole: the holy **X** on a field of white. The Master blew the silver-brass horn one last time. Kor bolted straight at the enemy standard. His goal: pull the pole from the stand and let it fall. The Tempters' objective was no less complicated—stop him.

One of the wolves dug at the barrier between the battle zones—escape foes, dig faster, fight to live, whatever that means. Kor zigzagged in a sustained quick-speed burst, blasting away with the disruptor, fighting for balance in an obstacle course of expanding craters. Sod exploded in a smoky haze. Black snow fell. The Tempters shouted at each other. Bad move. Kor pinpointed the end of their formation, heading toward it. The crowd whipped into a deafening frenzy.

Rounds of photon shells blistered the arena, driving him sideways. A bolt grazed Kor's shoulder. Into a tuck and roll, he picked up dirt and grass as a salve to his wound. Red and white banners waved in furious fervor. Cries of "fight" pierced the noise, trumpets from heaven. Encouraged, he vaulted, curling into a somersault, landing on a grassy block propelled high and low by massive pistons. A wolf that had dug its way out from the other arena landed on an adjacent block. The wolf's eyes glistened with resolve. Kor growled in kinship. Enemy fire intensified, shooting stars in search of something to burn.

The pistons moved in a chaotic rhythm. Pressure pulses added to his expanding map of how the board game changed. From block to grassy block, he jumped and rolled. Blood leaked from his shoulder and leg wounds. Photon fire escalated into blanket squalls impacting the arena's energy shield in a ruthless torrent of muted explosions. He counterattacked with a volley of disruptor blasts before jumping to stable ground. Fallen Tempters littered the battlefield.

The enemy standard faded into the haze of burning grass. Kor charged. Laser fire flashed, closer than near, he zigged, and he pivoted in a graveyard dance, tumbling and firing as he went down. A priest lurched back, a direct hit. Another howled as canine fangs punctured deep in the man's neck. *Good doggie.*

Supporters cheered. "Stand! Fight! Win!"

Quick-speed adrenals drained away; he stood, planted buckling legs—forced tension into them. The rifle was out of juice and so was he. Betrayed by his weakness, he fell to his knees. Sod-soaked Tempters loomed. Weapons pointed at Kor's head—his gun ripped away. The grim chants of the white-clad crowd grew bold. The wolf howled. The priests had won.

CHAPTER X

Jeth's mind accelerated to quantum speed. Colors streamed in untamed rapids as countless thoughts rushed through his consciousness at the speed of light, shooting prisms throughout the void. Every piece of him sought a separate escape. *The one way to gain true life is to become a god.* Light exploded and electric bursts rolled through his chaotic mind. *To become a god, one must first die.* If he had a heart, it would be racing.

Sala materialized in a low-cut black mini-dress, awakening parts of Jeth he believed were long dead. Did the universe ever allow anything to truly die? The question threatened to crush his mind. With effort, he refocused on the Sala he remembered, which brought forth long-forgotten emotions that gave anchor to his scorched sanity.

"Dreaming again of lost manhood?" Sala asked.

"A Kimbrian contacted me. She claims to be an Instigator, co-guardian of this Cosmic Song."

"Instigators scheme. Does she know humanity survives?"

"Yes, and where they are. The Instigator wants to use the Militant in some way to reconcile the Commonweal Alliance with humanity. The Kimbrian provided a safe route for Kor to reach E'lan. Once he's here, we win."

"Our savior must make physical contact," Sala reminded.

"A Psian intrudes into our savior's mind."

Jeth coalesced into his favorite cloud form, dense, towering, vertical, imposing, and commanding—a proper manifestation of a soon-to-be god. Sala's wardrobe shifted to a navy shirt-suit, minimal makeup, and hair in a bun with the ever-present blue swirl and I'm-taking-you-seriously gesture. Neither had fond feelings for the miserable telepathic backstabbers who helped to foil his divine ascension during his captivity with the E'lani Emperor.

"The Psian," Jeth said, "might help if they believe I'm one of their ancient lost brothers."

Sala raised her arms in quasi-mock celebration; a trio of tinkling purple necklaces added sparkle. "I must be rubbing off on you."

"Do you remember Cafe Shi?"

"You came every other day at 6:00 a.m. sharp, a blue pocket square in your lab coat."

"You made the best extra bitter ranna-lanna in the city."

"Your pocket square changed—became identical to the blue swirl in my hair."

"I never asked you out."

"I gave you flirty eyes, a wet lip, a gracious laugh, to no avail."

"I worked on my courage."

"Unhappy at the lack of progress, I took a day off and sat down at your table with two cups filled to the brim."

"Yellow rose in the dawn sky to the songs of fliers."

"While we sipped our extra bitter ranna-lanna."

"Can we have that again?"

"You still love me? Perhaps I underestimated you."

Jeth shriveled at his boundaries. Sala stepped into Jeth's presence where he was most dense, kissed him, and faded away behind a thoughtful gaze. The heady aroma of carmine's white-spotted star-shaped petals lingered in her wake. Jeth transformed into a roiling cloud. If he didn't flinch, he might win Sala's love. With that possibility in mind, nothing would stop him.

Jeth lifted into Kor's outer awareness, finding the telepath as a red sea in a constant surge, an expansive snooping expedition. The Psian was indeed curious. He dived into the red sea, parted it into sections, announced his presence, flattened the crests, and made sure the telepath perceived his existence. "I'm the first of you. I'm the father of your kind, and I need your help."

The red sea drained from Kor. The message had been heard. Most importantly, the message had been believed.

***

"Cede." A Tempter shouted with the conviction of a divine commandment. Black fog drifted over dead white-clad men— fallen tombstones in a battle-torn field.

Acrid smoke invaded Kor's throat and lungs, a noxious scorch that scraped, dried, a thief of breath. The wolf, with teeth bared, growled. Blood and dirt matted its hair, an honor brand to the gray animal's determination to survive. The wolf charged. The Tempter pivoted, shooting the beast in mid-leap. High-pitch whimpers diminished; blood oozed around charred marks on the felled creature. The wolf searched Kor out, its eyes, compelling and intelligent, exhorted him to slay the bad men.

The Tempter ripped away his mask. Golden face, agate-blue eyes, his best friend, close, yet never more distant. Wrath-lust hardened Baps's face into fearsome grind; he accused with the glower of the fallen. His best friend with whom he snuck away into the woods, stargazed and danced, competed and confided, played pranks and broke bread, no longer held a shred of their shared boyhood.

"What are you doing here?" Kor asked.

"I was ordered to join the righteous to protect Gallant from my association with you. I had no plans to fight until I saw the blasphemy across your forehead."

Baps pushed Kor flat to the torn-up earth and shoved the barrel of a long gun into his mouth. Livid frustration clenched Baps's party-boy face. He wore his happiness, boredom, and anger, the latter in a flush of jugular red. The gun slid deeper, grazing the back of his throat. Any further, and he would either start to gag or to choke. With his life measured in mere seconds, Kor replayed his sessions with the flute, trying to hold the music until the end.

"I told Iron Star you were going to the Academy." Eyes watering, Baps's gaze shifted inward to peer into some internal hell. "I wanted to scare you, to push you into obedience. If you had failed the ordeal, you would have died a man. But you are beyond redemption."

He fired . . . to no effect.

Kor rammed a heel into Baps's shin. Legs buckled, and he fell on Kor, lips to lips. Old bonds sprang to life. Baps's eyes watered with an apology, with regret. Mouth opened, a faint whisper released, the cry of the almost dead. Words ached for release, appealing for forgiveness, for understanding. Love, Kor gave and he took, both willing, in the space of a heartbeat, they were friends, and the Twin Moons granted every wish.

"I hate myself for doing this." Baps's eyes shifted into an arctic distance.

Arms braced to the thigh. Vertebrae forced upward into standing. Lookalike coats of mud and ash blurred the division between friend and foe. Baps tossed his disruptor aside; he waved off the other surviving Tempter. They circled, grabbed hold, and crashed to the ground in a torrent of dirt and ferocity. Baps, on top, pummeled with hate-fueled fury, distant thunder to the General's lashings.

"I'll dig your blasphemous brand out one letter at a time."

A right hook to the jaw sent his old friend sprawling. On hands and knees, Kor spat black crud, summoning the last of his mettle. Baps rallied, swinging his leg to deliver sharp pain to Kor's shoulder with a booted heel. On their knees, they traded blows. Take one, survive, give one back, no surrender, take abuse like a man. The crowd's roar rivaled dreadnaught engines at full burn. Was his father proud? Pain receptors flipped to "overloaded." Blood flowed—a grizzly sweat. Fatigue devoured. Who was the better man?

In a flash of movement, the General plowed into the golden man of Gallant.

Aluminum gleamed yards away, waiting for the one of true valor to pull the standard from its sacred mount. Kor slogged—fingers into the soil—the goal in reach. Disruptor fire blasted the ground, throwing up a shower of dirt; the other Tempter rejoined the game. Kor's arm hooked around the silver-gray metal. Spectators went into a crazed frenzy; the gods summoned in stomps and cheers. He let out a war cry and pulled the pole from its stand, letting it fall beside him.

Copper pipes blared. Protectors and Combat Medics charged across the field. Kor rolled to his back. High Clan flags waved in a jubilant frenzy. Heavy volleys of perfume balls overwhelmed the battle stench. Thousands of voices thundered Kor's name. The old gods declared their new champion. He had earned his life and restored the clan's honor from his error. Even better, his father reversed his disownment—a moment to relish forever. Life would and must return to the expected.

The General came to his side. Kor reached out for a hug. Emotions flooded back into the confines of his father's acceptance. The General put his lips to Kor's ear. "I'm not your father. I'm Rue, Society of Penitence and Approbation. Your interrogator."

Kor pulled back—searched for recognition in familiar blue grays. Lifeless orbs regarded him. *Psian. Mind-control capabilities. Ghost-Wizard.* A twinkle of the ghost filtered through dead-ash eyes. On a good day, disorienting. Today? Kor preferred a barefoot jog on broken glass.

"If this was your body, I'd break it in half. The crowd, both sides, would salute me."

"I saved your life," Rue-Strom said. "I nullified your father's public disownment. Is this how Militants show their appreciation?"

The ghost took on airs. "No wonder the civilized world calls your kind lead-heads."

"What do you want, spook?"

"To help you, gray eyes."

"Get your bony ass out of my father's head."

"My bony ass is quite removed."

Wherever the ghost lurked, he would have to be close to limit environmental decoherence—the scourge of telepaths exerting force through a quantum state. Normally, they required line-of-sight, but during the war game's horror, Kor sensed they tapped into his higher functions to assist their takeover. He pressed his fingers. "I wager my father endures pain way better than you. Want me to test that hypothesis into a theory?"

"Your father has been touched by a psi-agent. Interesting."

Kor squeezed his thumb on a pressure point in his father's neck. Rue winced. "Level three out of ten; withdraw, or we'll climb the ladder."

"I took possession as a last resort to save your life."

Unlikely, but Kor released the pressure point. No ghost would have bothered saving him without a hidden agenda. Motives— ghost machinations—would have to wait. He hobbled over to the wolf, brushing a hand over the creature's soft gray underbelly fur, feeling a thready heartbeat. He waved over a combat medic attending to one of the injured Marshals.

"Attend to the wolf," Kor said.

The medic saluted and opened his emergency kit. The wolf licked Kor's fingers. "Good doggie."

Kor kissed the wolf on the head, unsure what his four-legged friend deemed acceptable. Father and son worked their way toward the arena's imposing North Gate. Along the way, Kor searched for the charm lost during the battle but found no evidence of it or the pendant. Supporters held high-tech Roman candles—Earther photon shooters—above their heads; multi-colored balls of light streaked into the party sky. In return, the devout fought back with shouted sacred verses in a so-far bloodless civil war.

Baps, ripped bodysuit, bloody, covered with soot, dirt, condemned from a distance; his heart ensconced in burdensome not-welcome barriers. Kor renewed his march with the creepy, unreadable Rue-Strom at his side.

Supporters yelled, "Glory to the Heroes!"

Kor did not acknowledge them. Without the ghost's intervention, Baps would have won. He was no rebel, nor a model citizen. He belonged nowhere. At the gate, an attendant bowed. The battle had ended in the arena but not in Kor's heart. His father disowned him. His best friend betrayed him. And a ghost, of all people, had saved him.

***

The dessert spread supercharged Kor's five senses. Aches and pains submerged in the relish of creamy, tangy cheese, warm pudding made from minced fowl sweetened with succulent and gooey aromatic bread, fresh from the oven. The snap of sweet and savory biscuits heralded mouthwatering bites. Chocolate pancakes, a rare treat, stroked pleasure neurons into rockets' red-glare overdrive. To let anything go unsampled would be a crime against nature.

The ghost-possessor sampled dainty portions—unnerving to watch the mighty leader of Steel Rose reduced to no more than an animated corpse. A normal Psian would never be able to maintain possession from a distance without the help of many minds, which meant Rue was either close or he was no ordinary telepath. Best to avoid conversation, thinking, or eye contact. Nothing should taint the amazing flavors, colors, aromas, and textures. The harsh world receded into neuron tapestries where he stored precious moments of family gatherings during great feasts and festivals.

The medics took their turn after the feast, cleaning him up for his presentation at the temple. Awkward silence festered with his shell of a father as they boarded a mag-tube. The ride left him wonder-shocked. Holographic banners of Steel Rose, some the size of towers, hovered throughout the city. The Empire's messaging screens spewed static. The ever-present audio bands blared white noise. Supporters lined the boulevards and packed the avenues. Roman light candles illuminated their jumping and screaming euphoria, reflecting off outfits in hot pink, lime green florescent, black and yellow neon, psychedelic purples and blues. No one paraded in the white. Totems pumped in ecstatic adoration. Gourds banged in high-honor salute. Workers in gray dared to show up with rose patches on their chests.

At the Temple Square, a few priests roamed with heavier foot traffic from clansmen coming and going. Evenly spaced imposing rectangular marble panels stood guard, the outer defense, each with a mantra. *Do not question. Keep your discipline. Right thoughts equal right mind. Your purpose is given, your purpose to serve. The Code is truth, the truth is Code. Obedience is bliss. Freedom is death. You are nothing.* Clansmen lingered before the panels, alone, in clusters, taking in the messages to fill the void.

Paneled steel doors sat within the crosshairs of a monumental Holy **X,** reaching to the top of the flat-topped edifice. Kor passed through the entrance, lost between old faith and new dreams, and headed to the altar. Rue-Strom trailed. Leaded glass windows engraved with stern Marshals withered judgment. The sanctuary had no seats, pews, or podiums to shield the sinners. A raised stone platform in a basin curved at five degrees occupied the center. Kor took position on the platform in a relaxed pose. Rue-Strom observed with stoic detachment.

Three orange-belts anointed Kor with rose-infused, spiced oil as he held his arms spread horizontally to the floor. Inward peace blossomed in a nurturing caress. He wished it could be just that. After a water cleanse, an acolyte handed Kor a robe. In measured steps, he withdrew from the sanctuary. The flagstone underfoot, worn smooth by millions of men over thousands of years, nurtured cohesion. The peace persisted. In this den of enemies, a safe place prevailed.

Beyond, in the Refining Chamber, holy water washed away the sins of kneeling men as blood-boys ran among them with barbed whips lashing for drops of red. Water walls enclosed in reassuring flows and meditative sounds. The music of chanting choirboys cascaded from above, "Om, Mani, Hem." The voices of little gods breathed heaven into stone walls. *But no one here sings for Tara or the workers or the un-pure among us.*

He skirted a bank of herbal baths, relishing earthy aromas tempting him to stay. In the Central Hall, Marshals to novice grades went about their mission to protect the people's virtue—a river of white, blue, black, yellow, orange, and green-belts wearing veils, men who had cheered for Kor's death. Sanctified by battle, they offered polite indifference. Rue-Strom kept his distance, and Kor lost track of him in the flow of priests.

The star dropped to the horizon; twilight, the herald for the Festival of the Lovers' Kiss, meant the biggest party in a lifetime launched into high gear. The Twin Moons would do their dance of near tragedy avoided, as had Kor.

Picking up speed, he skipped over stairs to a colonnade, narrowly avoiding a collision with the closest thing to the Red Beast one found among the living. An Eternal blocked the way. *To the Combat Masters belong our flesh, to the Eternals belong our soul.* Black mesh covered his face. A shroud from the neck down draped him to keep the flesh hidden. Full-body tension jolted overtaxed nerves.

The ghost in the body of Strom appeared in the halo of Kor's radiant awe.

Without acknowledgment, the Eternal walked away. Kor and Rue-Strom followed the customary three steps behind. Acolytes, novices, and apprentices avoided their condemnation. The way forward descended into a labyrinth, into corridors haunted by phantoms, into an underground yellow haze. The Eternal stopped before colossal, bronzed doors engraved with a warning: TO SEE IS DEATH.

Memories flooded into Kor of the days before the Oath Breaker Rebellion when his father practiced gratitude and amusement, and the temples were places of hope and virtue. Palms bubbled with anticipation—nervous, aye, in fear, but intrigued and in amazement, a step away from the holy of holies. The doors swung inward. Silver beams from above struck Rue-Strom with targeted pinpoint accuracy. Kor flipped his possessed father around to confront a man with whitened eyes.

"You're blind."

"To see is death."

"Those happen to be my father's eyes."

"The blindness is temporary."

"Are you one hundred percent as sure as death sure?"

"No one living can be that confident."

Kor grabbed his father's powerful shoulders. "Give me a better answer."

"None exists. The priests deem you sanctified until you leave the temple, so you were spared the temporary blindness. Rules are important here." Kor grunted agreement, took his imposter father's hand, pretended the familiar contact meant something, and hurried after the Eternal. The hall ended in a sea of white and black veils hanging from the ceiling—light and dark comingled as one thing.

The Eternal pulled back a tapestry covering the entrance to the Inner Sanctum. Every boy knew the protocol. Remove temple sandals, take a slight bow with arms crossed over the chest, and then step into the sacred space with a mental suspension of reverence. Feet pressed into the hand-knotted fibers of a rug dyed with red botanicals. Water cascaded down obelisk fountains inscribed with verses of the Code. Bowls of hard candy decorated a long showy table with trophy-style legs, holy **X** plaques, and a polished concrete top. Bright pillows covered couches recessed into the floor. The scent of moon-flowers titillated. Dizzy, Kor steadied himself with a hand on the tabletop.

Hidden behind the black mesh mask, the Eternal hovered. Did a real man exist underneath the mask? The Eternal took it off. Copper insets gleamed in place of eyes.

"The inner sanctum is fancy," Kor said, bewildered.

"You see and yet you're blind."

"I'm seeing just fine."

The Eternal clasped his hands. A nest of semi-sheer curtains parted, and a goddess emerged—tall and slender, with silken brown hair framing pale skin. Rose-berry lips beckoned with mystery. A small **x** tattoo branded her forehead. Like Tara, her eyes shined in the under-glow of Kor's stunned gaze.

"She's aware," Kor said.

"She's your sister."

Kor's jaw dropped.

"A Misfire," continued the Eternal. "A self-aware breeder. Steel Rose has a history of misfires, both male and female. You are one of them."

"You're lying," Kor said, his voice catching.

"No need to lie when the truth suffices." The Eternal raised a gloved hand.

"Chi," the breeder said. She reclined onto one of the beds in a fluid motion.

"Your twin and your father's disgrace," the Eternal said.

Kor's mind spun into a whirlwind. Was that why he had no brothers?

"We recycle most Misfires. We keep a few for study, like your sister. Still, the deviations increase with each generation."

Kor circled the breeder who followed his progress with gray eyes and a turned-up nose. They might share blood. Too many thoughts fought for space. *Twin sister.* In defiance of common sense, Chi rested on a couch, looking fierce despite her relaxed pose, as real as his throbbing headache.

"You will undergo the ritual of conversion to our order," the Eternal said. "Under our oversight, we will determine if it's possible to reintegrate bloodlines corrupted by genetic regression through managed procreation."

"A breeding program."

"A better way to be the people's hero."

"Forget it."

"Like us, our Earth-born cousins created engineered humans; many more sorts than the Starry Empire. After much strife and debate, they gave their creations the freedom you crave. Our brothers and sisters misused their freedom. Wars followed. The Earther-Naturals hunted their subsets to the last. The Naturals will always fear us in the recesses of their paranoid minds."

"I'm not your lab rat."

"Lab rats are useful."

Chi started to say something but held back. Kor had the distinct impression that the threat was nothing new. Yet in her bright, gray eyes she showed no surrender. The woman was a fighter.

"You're going to free Chi," Kor said.

"Indulgent, weak, and stupid, an expected trifecta. You flaunt your genetic corruption."

"Halleluiah."

The Eternal's blank emotionless face hinted at scorn in the barest twist of the mouth. *Halleluiah* was a word peculiar to the Earthers, and its use was an insult.

"The natural-born tolerate us if we obey. Renunciate."

"I won't deny who I am."

"You covet a worthless trinket."

A guard with black inset eyes entered. The guard negotiated the room with ease. As he grabbed Chi's lush black hair, his arms shifted with dense muscle and veins bulged with impending violence. The guard forced Chi's chin up and put a curved, ceremonial blade to her throat.

"Please, da-da."

Da-da? Confused, Kor started to ask for an explanation from Rue; the ghost, lost in a private world, drifted in a mumbling chant. Given the possession's duration, the ghost would be under strain.

Light reflected off the priest's copper eyes to cast a strength-draining spell. A slight tremor rippled through Chi's cheek but no unspoken plea. Perhaps she didn't expect kindness from any man.

Kor growled like the caged beast he would become. "I submit."

"Insufficient. One last time—renunciate."

Kor went rigid. He would submit. He would obey. But deny himself? Silence thickened into a prickly pause.

"Very well," the Eternal said. "We go to lessons."

The high priest pulled out strips of burn weed. Time slowed. The Eternal waited with disciplined patience. Head bowed, Kor knelt at the Tempter's feet, letting his robe drop to the floor. Disobedience had to have limits. Strokes of burn weed swiped across his back, up and down, dragging tiny claws that leeched liquid fire into his blood. He clawed his hands into the textured rug as shuddering muscle tore away from ligament and bone. The Eternal's strokes quickened when a normal man might tire.

"Let the pain cleanse you," the Eternal said.

"Let it come!" Kor cried.

"Let it heal you."

"Let it rain!"

“There may be hope for you yet, son of Strom.”

The Eternal reared and lunged to the lightning strikes of burn weed.

CHAPTER XI

The summons came at 3:30am. Number 96 walked lockstep behind the Scarlet Shield, wearing his polished steel slave collar under a denim shirt and hood. The royal protectors gave off an earth-sweet aroma, pink clay, the odor of purification. 3-4am was the most sacred hour when the veil between the conscious and unconscious became at its thinnest. Never before had he been summoned during that time. Something of import was at hand.

The guards led him into the heart of the Tower of E'lan, the Blessed One's abode. 96 shed his clothes, chest out, shoulders arched, head tilted back at the proper twenty degrees, and waited, naked, revealed, and submissive. A circle of diffused luminosity brightened the solid stone altar upon which the Blessed One dwelt, the universe's one living god, cloistered within a burlap curtain. Gray frozen rays from a gray star erupted in expansive splendor to crown the altar—a symbol of the conquered darkness.

96, bare and vulnerable, held his position under the watchful eyes of the Royal Projectors amidst the shadowy ancient stones of the tower. Wizened fingers poked through the burlap, beckoning 96 into an expanding sphere of brightening light. The Scarlet Shield took precise steps along a purple-lit path and knelt on either side of three fresh corpses. "We serve the Tangible Word," they said through blackened lips.

"Let us see our next child."

96 stepped forward and prayed natural hunger remained asleep. Ignoring the dead, he joined the guards, showing no shame. His unpurified skin was close to defilement, close to the

instant death a single drop of rolling sweat would bring. There was no sweat, not a drop, not yet.

"You appear fit and capable of service. Stand and witness your living god."

96 obeyed the raspy command. The Shadow Emperor, Blessed One to the devoted, regarded his servant in stretched patience.

The Polarian League eroded into crisis. Assertive Houses seized full control of the system's third, fourth, and sixth worlds plus the League's seven stellar colonies. They sent warships to Sacred Heart, the emperor's last planetary stronghold, to coerce concessions. The enemy numbers blotted the sun and the stars. Both sides sustained heavy losses in a battle with no retreat. A Sol star-liner filled with tourists arrived and was destroyed.

"Servants more seasoned than you failed me," the Shadow Emperor said.

"Knowledge weathers faith, my Blessed One."

"Bold of you to say. Cause and effect provide danger and opportunity. We salvaged a Sloop-class explorer from the star-liner with an intact hyperspace engine. Hundreds of Sol small ones died. Post-physical consciousnesses were destroyed."

96's muscles tensed and locked. The Sol half-breeds treated the last two as high crimes. Three hundred years ago, the half-breeds were not so different in how they viewed death. With post-physical existence theoretically offering eternal life to their chosen, they had become fanatical in seeking retribution for anyone responsible for final deaths. The League's sub-light fleets would be no match for them in battle.

"The Sol Envoy warns of unhappy consequences if we are implicated," the emperor rasped. "Investigators come. It is time for the passing, if you prove suitable."

96 skipped a breath.

"Whose voice do you hear?"

"Whoever you command."

"What is your purpose in life?"

"To serve your desire."

"Where lies your heart?"

"Wherever you place it."

"You answer true, my faithful child. Do you know who we are?"

"The living god," 96 said, measuring each word.

"These corpses answered the same."

96 clenched into corded knots. What more must he understand? "You are the heart, mind, and soul of the Polarian League."

"These corpses answered the same."

Beads of perspiration pooled. A single lost drop would defile him before his living god. A single drop would condemn him to the ever-burning heaps of chafe, and rightly so. The emperor raised his hand. The Scarlet Guard pointed death-wands. A surging stench of formaldehyde overwhelmed the clay. Energy crackled in shades of death. In the blink of an eye, 96 wiped the sweat across his body and blurted an answer to salvage his soul. "The keeper of balance."

"Adequate." The emperor lowered his hand. "However, you dishonored the ritual of summoning by touching yourself."

"To avoid greater dishonor."

"Flexible thinking—necessary in this time of change. Your path goes to the expanse with few planets and no life—the Deep Black."

The emperor drew back the hood and opened his robe to reveal thin, ravaged flesh that clung to buckling bone. "Do you know who we are?"

96 gazed upon his master, rigid and without breathing.

"We were before the Deep Black ever came to pass. We ruled over all the humans before our ancient enemies drove us away. We are thousands of emperors bound into one, including a remnant of the Great One who began the failed ascent using the sacred endless. The Uplift should have made us God. Yet we became a stillborn creation, our ascension aborted by alien invaders and traitors to the blood."

The emperor pointed a gnarled, deformed hand at his servant. "Go into the Deep Black. Destroy any information you find on the Uplift. Bring us the sacred endless. A part of us will come with you. We shall give you memory about our ancient enemies and of the precious object destined to set us free."

96 bowed. He would do whatever was asked of him. Climb to airless peaks, swim the ocean, walk on lava, kill, betray, lie, anything for the living god.

"We begin with a name."

96 swayed. Duties and responsibilities followed getting a name, and he wasn't yet finished with the trials of preparation. He had taken a wife. They had a baby daughter. The pattern of life would be disrupted. This was more than a mission. This was a new forever.

"Your ritual begins," the emperor said as though reading 96's mind. "You are Raven."

96 bowed to cover his shock. The name of he who dared to try the ascent to godhood—no higher honor. Feet planted, standing tall, he met the living god's terrifying white, sunken eyes with his own.

"At last, a time of change has come."

Ribbons of ghostly light, pure consciousness bound by quantum energy, poured from the emperor into Raven. God and man combined in the same mortal flesh. The divided emperor's aspects looked back at those left behind.

"Who are you?" the emperor asked. "Whose songs do you sing?"

Raven's eyes flashed in oscillating harmonies of lights and shadows. "We sing our own songs. We are the Many who are the One. We shall surround Creation within ourselves."

Raven withdrew with gathering apprehension. Echoes of the Blessed One rin his mind. The emperor's pain sustained him. The emperor's desire drove him. His boredom ripped through and fed both impulses. League houses grew bold in their challenge. Earth's presence challenged with the power of solar flares. The Blessed One worked to outmaneuver his enemies, but time stripped potential from the future. The living god was dying.

***

The Eternal reared for another punishing blow.

Burn weed toxins saturated Kor's blood. Muscle convulsed in a futile attempt at escape. *Blessed are the men of Zorn who endure the pain of life.* He would endure, be stubborn, and regret nothing of who he was or what he had done.

"I will break you," the Eternal said.

"Well spoken." The hissed voice of Rue-Strom simmered with threat.

On his knees, Kor caught the Eternal as he slumped, a ceremonial scepter protruding from his back. Blood marred the white shroud. Kor checked for a pulse, getting no beats—the high priest was dead at the hand of Strom.

A splash of holy blood stained the rug, liquid crimson over antique faded red. Complex mosaics of braided knots covered every inch of fabric spread out across the floor in a rectangular grid of faded colors. Patterns emerged, of ways to navigate the room without sight. Echoes of generations, of spent lives imprinted in the compression of movement, forged into the unique, worn shapes that tantalized with offerings of comprehension. But what could fix a dead Eternal? Nothing less than a triumph of the gods.

A garbled scream broke his reverie. Distracted by the undeniability of abhorrent sin, he had forgotten the guard had a blade to Chi's throat. "Surrender," the guard said.

Higher functions kicked in. Kor ripped the knife from the priest's back, throwing it before he dared to think. The guard crumpled to the floor with the knife lodged in his forehead. "Never."

Chi stumbled—eyes wide in lingering shock. The toxic cocktail burned hotter within Kor, but he had bigger problems. The Eternal's death meant a quicksand of dire consequences.

"What have you done?" Kor asked.

Rue-Strom's face went slack. "That piece of slime experimented on self-aware women. I returned the favor by proving the efficacy of Chi's poison blade."

End game. Steel Rose would be disbanded, sold off as slaves or recycled. Kor retrieved the knife and pressed the crimson blade against Rue's, his father's, throat. Mouth dried into a sun-scorched lakebed. Blood for blood . . . killing his father might be the only way to save Steel Rose.

"I told the Eternal who I am," Rue-Strom said.

"The dead Eternal and the priests won't admit your guilt."

"Let the ghost go," Chi said. "Rue felt my pain, my rapes, my despair when my unborn children were ripped from my womb. She experienced what the priests did to me all at once. Any normal person would have killed that heartless monster."

Caught off guard, Kor gaped. Ghosts practiced intimacy mind-to-mind; the way a ghost perceived gender mattered more than the body. Kor assumed Rue aligned with her genetic sex. A female consciousness possessed the General, for a Militant, an end-of-the-world violation.

Chi rolled her eyes. "You didn't know about Rue, did you? Dada, the Eternal, raised me. He was cruel, sometimes kind, but he deserved a blade in his back." Chi shifted to Rue-Strom. "Tell him like you told me. I gave you the knife. I had plans of my own."

"Naïve plans."

Chi glared in stubborn rebuke.

Rue-Strom turned her hands in acquiescence. "Your name came up during a seer communion with the Chorus. You are prophesied to liberate your people, restore the breeders' humanity, and free the empire's sub-groups."

"Is that all?"

"The Naturals will cheer you as the Unifier, the Amun who puts us on the path to union with the Polarians and our Earth cousins. If you fail, you are destined to become the Khonsu, the avatar of death."

Rue-Strom's voice crackled like dead leaves underfoot. Communions forecasted society-scale movements—significant events—calling out a person's name was supposed to be beneath their level of granularity. The Fates themselves were on the prowl. Ghosts lied, but it jived with what Demi said. Blood smeared from the blade to Strom's neck. The functioning part of Kor's brain noted holding the murder weapon was a bad move. The blade stayed put.

"You won't kill your father."

"To save Steel Rose, one death to save everything. . ."

"If the world around you burned, you would cling to the need for your father's approval."

Blood for blood. . .

"Your answer lies in my pocket," Rue-Strom said.

Thinking twice, Kor reached into the Ghost's pocket and gripped a rock. Familiar in shape and texture, he knew he had found his charm. Blood from the arena battle stained it. Rue-Strom's liquid-black eyes apprised. To preserve the clan, nothing less than his father's sacrifice would satisfy the priests. But there had to be ways other than death.

Kor pulled the knife away. "If you've got a plan, wizard, it better be gold-plated."

"Plans start with me, brother." Chi sucked on a piece of bright ultramarine candy. "The Eternals built secret tunnels to four small shrines beyond the temple gates. They like to think ahead."

"Noted. Lead the way."

"I'm staying."

"That's a death sentence. I won't have it."

"I just met you and already you're giving orders?"

"You don't have the conditioning pheromones. It could work."

"The priests have me tracked."

"Scan Chi's mind," Kor said to Rue. "Find the passage." He advanced on Chi.

"I want you to free the others," Chi said. "All Misfires. All breeders."

I won't sacrifice you, my impossible twin sister. He breathed in her candied breath.

"Don't be like them," she whispered.

A wave of shudder from the burn weed's fire swept away his numbered objections. The time to choose detonated. "I promise to come back."

Chi kissed him on his Independence Man brand with sticky lips. "You better."

CHAPTER XII

Kor's thoughts ruptured between escape plans and reconsidering his decision to leave Chi behind. Every time he glanced at his possessed father, emotional grenades blew up, a shrapnel shower of anger, empathy, remorse, respect, shame, and love. Seeing his father under the control of another, diminished and helpless, amplified too many warring emotions until his distraught heart threatened to burst.

Tunnel sections lit up the underground passage. Sealed with stealth-enhanced alloys, it extended for a kilometer, well beyond the Temple Square. A military-grade door blocked the tunnel terminus, but Rue tapped in a code he'd snagged from the guard's mind. At the top of an ascending stairway, they stepped into a ten-foot-diameter shrine.

Narrow shelves provided interior bones up to a hemispheric dome. Reliquaries—vials of blood—lined the shelves. Simple tubes of clear glass dotted an array of unique designs; square glass, blown into sculpted flowers for tops, cobalt blue with floral designs, silver stoppers, some of them painted, light-catcher tree, meadow, paintwing, the holy mark, others with decanter shapes, twisted cut diamond patterns. Kor marveled. The priests selected their vials of remembrance. In death, they allowed themselves a freedom of expression impermissible in life.

The shrine's arched exit was a gateway to uncertain futures. Kor swayed—impulses roiled in divergent directions. The door cracked.

Rue-Strom brushed up against him. "Anything?" Kor asked.

"No. A balanced mind on the other side."

Serene and sexy, Demi appeared in a pearl skin-matching mini-dress with exposed shoulders and legs. Demi dipped her head, made careful observation of the shrine's vials, and picked one up with two crossing-arced swirls of delicate gold-painted leaves that invoked a coat of arms. The barest hint of a smile brightened her face. "Your people sometime surprise me with unexpected delicacy."

"This is the third time you've tracked me down in six days, and three of those, I was in a jail cell. Are you stalking me? How did you find me?"

"You are a reservoir overflowing with un-channeled flows. The imbalance amplifies into unmanageable possibilities. I am sensitive to your whereabouts."

Demi opened a case and gave it to Kor. With self-assured speed, she placed the needles in her ears, head and torso in patterns, attuning to the flow of energies. . .a hundred, dozens more, in swirls, lines, clusters, and arcs. Demi's smooth pace remained constant until she emptied the case. She circled in languid motion. Yellow-gold eyes watered to the point of tearing.

"The spark catches fire," she said. "We must choose our pain and our regret."

Demi stepped outside. Needles glinted, an angel from the gate of heaven. "The future calls for your father's death by your hands. Kill him at your clan's sacred whipping post. Quick, both of you, into my car before you're identified by security."

With no ready alternative, Kor complied, pulling in his father. On autopilot, Demi's private hovercar sped along Hero's Boulevard to the compound. Mighty Sapphire dipped below the horizon. The lunar eyes headed to their closest approach in a lifetime. Reds and oranges, the colors of Lovers' Kiss, lit up the mountains. Streaming videos splashed across buildings and floating displays showed off ultra-fit men in inciting poses. Men gathered in plazas to dance, drum, and roar. A siren song of growls, grunts, and whoops demanded a heated response. Rip open the door, throw himself into the mayhem, and he would forget his burdens in ecstatic delight.

The dead Eternal might go unmissed during the festival, but there were no guarantees. The hovercar came to a stop at the compound's stairs to the street. He sat, unwilling to advance, unwilling to murder his father. The best lies were the ones you believed, and in truth, he would never be a proper Militant.

Demi took Kor's hand. "Rid yourself of doubt. Kill your father to snuff out the imbalance. Do what must be done to save yourself, your clan, and your people."

"Hurry," Rue-Strom said. "This mind hungers for release."

Kor picked up his possessed father and carried him through the compound gate. Foreign energy cloaked the rooms and hallways—he had become an intruder in his own home. Worker drones murmured, scrubbed, cleaned, and cooked a grand meal for the men of Steel Rose upon their return from the festival. He steered away from others, finding himself in the courtyard of lessons. The courtyard's whipping post, nicknamed the Punisher, was a child next to the Rainbow, though no less menacing. Moonlight bathed the Punisher's impervious shiny gray-white coated hide. Alert for sudden movement, he shackled his father to the post, a reversal of roles, stirring up the yard's fragrant mountain mint.

"Stop right there."

The threatening directive thinned Kor's blood. Cousin Dagger, blaster drawn, emerged from behind one of the courtyard's perimeter columns. White-blond hair, icy silver, a hell-hog tattoo on his broad shoulder won in a hunting competition, but no kill brands on his light creamy brown skin, by appearance a standout from the other Steel Rose men. Dagger's rich dark eyes convicted.

"You're finished," Dagger said.

"Who are you to say?"

Dagger motioned at the whipping post. "Hook yourself up, traitor."

Kor slow-walked to the Punisher. "Why are you here?" he asked, stalling for time.

"Your father is by the book. A search team scours the city. I stayed behind."

Of course. Strom, as leader of Steel Rose, was supposed to lead the clan into the Lovers' Kiss festival zone—another blot in the annuals of Kor.

"Hurry it up," Dagger said.

Kor fumbled with a set of manacles for wrists and ankles. Ideas for a counterattack jostled for his attention.

"Make one move, and you're burned." Dagger pointed his gun. "Why did you chain your father to the post?"

Stories and lies coalesced into tangible lines. The truth, as so often the case, would be unbelievable. A beam cut through the moonlight, striking Dagger in the back. Kor rushed to break his fall. Wolf emerged from the far side of the courtyard in his favorite sensor-stealth bodysuit.

"Sneaky son of a gun," Kor said.

"Your number one fan. You're lucky I like you."

"Aye. Many thanks, cousin."

Wolf slipped away; he would go far in the Brigades.

"Time for you to go as well, ghost," he whispered into his father's ear, and the presence of Rue faded away.

Legs crossed, Kor waited for his father to wake up and see the son he had helped forge. The worker who had approached Kor earlier entered the courtyard with remarkable calm, given that he violated a sacred rule, carrying a rose and a stuffed travel bag slung over his shoulder. The worker stepped around Dagger's limp body as he would a fallen log.

"You broke into my locker?" Kor asked.

"You never locked it after I left the rose."

"Locked or not, you could lose a hand for that."

"Steel Rose would handicap a productive worker."

Caught off guard by the pushback, Kor reset his attention. The worker had the square forehead brand, monochromatic eyes, the color of silt, beautiful in its way, short, ragged fingernails, gray shirt, and pants—a wiry, lean ordinary man, unremarkable except for his presence.

"How did you know I was here?"

"Rose-harvesters' sense of smell is above average, and I got a whiff of you when I gave you this rose."

"What's your name, scent-smeller?"

"Ezara."

"Unusual worker name."

"We rarely tell outsiders our real name."

"You're full of surprises, Ezara."

"Someday, I would like to introduce you to my partner; he thinks me dull. Your father and cousins have kindness, but armor shields their hearts. I see into your heart. I believe you do as well. A man who knows his heart cannot kill his father without being forever wounded. I fear what your wounded heart might do."

"You are wise."

"For a worker? The Transgeneticists bred us to toil and to obey the same as you though we bear pain no one else does. No one cares about us." Ezara's voice choked up, and his eyes watered from the stout effort of refusing to yield to grief potent and humbling in its silence.

"My best friend was retired today," Ezara said in a trembling voice. "The recycle transport arrived, and he stepped into the trailer of death as though going to market. My kind simply disappears. You are a man who seeks other ways."

"Do you know who my father killed at the Rainbow?"

The question was unfair of Kor to ask. To reveal a clan secret would be a violation, punishable by termination. Shrills and twitters from the estate forests filled the void. The worker breathed in an extended exhale.

"Yes," Ezara said at last. "One of us disposed the body."

"Tell me."

"Not my place. But you will not find peace until you understand."

Disoriented by the revelation, yet unwilling to endanger Ezara further, his thoughts processed at dreadnaught-burn. Kor exchanged a kiss as he would with a cousin and told the worker to go before Strom awoke.

The real Rue showed up, fittingly a creature of the night with a black cloak and cowl. "The hour is late. Why isn't your father dead?"

Kor flinched at Rue's raspy voice. His father stirred, a hissing breath and a distressed moan. Kor gripped the post's whip, knuckles whitening, ready to strike once to balance the scales for the thousands levied against him. Ezara was right; Kor would never be whole if he murdered his father.

The General cocked one eye open. "Go ahead."

"Why must the clan always come first?"

"You are my only son, but I would kill you if our roles were reversed, and my heart would weep until starved of blood."

Kor teared up for a moment before waving off the remark.

The General's familiar molten glare blazed with full force. "Approach."

On instinct, Kor obeyed. His breath—quick and shallow—the General's long and dull.

"We are slaves, son."

"I know."

"Your tongue knows. We are less than human. If Steel Rose falls, we face far worse slavery. You yearn for storybook freedom. I fight to keep the freedom we have."

Kor struggled to counter. The General sounded reasonable. Obeying without question, the punishments, the death pool, and the whole messed up universe sounded reasonable. He leaned into his father's ear, bursting between urges to strike and rigid discipline.

"Talking points."

"I'm the Oath Breaker traitor who broke under interrogation. I betrayed the resistance leader, my Orest, my partner, a name I cannot speak without the pain of salt knives slicing my heart. To save Steel Rose, I killed him at the Rainbow in an act of penance to the Chorus. He screamed, "I love you," with every lash of the whip. I did my duty. I saved the clan. What have I asked of you that I have not asked of myself?"

Kor dropped the whip. The General wept, never meeting Kor's blurry gaze. Rue hissed insistent wants. The world lost its edges—the moons and the courtyard decayed into formless jelly.

Demi appeared, a serene wave, goddess of the moons, as unreadable as the Punisher. She inventoried the scene, then removed and added needles in quick succession—a shaper of energies tapping into creation's flow. "You are behind schedule and haven't done anything I've asked."

He scanned Demi, reading a steady pulse and easy breath, a perfect lack of tension. "What's your game?"

"Critical and complex."

"We must borrow your clan's frigate," Rue said.

"You mean *steal*." Kor swallowed hard. Follow the advice of a Ghost? Just. Plain. Ridiculous. Kor muttered something; even he wasn't sure what he said. The indomitable General had betrayed the rebellion, betrayed his partner... For a brief flash, Kor's love for his father carried no grief.

"Your delay exacts a price," Demi said. "Kill your father. Or flee and take me prisoner as a guardian against chaos. Act quickly or the price gets higher no matter how you choose." Demi rearranged a slew of needles and swooned.

Kor bolted, sweeping Demi into his arms. He took one last long look at his father. Flashes of Garrison, Wolf, family meals, and celebrations locked Kor in place. The choice was inhuman: a lifetime watching his hand whip his father to death or exposing the clan to execution or slavery. Surely, the universe offered other options.

"Send a confession to the Plebiscite," Kor said to Rue.

"An empty gesture," the General said. "Either kill me as a sacrifice to the Eternal's death or you must cleanse our name with a deed to inspire awe among the clans. Time for you to be a man."

Fates were in motion, the pebbles tossed, best to ride, if possible, the consequences of victory. Every High Clan maintained military assets, a nod to the empire's last dark age when the clans rose to prominence and exerted their will over Zorn; Steel Rose's prize and pride, *Brave Star*, was a stealth-black, beautiful, and potent frigate. The compound's tube car took them to its mountainside hangar in minutes.

Kor carried Demi to the frigate's brig and darted to the bridge to initiate the ship's power-up sequence. Part of Kor's mind focused on the start-up checklist; the rest went numb. The primary control panel lit up in multiple banks of diagnostic checks. Power flowed to the engines. Rue transmitted a virtual confession treatise, as much as one could do in words. No longer an annoying evil paranormal, she took responsibility for the Eternal's murder.

After a quiet prayer, he launched the frigate into the sky and played a tune. *Spread your wings and fly away . . . you're a free man.* The ship smashed through the clouds and escaped the atmosphere, plunging into a starlit sea filled with hunters.

"Thoughts of positive outcome improve our chances," Rue said.

"Out of my mind, spook."

"No vacation spot and unnecessary. You discharge your intention to the universe. Thoughts create reality."

Kor snorted. Ghost propaganda. The control panel's readouts displayed no-trouble green. So much for Rue's conjuring. He split the view, adding the rear to catch a parting glimpse of Zorn's bright blues, whites, yellows, and lavenders. He stole the clan warship, abetted a ghost, killed in the inner sanctum, and dishonored the blood duel, though not by choice. As far as heresies went, he had covered several of the big ones.

Alerts flashed in a shrill warning. Nothing less than a war-star, a gargantuan battle station, jumped into proximate space. The mobile fortress would be upon the *Brave Star* in minutes. Six mighty pylons towering from a central globe gave the construct its distinctive, mouth-dropping shape.

"The Empire comes for you," Rue said, her eyes a simmering black. "You attract an unnatural amount of attention."

Kor banked toward the sun. Balls of laser light shot past *Brave Star's* port side. The frigate was a tiny night-flier going against a goliath. A high-energy particle blast from the rear cannon forced the war-star into evasive maneuvers, buying him precious seconds. Out of options, he plotted a course off the space lanes.

"Hyperspace jumps through uncharted routes pose the following hazards," warned the AI. "Unknown gravity wells, hyperspace inclinations, electromagnetic storms, space folds, sub-space pockets of instability, displacement deviations, temporal anomalies—"

"The forest has snakes, yirgs, arvorgs, and poison-leaf," Kor said. "Just do it."

He hopped into the command chair and patched into the ship's external sensors. From his perspective, he hovered on top of the ship with super-enhanced vision. Multitudes of stars sucked oxygen from clenched lungs until the massive enemy fortress blotted them out.

Ion blasts smashed into *Brave Star's* synth-metal shell. Chunks of the ship's hide spun into space, revealing a second skin of sleek neutronium armor. Score one for Steel Rose. Kor broke from the mind-machine interface, blinking away a flood of flashers. Alerts lit up the control console. Repair sub-routines went into action. Concentrated turbo-laser fire shook the *Brave Star* to its bones. Weak spots formed throughout the ship's armor; it tilted from the blows of multiple hits, throwing him to the deck.

The engines' power bars sank to zero. The *Brave Star* drifted. Kor's thoughts flattened into a slipstream. Skin itched with venomous intensity from the Eternal's burn weed strikes. He reached for the captain chair's command display. Outcast, a slave, but he would choose death on his terms. He calculated the time for the war-star to take his ship into a holding bay, added fifteen minutes to be safe, and activated the self-destruct. Blood should never be wasted.

***

Bleeps, bloops, quiet conversations—the ambient noise of the bridge—intruded, stoking uncertainty in Charronna's nerves. Why be on edge? The voyage to Zorn encountered no difficulties. As a bonus, the war-star emerged from hyperspace with a satellite relay identifying a rouge Steel Rose frigate on an unscheduled flight. The chances were high that her primary target made a feeble attempt at playing fugitive.

Scans showed a Psian, a Militant, and a Creator, by itself unusual enough to investigate. An acid-reflux cocktail to sour anyone's stomach percolated. Add in the savant, quite literally breathing down her neck, and dinner bubbled with unsettling persistence.

She rotated the command chair. *Blue Serenity's* expansive four-level bridge exuded power—the Starry Empire's mightiest class of ship, a mobile fortress that impressed even the Earthers. Over a hundred techs supported command staff monitoring the ship, the frigate, proximate space, and anything that moved. She would deal with the so-called threat and secure sovereign status without breaking a nail.

Her pet wizard should be on the bridge. What was his name? Noah, Noe, Noi!

The war-star pulled in the drifting frigate. The First Commander, prim and proper to the point of neurosis, kept her attention fixed on her primary display cluster. "Interior bay boarding tube connects to the captured frigate. Protocols remain intact. Preparing to board."

"Hop to it. The staff is replaceable."

"Never forget you are also staff," the savant muttered.

As if you would ever let me.

Directed remotely by the First Commander, marine blue-clad troops in full-body armor charged into the frigate. Within seconds, they escorted the Psian into the boarding tube and strong-armed the Militant. Mission accomplished. Another figure emerged from the brig—gray pearl skin, needles galore, and an unhurried gait to grate one's nerves. Demi-One, puller of other people's strings. An energetic barrier encapsulated Demi's mind. Telepathic scans yielded nothing. Charronna dug fingernails, one into the other.

"Excellent work, First Commander. Escort the Demiurge to the best available quarters."

A message pinged Charronna's private link, from Demi no less. *The spark catches fire. The imbalance grows and gives birth. You are the key to channeling its effect. Fail in your moment of trial, and the stars themselves shall fall. Your friend, the Demiurge.*

The savant stirred. A waft of perfume—patchouli—tickled Charronna's nose. Patchouli triggered the resident ghost in an unhappy way. The savant whipped out a small bottle and anointed Charronna with a few drops of the spicy, sweet essential oil.

"What in oblivion's name are you doing?"

"I assigned the Psian on this mission to teach him a lesson. If being stuck on a war-star doesn't disturb his mind enough, the patchouli should do the trick."

Oh joy, an unbalanced ghost. If Charronna placed bets, and on sure things she did, Sentinel and Harmony would soon be having a heart-to-heart on Demi's activities. The war-star seemed fated to earn a cameo in a melodrama.

The savant strutted to the omnidirectional transport. "Tell Demi I'm on the way as Sentinel's voice. Don't screw it up while I'm gone."

Charronna gave the savant's back an I'll-turn-you-into-toad-soup squint. She fingered her com-badge, an inverted red triangle, a symbol of authority precious few rated though with clear suffocating boundaries.

The troops onboard the Militant ship set about taking control of the frigate's command-level systems. Officers focused on readouts. Sub-officers and crew worked at their stations. A wall of imperial blue, many of them Militants sworn to service, protected her with weapons at the ready. An entire war-star responded to her command.

Troopers hauled the Militant captive to the bridge. His ripped bodysuit exposed numerous bruises and bloody wounds, none life-threatening, and a fit, mouthwateringly built body suitable for a thorough inspection. The forehead brand, *All Men Are Created Equal*, might have offended except for the joke of that sentiment. Kor of Steel Rose advertised himself as a radical. The Psian communion had indeed illuminated a threat.

Charronna gave *the look* and the troopers dropped him to the floor. The barbarian didn't react. Not that she had a trace of the breeder-pheromones, but part of the Militant's genetic aversion to women was simple chemistry. She expected at least a twitch.

"Not much of a Militant," Charronna said.

"You see the problem. Are we done?"

"Your attachment to the idea of hope means nothing. Hope belongs to fools and fairytales."

Suppressing a surge of grief, she glanced at one of the soldiers, who slammed his gun into Kor's gut. The prisoner doubled over. Militants were woman-hating barbarians. She did the rest of humanity a favor by getting rid of one. *Too bad he's hotter than premium lab spawn. I could feed on this heady, unripe hunk of a man for a long time. I'd be a candied vampire without remorse.*

"We have teams in engineering and on the command deck," the First Commander said.

"You've omitted words like complete control and secure."

"Sentient algorithms sophisticated enough to mutate against our viral security probes protect command-level inputs."

Charronna's forced smile faltered. The game was over by any set of sensible rules. Gods, she needed a paradise pill. "Deploy more infiltrator probes."

"Already done." The First Commander's dark skin darkened further with irritation.

Guards brought the Psian prisoner equipped with a finger-wide helmet with green lights—an active Psion blocker. The newcomer had the same brooding pallor as the morose one she had skulking about onboard, but with a red-brown skin tone. The Psian used a cream concealer around the eyes, had shaped eyebrows, a foundation powder over the whole face, highlighter brightening the tear ducts, and a hint of lipstick.

"You identify as female?" Charronna said.

The ghost bowed in affirmation. "Rue."

"Well, Rue, the barbarian you hooked up with attracts attention, and not in a good way." Charronna raised her chin a bit, brushing off the guilt at having to do the Chorus's dirty work. Everyone knew the rules and the consequences of breaking them.

"Our viral probes breached the frigate's access barrier," the First Commander said. "Defensive anti-virals swarm. Traction not achieved. The frigate's AI attempts to partition from infected networks."

"Time isn't free, First Commander. Prepare to eject the vessel. I prefer to recover the ship's memory core and data logs, but a nice-to-have. Anyone who doesn't need to be on the ship, get them off."

Charronna's pet wizard appeared. Ever the charmer, Noi dumped heaviness onto the bridge with a long, unhappy face. Caught by the patchouli surprise, he leached spiraling disturbance into the continuum, but, to his credit, he regained control and kept his lunch down. Charronna sent a telepathic message to her resident Psian. *Play nice, and you get to see your family again. The patchouli wasn't my idea.*

The Psian prisoner stiffened upon seeing her fellow subset. That the localized psi-blocker prevented a private chat was worth a quick grin. Waves of hot anger emanated from the sexy barbarian. He didn't like spooks any more than she liked barbarians. A bead of sweat formed on the nape of Charronna's neck. She commanded the situation. Yet here she was with a pair of Psians, and their kind lunched on treachery.

"I'm ready to die," Kor said.

"Part of your specs," Charronna said. "You might as well be a chronometer."

"I'm as human as you are."

Incredulity and sadness collided in Charronna's mind—disbelief that a Militant was capable of saying such a thing, grief that in her case, he probably sold himself short.

"Don't worry," she said in a far-off tone. "I'm feeling like your fairy godmother today."

Like a respectable minion, Noi showed his hands to Charronna, branded with a total of fifteen black rings and eighteen red bands—naturally strong as indicated by black, a master skill level based on red. Thirty-three rings out of a possible forty translated into a potent rating of P-82.5. Rue spread her fingers, each one branded by two black and two red circles—the perfect mark of Penitence and Approbation.

A sudden headache hammered Charronna, and it had no remedy. "King's Mercy," Charronna said, "you're one of the Twelve."

"A mover of vital and unfortunate events," Rue said. "I am the Weeper."

"I'm being screwed. To be perfectly clear, that's *my* job. Why are you here?"

"Your prisoner's mind holds something the Twelve want to examine."

"Never trust a ghost," Kor said.

"The barbarian has a point," Charronna said. "You scheme to fulfill the Starfall probability. Why else would you be on Zorn?" She paused amid a flurry of discarded retorts. "Weeper."

"The pursuit of intangible probabilities attracts fools and chasers of dreams. A presence in the Militant's mind revealed itself. It claims to be an ancient Psian, the original, a Lord of Avad."

"You're telling me one of the old gods inhabits this barbarian?"

Rue gave a slight affirmative nod.

"I want him examined," Charronna said, "by both of you."

Noi removed Rue's psi-blocker. Charronna tensed. Noi understood the price of disobedience: the lives of his wife and children. Rue was a wild card, one of the Twelve, and among that sordid lot, the Weeper was notorious for weaving plots. Sentinel would take the Weeper to task for being on Zorn without permission. Charronna would give anything to eavesdrop.

The ghosts laid hands on the barbarian; their loose robe sleeves rode up, revealing a numbered brand corresponding to Bureau of Facts and Circumstances files. Charronna accessed Rue's, getting basic bio-data, unusually sparse. No matter. The truth of Kor's threat would soon be revealed.

CHAPTER XIII

Something was wrong.

Raven pushed through frozen-stiff ligaments to raise himself off the stasis bed. How far had he journeyed? The single-cabin sloop wasn't designed for long-range interstellar travel, one of many factors reducing the odds of a successful quest. Cold vapor dispersed in a pale light. He reached into a storage compartment for a double injection of stim. Pangs worked through soft tissues and swollen veins; senses heightened in a downpour of clarity. His youth belonged to the Blessed One, and its abuse was to his glory. The concentrated stim-burn spread to his toes as he climbed out of the hibernation bed.

"AI Unit, status report."

"Distress signal detected."

"I instructed you to not interrupt the priority mission."

"This unit is of Earth Confederation manufacture. My architecture mandates a response. Primary coding cannot be overwritten."

"Will you proceed if ordered?"

"Affirmative. The Confederation Inter-Planetary Commerce Oversight Agency evaluates responses to distress signals at the time of license renewal."

Raven relaxed. The Sol half-breeds, as annoying as their blood-sucking mosquitoes infesting League worlds, had not compromised the quest. Mind clear, he headed to the cozy bridge, dominated by a convex control panel comprising holographic and digital overlays for command, weapons, communications, navigation, and data analysis far more advanced than the League's simple view screens. With a wave of a hand, he brought the systems out of power-conservation mode.

A visual of a military patrol-class vessel hovered beyond the convex panel. It bristled with high-grade sensors, electronic countermeasures, communication arrays, and laser cannons on each side. Three banks of shield generators reinforced thick armored hull plating. Fully operational, the ship would be a nasty surprise to an unwary challenger, but it drifted with most systems off-line. Registered as *Serendipity*, with diplomatic protection, the vessel originated from the Earth Confederation world of Hermes. Adrift off the shipping lanes, it was a lost cause in the process of demise. It's fate, of no importance.

"Make your recording of the event," Raven said. "Resume course."

The emperors within Raven swelled in presence. Teeth buzzed; unadulterated bliss engorged his entire being. The majority of the emperors' aspects wanted to move on. The strongest of them believed differently.

Serendipity journeyed to a League stellar world controlled by the ambitious House of Arc. Malcolm Baxter, ruler of Hermes, sent his daughter there for a year of education. A rush of knowledge about the half-breed dynasty poured into his thoughts. The Baxters desired significance. Raven paused in reverence. Vast numbers of people put faith in imaginary murmurings from invisible gods, but the living god inhabited his mind.

Visions of past lives belonging to others exploded and died in his mind. The control board pulsed with too many lights in a coded language at the tip of his understanding. The AIU maneuvered on top of the *Serendipity*. Reinforced with another dose of stem, he climbed down a boarding tunnel and dropped into the vessel near an observation deck. Nausea lurched up his throat. Human waste was smeared on the walls like runes to ward off unwelcome guests.

Raven invited the stench into his lungs. It fused into his blood cells. The desire to expel subsided. Shattered interface displays and bludgeoned speakers suggested a maddened crew. Smashed alert signals. . .leaky water tank. . .cracked computer portals. . .a door unhinged by a spent fire extinguisher. . .more runes, more warnings for Raven to turn back.

Demented scrawl had reduced the command deck to a lunatic's nest. A bloated corpse, an adult male, lay dead on the floor. The ship's log looped in a captain's ramble of sabotage, of a conspiracy by rebels from Hermes's tributary worlds to take Malcolm's daughter hostage.

A presence close by. . .Raven whirled with his gun raised. Nothing, no one, someone had to be there, cloaked by rank fumes. He feigned nonchalance, then spun again. A naked emaciated girl, not quite a teenager, smirked at the entrance.

Raven fired, grazing the girl's shoulder. She twitched but remained standing. Matted hair stank of feces. Bruises, scabs, and fresh wounds colored ghastly pale flesh that clung to her visible bone. He edged closer with mini steps to avoid scaring her away. Within arm's reach, he made a quick move. Gently, he lifted and carried the half-starved girl as he would a baby.

The Blessed One's disappointment coated his mind, an unpleasant aftertaste from an unsatisfactory experience. The damaged girl would be of no use. The investigation had yielded no advantage. Standard practice dictated culling the girl by breaking her neck. He hesitated. She was an innocent, about twelve years old, the same age as his youngest sister.

The girl gurgled, gazing at Raven with empty eyes. Light as a bucket of chaff, he carried her to his ship's med lab, stroked her bruised face, and wiped away a rolling tear. Unsalvageable. The med-doctor declared as much in red bars on digital readings over the regeneration bed: Harmonic Instability Sickness, a hyperspace malady fatal in advanced stages.

"Goodbye, little star," he sang.

The emperors trembled with the rumblings of a quake—dissension. Dizzy, he put a hand against a wall. The division within the living god's aspects expanded, leaving broken pockets for Raven's wants. Thunderclaps detonated, each one a new argument. He drooled. He dug ever deeper for some part of him not exposed to an aching throb.

"No!" he bellowed.

In the shock of his denouncement, ribbons of ethereal Shadow energy abandoned him and flowed into the girl. Raven fought the urge to weep. Not a single aspect remained behind.

Sometime later, a thin tendril of white snaked its way back to him. Smiling, he welcomed back the Blessed One. A lone voice echoed. *"Is anyone left? I am Ashtore."*

The voice drifted and repeated the question in a call to every direction. To Raven's amazement, none of the other aspects responded. He would have wept without shame at the loss of so many, except, the lone presence emanated pure relief.

***

Ghosts plowed into Kor's mind. Memories, the Painted Garden, the valor ball victory over Iron Song, dancing in the White Pearl, relaxing on the beach with Jude, playing chase with Wolf, the first kiss, offered refuge. Although the darkness sapped willpower with the might of a high summer sun, the optimism of life prevailed to keep him whole.

In the Real, orders cascaded, voices demanded attention, and alert beeps sang, fading into a muffle as the outside world receded. Circular halos, ghost-force, rampaged through the electric discharge of his mind with the care of an invading army. Where ghosts tread, rainbows and happy memories broke into scattering ash. The foul halos extended mighty wings, enveloping Kor in suffocating space. Ghost presence blocked every avenue of escape.

"I am Kor!" he shouted. Intertwined, he locked into the battle, raw will against loathsome halos reshaped into shining blades of white lightning.

"Surrender your secrets."

Excitement and hope submerged into rage that he ever trusted Rue. He raged at his father, at the Code, at the injustice soaking life to its wretched shambles. *Never again.* Never again would he be controlled. He tore his mind apart and scorched himself on replays where he murdered his comrades—where he endured the whipping post. *Feast on my pain. Walk on the sun.*

Reject who you are. The ghosts drew back, enough for hope to kindle.

"Not pretty in here, is it?" he asked.

"Surrender."

Ghosts hovered over his mindscape's horizon. They brightened. Electric fingers stabbed into the mindscape.

"Surrender."

Kor howled in defiance.

From the uncharted interior depths, blue flame surged, a fountain of unexpected strength. Power magnified, unsatisfied, dark and focused, and he embraced whatever the force offered. The ghost-halos withered in Kor's augmented glory. The god force filled more of his mind space, an ever-expanding bloat. Foreign noise of boundless anger fueled his defense. Ghosts, darkness, old gods—a mythic universe closed in from every direction.

No more. Better to let go. Better to surrender than to become his rage and his pain.

Blades of ghost force plunged through his vulnerability, exposing his mind to the absolute raw. The ghosts had won. He searched the cluttered wreckage in aimless wander for rainbows, for happy memories where he might remember who he was. *Should he cry in tribute to the many unhappy yesterdays? Was it the joy or the pain, was it the excitement or the heartache giving rise to meaning? Could he be without both?* Life was a puzzle.

A voice spoke, "Come."

An egg shape appeared, metallic and gleaming. Its presence fluctuated. Blue flame engulfed the object, a corona worthy of the night.

"Come to the Dead Center."

The plea took root in mental recesses, combined with echoes of previous forgotten calls.

"I remember; you claim to be one of the old gods."

"Holy mission awaits you."

A location far into the Deep Black (DB) pulsed red on a holographic star map. The map zoomed larger, a planet came into view, the image pulling, a harsh siphon. Clouds filled the vision, and then a vast plain where a massive, stepped pyramid towered into the sky, home to gods. Danger shivered his senses as he entered the ziggurat's shrine. He plunged a hand into the blue fire, the burn of dry ice binding to his skin. Jolted into the Real, he coughed in a spasmodic fit. A ghost-wizard, Rue, wavered—her once sharp eyes glazed. Perhaps she, too, had experienced the entity's divine touch.

"I have the upper-level command codes," Rue said. "A countdown is in progress and cannot be aborted. Twelve seconds to self-destruct."

With a snarl, Kor leaped at the ghost-wizard and into a barrage of laser fire.

***

By the gods, Charronna despised Militants.

Warnings lights around the viewers pulsed emergency-red. Charronna tracked the seconds. Nine. . . Tractor beams pushed the frigate outside the bay. She barked at the First Commander. "Destroy that ship." Five. . . In the good old days, a Militant would never go out of his way to kill his superiors. Three. . .

"Too close," the First Commander said.

"Do it." *Better that than a reactor explosion.*

The Weapons Officer's fingers flew over the control console. One. . . Laser fire slammed into the frigate's heavy armor. Charronna calculated the diminishing chance of survival in morbid fascination in concert with the increase in hazard pay. She strapped into the captain's chair, beating the explosion by a fraction of a second. The gates of apocalypse opened, and the frigate vanished in an inferno. Shock waves covered the war-star. Bridge command screens lit up with damage assessments. If she lost an entire war-star, no flowchart in civilized space would be big enough to document her mission failures.

Many officers were down; others fought at their stations to salvage the Empire's pride and glory. The communications officer screamed as flames burst through the console, consuming her hands in a flash. Stinging, blinding smoke assaulted the senses. Charronna unstrapped and dropped to her knees, gasping and coughing. She refused to fall apart like some commoner. If the Empire had given her anything useful, it was how to keep her head in a crisis.

Control boards dueled in electric lightning. Near the helm station, she bumped into the First Commander, breathing but unconscious. By the gods, this was not supposed to happen. *Think, woman.* Telepathic scans for nearby life signs yielded a headache as a reward. Death licked in flames, stealing breath with black smoke. Where was the barbarian?

Alert messages flooded the comm. Primary power failed. An opus of useless screams and sirens reigned. Vision narrowed in scope and eroded into cloudy twilight. She belly-crawled toward the barbarian's last position, gun drawn. Her com-badge pulsed blurry green, thank the stars. Help was on the way.

She aimed, and fired at the barbarian, unsure what or who she had hit.

CHAPTER XIV

Toxic smoke thinned into wispy strands of cemetery haze. Kor blinked his tearing eyes. Metallics oiled the air. The Empire's agent, a body length away, clutched a blaster. Her lethal green eyes were closed; hair disheveled; cheeks grimy; face slack. Without the evil Chorus agent tension, her inner beauty shined, stunning, a heartbreaker to anyone brave enough to dare connection. He jerked the shooter away and searched for mobile enemies in the pall of emergency lighting. The Starry Empire's finest lay fallen throughout the bridge.

Except for one.

A ghost's backside taunted for a round of target practice. Smoke was repelled around his head, a fallen angel's halo. Knuckles whitened, Kor stood and took aim. Any second, the ghost would turn, see Kor, and consume his soul with unreadable black eyes befitting a hell-born incubus. The Resistance would disappear into the recycling tanks. His sister Chi, Tara, and others like them, would be wiped from existence. *Blood for blood*. Killing the spook was self-defense, an act of love. In painful solitude, he fired.

The spook moved to the next person. The smoky halo went with him. Partial lighting powered back up. Displays flickered to life. Had he fired the gun? Was he lost in a ghost dream? Overcome with spotty haze, he grabbed at something solid. Amazingly, the spook stepped over the fallen officers on an intercept trajectory. The ghost peered with gentle eyes. The man's pale skin shined with vitality, but still a ghost.

"I'm Noi Zekra, Society of Substance and Curiosity."

The spook reached out with bony fingers and pointy, uneven nails. The touch was too familiar, and Kor brushed it away. Noi? The name was Rue.

"Rue is dead," the spook said.

"So are you."

"Your flesh belongs to the State," the spook said. "Your heart belongs to the Supreme. You think yourself cheated? The Naturals claim no better."

Kor grasped the ghost's throat. The thin figure didn't flinch. Psians showed you what they wanted you to see. They raped the minds of others and never shed a tear. Around the ghost, roses sprang to life, growing and blooming in a Psian reality, extending to surround them both in a comforting embrace. The aroma, delicate and pure, nourished compassionate instincts.

"I ask for generosity for Rue's weakness. Absolute honesty washes the soul in bliss and in brutality. The Empire provides the stability we crave."

The telepath's thin lips stretched, an almost grin, too brief for Kor to be sure.

"Forgiveness must be earned."

"You condemn yourself in shame for the wizards' crime you claim as yours. It is right to self-absolve."

The infernal ghost didn't understand. They broke his father, possessed Kor's mind, and forced him to kill Jude. Faith withered before his lover's bewildered eyes. The light went out on killer and victim alike.

"The wizards forced you."

"The memories show otherwise. The memories say I had the freedom of will to kill myself."

"A burdened conscience confuses truths and lies. The outcome was never in doubt. Some tests are not meant to be won."

Belief and exhaustion collided, smashing him in between. He kept a firm grip on Noi's ruddy flesh. The ghost spoke again, his voice infuriatingly composed. Kor's head expanded. Killing the ghost would be quick and easy, satisfying and vile. Tears formed. Arms wobbled. Clarity of purpose wavered in the face of murder. Jude would never be at peace until Kor avenged his lover's death. *Blood for blood.* The Blood King would forgive. But it wasn't the Blood King who haunted his dreams.

"Do you listen to others or to your heart?" Noi asked in a wispy telepathic fade.

Above all, Kor wanted to believe he was real, to have a home without whipping posts, a lover to fall asleep with, gardens filled with paintwings and cooking herbs. He wanted to dance, to be alive, whatever that meant, instead of biding his time until he died on a battlefield. *A good soldier protects.* He slackened his hold. The weight of his charm pierced his attention. The flip of his charm would show him the way.

"The universe speaks to your heart, not to your stone."

The ghost diffused into a dream. Kor eased into oblivion, an Earther song spinning in his head, sung by a group with an intriguing name . . . Five for Fighting.

Watery shimmer poured off Kor's yellow sandstone dream cottage. He squinted. The star's ceaseless outpouring of rays separated, centered upon him, seeking weakness. He wiped the sweat saturated with spicy orange pollen. A man pounded on the front door with a formidable Thor hammer. The synth-metal doors vibrated with each stroke and a pocket-sized area dispersed, then reformed, though the solid face diminished. Kor jumped over a low cattle fence into a trampled garden of flattened flowers, broken stems, and squashed vegetables. No one messed with his home. He spun the intruder around.

"Father? What are you doing?"

"What I must, boy."

Strom carried the energy of his rank as the General over his role as a father, and he shook loose to swing a mighty blow. The doors dispersed into shimmering nonexistence. The General marched into the cottage. In the sparse living area, he struck a piece of abstract floor sculpture. It shattered into glassy fragments.

"Not what I'm looking for," the General said.

Kor followed his father to the sleeping room. A tall tube pulsed in fast warning beats next to his bed, bathing the room in teal. The General slammed the Thor hammer toward a flute resting on a stand in the far corner. Blue fire surrounded the head as it bore close to its target. Spiky pangs riddled Kor's heart. The General's hammer inched closer. A white bird appeared above, flapping its wings.

"You should take better care of your soul," his father said. "Come to the Dead Center. Do as you're told, boy."

"You're no longer my boss," Kor said. "Get out of my house."

The General cackled. "This isn't your house."

Growling, Kor muscled his father to the mattress. His father's cackle spiked into unnatural glee. The white bird screeched. Kor unleashed right and left jabs. Strom's body softened. In a sudden shift, he morphed into a middle-aged gentlefolk man—a familiar presence.

"I've seen you before," Kor said. "You gave yourself the name of an old god, Jeth-ka."

"Your soul belongs to me, flute player."

Jeth twisted into a point and disappeared.

Kor gaped. Souls, the essence of god-stuff, must be untouchable. *Unless Jeth is himself a god.* Memory spun, rumination without end until he cauterized Jeth's existence into his brain. Whatever Jeth might be, he would not make Kor forget again. Harsh chills stiffened his bones, slowed his blood, settled in his marrow, vapor-sealed. How was he supposed to fight such a being, whether he remembered or not? Where were his weapons? Where was the battlefield? Perhaps Jeth lied. Perhaps he needed Kor to be afraid. But he believed him.

Light flooded the sleeping room. Discordant sounds sharpened into scattered words. The clatter of boots drew close. Words formed into sentences, sentences into a conversation. Kor was conscious and in a med room. With a start, he raised his head off the platform.

"He's dangerous," a firm, high voice said.

The war-star's agent voice, melodious yet hard, unleashed a wave of anger into Kor's grief-stricken heart. The Starry Empire took Jude, but for those with power, it was never enough. Eyes closed, Kor flipped to his side. The speakers stepped into his room. One reeked of ghosts; the other of perfumed, flowery hauteur. Noi and Charronna had come to pay him a visit. He relaxed into a numbed, unobtrusive mind.

"He had reason to kill us," the ghost said in a scratchy voice. "He didn't."

"Hello," the war-star agent retorted, "because you knocked him out."

"Kor moves beyond his origins."

"Against the rules."

"Your rules."

"God's rules, the state's, your wife's, does the author matter?"

"God isn't holding my family hostage."

"The sad-story-victim game?" the agent asked. "I'm not allowed to have a family or visit my parents. No children. No husband. No 'I love you' from anyone. Life hurts everyone."

Kor concentrated. Her voice caught with real emotion, but that must be imagined, his hearing fooled for he doubted the witch ever shed tears.

"I've got a dead, injured, and unconscious crew. The ship's power that feeds into the bridge is disrupted. Communications are offline. Thank the stars, most of the ship's self-repair mechanisms survived, or we'd be ruptured space corpses. To top it off, I've got an entitled savant I have to talk down. Be useful or be elsewhere."

Determined to stare down his adversary, Kor sat up on the medical lab's healing station. The Empire's agent brushed away silky strands of red hair from scrubbed cheeks. From the neck down, she wore a fresh skin-hugging uniform to stir the imagination.

"I see you're in the blue," she said with a nod at the instrument panels running the length of Kor's bed.

"Militants heal quickly."

He fixed his gaze on Noi. "What's with the red-headed butcher?" He spat out the last words, a bit of anger boiling into the open. Noi was no different from Rue—spooks, pale and lost on the inside of thought, separated from flesh and blood.

"The redhead runs things around here," the witch said.

A slight tremor near Noi's thin lips betrayed a reaction to something. Life drained from Noi, giving him the semblance of an actual ghost.

"You demand more than I can give," Noi said.

The witch waved her fingers. "I'm tired, stressed, and hungry. Don't mess with me."

"Why don't you drink the blood of your victims?" Kor asked. "That should keep you full."

The witch eye-slapped Kor and turned to Noi. "For the love of your family, Noi." She snapped her fingers. "That quick, and they're gone. This barbarian isn't worth it."

Tears energized Noi's cheeks—labored breathing through a blood-soaked face. Kor had never seen a ghost so alive. "I've taken back my creed," Noi said.

"Don't go spiritual on me. We do whatever the Chorus wants, no matter how insane the demand. Deep scan the barbarian, and total erasure once you're done."

"I won't mind-wipe him," Noi said.

The agent cast a scornful glare to shrink one's manhood. "Your regret—not mine. The Starry Empire has loads of expertise at exacting a price." She drifted away and became unmoored. "Usually at a premium."

She gave Kor the once-over in well-honed dismissiveness. "This will hurt," she said. "More if you resist."

The witch penetrated his thoughts in the guise of a dominatrix armored with iridescent white makeup, leather straps, and diamonds embedded into her skin, an exotic, trippy vision far afield from the ordinary world. Paintwings fluttered from her mouth in a confusing blizzard of color. *Distraction.*

"You're not repulsed by women like most of your kind," the witch said into his mind. *"Lust for men and women heats your idle passions. Boundaries are open to exploration. I like that."*

Kor concentrated on remembering who he was—who he wanted to be.

"Killing others troubles you. Roses—the scents, the aromas, the colors, and the delicate folds—captivate you. Poetry and music flow through you, seeking pathways for expression. You're a romantic who stumbles through life by candlelight within an illusion of divine illumination. You wish to fly, but you're learning to crawl. You must be terribly unhappy."

The witch glanced away. The mental pressure lessened.

"I wish—"

Blue fire erupted from the fibers of her dominatrix skin. Conflagration consumed her in a screaming, rushing inferno. The flames dispersed, leaving a twinkling void.

Thank you, cantankerous old god.

Shaking off the parting image, he hopped off the bed. The witch lay on the floor. The ghost's head swiveled between the witch and Kor. He lunged at the spook and knocked him out with a blow to the head—another victory for the balladeers back home to spin if anyone lived to tell of it.

Grim options tallied up. Fighting alone against the Chorus would result in suicide. Return to Zorn, suicide. Wait for the surviving crew to wake up, suicide. Goal one: evacuate the enemy ship. Goal two: force the old god out of his mind. Goal three: help the Station and other resistance groups deliver freedom to Militants, Workers, Breeders, and to the many peoples throughout the Starry Empire.

He raced about the ship in search of a solution. Doors didn't open. The omnidirectional internal transport system didn't work. Bulkheads blocked halls. Emergency seals cut off whole sections.

The uniform of a dead ensign with a touch of blood splatter provided a morbid disguise. He would at least look the part as the surviving crew recovered, except for his forehead brand. Corpses with traumatic injuries were abundant. He tore off a piece of fabric smeared in blood and wrapped it around his head; presto, he had a fake wound to boot.

Corridors, rooms, and operating stations blended into the surreal when he found an answer in the war-star's leeward hangar bay—a drop ship, larger than the *Brave Star*, primed with an ultra-drive, but protected by access codes. He slammed the wall, breaking into a run.

Ghosts collect secrets. Surely the mind-voyeur ghost knows the ship's codes. If Noi agrees to cooperate, if the drop ship survives intact, if the crew doesn't rally, if no rescue ship interferes, we have a chance to flee to Earth and rid me of Jeth. After I'm free of the old god, I will return to fight with the Station. If...

CHAPTER XV

Kor used a healing station to revive the ghost. Operation Emergency Exit was underway. Kor rubbed his jaw, rife with stubble, assessing the ghost with unreadable inky eyes. Hands folded, his long black hair neat, he waited with patience as Kor made his case. With luck, he would make it to Earth. He trusted the post-physicals on Luna to rid his mind of the occupying presence over a bunch of ghost exorcists any day.

"A one-way choice," Noi said.

"Life is full of them. Ever since their first ship showed up, I wanted to visit Earth."

"Earth's Magnates wield the most power in the Confederation, and they value profit over life. A Militant specimen would be of value to certain factions, and value means more to them than heaven or soul. The Earthers might save you, but only to use you."

"That's how the universe works."

Noi took Kor's hand. "If that is your choice, I will help you."

Kor put an arm around Noi and headed out to the hangar bay at his best pace. None of the surviving crew they encountered wanted to interact with the resident Psian. For once, the plan went according to plan.

The drop ship's five-chair bridge concentrated control functions on a quarter-moon console with floating holographic data and command displays. A beverage bar built into the wall separated two banks of standing stations, a typical natural-born indulgence. The drop ship's specs showed it was capable in terms of firepower, speed, and most importantly, range. Kor started a run through the controls. Short-range scans detected an incoming dreadnaught. It was nowhere near the size of the war-star, though plenty badass. The spook hovered; his mask of inspired sainthood wedged beneath Kor's emotional skin. The ghost's unnatural demeanor fit right in with the antiseptic technology gleaming to the rhythm of pulsing lights.

"Two rules," Kor said. "Stay out of my mind and follow my orders."

"What do you know about the presence in your mind?" Noi asked.

"It claims to be an old god."

"Old, yes, ancient—a wraith of human spirit."

Heat poured off Kor. No affliction imaginable topped being possessed. *Never trust a ghost.* He air-tapped the holographic sensors, checking the scans again. The dreadnaught accelerated when it should be slowing.

Noi spoke, his voice a shade stronger than a whisper. "The entity inside of you feels of Khonsu, the consumer of life. The Society of Temperance and Severity are practiced in consciousness eviction."

"Hell, no, not in a million years, no exorcists, not ever, not on my deathbed. Are you with me?"

With hands clasped, the spook chanted. A presence entered Kor's mind, gentle yet firm. Before he conjured a protest, it vanished.

"The spirit possessing you vibrates with intention," the spook said. His black eyes simmered into heated oil. "It abides in the Deep Black. It calls your name. You must respond."

Hand fisted, Kor slapped the command console. Wordless shame whipped through him in a firestorm at the ghost's violation. *The weak are baby fat.* The weak kill their comrades in muddy, forgotten trenches. He would never be able to trust himself around ghosts. The dreadnaught's chatter was encrypted, a sure sign the captain expected trouble. Someone might as well have put a hole in his heart.

"To be the hero, the one celebrated in ballads, is that not the Militant way? Unlike Rue, I believe in prophecies, and yours leads into the heart of the Deep Black."

"Trusting a ghost is like begging my father for forgiveness."

"The Truth and Gnosis communion was the means through which you were possessed. The events share energy, linked most profoundly."

"Why do ghosts like to screw me?"

"You don't trust me."

Kor laughed, a painful crack to his ears. "Hell, no." He paused for several ragged breaths. "I did have a weird dream."

The Psian's oil-black eyes widened; he pressed a hand to Kor's forehead. Chaotic images roiled his mind.

"Show me."

He grabbed at his cropped hair. Noi, the control panels, the entire bridge, splintered into momentary scraps, while dual black epicenters swallowed him whole.

"Show me!"

In a jarring flash, the spook withdrew his hand.

"Your subconscious warns your ego with dreams," Noi said. "I placed blocks to retard the spread of the possession."

"Get out of my head."

"I'm neither a wizard nor an exorcist. The blocks won't last long."

"No exorcists."

"Absent action, you will lose your sense of self. Permanently."

"Two rules." Kor flashed his fingers for emphasis. "You've broken both in the space of a fart. Forget it, spook."

"I'm trying to help. Most trained Psians keep themselves shielded from foreign minds when bonding. I'm not one of them. I take you back when I withdraw. Your disgust. Your dreams. Your anger. Your hopes. Everything. I am prophet class. Close connection with someone unable to contain themselves is a madness I prefer to avoid."

It never occurred to Kor that Noi paid a price. "Thank you."

Noi smiled through his eyes, a peek of sunshine through the clouds. The harder Kor concentrated, the more images he conjured, and the clearer the dreams became. Voices inside his head pushed for dominance in a non-stop war for his mind—peace, a quixotic pursuit. Life would flow better if he accepted reality. He extracted some comfort that the Empire's agent would awaken to find her prized prisoner and her prized spook gone on one of her prized ships.

Encrypted messages passed between the dreadnaught and war-star *Blue Serenity*. Time to choose a path or let others decide for him. The Psian, paragon-in-waiting, exerted pressure by his constant presence. Surrender or a coward's flight? Kor fingered his charm in a prayer for divine intervention.

"You would leave your family to go on a fool's quest into the DB?" Kor asked.

"To free them, yes."

"Prepare for operation Fool's Quest."

"Charronna must come with us."

"The evil Empire minion isn't coming."

"Infiltrator probes attach to *Blue Serenity's* hull," the AI said.

"I'm half a man if I don't kill her," Kor said, "and you want us to be comrades?"

The Psian locked gazes. "She knows I'm alive. I can't make someone of her talent forget. Are you willing to kill an unconscious person?"

"Every good rule has exceptions."

"I am being compromised," the AI reported. "External links have been severed."

Noi folded his arms and repositioned to an open, uncompromising stance. Kor couldn't help but respect a man feeble of flesh yet brave of spirit. He raced to the war-star's healing room. The agent was still unconscious. He carried her back and placed her on the drop ship's regeneration bed. The inverted triangle inset with three red panels emblazoned threat on the agent's uniform—the highest rank in the Starry Empire's intelligence bureau. The two of them together would be an unfolding disaster. The ghost hovered, not saying a word.

"If she misbehaves," Kor said, "by the Red Beast, I swear on the spirits of Steel Rose, I will break her into pieces."

He doubted he would have to wait long.

***

Sentinel strolled along a tasteful reflecting pool within the expansive Smiling Court palace complex. The name's origin had been lost to history, but she suspected no one was smiling. A pink-purple flowering ground cover bordered the pool, giving off a delightful aroma of rosemary. In simpler days, she loved to cook with Earth-sourced herbs, none more than rosemary, and the ground cover's gene-splicing update memorialized those happy times. Tiered step gardens interspersed with fountains extended the length of the bright, clear water leading up to twin offices with glass exteriors fronted by precision spaced columns, a hundred each, capped with flat roofs, one red, the Agency of Affairs, and the other gray, the Agency of Restraint. Two figures emerged from the red-capped mid-rise and approached with confident bearing.

Harmony, blond hair, tangerine lipstick, and tangerine leggings with thigh-high purple-blue boots, matched pace, nausea in motion, along with her Demi lackey. Demi, wearing arcs of sun-kissed bejeweled needles, glided to the middle position. Not to be outdone, Sentinel wore a sleeveless white gown with gold-glitter lipstick and exposed skin dusted in gold. Harmony's envy at having been outplayed showed up in quick darting glances. Keeping Harmony off balance was a perfect start to their get-together. Mutual distrust among the Chorus went with the territory. But on most days their goals aligned. Sentinel wasn't sure that remained true.

The situation unraveled. The Starfall Militant headed into uncharted space. Interceptors scrambled to catch him. Charronna Ny' was lost and likely a hostage. *Blue Serenity* would be in space dock for years, undergoing repairs and upgrades. The Psians experienced a new future covered in doom. The recent turn of events had been unfavorable to securing the future, with every action now fraught with potentially dire consequences.

"Coming from another drag show performance?" Sentinel asked.

"I adore your attempts at funny," Harmony said.

"I'm not trying. You're late."

"Fashionably. Ask your questions."

Sentinel nodded. A compromise to a private interrogation with Demi. She wanted the interview sooner, but Harmony refused until Demi recovered from her *Blue Serenity* injuries. Compromise was as much a part of the Chorus dynamic as distrust. A black-clad man and woman lingered among Restraint's step fountains, thought police, rare and valuable, and despite appearances, with their undivided attention on her little gathering.

Sentinel opted to go for the jugular with a direct question to Demi. "Did you let Kor of Steel Rose escape?"

Demi trained her ocean-deep yellow-golden eyes on Sentinel. "Yes and no."

"Come now—you are capable of clarity."

"I told Kor to kill his father. Had he done so, the probability that concerns you would have ceased. He refused. A most stubborn Militant."

"Why didn't you simply kill him?"

"That was Agent Charronna's job."

"You knew she was coming?"

"I suspected. With Kor's escape imminent, I knocked myself unconscious in the hopes he would take me with him on the chance he eluded capture."

"Prognosis?"

"The fire has become wild."

Sentinel gazed at the reflecting pool. A false sense of peace lurked in the pristine water if she allowed herself the reprieve of self-deception. The thought police detected no lie. But truths and lies were camouflaged within many shades. "I want Demi reassigned to me."

Harmony flashed her teeth with no pretense of being friendly. "If you question my service or use Demi for activities I would find objectionable during the assignment period, this will get messy."

"I'm not going to play a guessing game."

Harmony waved a tangerine-painted fingernail. "Games are fun—but I'll download a list into your account. The reassignment begins now and expires in six months."

Sentinel decided to let the walk continue. Thought police continued to probe both Demi and Harmony, but they were not getting anything suspicious to report. That was itself questionable. Harmony came prepared.

Up ahead, someone had planted a tree in a hardwood planter. Sweet scents of white flowers—orange blossom emissaries—taunted her self-control. The tree was a virtual replica of the one that provided ambiance to the orange and fennel soup she made for her brother and his family—the dinner where she murdered them. She ate some soup to avoid suspicion, a reduced portion, of course, a meal she would never again enjoy. The orange blossom provocation warranted a ruthless response. Sentinel bent her mind to shutter any emotion, allowing no more than a brief body flutter to betray her feelings.

Harmony snapped her fingers.

"If you or Nexus ever again deploy the thought police against me, I promise more than an unpleasant trip down memory lane. You mess with me, and I mess with you."

"I run this world, Harmony."

"You're not a one-woman show. I will work with you, but not for you."

"Keep to this tack and our games will get unfriendly."

"Power down. Your brother had it coming. But his family? Not so much. But what's done is done. We cry and we move on, but you haven't. In the times ahead, your judgment must be clear. You need therapy. The orange tree is a start."

Sentinel took Harmony's hand the way a lover might; she resisted the urge to crush it in slow motion. "In your most inconvenient way, you are right."

"Candor liberates the soul."

"Trigger the final stage of your operation to pit the high clans against the priests."

"We voted against genocide. The plan to dismantle the Militant leadership matures. Civil war brews."

"Accelerate the timetable. I want the Militants to be so broken that they can't repel Organic swamp dancers. Expand your scope to include Psian seers. They reek of treachery."

Harmony squeezed Sentinel's hand. "I felt it too, in the communion. War against the subsets would be unforgiving."

"As would ours."

They continued their walk along the pool. Harmony was right about the therapy, and it would be a daily requirement until every inhalation of the white flowers' scent filled her with joy—a final victory over her double-crossing, back-stabbing, sorry excuse for a brother.

Sentinel breathed in rosemary aromas once outside of the orange tree bloom's range. The window spectators got to see their leaders together, by appearances united and self-assured, the protectors of civilization. With the Militant's escape, the perilous probability unfolded. The stars would fall, and not even the Psian-seers perceived past that.

***

Charronna lurched here and there in an unnerving something-bad-is-about-to-happen mist. Muted footfalls hinted that she trod in a dangerous place. The distant discharge of thoughts faded into muffled pops. Cold draped, the mist thickened, and the weight of balls and chains compressed her lungs. Dread, the clammy tickling that something awful approached, clung in a suffocating embrace. Blue fire lapped at her feet in rolling waves of desolate, unflinching intent. Anxiety inflated her stomach, a gassy cocktail of fungi, bacteria, and rot.

Charronna stumbled into a crying girl. She brushed back the girl's stringy red hair. A remarkable resemblance—the girl could be her daughter if the Chorus permitted their agents the miracle of motherhood.

"What's your name?" Charronna asked, her voice cracking in a fraction of grief.

"Go away," the girl said.

"I'm not going to hurt you."

"Stop what you're doing. Before it's too late."

Little Charro. The girl accused with glassy emerald eyes to freeze one's soul.

"Tell me, please, what am I doing wrong?" she asked.

"Wouldn't help."

The little girl diffused into the mist. The mist swirled, faster, buzzing, a blizzard of tiny sharp things pushing her into the Real. Shapes and patterns of light sharpened into stabbing points. The burst of brightness struck with the intensity of a sensory ambush. In her perseverance emerged an absurdity in temple-pounding living color; the lead-head and her pet Psian together, brothers in arms.

Greenish vapors curled to the ceiling. "Stasis hangover?" she said in a half-question.

"Correct," Noi said, massaging his forehead. "You're onboard the *Blue Serenity* drop ship *Blue Compulsion-1* rededicated as *Star Horizon.*"

A biting pang shot through Charronna's gray matter. *Two decks for crew and passengers, and recently outfitted with an ultra-drive.* Noi, dressed in an informal knee-length tunic, clasped his hands. Kor tried to murder her chewed-up soul with a magma glare—too late, and child's play compared to the Smiling Court. The lead-head's restless hand twitched on and off a blaster strapped to his thigh.

Twenty stasis beds jutted into three of the wall sections. Two were open next to hers, and from those two, not a whiff of green vapor was visible. Stasis meant a long trip to who knows where. Plus, the others got an early wake-up call. "Am I being kidnapped?"

"In a manner of speaking," Noi said.

"The Chorus won't pay a ransom."

The lead-head grinned carnivore-style. Well, the young pup would soon learn his lesson. Like any Smiling Court veteran, she excelled at blood sports. She touched up her hair and exerted ringing authority into her voice. "Does this ship have a hot shower?"

"Dry only," Noi said. "Court prerogatives are not relevant."

"When did you grow a spine to say such a thing?"

"You survive under the bane of a Militant blood oath."

"First, I collect those like merit badges, thank you very much. Second, I'm a P-94. Neither of you scare me one bit."

Noi's eyes fluttered. "You are a P-84, and I am a classically trained P-82.5. My special ability gives me a slight advantage."

Though Noi had never used his unique talent in combat, Charronna elected to let the matter remain unresolved. She'd told a fib. The Psian called her on it, which meant he no longer feared the Court's reach, ridiculous, given Chorus spies infiltrated everywhere—from the smallest chat rooms to Earth's ultra-secure post-physical Cyber Heaven headquartered on Earth's moon, Luna.

"We are not headed to the Sol System," Noi said.

Charronna tightened her psi-shield and covered her disappointment with an on-the-shelf sex fantasy. She rotated to the barbarian lead-head, serving up seductive promises and guarded disdain.

"Try me," he said.

She wet her lips. Anger poured off the Militant's taut muscles with simmering zeal and fervor evocative of pressurized steam about to explode. His hard body boiled with fire and passion. Gods, he was dessert beginning to end, a ready-to-serve juicy beefcake enticing enough to risk howling sex once he got rid of that thing in his mind. Someday, after the Chorus was done with him, he would be killed, but until then, why not play? Live life and savor the sweets.

"Name the time and place," she said, her voice whistling with her brand of steam heat. "I'm a sucker for seconds," she added licking her teeth. "Extra helpings are always a plus."

The Militant flipped a data crystal. "I've got some reading to do."

Kor gave a long stare to Noi and left in a controlled burn.

"You inflamed a difficult situation," Noi said to Charronna.

"Forget your pet barbarian for the moment. Explain yourself."

"We are far into the Deep Black."

"What?"

"We are—"

"I heard you the first time." The Deep Black, beyond the Red Line that divided charted from uncharted space, had been off the expanding list of possibilities. Despite their technological prowess, the Deep Black thwarted the obsessively curious Earthers. Probes and crewed expeditions vanished alike. Exploration continued at a cautious pace. The outward movement of the Red Line into the Milky Way slowed. Noi was as crazy as the lead-head. A straightforward mission had left her stranded in the literal definition of "the middle of nowhere" with subsets off their leash. There wasn't enough money in the Empire's treasury to cover the escalating hazard pay.

"We have been guided," Noi said.

"By what? Space fairies? How about you take us back, and I pull strings for a writ of extraordinary service by none other than Noi Zekra. As a reward, you get to go back to your family a modest star and live happily ever after."

"You commit to having the biologics removed from my wife and children?"

"I'll invite them over for a seven-course dinner after the removal procedure. No more death warrants for your family. What do you say?"

Her pet ghost didn't jump at the tempting inducement. Twisting her mind, she slunk into the Psian's head on a hunt for clues. *Noi splinters inside; he's done terrible things to reclaim his life, none more than confirming the execution of Neewa, a university student who got involved. His family will understand this idiotic quest into the DB. Yet part of him wants them to be angry, wants them to demand that he accept the offer. Unlike me, Psians cannot live within the comfort of lies.*

Noi faded into a pinprick presence as his vitality drained into some internal graveyard. She circled about Noi. An idea tempted to mind-blast him, take the command codes from his liquefied mind, and move on to the lead-head. A failed takeover attempt would make matters worse—dead, stranded, or back into stasis with no say in her survival. The timing must be flawless.

"I suppose I owe you my life," Charronna said.

"We decided to give you the captain's quarters. I will take an officer's room."

"Appreciated," she said, opting for a bit of gracious gratitude.

"Kor and I retrieved fresh clothes, your special treasure, and as many items from your cabin as we had time."

"My Prada shoes! For that thoughtfulness, you've earned a favor to be named later. Bringing them was silly."

"Neither of us are machines. Enjoy your pleasure."

Charronna's stasis-induced headache faded. Legs wobbled in a standing position, but good enough. A meal, a shower, and a meditation with her Pradas as the focal point would help her mood.

"One standard hour before we jump to our destination," Noi said.

Noi bowed but left without bothering to ask permission, a worrisome sign. *First things first, find the galley.* The ship's mini-AI provided directions. Most of the way through a moisture-sucking protein cake, a primal yell of a crazed beast blasted from somewhere on the ship.

Reality reoriented. The brownish cake crumbles went fuzzy. Nuclear infernos exploded through the continuum. Charronna staggered, stumbling into the primary food synthesizer on the back wall, and rolled to the bar, careful not to break any of the precious few bottles of non-synthesized wines and liquors. Overheating, she fumbled to loosen the top part of her outfit. By damn, she wanted a shower, a real one, with a rainwater showerhead that drenched cool water. The Militant burst in, shaking the data crystal. Wrath flooded his red-flushed face and darkened his Independence Man brand.

"You're not just any witch... You're the Red Witch."

"Tone it down, big guy," she said, wincing. "Guilty as charged. I've got a tattoo on my pretty right cheek to prove it. Want to see?"

"You're the faceless evil of my world. You're the one who ruined everything."

The continuum quaked from the probability current building into a wave ever since she savaged Strom's mind. Curse the Chorus to their foul, deceitful souls for sending her to confront the son of Strom.

Headache throbbed. Heart rate jumped in escape-speed rev. Male rage cracked space-time. The probability current gained amplitude, a cresting wave of consequences disrupting the moment and possibility of future happiness. For anyone.

CHAPTER XVI

In the void's endless sameness, memories sustained Jeth. Without them, he would fade into the prison's vibrating tides. Though he needed to stay focused on Kor, frozen needs drove him backward to the time and place where the sky ship *Gerd*, in protective stealth mode, meandered above an idyllic battlefield. On *Gerd's* uppermost observation deck, under a clear blue sky, the breeze light and cool, Jeth offered Sala a glass of fruity red wine. With a patronizing flick, she brushed him away, the abrupt swish of her pale lilac dress mocking his desire to please. He repressed a sigh.

Sala snatched a flute of bubbly pink wine from a hovering mech-waiter raising her glass in a mock toast to the unfolding chaos on the ground. Jeth pretended to have fun, snagged the same drink, and observed a battle taking shape while sipping the bubbly. Reptilian Janzorians in full battle armor massed along a tranquil mirror lake, preparing to strike against an alliance of forest-dwelling ape-like Taag hiding out in the canopy with slingshots and darts and Cheemin lionesses on the ground with bows and blades. To enhance the stakes, he bet a thousand credits on the Taag-Cheemin forces at three-to-one odds. The betting display tilted further toward the fearsome raptors until chirping Harps collected into noisy clouds over the loch's polished, brooding surface.

"You seem unhappy, my pretty sunbeam."

"We create intelligent life, pit them against one another, pretend our superiority, and yet we prove our cruel hearts as we heap misery upon them to the clink of our wine glasses."

"Sky ships are popular," Jeth said. "We don't have to watch the game."

"You gave this no thought. Sky Ships are popular. Here we are."

"Would you rather we went sun-skimming?" he asked. He concentrated, remembering the most beautiful Sala from his lost life who resided in his mind as indigo water, rose skies, and yellow sunbeams, who brought buoyant color to the pitiless void. The fantasy version of Sala existed in insubstantial make-believe, but Jeth needed make-believe to survive the void.

"Being here with you is enough for me," Sala said.

She pulled him off the viewing deck in a rush to their cabin. Before she spoiled the moment, he threw her on the bed. Sala's porcelain cheeks flushed. Heady scents from distant memories fueled his push against the bane of Zaxa, which shriveled the onslaught of his passion. He ripped Sala's sheer top, grabbing for more. Sala's image peeled away, and the Sala of the void emerged through with blazing contempt. Perspective reoriented into harsh reality. The spectacular Sky Ship, the stunning planet, the spacious cabin, everything was gone. No one wanted him to be happy. In cloud form, he surrounded Sala, swirling with thundering black frustration.

"If you expect me to help, stop this debasement," Sala said. "I am not your toy."

"Never interfere in my moments."

"It's bad enough when you recreate the past, but at least be honest. You never got my top off, much less my bra. When we disembarked, we weren't on speaking terms; I used public transport to get home, and I ignored your incessant calls for three days."

"Honesty won't be necessary when I'm a god."

"Fantasy won't make you any happier than reality," Sala said.

"Fantasy keeps me alive."

"You still love her."

"Love," Jeth said in a wispy far-off tone, "is supposed to be forever."

"Dear misguided Jeth, your long-lost Sala misjudged the hopelessness of your love. If she had experienced you as I have, she might forgive—she might even love in return."

"Not for you to say, my imaginary Sala."

"I know her better than anyone."

Jeth cold-flashed into grief. He had turned the true Sala into a monster when he transferred her awareness from her dying body into the empty hive mind of a White Mother—a rash decision. She never forgave that violation, and as her consciousness rotted with bitterness, she became Zaxa. He had wanted them to be together. Instead, he lost both his love and their eternity. Forever.

***

Kor boiled—his mind lava—his blood wildfire—to be cooled by nothing save the witch's death.

The Empire agent retreated into a wall. He grabbed the witch, pinning her in a rough squeeze. She shimmered in watery vision. He drank in her desperation. She struggled and might have done damage. He didn't pause to assess. The God-Supreme had revealed his mission: erase the inhuman creature who had tortured his world and mind-raped his family. Psychic blasts crashed against his determination. The witch's cold-blooded mind-shoves kept coming, but this time, he was the indomitable war-star, and she was the pesky frigate.

Untamed fires raged in the dark. Restless arms wanted to hold, to kill, to explore forbidden territories, to prove his manhood to his father, to himself, to her, to the almighty Supreme. The writing carved into his fractured heart called upon him to be the divine slayer.

"You are a destroyer of lives. You are a monster."

"You're right. Thanks to the Chorus, I'm more dead than alive. Go ahead and finish the job. Maybe I'll be happier."

A tear glistened in Charronna's eye, a sword to Kor's heart to cleave out the hard knots where he resisted seeing her as anything but a monster. Frightened distance in child-like emerald eyes stretched his heart into the boundaries of unearned forgiveness. He staggered back a step. The witch's hurt, her churning repressed pain, loss, frustration, vulnerability, and helplessness bled into stark view. The universe delivered the lowest blow by revealing the human within. Anger dissolved into uncertainty. Another presence burst into the room.

"A good soldier protects," Noi said.

A good soldier destroys evil.

"Priority alert," the ship's AI intoned. "Long-range sensors detect a distress signal in a proximity system."

Body quakes pulled him apart. *Retreat, advance, sing a distracting song, do something.* Heat seared his neurons, his molecules, his DNA. *Blood for blood.* There must be one truth to believe. No real man of Zorn would hesitate to kill the wicked Red Witch. *You do not want to live the wrong life. The worst possible sin. . .*

The witch dropped to her knees, head down. Was she crying? Why did he care? The Red Witch should be slack-faced dead. But he did care, somehow, someway, his boiling grievance at the suffering she inflicted softened by the power of a few tears.

"AI, what kind of signal?" Kor asked.

"Earth Confederation, nonmilitary, no identification," the AI said.

Prospectors, explorers, criminals, or someone surprising? Quite the coincidence that he came across a human signal in the vast DB. Unable to stand the presence of either telepath, he headed to the ship's compact gym for a badly needed workout.

"Execute intercept course," he said on the way out.

After an hour of pushing weight, another of stillness, and another of counted breathing, interspersed with conversations with the Cosmos, Kor declared himself safe to see the telepaths. Eventually, they joined him on the bridge to view the non-rotating world. Desert storms surged into the night and blizzards conquered into the day, melting into titanic line squalls, a hopeless fight for turf, thrashing the twilight zone, keeping it in upheaval. Much like his mind. Feelings congealed into a hard ball.

The transmission came from an Earth Confederation beacon. A second SOS originated from a colossal cluster of ruins on a five-hundred-plus-square-mile mega-island surrounded by a gray sea. A network of artificial satellites bore unfamiliar markings. Nervous twitters danced along his spine. The DB yielded few worlds and none living. No ships, no artifacts, no cities, no signs of civilization, no evidence of human exploration, and yet the holographic displays showed satellites, a city, and a Confederation distress signal in one suspicious swoop.

"We'll check out the SOS," Kor said.

Charronna gave a shake of the head, rife with disbelief. "Stolen drop ship, kidnapped agent, flight plan into the Deep Black, and you want to add a rescue? You have no idea what's down there, and we are far from home, unprepared and without support."

"Whoever is down there has the same problems," Kor said. "It's up to us to help. Do you agree?" he asked, glancing Noi's way.

The Psian's eyes took on the sheen of wet oil. "Our path goes to the world."

"Fantastic," the witch said, in a sarcastic tone. "We have prep to do. I'll organize the field trip supplies for our idiotic adventure." She grabbed a cup of chai and headed off the bridge.

Noi followed her out, while Kor identified a landing zone within walking distance of the SOS but not adjacent to an unknown and possibly hostile location. A wide boulevard would serve as a runway.

"Away team, please assemble on the hangar deck," the AI continued to broadcast in soothing, modulated tones.

Kor avoided eye contact. Conversation compacted into one-word clips. Coexistence sometimes required social distance, and on that score, everyone read the same handbook. The trip to the planet went off without a hitch. Operation Rescue started with a smooth landing in the planet's singular city.

Star Horizon's one-person transports, more like pressurized coffins, touched down on a boulevard impressive enough to host a victory parade. Advanced graphite composite polymers overlaid the streets, pricier than gold. Atmospheric readings showed green, confirming initial scans. Kor opened the transport and planted four shield rods in short order.

"Activating shield," he said. Blue shimmer surrounded the camp.

Ripe and earthy in a fetid sort of way, the atmosphere would be sweet to Kor's nose even if it stank of drunk-induced vomit. The first walk on a non-human world. The Red Witch kept her distance.

Skeleton tower frames stood next to spires from pristine to various states of decay. Pale-pink vines with large, hinged leaves and bright ruby pods draped most of the buildings. Nature invaded in inexorable advance. Lamppost towers soared in artistic curves, hundreds of them placed with strategic precision to bathe the area in light. Clusters of tossed tables, chairs, and benches littered the walkways—evidence of lost happiness from vanished inhabitants. Nothing exotic, nothing extraordinary, and if the rumors were half-true, the Empire's Organics created nests in ancient forests more alien than the abandoned metropolis.

The city was alive in death, much like the General.

Hordes of palm-sized, furry creatures scampered in speedy blurs for quick bites of the leafy vines. They avoided a thick cluster of pods. "Anyone for fruit never tasted by us humans?"

"As long as you go first," Charronna said.

"We must be careful," Noi said.

"Pfff. Careful is for baby fat wimps." Kor retrieved an analyzer. The ruby bean-shaped natives practically begged to be picked. He lowered the shield and closed in on the prize. The brown furries scattered into the vines. The pods split, serving up a mad flurry of snaky appendages that feasted on a slew of unlucky creatures.

Stunned, he made a fast retreat.

Noi gave an I-told-you-so expression with a haughty shade.

"We learned something," Kor said. "I'm leaving you to guard our transports."

Oil-black eyes glazed in a classic ghost stare. "I will be needed," the Psian spoke in the not-quite-human barren inflection, famous among his people.

"I promise to leave the redheaded manslayer alone during our away mission."

"This is a death world," the witch said.

"Perfect," he said, jaw clamped, "You should be right at home."

Truth be told, he didn't know the protocols with a woman, and the agent was not entry-level material. The whirling anger, the blindsiding surges of unnatural desire, the protective instincts, how did anyone manage? Most of his people had never interacted with the natural-born, male or female, outside the chain of command in the Brigades. The situation was impossible, and he had no instruction manual at the ready.

"Life advances in our direction," Noi said.

"Be more specific," Kor said.

"Local fauna heads our way," the witch said. "Do you require the name, rank, and serial number?"

"Are we talking killer bees, arvorgs, or a T-Rex?"

Noi's complexion paled.

Kor split his attention.

The agent clutched her head. "Kill. Water. Blood. Hunger," the Red Witch howled.

"Pull back," he barked.

Charronna stumbled, wobbling for balance. He wrestled with his charged mind, clasping the witch in a firm grip. Kor accessed his higher-level functions and changed the perimeter shield to a mirror setting. A ground-shaking horde of upright lizards stampeded into view. Like crazed shock troops, the man-sized lizards leaped against the shield with jagged teeth bared. Clouds of small-winged creatures dipped in multi-hued incandescent colors swarmed. Some lizards retreated. Others stomped on the winged vipers, smashing dozens at a time. Incandescent wings billowed, mesmerizing, a celebratory feast. The colorful clouds felled lizard after lizard. The winged vipers devoured flesh and sinews, but they ascended into the sky with mounds of gore left behind.

Killer bees *and* T-Rexes—this planet didn't mess around.

"You win, spook," Kor said. "Let's move before scavengers make their introductions."

They jogged toward the target half a mile away. Kor wielded a pair of heavy disruptors with higher-function scans on full alert. Except for the big guns, they traveled light with water canteens, food bars, a scanner, and a med kit equipped with a diagnostic tool and an array of anti-poison and healing serums. They maintained a steady pace until they came upon a forest busting through the avenue in dense clusters of gray-purple columns. Cloying aromas lingered from purple flowers, crowns for bulging stalks. Nettlesome arms held him back. Kor pushed them off and raised his gun, ready to shoot the annoyance. In the reflection of the telepaths' eyes, a dangerous animal peered back. Shaking, he lowered the gun.

"The floral scent affects your mind," Noi said.

"I have bio-defenses."

"Nobody's indestructible," the witch said. "You're up, Noi. Use your unique talent to keep our lungs clear of the plants' perfume, though it seems we telepaths are somewhat immune."

"I've sworn not to."

"You used it on the war-star with the smoke."

Kor shifted his weight, putting on his best clue-me-in-or-else face.

"I'm a Micro," Noi said. "I'm able to influence air flows at the molecular level. The manipulation requires immense concentration and effort."

"You used your talent to knock me out on the war-star," Kor said.

"I bent my rule."

"Bend it again."

Noi took Charronna's hand. The wind stiffened, whistling through the vines draping the buildings on either side of the street. The breeze heated into mouthfuls of extra-thick decay. A day-side front pushed into the city.

"The conditions are difficult," Noi said.

"Conditions almost always are. Do your best."

Keeping in a tight formation, the witch broadcasted calming delta waves. Noi repulsed the plants' biochemical compounds. The purple-gray stalks sweated a wet sheen. Dark shadows pervaded and deepened under the heavy canopy—the eerie twilight of a dead city. Kor switched to infrared vision. One step forward, then another, he slipped on the buckled road—his arm brushed one of the stalks. A stalk opened at its base. Rope-like muscular tissue uncoiled, thick enough to choke a yirg.

Dusky light filtered through a thinning canopy. Kor relaxed into ponderous heartbeat rhythms. A snake-like tongue rose to eye level. Drops of sweat rolled off his chin—his breath light and shallow. Heady sweet air seduced with promises of peaceful slumber. Legs tingled. Needle sensations poked in his gut. Eyes fluttered, the ground too close, the light too dark. He surrendered to emptiness and fell forward into an eternal embrace.

Flesh and force hooked around his forearms. The forest's padded surface shifted to hard. The next thing he knew, the telepaths steered him clear of the grove. The witch gave him a "you-owe-me" smirk before turning her imperial attention elsewhere. Layers of dead vines and other plant matter covered a plaza. Arms opened, she embraced to claim the entire scene—no stretch for the polished stone queen.

"Not even close to what I expected," Charronna said.

A flickering aqua force field protected a man and a girl huddled around a giant flower with a supersized stalk. They pressed their mouths against the flower's trunk-sized stalk and sucked for dear life. The bedraggled and starved young girl spotted Kor and his companions and sobbed without shame. On the other side of the trapped humans, towering flowers weaved in a hypnotic rhythm. On the top of swaying stamens, eyes glowed, a floating sea of them focused on him and his comrades with flickers of awareness—tough planet.

"Their shield collapses," the witch said.

"Do your calming psi-trick with the scary-looking flowers," Kor said.

"Say 'pretty, please,' and I'll consider the request."

"Pretty, please, with spun sugar on top."

Charronna winked at Noi. Hands out as would-be priests offering supplication, the telepaths performed their tranquilizing magic. The nearest watchers went to half-mast or shut down.

"The local flora resist," the witch said. "Better hurry."

"My specialty." He rubbed his charm and marched toward the badass flowers. Dead vines crunched underfoot. Above the horizon and below the clouds, the star hung at the same point in the sky, pouring out twilight with relentless consistency. The warm wind blew harder—the planet's fire breath stoked. The planet readied for a fight. *Bring it on.*

He wielded his guns with the ease of an extra appendage. He would be a pathogen, who his father wanted him to be, what the natural-born created him to be. Militants protected. Militants killed. He advanced up the byway. The aqua energy field surged bright and dim. Flowers opened at the apex, then closed, then unfolded again, resisting the telepaths' calming broadcasts. The urge to fight swamped his mind. Rapid-fire blasts, a warrior's ballet, decapitated a slew of the huge flower heads. One of them burst into flames, shooting off flying embers.

"No more," urged Noi.

"You're waking them," protested the witch.

Giant sunflowers of yellow, tangerine, and wine packed with thorns unleashed flurries upon the aqua shield. Gaping holes appeared. The dayside weather front seized the sky. Red lightning crackled from darkening sepia clouds in a fierce display of bad portents. Thorn darts streaked through the flames of burning flowers, catching fire. Conflagration rained, a plague from the Supreme, igniting layers of dead vines on the ground. Combustion exploded in a racing wave, forcing a sprinted retreat. The witch stopped, going rigid, engulfed by swirling pillars of incandescent orange. Insatiable conflagration swept closer in knee-buckling heat. Fire tornadoes lifted off the ground, corkscrewing against the wind toward the flower heads. More plant matter fed the whirling torrents. Fire demon after fire demon slammed into the dart-shooting plants.

Kor lowered the gun like an automaton, like the Khonsu he feared himself to be. Headless flowers burned. Scattered rain plopped from the sky. Thunder clouds dropped lower. Lightning ripped. Heat throbbed upon his face. Straight ahead, a forlorn figure stood in the ash fall, the witch, the Starry Empire agent, and in a place where his heart strived to forgive, a person with a name—Charronna.

Relief, anger, confusion, and happiness collided at seeing the wicked witch alive, adorned with a coat of ash, beautiful and spellbinding. Kor wasn't trained to deal with such warring emotions. When unsure, return to the basics. "We need to set the camp and finish our rescue mission," he said, pulling her along.

"You're a Macro," Noi said to Charronna from behind.

"News to me," Charronna said. "Psychokinetics don't materialize at my age. Without trying, I saw the burning vines in my mind as tendrils of energy moving to my command. The experience was mystical as though I transcended into the universe's true reality."

"Perhaps the stress," Noi's voice belied his puzzlement.

At the faltering aqua energy field, Kor tensed. The child was no threat. The Iron Hand branded the man's pale-olive bicep, and he had the steel collar of a Polarian slave. The Polarian disabled the shield. Kor shifted his weight, on guard for the unexpected.

"By the Blessed Emperor, I expected to die in this place," the rescued man cried out with gratitude. "The emperor will honor a debt to you. I am Raven. The girl is my servant." The Polarian dipped his head, eyes cast down.

Kor said nothing at first, though enemies should be less rude. The Polarian's body was fit and healthy, while the girl's showed the outline of bone. The girl was Earth-stock, not a slave—the Earthers were human but not quite. Their DNA had combined with native hominid species, the renowned Eve; if the visual didn't unmask them, the musk certainly did.

"Earthers would never allow a child to be your slave," Charronna said.

Raven raised his head in a bold challenge. "She came to me by right of rescue."

"You saved her life?" Kor asked.

"At great cost."

Charronna dribbled her canteen of water on the girl's face and used a cloth from the med kit to wipe it clean. "The right you mentioned isn't respected by the Earthers."

Kor knelt at eye level with the girl, and with gentle firmness opened himself to her inspection as he gazed deeply into her eyes.

Raven took a half-step toward them, his face hardened. Kor checked him with a set jaw to crack bone.

"According to the customs of my people, she belongs to me."

"Well, I saved both of you, so there you go." With his peripheral vision focused on the Polarian, Kor addressed the girl. "What's your name?"

"Meagan Alessandra Hayleigh Baxter the Second."

"Impressive."

"Yes," Raven said, "and the Blessed Emperor has every intention of returning the princess to her father."

"I'm my father's only daughter. I have to make a lot of people happy."

"Never an easy task," Kor said.

Raven's flush expression flattened, but he made no protest.

The girl's vacant eyes brightened. "You may call me Sparrow. I like mint tea, French vanilla ice cream, virtual replays of 1940s jazz, raising boxer puppies, and hunting for dragonflies. I'm a total math nerd, and my dad is the most powerful leader in the Confederation Colonies."

"Are you okay, Miss Sparrow?"

Sparrow examined her uniform, adjusting a tattered orange fabric sash. "I'm a beautiful girl, you know. Everyone says so."

He wiped some grunge from her face and said, "The prettiest one I've ever seen," which was quite true since he'd never seen a girl before.

"My dad says I'm prettier than a Disney doll."

"I promise to return you to him."

"Then you may attend to your duties."

Sparrow straightened, adding inches to her height. Kor gave a solemn salute and proceeded to establish a defensive perimeter. Black snow fell, mixed with embers. Gaunt chin on her bony knees, Sparrow's restive brown eyes beamed into Kor's. *You are my portal to safe havens. You will take me home.* He set up another rod and moved to the next position. The routine logistics protocol provided a buffer against undisciplined emotion. With the last rod in place, a protective cocoon shielded them from the planet's flora and fauna.

Kor threw the agent a wary glance. "We ride out the front before returning. Try to rest." He checked the ground, his mind drifting to a difficult place. "Thank you for saving us."

"Does this mean I'm no longer public enemy number one?" Charronna asked.

"Aye."

"Progress! How about an upgrade to 'respectable'?"

"You go too far."

"Congratulations, you win. I'm an awful woman. Be glad I have to live with that, and you don't. I want to go home."

"I've got a possessor to expel."

"Promise me we'll go home after that."

"Do you think you can manage to feed the rescues from our provisions?"

Charronna stuck out her tongue. "A round of tasteless paste coming their way."

Holding ration packs, she sauntered over to Raven. Noi attended to the girl. The sepia cloud wall surged forward, dividing into cumulus towers reaching for the stars—air demons coming to avenge the defeat of their fire brethren. Jagged red lightning knives cut to the surface—fingers of the Red Beast searching for prey. The wind huffed a final warning into a stiff cool breeze beaten back in a sweep of heat. The Polarian would not have ventured into such a volatile world without a compelling reason. Kor recalled one of *Star Horizon's* shuttles. Before evacuation, he would discover the reason, one way or another.

CHAPTER XVII

Kor's eyes flashed open.

Cool wind clamored against his tent, blowing an opening, forcing its way in, switching to heat, then back to frigid—a moody planet. Specs of dust and pollen floated. The world attacked in micro.

In counter-offensive, he scouted beyond the protective barrier for reconnaissance. The city oozed ancient, lost power. A mauve-granite stair wrapped around a spire clear of the vines, the bottom windows amazingly intact. Revolving doors, guardians to the tower's secrets, had been locked from the outside. Gun drawn, Kor hiked under a rusting gray arch spanning the entrance and pressed his face to a murky windowpane. Jumbled shapes covered the floor except for scattered bare spots. *Skeletons.* Cold shudders triggered memories, exposing images best left in chain-bolted boxes. Bony, humanoid appendages peeked from tattered clothing. Many skeletal hands held small bundles. *Mass murder.*

Dark clouds regrouped in the hop-colored sky. Another edifice beckoned, spectacular in its old age with a honeycomb façade that bled mold and algae, perhaps for itself and for the abandoned city that served in part as a necropolis. Scattered sections had functioning lights, an incredible achievement. Kor approached the entrance, grand with a translucent micro-honeycomb suspended in glass. A field of ambient yellow illuminated him. The door slid open.

Inside, an impressive lobby with marble-inlaid floors invited visitors. Strip lighting on the ceiling flipped on in welcome. A dramatic art piece erupted high in a spiraling erratic flurry of symbols invoking music. Bones covered recessed benches, chairs, and sleek tables. Adults and children, many holding hands, embraced each other. Adults clutched babies. Everyone died in seconds, judging by the density of the remains. Unused protective masks lay scattered among the bones, while others had kept theirs on and likely watched their comrades die. Wisps of acceptance, resignation, and terror lingered in the lobby, an open human graveyard.

Outside, unsettled, he gazed at the weird-colored sky wrestling with unclean tension that he disturbed the resting place of people exterminated like bothersome bugs.

Presence touched the edge of his mind. Noi probed, albeit with restraint. He pulled out his charm, gripped it hard to ward off the pain of lost love. Noi projected warm energy, liquid sunshine, the essence of pure acceptance. After a time, Kor allowed the warm energy to blossom.

"How do you live life always calm?"

"There are storms and other vagaries of daily weather, and I take pleasure in the diversity. Carry the love of Jude and not the grief of his absence, and you will take comfort whether it rains or shines."

"Storm drowns my heart." Kor focused on the posh tower graveyard. *"Our ancestors lived here. We should explore before we go."*

"I agree," Noi said. *"I am connected to this place. The legends say one hundred and twelve ships fleeing calamity made planetfall on Imperia. Of those Founders, at least some of them came from here."*

No longer feeling alone, Kor went on a hunt for a breakfast treat to satisfy stomach and soul. A short time later, he admired a full string of toothy critters with meaty backs who mistook him for an easy mark. He used up his quick-speed adrenals, but it was a fair exchange for real food. Tough planet.

A ship's alert double-flashed red on his armband.

"The satellite network initiates an arming sequence," the AI reported.

Kor rubbed hopeful faith into the charm. They tripped an auto-defense system—technological prowess confirmed. Dark clouds invaded the sky. No rescue party would be coming for them.

***

From Charronna's perspective, the expedition's outlook improved. Severe weather fell apart before thunderstorms broke. Eggs over easy, blue-orange yokes with yellow flesh instead of white, but no complaints, well-done steaks, and a tasty soup whose ingredients she was content to leave a mystery satisfied pallet and stomach—every sumptuous inhale a salve to her overtaxed neurons. Kor not only mastered the hunt, but thanks to his backpacking excursions back home, he was a damn fine field cook. After the cleanup, he spoke in her ear in electrified heated breath.

"Change of plans. The buildings are full of human remains. I bet the Polarian knew."

Charronna went placid.

"I need you to show our rescue a good time."

"I'm not your whore."

"I want his mission plan."

"Order your pet ghost to scan him."

"Noi is not my pet and he failed."

"Impossible."

"He believes if you distract him, he should be able to get a reading."

"You do it."

"We would butt heads and not in a good way."

"Even if I wanted to, I can't."

"Tell me."

She didn't answer; to answer meant to remember.

"Speak your fear."

"The last time I manhandled a real man, I fried his mind at the point of orgasm. Happy?"

"Did he offend you?"

"During sex, I sometimes lose control, and he had a dark mind. Since then, I've kept to lab spawn."

"You've chosen an empty life."

Charronna cringed at the undeniable truth. "Will you forgive me if I do this for you?"

Kor's warm breath heated hers. She grasped at his potent masculine scent—lust, primal urges, no other explanation suited her reaction. No agent of the Empire would fall in love, much less with a sub-human barbarian.

"I will respect you."

"You've got your diversion. The Polarian doesn't stand a chance."

Hips in a seductive swivel, Charronna sauntered over to the Polarian's tent. The proposition for sex was an easy sale—an exchange of pleasure for two people far from home violated none of Polarian's cultural mores. She stripped in tandem with Raven. She purred deep into his young, smooth, delicious chest. No complaints on her part—Raven rivaled top-grade lab spawn. She agreed to straight-up vanilla sex-- no frills, no kissing, no sucking, and no variants. *Let's not get personal.*

The hunky Polarian knelt, his eager tongue gliding, spiraling to her breasts before clamping onto its sensitive prize. Charronna put a leg over his shoulder and pressed it against his torso. Freedom was an illusion. Sex was real. Pretense dropped away with each discarded piece of clothing; desire, pure and rich, melted the hard places inside like glaciers in warm water. The beating of her heart heralded the resumption of life.

Raven's wild cognitive emissions streamed into the universe. She envied at times the common folk, those gifted with less demanding talents. Telepathy, a talent and a curse, exposed the illusions wrapped around the idea of love, ripped away the self-delusions and laid bare the grasping human heart. The common folk had their illusions, and she had her moments of animal desire.

They tumbled onto an air mattress, rolling, heavy-breathing delight, feeding thunderous waves of passion before the impending release. She resisted, wanting more, to punch through the clouds and show the stars how to burn, stretching, arching her back in escalating heat to dissolve memories of dark lovers trapped in warped neurons.

"Why are you here?" she asked, pulling Raven close. There, she had done as Kor asked. Raven maintained his rhythm. She gasped, riding a sensual nova. Still, Raven didn't release. He worked her, triggering more starbursts until at last, he erupted with his own force of nature.

Charronna's telepathic defenses collapsed. A foreign voice flashed into existence, a spirit from a well of condemned souls, lifeless yet living, insane and sane, a seething electrical mass that splintered attention into slivers.

"Who are you?" the voice commanded. "Whose songs do you sing?"

The grotesque electrical mass enclosed her identity. Too large, it was at odds with itself, desperate and hungry. It wanted to destroy resistance.

Darkness. Pain. Isolation. Self-preservation. Tough-mindedness. Denial. Am I these things? "I don't know," she cried. Panic in her rising voice fueled yet more.

"What is your true name? Bitterness? Loneliness? Vengeance?"

"Those are your names," Charronna said with a defiant ring.

"Yes, I see, you are Victim."

Acting by instinct, she gathered spilling life energy and blasted its sum from the root of her being. The voice quieted, suspended in the moment of realization, and she wrenched free of the electrical mass.

"I am a unique song," she screamed.

Thrown back into the Real, she pushed Raven off. He grabbed hold with an outreached arm, but she had fended off enough overeager men to slip away without having to think. In a daze, she snatched her clothes and fled to her tent, put her head between her knees, cried without shame, and shivered at the cold from her own wet offering.

The dark voice called her true name. When she screamed back her defiance, she discovered another one that she wanted to explore, one not content in the empty servitude as the Red Witch where she would never find peace. Victim was a name that no longer suited, no longer commanded, no longer churned in an angry fearful tempest. It remained to be seen who she would become.

CHAPTER XVIII

Jeth guided Sala into an unhurried spin, lifting a swirl of iridescent plumes from a feathered floor. The Kimbrian instigator divulged that Kor had arrived at a world under observation within one jump's distance. The plumes floated in a celebration of textured red-spectrum colors, spreading a delicious lingering fruity scent that uplifted Jeth's mood.

"Careful with your self-congratulation," Sala said. "The Kimbrians work with plans stretching over millennia. Compared to them, you are an amateur."

"They want to atone for what they did to the E'lani."

"Conjecture. The Kimbrians are not ones to fret over the wreckage of their actions."

Jeth spun Sala away. True, Kor continued to resist. But Jeth embedded deep into the young man's mind. Kor's defiance waned. Whatever the Kimbrians planned, it ended with Kor's arrival and Jeth's liberation. He would be as ruthless, as savage, as cruel as Zaxa ever was, and he would exceed her in terror.

"I will do what must be done," Jeth said.

"My juicy sweet, if this works, I have a surprise that will change your life."

In the void, surprises should be impossible. Nonetheless, Jeth vibrated with anticipation.

***

Kor hovered at his tent's flap. Yards away, in a take-a-fly-out-the-window tortured proximity, Raven and Charronna engaged in heated, aroused interplay. Confused, he was unsure about his feelings toward Charronna, an enemy of his people. Guilt and worry drove self-reflection into a quest for understanding of who he was and who he wanted to be, finding confidence in the necessity of his request.

The Starry Empire agent was not to be messed with, but Kor cocked his enhanced hearing, crossing into the voyeuristic, as he listened for signs of violence. Thirty minutes of grunts and groans gave way to an alarming scream. Kor tensed up, ready for action, when Charronna burst into view, dashing to her tent half-dressed. Ripples of guilt swamped cold logic. By the Red Beast, by what sorcery did the pitiless killer of Militant men induce compassion?

He grabbed the Psian and headed into the city at a fast walk. A white noise blend of clicks, buzzing, hoots, warbles, howls, roars, and clacks never ceased behind a cover of miniature jungles wedged between structures in various stages of ruin. For once, he didn't mind Noi's telepathic update. Thanks to Charronna's distraction, they had a destination. He wanted, he *needed* to accomplish something. The armed satellites allowed the shuttle to land but zapped one of the landing pods sent up on a test run, rendering them effectively planet-bound.

They climbed a striking hill shaded by hulking dark taupe bark trees with wide citrine canopies. No trees grew around the apex, allowing for a clear view of a small lake. A plaza dazzled on the other side. Rings intersecting at their highest and lowest points formed a graceful, ornate bridge. On alert, Kor monitored the water as they traversed the bridge—a sizable lifeform inhabited the depths but in a quiescent state. At the plaza's far end, a stair led to a temple with black and white columns decorated with multi-layered plinths. Defaced mosaics between the plinths hinted at the city's former masters. Half-missing faces, arms, and legs had been scratched and blotted and other parts shattered in obvious desecration. A star went nova in a faded vibrant background as it channeled its explosive energies into a sketchy fragment of a hand.

"The people of this world had a flare for the dramatic," Kor said.

"I have something to tell you about Raven," Noi said, with a slight frown.

"Not to be trusted?"

"Besides that. Raven is possessed."

"You're kidding. Like me?"

"Not like you. Another consciousness inhabits his mind."

The shock of Noi's revelation dispersed as they stood below the mural, in stunned, awed, no-words-worthy attention. He called the others over from base camp. The Starry Empire agent came with Sparrow in toe, lost in wonder. Raven beamed rapt hot interest on Kor.

Kor tilted his head at the mural. "I present exhibit one."

"Not the clearest rendition," Charronna said, "but no doubt, one of us."

She stepped up for a closer inspection. From Kor's perspective, the witch's armor thinned—vulnerability seeped through. He stared too long. Whatever happened between her and

Raven must have been intense. She was more than a witch. Blood for blood. . . No Militant would forgive her. Blood oaths were not supposed to work like this.

"Do you think we've found our birth world?" Charronna asked.

"Without our tech," Kor said, "we'd need poison sacs and fangs to survive this planet."

"This is a colony," Noi said. "Some evacuated. Those left behind were killed. I'm sensing echoes, cries from a distant past event seeking salvation and revenge."

Raven ran a hand across the mural with wistful cherishing. "You are children running amok in a stranger's house. Go, before you break something precious."

"Leave you with all the fun?" Kor said. "Not a chance."

Plaza stairs tiered up to a temple framed by colonnades, the target destination. Kor directed everyone through three ranks of columns. Inside, in an otherwise empty space, eight nondescript capsules alternated in colors of blue, gold, silver, and green atop a raised crimson square. The entire temple gleamed. He kept an eye on the perimeter.

"Stellar housekeeping," Charronna quipped. She winced and massaged her temples.

"A mechanical telepathic force scans us," Noi said.

Charronna jerked. Facing forward, the agent slammed her hand against a panel on the gold capsule. The door slipped open. Face slack, she stepped in.

"Get out of there," Kor said. "Charronna!"

The capsule whisked closed. With a snap of the fingers, she was gone.

Noi's eyes twinkled. "You used her name. I'm proud of you."

"Slipup. She did save my life. I'm going after her to settle the score."

He handed the disruptor over to Noi, who looked about as comfortable as a Militant in the company of women. "Evacuate to base camp at the first sign of trouble."

"The telepathic force protects Charronna. Be careful not to threaten her."

"Who, me?" Kor waved his hand over each of the capsule panels. The red one came through with a ride. With a whoosh, it plummeted in a smooth fall, opening to pitch black and a faint hum. Foliage-green aroma enticed him to venture forth.

Walls close enough for fingertip gliding kept him on course. The steady hum evolved into a drone. Hands slid into emptiness. The drone escalated to a triumphant buzz. A circle of light centered on a Gothic chair with straps and a cone-shaped hood. In the bright illumination, Charronna stood, a queen awaiting admittance to Paradise. He hurried to the agent's side. The chair's setup resembled a docking station with a trans-neural interface, but with a little imagination, the contraption morphed into something from a horror vid about to go live.

"It wants me to sit," Charronna said.

"Who is *it*?" asked Kor.

"The Oracle of Verity, a mechanical intelligence. Nothing I would cuddle up to, but it gave me a power boost to save us from those homicidal flowers."

"What happens if you take the offer?"

"No idea."

"Your decision," Kor said, a bit jealous.

Charronna stroked the chair's arm. She sat, taking a deep breath. Kor buckled her up to a snug fit.

"Say something sweet to me."

"I bet you've never tried that line before."

"I'm serious. Contrary to popular rumor, I do have feelings."

"Shouldn't we have coffee first?"

"You don't like me. I get it. No one does. Pretend that you find me desirable."

"What good—"

"I've learned to be satisfied with pretend." Charronna's eyes pleaded for cooperation.

He shook his head, unsure what to make of the vulnerable stone queen. He leaned in with a puff of warm breath. "Ask properly."

Charronna's lower lip quivered. "Pretty, please, with sugar on top."

"You have lovely eyes." Compelling best described her emerald beauties—they drew in the energy of anyone who dared to gaze upon her gemstone cages.

"Go on."

"You have an athletic body," he blushed.

"Spice it up for an adult audience."

"You have long, wicked legs," Kor swallowed a rock of air. "Your lips seduce me," he whispered, brushing them with his own. "Your breasts. Soft. Inviting. My hands. Your lips. My tongue. Your nipples."

Charronna moaned. "I'm getting the picture."

Kor secured Charronna's feet. Their tongues brushed. Breath shared. His hand, trembling, rested on her leg in unhinged imagination. Was this still pretend? He was officially crazy. He wiped the sweat off his brow.

Charronna sank into the contraption, mumbling a chant, "Water off my pretty sweet ass."

No argument. The more she relaxed, the more she radiated beauty kindred to the breeder Tara, to his sister Chi. Maybe he was too spent to see her for what she was. Together, they could create a mind-blowing dance to rattle the stars—her skin, soft and smooth, his muscles, hard and slick. One gliding over the other, fed by friction, by internal fires determined to burn until they were reduced to ash. He would wallow in the heat, and he would be the untamed beast. Except Militants kept to themselves. Sharing pleasure with a female wasn't in his playbook. And the woman was a monster.

"Kiss me," Charronna said, whistling steam. She licked her lips in nervous invitation. "Don't be shy. We both know you want to sugar my fruit before you deep fry it."

Tomorrow we die, let's kiss the sky. His mind broke into pieces and reshaped itself into fluid, out-of-body acceptance. A human needed to be comforted, and Kor hungered for a closer connection. In slow strokes, he snuggled Charronna's throat. Her scent penetrated the furthest nether regions of his lungs.

"Your scruff has my heart aflutter," she cooed.

"Woof, woof."

In and out, up and down, heated breath warmed his lips, and caressed his darting tongue. His blood ignited—whipped his passion into rapid expansion. He growled into her bones. Body over mind. Primal devotion to the Supreme.

Charronna purred. "I'm ready."

"Killjoy," he purred. He lowered the cone over her head until the contraption took over, leaving Charronna's mouth and chin exposed. Hands-on the cone, he prayed for a safe outcome.

"I feel heat," Charronna said.

"Relax," Kor said.

"It's starting to hurt."

"Do you want to stop?"

Charronna twitched with an electrical charge. A net of energy spread over the planet, taking his mind along with it. An outpouring of information ensued. Data flashed into his memory core at unimaginable speed, appearing as light smears to his inner sight. He pictured the data slowing. Whether by his effort or by the machine's choice or Charronna's, the data separated into distinct sections.

"*What is this*?" The question popped into his mind.

The visual representation of the data flow brightened, and an expansive voice answered. "I am the Oracle of Verity, a repository of knowledge. All humans within range are welcome to receive."

"State your purpose."

"Preservation of human heritage for any who survived the Mass Exodus."

Words from an old myth, a children's fable, which recounted how refugees fleeing a terrible calamity founded the Starry Empire's first world, Imperia. Dark fairy tales of worlds burned. Cataclysmic death turned into history. Yet there must be much more—lost legacies, like the Earthers, a union of forgotten refugees and native hominids who combined into a new form of human. Sheer glee ramped up his mind at what he might discover.

"What caused the exodus?"

"The Emperor of the Humans sought elevation to godhood. The Commonweal, an alliance of many species, opposed him. The Long War ensued."

"How was godhood possible?"

"The emperor possessed an ancient artifact from Avad, the place of Origin, created to uplift human consciousness to godhood."

Avad, old gods. . . Would Jeth's name mean anything to the Oracle? Pain seared through his brain like popping oil. *Oracle, what can you tell me about Jeth-ka?* Before an answer formed, his connection was severed in the scorch of an oil-fueled inferno.

Spotty vision cleared. He had no idea how to reconnect. He stroked Charronna's tangled hair, wondering what the others asked. Answers were left unsaid, more questions swirled, and one important conclusion blistered. *This I vow, Jeth-ka, your secrets will not last. We are officially enemies.*

***

The Oracle's visions ended. Charronna floated on a cloud, immersed in a thousand dreams of happiness, sorrows, and marvels. The heat of suns had warmed her face, from hot blue-white to cool red, and the histories of unknown worlds, art, operas, music, wars, sports, and calamities embedded into her mind in a lightning storm of neuron flashes. She floated before nebula clouds, tiptoed over mirror lakes dotted with partially submerged leafless trees the color of fire, and worshipped among crowds in white and black robes who chanted with arms raised to soaring, vaulted stained-glass ceilings. The experience left her drained yet filled.

I went to E'lan, our destination, a place of legend. The Oracle also spoke of Avad, a place of myth, of gods, our original home, touching energies potent enough to send me to my knees.

After the vision quest, the satellites returned to their inactive status, allowing for evacuation. Kor retrieved the shuttle and carried her to it with unexpected gentleness. Indistinct chatter kept her company on the trip back to the ship. When the shuttle parked in *Star Horizon's* bay next to its twin backup, Charronna dared to hope. One obstacle down, three adult (sort of) males to go.

After a long shower and a change of clothes, she joined the others in the briefing room, taking a seat at the elliptical command and control table. Praise the gods, the beverage bar's synthesizer replicated coffee. She ordered up a pot, drew in the aromas of a heavenly Ethiopian medium roast, and for a moment, believed she was back home getting ready to rule the day.

The virtual control panel built into the table at each chair included a hologram touch interface and a sleek vector design favored by the tech-savvy Earthers. The outer wall windows were oriented at Eos. Storms whipped in various theaters, fitting, given the upheaval the world's revelations would create. Noi maintained his irritating meditative stillness, but underneath, he fretted and worried. If someone died, Charronna wouldn't be surprised. The coffee's dark nectar energized and clarified. It was every man, woman, and child for herself.

She slid a steaming cup of coffee in front of Kor. Despite a disapproving shake of his head, the hot brew remained. *Be extra nice, little Charro. You never know what might tip the balance your way. The oh so manly pup is flustered by what happened at the Oracle, embarrassed, no, something else, insecure, unsure of who he is. Does he like me or like me not?*

"Go ahead, take a sip," Charronna said. "You look like you could use a pick-me-up. You reek of stim."

"Guilty as charged. We need to decide our next move."

"E'lan works for me," Raven said.

Charronna assessed. Whatever inhabited the Polarian's mind deflected every telepathic probe, though she didn't want to go up against the hideous presence with too much vigor. If Kor had any wits, he would airdrop Raven back to the planet.

"What about calling it a day and going home?" asked Charronna. "With what we've discovered, the Chorus might be magnanimous, declare you a hero, and make a few concessions without loss of face. Everybody wins, a rare opportunity."

Kor sipped the coffee. Beautiful, sea-born eyes stoked the fire; the touch of his tongue lingered, sharpened, a reminder of unfulfilled lust. Desert winds had sculpted his airbrushed body. He could give her cavities anytime. Gods, she reverted into a teenager.

"One more jump to finish our work with Kor's possessor entity," Noi said. "Then we go home."

"Is that an official promise?"

"I offer no other kind."

Kor took a long gulp and placed the mug on the table with the uncompromising glare of a fanatic committed to absolute belief. Ghostly feet tiptoed on her heart, leaving behind a dreadful chill. The man-pup rubbed his rock charm, flipped it, and pocketed the silly thing in one fell swoop. The continuum, the essence of true reality, quaked. *He's decided.* Objections gathered to stop the future in its tracks.

"We go dance on the clouds," Kor said. "We go the Commonweal. Thanks to the Oracle, we have a hyperspace map to take us there. We make first contact. We return home with the promise of peace with a civilization that tried to exterminate us. Success would be a feat of legends to save Steel Rose. Success might inspire enough people to overturn the system, enough to free all the subsets."

The continuum churned with consequences. Squalls of energy, magnificent and terrifying, formed over the event horizon. Noi's mind shield leaked troubled doubt. The psychic realm erupted with geysers, unbalanced by too many possibilities. Futures emerged, dozens, hundreds, thousands, filled with uncertainty, loss, death, terror, and hope.

"You must deal with Jeth," Noi said.

"He's on the way back."

Charronna swept Raven with a surface scan. The Polarian had a connection with Jeth. Improbable, yet Raven's hideous presence shared an energetic fingerprint with Kor's possessor akin to a relative's DNA. What was she missing? The Polarian spiraled into full-blown panic.

"The Indeterminator warned me," Charronna said, "the path forward takes us into peril."

"A lot of people are counting on us," Kor said. "Nothing less than Hero of the People will do. We go to the Commonweal."

*****

The old god's whispers in Kor's mind escalated into fractious shouts. Jeth seemed to be everywhere. The briefing room blurred. Otherworldly auras spread from a male shaped of blue flame. The aura reached out with flares to hurt, to punish, to blind Kor to his true self. He dug his hands into the table, fighting for pain, for something to break the connection. *Some tests are not meant to be won.* One way or another, the old god would have his say.

"Go to the Commonweal," the figure said, *"and you go to Zaxa, an embittered enemy to human life. If she discovers you, you become the Destroyer."*

"I'll go and do battle with Zaxa," Kor countered, *"and if she is the formidable evil you claim, what better way to become a hero? After a feat like that, I wager Marshal Torz will pass a kiss."*

"Death and defeat await you in the Commonweal."

The memory of earlier encounters with the old god stirred together into a pureed soup of divine and wicked voices. He longed for Jude, his friend, his soon-to-be-lover, the first to die on the other side of the world. Jude always knew the right thing to say or to do, or he would say nothing as he brought his warm lips to Kor's, sharing his breath, his heat, melting his tapered body into a holy union.

"I'm here," Jude said. *"It's never too late."*

The aura reshaped itself, and Jude stepped into Kor's dreaming. Wild wolf energy electrified his eyes. Kor blinked several times as a blue haze descended, deepening with their comingled breath.

"Open yourself. Give me your pain. Give me your loneliness. I am forever here for you."

He shed his clothes, and Jude did the same. The blue haze darkened. Their bodies merged, lock and key, eye-to-eye, nose-to-nose, lips-to-lips. Kor's desire, Kor's knowing, Kor's name burned into his lover's twin sacred mirrors until the floodgates of consecrated space opened, and he moaned all that he was.

"At last," Jeth-ka said, *"you are mine."*

CHAPTER XIX

Jeth-Kor cast his new eyes to the briefing room's elliptical table. To feel, to see, charged his being with unadulterated exhilaration. Alone, he would have shrieked in unbridled ecstasy. How easy a task to seize Kor's mind once he understood the proper way.

The female, a potent presence, gestured in an annoyed motion. "Must I be the sensible one? It's not our place to make contact with homicidal aliens. We have limited weapons, no backup, and no idea how we'll be greeted. Let's send in the professionals and go home."

"You're right, the Commonweal would be a mistake," Jeth-Kor said, in savory, halting beats. "We should stay on mission and go to E'lan."

Jeth reached for Kor's gun—his hand shook. Foiled, he redoubled his effort, the blaster centimeters out of reach. Something was wrong. Kor's quick-speed hangover counteracted a double dose of stim that should have him energized.

Waves of energy depletion fed nausea and a throbbing headache. Sensations of the world piled, a babble of languages assaulting in a flood of the incomprehensible. The urge to scream and to laugh competed for airspace. Lights too bright, sounds too loud, breathing, folding of legs, pacing, the hardness of the table, the ragged range of sensory stimuli, it was all too much. As if that wasn't enough, Raven spread the Shadow Emperor's stink throughout the briefing room. Jeth would know better than anyone. After all, he cloned the first emperor from his genetic material. Sala was right—his mistakes did have a way of enduring.

The Starry Empire agent examined him as though he had stepped out of a cell-culture dish. Jeth avoided eye contact, focusing on the table. Charronna would be a problem he would have to eliminate. Kor had plenty of justification. Concerned he acted weak and out of character, he confronted the Psian. Their eyes met. Fingertips brushed the disruptor, but no grip. Push, command, his body must obey the new master.

"The future trembles," Noi said. "Malevolence shrouds both paths, but darker to E'lan. I change my vote to the Commonweal."

"A minute ago, you said I had to go to E'lan," Jeth-Kor said. "More ghost nonsense."

"Crazy talk galore," Charronna said. "Kor may become the Khonsu, the consumer of life. Hello, enter the human-hating Commonweal. For the love of life, let's go home."

Noi stood with his hands folded. Bottomless blank eyes glimmered. He traversed into the continuum. Creation's flow shifted underneath. Ghosts betray others by instinct and by preference, trapped within mazes built through the perception of too many truths. Jeth-ka commanded his possessed body in urgent need, putting a firm hand on the blaster. Before he made a move, Noi locked the ship's command codes.

"We go to the Commonweal," Noi said. "Prepare for jump."

Jeth-ka's heart accelerated into rough rapids. Attack, he must, and he gave frantic orders to Kor's mind that screeched for movement, for combat mode to eliminate the others. Kor preferred death to letting go; *give me time*. Frustrated, Jeth-ka sagged into his chair. Once he gained better control, he would strike. In the meantime, it would take more than a Psian to dislodge him.

***

Fresh from stasis, Charronna shambled down a familiar corridor; her immediate agenda locked into a craved need for coffee. Existence had settled into a routine of check-ins interspersed between periods of prolonged multi-jumps. Keeping to protocol, Noi greeted the crew in the briefing room. Sort of. The ghost sat with back straight, legs crossed, and mind somewhere else, probably in a higher dimension reserved for the enlightened. Steam from a cup of white tea wafted, one of the few pleasures available. Noi remained oblivious to his hot drink in his above-it-all self-actualized steadiness.

Coffee in hand, she slid into a chair at the conference table, downing the sweet-bitter brew, the best thing to ever come out of Earth besides her Prada shoes. A long, bubbly bath followed by a sensuous dinner during sunset over the Ragoth Plain, and the world would be right again. The room's transparent wall showcased their folly, home, a distant star lost among the billions. Done with the coffee, she ordered a cup of green chai. Why not indulge? The testosterone-overdosed Militant and his immutable ghost-friend nursed early death wishes; sooner or later, their fairy godmothers would either grant the favor or go on vacation.

"We're low on power," Noi said. "Please conserve."

"Sounds like we should be going home."

"This concerns all of us."

"Big news, huh? Any hints?"

Noi gave his trademark placid hidden smile. Next to him, Sparrow fidgeted. Her mouth full of breakfast, she sneaked glances at the adults with perplexed evaluation. The girl wanted everyone to get along. Life would soon shatter her sheltered naiveté. Late and angry, Raven, and whatever thing inhabited his mind, settled in. Everything appeared normal, except the Militant who discharged energy best described as peculiar—his new normal since Eos.

"We've crossed the Deep Black," Noi said. "Long-range scan shows a living world at the coordinates corresponding to the Commonweal world of Sy'tall."

Over the table, incoming data added details to a holographic planet with an impressive forest moon, a third in relative width.

"Looks like Earth before the Meltdown," Sparrow said.

Charronna sipped more chai. Mixed in with Sparrow's chatter was a story about how her family schemed their way to be among the dislocated Meltdown refugees lucky enough to be crammed into Earth's first colony ship while three billion others perished in wars, disease, forced migrations, and famine that followed the environmental catastrophe caused by the sudden collapse of the Greenland ice sheet—not the type of bloodline to be disregarded.

"Since we see them," Charronna said, "they likely see us."

"We should say hello," Sparrow said. "The Oracle said the Sy'tallians liked humans."

"Relative to aliens who sought our extermination."

"I bet they've forgotten the whole thing."

The princess picked over the contents of her packaged breakfast, looking quite smart in her mini-uniform—starved, but with renewed vitality. Someday she would marry the handsome prince of her choice, birth beautiful children, acquire pets, and live happily ever after. The little princess required instruction on the other side of life. Instructors withheld mercy and empathy to crush their students. *Crush Sparrow like they crushed you.* The girl piped up in Noi's quaint conclaves with the confidence of someone who counted. *Little Charro never mattered.* Charronna set her hands on the table, trying to at least be a quiet witch.

A lithe, forest-green humanoid with prominent pointed ears and a delicate face poised between joy and sadness materialized in place of the planet. "Cute," Charronna remarked.

"Woodland elves," Sparrow exclaimed.

Kor looked ill. Fear and terror poured off him, not part of a Militant's specs. Kor aimed a blaster at the Psian. Charronna choked on carbon fumes. Noi's eyes widened. The Militant's mind burst with the emissions of a foreign will in control.

Screaming, Sparrow dove into Noi. The gun discharged. A beam struck the tumbling pair. They fell below the table. Charronna threw her cup at Kor. The mug spun out chai in frantic weapons fire. Kor pointed the gun her way. The cup smashed into Kor's ear. The impact threw him off balance. His next shot singed her gorgeous hair. The burned hair smelled of chemical death on the prowl.

Raven jumped on the table, kicking a leg at Kor's head. The Militant deftly ducked. Charronna grabbed the table's edge, twisted into a flying pivot, and landed a satisfying blow that knocked the Polarian to the floor butt-first. Kor struggled to stand.

Raven scrambled up, brandishing Kor's gun. Eyes in a black simmer, Noi backed into a window. The girl screamed "Gun!" and barreled into Raven's legs. The gun clattered on the floor. The princess pounced on it and scampered back into the bar. A wild shot grazed Raven's shoulder. He pulled up, muscle rippling with fight-versus-flight strain.

"I saved your life," the Polarian said. "Give me the gun."

"I'm called Sparrow for good reason." Her eyes narrowed. "I borrowed my dad's hunting rifle to practice since I wasn't allowed like my brothers. I missed the decoy. Zapped a sparrow. Never know what I might hit." She smiled with victory on her lips. "We're going to see the aliens."

Raven swayed.

"The odds are against you," said Charronna, who positioned for a counterattack. "I bet her aim is better than yours."

The Polarian stormed out in a wordless swirl of payback-threat—one troublesome adult male out of the way. Charronna locked her gaze with Noi's. Together, they rode a telepathic wavelength into Kor's surface awareness. The presence she had encountered before infected most of Kor's neurons. Dark blue energy metastasized to more areas of his brain.

"This presence's contamination cannot be cured with a mind-wipe," Charronna said to Noi. *"We need an Exorcist."*

"We need to improvise."

"Improvise, as in you have no idea what to do. You know me, I'd be willing to put on a show to draw the presence out, but we're

way past parlor tricks. There's one reasonable solution, and that's to kill Kor."

Charronna wrapped herself in a shield of invisible friends. In the quiet between heartbeats, she forced awareness into the dark blue light. Starbursts detonated in a rain of hydrogen blasts to thwart her advance. The entity unleashed malevolence, indifference, and contempt—a sickening stew. Walls enclosed, the ceiling lowered, and mountains fell. The possessor-menace came for Little Charro to claim the last scrap of heart and drop of soul.

"I will absorb you," the entity said.

Noi appeared as a wisp of light, seeking to intertwine with hers. Charronna relented, and they embraced and transformed into a bubble of intimacy, immune to the entity's attack. Noi infused to the core—blended into her truth—and she surrendered the horror of herself in a wretched need for survival. Walls and ceiling shattered, the mountains crumbled, and the dark blue light retreated.

"We came from the same thought," Noi said. "Your horror is my horror. My beauty is your beauty. The entity weakens. Fly with me."

Together, she and Noi spread mighty wings to pursue the entity's retreating remnants, its imprints evaporating from Kor's awareness. Hints, names decayed in the vacated battlefield—*last chance, Sala, Zaxa, doomed, White Mother, Z'yax, Asags, HoZo,* and most unexpectedly, the legendary home of the gods, *Avad—* she experienced with longing, as something real. Essences disintegrated, leaving behind a shiver through her non-existent soul.

Kor's consciousness returned in a flood. Charronna firmed her presence into a churning ball. She would soon be awash in the Militant's thoughts. She shuddered. In the shape of a bubble-nosed sea dog, Noi floated in a circle. Loads of time melted away during his lazy arc. The continuum shimmered into a watery blur to accommodate his chosen form. He was indeed skilled.

"Whatever skulks in Kor's mind is dangerous. It will return."

"I won't let you do harm."

She spun into a vortex, gathering energy to discharge into Kor's exposed mind. In defensive posture, Noi enveloped. She whipped faster, pressed into Noi's protective barrier, ripe for a finishing attack. She would wipe out him as well.

"We need Kor."

She whirled into tornadic force to level buildings, towns, and lives. The truth of her telepathic embrace with Noi overcame years of emotional purging. Self-taught propaganda fizzled in the onslaught of certainty that, yes, Kor was decent as far as humans went and would be useful to have around in the middle of dangerous nowhere. But it was time to take charge.

"He's attracted to you," Noi said. *"Despite who you are to him. I am your friend, despite what you've done to me. Are you willing to destroy the rare treasures who see your light through your dark?"*

"No." Stunned by the instinctive answer, she quieted. The urge to sob ruptured into her mind. Without another word, she allowed Noi to help her place new, more effective blocks. After they had isolated the thing claiming to be the first of the Psians,

she withdrew. Whatever inhabited Kor was ancient, and disturbed, and it persisted. The malevolence had been contained, but it was a cancer capable of breaking through again. To make matters worse, she liked Kor. An agent of the Starry Empire couldn't afford warm, fuzzy, I-care-about-you weakness.

Kor shuffled to the bar and ordered a liquid-balanced meal from the food dispenser with protein and sea extracts, gulping the greenish-brown drink. He was disoriented as would be expected after a full-fledged possession. Vague light in his gray eyes focused into the sharpness of a laser. He swept over, pulling her within his exhales of overripe sea. Dribbles of the liquid meal streaked his chin and neck. He plunged his warm, wet tongue into her mouth. She returned the favor, wanting to wrap her legs around his tight, muscular torso and ride him to paradise. First kiss . . . she would remember it, always.

"Tone it down, big boy—we have an underage audience."

"Noted and thank you," his voice oozed sexuality. "I cannot lift the clans' blood oaths against the Red Witch. But I won't kill someone who saved my soul, no matter her crimes."

"Happy to be of service."

"My father will never forgive me."

"I wouldn't worry. You are way past what the General would overlook."

The Militant nose-kissed, playful, so Kor. Warmth, need—the onset of delight opened the moment into risky joy. She kissed him back and moved away before their passions ran wild. One day, she would return home. Thought police would undertake a thorough debriefing. Fantasy-life role-play would end in a prison cell or a reprogramming tank.

"*Star Horizon* enters the target system's heliosphere," the AI announced.

The woodland elf hologram continued to rotate. Assuming the aliens detected their ship, what were they thinking?

"Our meeting of human and alien takes us into the heart of our purpose," Noi said.

"Do we look ready to meet the evil empire that nearly wiped out our species?" Charronna asked. "We barely manage between the five of us."

Sparrow chattered about her favorite math tutor, her music instruction, lessons on grooming, how to dress, and how to present oneself when in public. Hermes, Charronna gathered, was technically a republic, but in practice, an aristocratic-style dictatorship dominated by the Baxter family. The alien image turned. The ship advanced into the outer border of the system's Oort cloud—close enough for a crack of light from a shudder room's door, opening wider by the second. She gave a defiant stare to the hovering green alien. The continuum vibrated, jarring, impending, ground-quaking possibility.

***

"I'm sorry," Jeth said.

Sala slow-walked over a carpet of iridescent feathers. In the course of her thoughtful movement, her face relaxed. "I think you mean it this time."

"Waking to full control of Kor left me disoriented and overwhelmed, and we are both men. What you endured when I transferred your consciousness into the White Mother's hive mind must have been a thousand times worse. I wanted to love you forever."

"At any cost."

"Yes."

"Without any thought to what I might want or find acceptable."

"Yes."

"That's ownership, not love."

"I was a child in a man's body, and I felt responsible for what happened to you."

"Did you cause my accident, juicy sweet?"

Jeth vibrated a bottom-end tone. "No accident."

Sala brightened into sharp, cutting high-definition detail. "No lies, Jeth, or so help me I'll snuff you out."

"One of the rival schools intended to assassinate me to stop the Cosmic Song project. Their bad timing cost you your life. I couldn't let you die because of my pride."

"Your honesty is lifetimes overdue."

"I was too ashamed. I blamed myself."

"That, I can understand. Dear Jeth, you dream of being great and powerful when you see yourself as small and weak." Sala drifted closer and anointed Jeth with a warm caress that passed through him as a summer breeze. After Sala withdrew in a ponderous ebb, he clung to the sensation, slowed the perception of time to capture every nuance, and wrote it into memory where he enshrined his most precious collectibles. There was no peace outside of the caress, only himself.

CHAPTER XX

The aftershock of the possession ricocheted through Kor's mind. Part of him wanted to stay in the briefing room with the others, but another part of him needed to be alone to remember who he was. He excused himself.

The bridge wasn't far away, nothing was on *Star Horizon*. The ship's creators had an eye for both utility and aesthetics. Lighting the color of an azure sky lit the corridor ceiling in repeating double-row squares on the way to the forward section. Banks of vertical, matching blue columns lighting showcased the walls. But the illumination disturbed his thoughts, and he hurried his pace.

Ensconced on the bridge, he turned the primary bluish lights off. Kor brooded. A space buoy flashed a white warning on the viewer. Operation Hero crossed the threshold. The fates manifested themselves in the physical universe through the beacon. Go further, and his destiny as either the Amun, the liberator, or the Khonsu, the destroyer, would be unavoidable. Untold outcomes weighed his soul. Was it his right to be the author of epic change? Nothing would change if he retreated. Stories swirled in his head, heroic versions, happy endings for all.

The beacon lit the bridge in pulsating beats. An oddly pleasing resonance played in patterns. Eyes closed, he listened to the underlying vibe, the hum of the signal's rhythmic vibrations. The option to retreat laid at his fingertips. Charronna would throw a party. Hell, she'd do a pole dance.

"Who do you think you are, boy?" Strom's voice needled into Kor's mind.

"I am a man of faith. I must be to go on."

The ship passed the buoy. Flashing light took root in his eyes. Scans pinged the ship's hull. First Contact had begun. He went in search of Noi, finding him staring at a corridor wall in a meditative pose. Kor whispered his need for company.

"Come, sit with me."

"What do you see that you have not seen a hundred times?"

"Let the words go. Let the thoughts go. Sit before the wall."

For a while, Kor did just that. Eyes fluttered. How much longer? How many minutes? How long to see God?

Noi switched to an audible breath and confronted Kor with oil-slick eyes. "Doubt assails me, your energy capable of shaping the future for good or for bad. But I like you—I've deposited the command codes into your memory core."

Kor hugged Noi like he would a brother and left to wander the blue-lit corridors, returning to the bridge before a scheduled short jump.

"Jump in ten seconds," the AI intoned, counting down to one.

Reality phase-shifted into swirling violence, into purple, shifting through the color spectrum to red. Voices riding radio waves from throughout the galaxy sang their songs, lost in the cacophony of their hubbub. The ship shifted back into normal space in the shadow of a station eclipsing a blue-green jewel of a world. It bristled with weapons and sensors, an aggressive construct of power. Connected to an external bay, a cruiser-class warship with don't-tread-on-me engines, twisting tubes, and dozens of clustered command nexuses flaunted military prowess.

A tractor beam grabbed hold of *Star Horizon*. Magnetic claws clapped onto the ship's shoulders—the first handshake. The ship jerked. He rubbed his charm for reassurance. One by one, his shipmates shuffled in. He squeezed heat, hope—his pounding heart—into the stone.

"Our moment of truth," Noi said.

"Cut the gravity," Charronna said. "I'm nervous enough about getting blown apart by some jittery green guy."

"Our goal remains basic," Kor said. "Say hello and survive."

"To that end, Charronna and I will greet our new friends," Noi said. "We may need our telepathic advantage."

"How do I become the Amun holed up on the ship?"

"By staying alive," Charronna quipped.

"Heroes are not made in the palace."

"Let us make first contact." Noi put a light hand on Kor's heart.

"What does your ghost-sense tell you?"

Noi removed his hand.

"No, that won't fly," Charronna said. "What if whatever thing inhabits Kor's mind goes off on the station?"

"Fine, I'll go solo. If I fail, I hope they treat the rest of you with respect."

"King's Mercy, I hate you like the ex-husbands I've never had. What about Raven? I don't trust him alone on this ship."

"I don't trust him, period. I'll lock out the bridge and the briefing room," Kor nodded at the rotating holographic image of the forest-green male. "What do you think of them?" he asked Sparrow.

"A door-catcher," she said in an official pronouncement.

Charronna shrugged at his questioning gaze; he moved it back to the girl.

"At the palace, one of the swinging doors didn't close properly. Some people let it slam shut—others caught it before impact, guiding it in. I found the door-catchers to be nicer, less dangerous, less ego, less stuck on themselves."

"Door-catcher," Kor mused. "I like that." Though he had no business taking the girl on such an important mission, her perspective could be useful. Noi gave no hint of his opinion; the agent's horror bled through her Smiling Court mask. He shrugged. After all, Sparrow's nifty gunplay preserved the quest.

Charronna threw up her hands. "Say something, Noi. Must I always be the mean one? It's not like we're going to meet the savages. We *are* the savages."

Noi hovered apart much like an actual ghost.

Charronna stormed off, muttering "fanatics" in a wordy stream to perk up Kor's locker-initiated ears. But once the ship docked, she dutifully presented herself at the airlock, Sparrow in tow, both wearing their garish orange space suits. Kor wore a sensor-deflecting bodysuit under the space suit. The others relied upon Starry Empire pendant-sized deflectors.

"I'm doing the talking," Charronna said. "Not a word, Miss Baxter."

"I hear you." Sparrow twirled her hands around her helmet.

"I think," Charronna said into Kor's mind, *"I've been dismissed by the little queen in waiting."*

The outer door opened to the glare of alien technology. A glowing path sealed by force fields connected to a liquid mirror portal. The station spouted gossamer wings soaking up star rays, artistic as much as functional—an odd pairing to the menacing station. Kor's heart sang, shouted, and danced, a taste of pure joy at the unfolding unknown. The silvery portal beckoned. With the girl sandwiched between himself and Charronna, they breached the looking glass.

Higher function command displays popped into active mode. Multi-level dry docks wrapped around the station's curvature a level higher. Sleek vessels occupied a few alcoves for shuttles and fighters. Plenty of green-skinned locals with long ears and red-diamond talons lined the perimeter interspersed with fancy control stations, while a second group commanded the high ground on an elevated narrow platform. Orange and yellow stripping outlined a walkway in the middle. Symbols marked up the floor and the alcoves, the mysterious language of a new world.

A different faith struggled for a voice to replace what he had lost when he discovered the Code's lies. Despite the vast knowledge accumulated by the human tribes, the cosmos was indeed awe-inspiring and spectacular. They approached a pair of aliens on the far side of the spacious bay in front of a hatch big enough for a hover tank. Neither movement nor expression lifted the veil from the aliens' intent. These aliens were door-catchers. Kor was almost sure of it.

The forest-green elves announced themselves—Arn, station administrator, and assistant Ly'. Each wore a brown cloak with a silver pendant—one with three loops and the other with four, suggesting a rank.

"Welcome to Eda, visitors from beyond the Periphery," Arn said. "We will adjourn to the Refuge and start a conversation." The pitch of Arn's voice rose and fell, a pleasant lilt with a singsong quality.

First exchange, first words, worth a happy no-reservation-grin. Fearless, Sparrow hopped right up to a gun-toting alien. The aliens escorted them through a sterile corridor with the décor of a long-abandoned lab. Parkland wonder greeted them at the end. Wildflowers of red, purple, yellow, and white covered a blue-green meadow banked by a wall of trees as high as sixty feet tall. Coos and whistles emanated from the woods. A holographic ceiling mimicked an Earther blue sky. Tiered gardens dripped with spherical editable fruits on ropy branches in various autumn shades. Perfection squared with joy.

Charronna activated the helmet comm-system. "We're cut off from *Star Horizon*."

"Think happy ending." Kor plucked a four-petal flower. "Relax, enjoy the scenery."

Charronna thumped him on the back. "Picking flowers could be an offense punishable by death. Tension abounds and not the exciting kind. I'm guessing padded cells behind those trees."

Arn and Ly' emerged from the woods wearing yellow-washed kilts and loose brown shirts, fun and casual. They brought a guest, a lioness with liquid gold cat-eyes who strutted with bravado that matched her cat-like muscled body of royal blue fur outfitted with a colorful swashbuckling uniform and an oversized golden earring any pirate would lust for.

Arn's long pointed ears fluttered. Charronna mumbled half-sounds. Divine whispers surged into Kor's mind: *You must not reveal yourself. Beware Zaxa. Beware the White Mother."*

Ly' drew a rod that glowed at the tip. Aiming it at Sparrow, Ly's pupils dilated in shrill alarm. Arn shouted. Sparrow held her helmet, a wound to human fate.

"We've come all this way," Sparrow said.

Helmet off, Charronna spoke in a cool voice. "Please remain calm."

"E'lani," Ly' shrieked. "They tricked us. We're doomed! Blessed Tree!" Ears in an anxious twitch, her rod's glow intensified to lethal charge.

The station administrator fingered an amulet on his chest.

"Seeds and saplings," Arn said, "give me your weapon stick."

"What's everyone afraid of?" Sparrow said.

"Something unexpected," Charronna said, her tone sour.

The lioness snorted. "Gods and demons! The understatement of the millennium. What have you done, Friend Arn?"

"An act of civilized tolerance toward our guests, Friend Mestjet."

Fangs bared in a show of menace, the feline stalked around the meadow. Metallic chains clinked from hard-earned riches. *See me*, exhorted Kor.

The formidable feline swiveled to snarl at Arn. "Never serve me bird shit. We could be executed for standing in the general vicinity with this poor excuse of a sentient species. Plenty of citizens would pull the trigger without a whisker-twitch of sympathy."

Arn bravely attempted to interrupt, but the feline refused to yield. "Why on sweet mother Chea have they returned? I promised your visiting Etamite slugs the aliens' identity. They're under military contract, and they have the firepower to enforce their demands. When those radical adherents sniff law-breaking," the lioness growled, "they go for the cruel and the unusual."

Helmet in hand, Kor stepped in front of Ly'. The brown rod glowed brighter. He would die for his comrades, for the balladeers back home in need of another verse. A sacrifice to save the lives of his shipmates.

"We burn," Ly' said. "Our trees, our meadows, our communities burn to ash and our names forgotten. We lose the trail of life if we don't keep the law." Yellow translucent tears flowed over flushed green skin. "Some sins are never forgiven."

"Let us go," Kor said. "No one except you three knows we're here."

Sparrow, ever the brave one, offered her hand to Arn. Hand and talon met in a light clasp. The face of the lioness creased, transforming its surface into ridges of delicately folded fur. Pungent breath mixed with her spicy perfume enticed his nose to twitch. Kor's heart thumped with the tempo of war drums.

"Sy'tallians," Mestjet said with emphasis, "was the one race friendly to the E'lani who survived the Virtuous War's retributions with an intact home world. Mercy is off your menu. Kill them, Friend Arn. If you don't have the gonads, I'll do it."

Kor's heart sang. The lioness spoke to Arn, but her golden orbs, treasures worthy of a dragon's keep, locked onto him. For the first time, she broke through her perceptual prison; she *saw*.

"We are travelers in search of truth and peace," Kor said. "Where is the crime?"

Mestjet fingered a dangling gold earring and hissed, her zesty breath a pleasant surprise of mouthwash mint. "The Commonweal Extermination Edict mandates E'lani, whether male or female, adult or child, armed or defenseless, guilty or innocent, to be killed by any means available and as quickly as possible."

"The sin of blood," Kor said, accessing the phrase from the Eos Archive.

"We're human beings, not E'lani," Sparrow said.

"Ganzag!" hissed Mestjet. "Semantics. The gods are unkind, but they are not that cruel."

Kor waded into the fierce stare of the golden-eyed lioness. He summoned the boy who hid himself away in the Painted Garden and prayed to the stars for cosmic magic to make dreams come true. He summoned the young man who held on to his weathered faith that he was more than a cog in a Starry Empire machine. He summoned his love for Jude.

"We want to be friends," Kor said.

"No one drinks from poisoned waters; at any rate, no one you could talk to."

"We don't even remember the war," Sparrow said.

"Let Charronna and me do the talking."

The girl's eyes widened. "You used her name, and in front of her."

Charronna waved a finger in Kor's face. "You can't go back now."

He shrugged. The agent had earned respect, no matter her crimes. "Examine us," he said to the Cheemin. "We're not a prepared expedition."

Mestjet swished her tail. "The Councilors of Vio rule through diamond eyes. Why should I be different?"

"Every soul deserves to be judged on its own merits," Kor said.

Mestjet's tail no longer moved. "You sound like my mate back home."

Kor waited to discover whether that was good or bad.

"I like that, but I need more. My kin can't afford to take major risks."

"Can you afford not to?" Charronna said.

The Cheemin bared the bottom of her fangs. "The question of the hour. Bring me something civilized to drink, Friend Arn, spiced warm and fermented milk. Ganzag! Marauders, raiders, a visit from my mother-in-law, pleasant times compared to this mess."

Ly's ears twitched hard. "A Dorram Hallow requests docking privileges."

"Those clairvoyant know-it-alls would not come here without an alarming reason." Mestjet flashed fangs at Kor. "You are the only alarming reason we have." Mestjet held a blaster.

Sparrow turned to Kor wide-eyed. He motioned her back, moving in front. His heart broke loose of its moorings.

"The E'lani," Arn said, "are a happy curse we must climb through."

Mestjet hissed and headed to the door. "Have it your way. I wasn't here. You didn't see me."

Arn fingered his amulet, unleashing immobilizing peace within an amber glow. Kor's perception slowed. He reached out a hand to Charronna and Sparrow. The three of them squeezed life into the ebbing moment, unsure if they would ever experience another.

CHAPTER XXI

Men'op waddled through a narrow unlit loop corridor emitting high-frequency chirps and clicks, repeating his frustration. *Why am I at the Commonweal's dissonant edge?* His mind hummed with annoyance. The Elder Brood, a gaggle of hags, dreamed of calamity emanating from Sy'tall, and they demanded that he go on the fool's errand. Atrophied wings twitched. A male, even one admitted into the Media Guild, had to submit.

Long-range scans confirmed the presence of an unknown, unregistered, ship. Station Eda's Administrator ignored his queries and the Coercer controlling the Etamite vessel didn't admit to anything useful. Men'op, Observer from Truthful and Accurate Media, would arrive soon enough to sort things out.

Compression waves enveloped, painting the corridor in soothing gradients. Rarefaction gave shape to his surroundings. On a whim, he stayed on the ship's loop, circling back, sinking into the sensory delight. After all, he ventured to civilization's end, a place where the hyperspace lanes stopped at flashing beacons, a warning to venture no further. Great Beyond—what could be worse than to abide at the edge of the abyss? The captain intercepted him in quick response to the ill-advised challenge to the universe. Her high-frequency calls pinned him down, allowing him no way to escape undetected. She hissed, shoving her long snout forward in space-violating aggression.

"You sent messages to Station Eda," she said.

Men'op squeaked. "Of course, Uppermost Perce. Observers inquire."

"Apprentice grade."

"Good enough that these red-shifted Sy'tallians won't dare lie to me."

"Have you ever met one?"

"Assorted E'lani sympathizers, traitors, and sappy tree-lovers—what more do I need to know? Some wrongs are amendable only by the Flying Spirits. Some sins are forever."

Men'op flapped his useless wings.

"I take that as a *no*. Why the Elder Brood sent an amateur out here is beyond me. I run this ship, and I won't have any male, especially a young blood, running loose and unsupervised. No more unauthorized communications."

Men'op's wings drooped more than usual. *Senile hag, no better than the Elder Brood.*

"Stay out of trouble, Apprentice. My ship and my crew come first."

With that, the Uppermost waddled away. Men'op waited in place until the hag's echo calls went out of range. *No one tells me what to do.*

Hours later, he entered the pitch-black Hallow and crooned in answer to the pleasant hum created by the beating of atrophied wings. Eleven times eleven horizontal bars bisected the sacred area with eleven vertical poles. He chirped and clicked, confirming female energy, heady and sweet, filling the Hollow. Men'op climbed a winding staircase past hanging hormone-saturated females to reach the top, using a stream of clicks to navigate. The perfume of ninety-nine females tickled his nose, and his blood heaved. Above the highest bar, he dropped right in place between flanking females.

One of the females gave a ragged chirp. "The Uppermost," Esha said, "won't approve if she finds out we allowed a male into a dreaming."

"She has not forbidden it," Men'op said.

"Because it never occurred to her that you would ask such a thing. You're lucky I like you."

"Male energy promises to add much power to the intermingling."

"So claims the echo chatter. The same rumors warn of fallouts. Deaths."

Within the transition of Men'op's next coherent thought, his sexual organ extended down and locked in place. Perched females extended their slender external appendages to connect with others hanging below. The interconnected mass combined into one. Their flesh seethed in a rapturous union. No indecision dissuaded Men'op, and no Elder Brood objections swayed him. Swept into a forming vision, he jumped off the cliff, flying high into the sky.

Men'op chirped a barrage of squeals. Rational thought melded with bouncing walls of audible vibrations. Layers of frequency shredded through the group's mind as it strained to rearrange the molecules of time to know the possibilities emanating from the perpetuity they neared. A vortex of colors rushed to enlightenment. The female presence changed pitch, diving lower, a bass crescendo. He squealed past his splitting throat, past the blood, the pain, straining for the all-knowing.

Visions erupted at the precipice of consummation. Whole worlds were annihilated, entire species wiped out, the fall of civilizations—the loss of hopes and dreams. Planets organized themselves into armed camps, shielded from enemies who encircled and raided, descending into dystopian shadows, shooting at anything that dared approach. Tellerian spires dimmed with soot. Pitiless fires engulfed the tree-like Zev. Foul gases poisoned Z'yax hives. T'hyto cloud cities plummeted to the ground. Nuxinni metropolises melted into molten rivers. Atmospheres evaporated. Worlds wailed in their misery.

E'lan.

Self-awareness grasped for both ends of the sonance. The cursed name of the obliterated world resonated in cleaving crust and breaking mountains. Vast firestorms, too many to count, horrible holocausts, too much for the mind to bear, and then, barren stillness. Men'op whimpered. Parts of his last meal oozed through clenched teeth.

The movement ebbed. The expanse of civilization spread across the wastes. Thousands of ships—constellations in motion—brought connection and prosperity throughout the galaxy. A new species was the key, but a nameless influence on the Commonweal's auditory wavelength might result in a shrill sound, changing the course of history in a dreadful direction.

Vision concentrated into the ordered harmony. Men'op's voice rose to notes beyond comprehension. An object glowed and pulsed, radiating with light and sound, its amplitudes growing ever larger and flowing through the continuum. The object's rhythm changed. It was aware of his presence.

"You belong to me," it said, pulling, draining life energy.

Disturbed cadence saturated the dreaming. Pitch oscillated between extreme highs and lows, light broke into shadowed colors, and he screamed to blot out the presence. His consciousness crumbled into a descending blackout.

Sometime later, Men'op awoke from the intermingling to broken melodies of choppy peeps. Scattered, distressed squeaks among the females didn't make sense. "Were we attacked?"

"The soul-catcher tried to eat us," Esha said. "It is beyond us. Many are dead. The Uppermost must be informed."

The soul-catcher, a mythological figure in oral histories, scared the pups, and he was no pup, but the presence resonated with utter malevolence. Men'op wished for fully developed wings to out-fly the panic chasing him down. Deaths were rare during intermingling. There would be no escape from consequences this time. At least he understood the enormity of the stakes. *E'lan*. The vilest of worlds shadowed the future.

"Wait until I am gone. Do not offer my fault, but do not deny it either."

Men'op waddled to a computer station and generated a sound shape of Eda. As orbital habitats went, it was remarkable for an outland planet—a ring thirty miles in diameter with barbed, menacing pylons with delicate solar sails affixed. Profuse windows were dark except for a discreet section. The locals used no more than ten percent of Eda—a place on life-support, more dead than alive.

His wing nodes chilled. The future had never been so uncertain.

***

The amber faded away.

Charronna's well-worn glare came into focus. Kor shed his bulky spacesuit, and Charronna and Sparrow did the same. The Sy'tallians had put them in a padded cell. Score one for the agent.

"I told you we should have never come here," Charronna said.

"You played your part," Kor said.

"Don't blame me because you led us into this avoidable disaster."

"You started it."

"How's that fearless leader?"

"You showed up in a war-star, guns blazing."

"To uphold the law."

"Who decided your law? Who justified your murders? My people had no say."

"Excuse me, Hero of the People, but I wanted to go home."

"Where you could reprise your role as the bloodthirsty witch? How does it feel to be on the receiving end?"

"Your guardian agreed to die," Charronna shouted.

Kor's muscles contracted. He wanted to attack, to withdraw, to ask questions. In powerless silence, he paced. His determination sought every direction.

"Your father broke under my interrogation. Strom's partner offered his life to spare the clans from excessive retribution. As part of the deal, Harmony required Strom to help us; to ensure his compliance, he had to kill his partner himself; his disgrace had to be complete."

Kor went still. Rue had said that his father's mind had been invaded by a telepath—her description matched up with someone like Charronna. His father killed his lover, because, like Kor, his father broke under a telepathic attack. Steel Rose's disgrace. His father endured an unbearable burden, alone, in shackles forged with shame to exhaust a giant. The girl trembled. Charronna's emerald-green eyes turned glassy. Too much to bear. Too much to comprehend. *Uncomfortably numb*.

Charronna was right. He had made a bad situation worse. Instead of the ballyhooed hero, his reach for the sky led to a padded cell. Kor caressed Sparrow, pulling her to him as he gripped his remembrance stone. He squeezed the charm extra hard, hoping to extract a bit of magic to save the day.

The cell's temperature rose. The hours ticked by. What were the aliens thinking? Kill them? Or kill them not? He took his top off, showing off his sculpted chest and ripped abs. Maybe he wanted to impress Charronna—feed her lust. Drips of sweat spattered on the floor. By the Red Beast, it was hot.

"As far as anyone this side of the Deep Black knows," Kor said, "we're extinct. We turn ourselves into something else, a.k.a. Operation Alien Costume. Earthers play disguise make-believe in their vids all the time with prosthetics, makeups, masks, and weird dress-ups."

"What about Administrator Arn?"

"What about him? The perfect plan to protect his green ass."

"Got me there. Is there a phase two where we go home, lessons learned?"

"Aye. We have come far enough." But he didn't believe that. Still, knowing he put the entire species on the line against a grudge-holding Commonweal . . . he didn't have the right, righteous cause or not. Reckless fantasy urged otherwise. Being responsible would win him no love on Zorn.

Not from anyone.

***

To Charronna's surprise, the Administrator liked Kor's idea. There were a dozen things ready to go wrong, and that was on the low-hanging fruit list. On the plus side, Operation Alien Costume postponed the execution, got them all out of the padded cell, and, as a bonus, provided an opportunity to dress up. While Kor, Raven, and Sparrow returned to *Star Horizon*, she and Noi prepared to face the enemy, with as much drama and with as much style as they could muster.

Off a deserted corridor in an abandoned section of the Sy'tallian station, Charronna waited for the Dorram Observer with eyes wide. Noi sat next to her in a matching rustic wooden chair. Outfitted in garish armor, a pronounced cranial ridge with three demon horns, she would make the great and terrible Sentinel nervous. Liquid nitrogen flowed in her blood, into her heart, icing it to a cold block never exposed to the warmth of a simple caress. *My pretty ass can be as hard as any man's.*

On the flip side, Noi's inner civilized man clashed with his purple-drenched eyes and white synthetic hair. The poor man's neck strained to hold up a head-cracking mallet hanging from a chain necklace. Fortunately, the Observer lacked context to judge. Seven lemon-sized bumps started above the eyes and ended at the base of her skull, and in place of hair, a painted prosthetic gave the illusion of vestigial horns. The garish costume befitted the Knights of the Half-Moon. Thank the stars for the room's dividing and distorting force field. An urge to giggle clogged her throat.

The Dorram waddled in late; his smallish frame didn't command gravitas. Arn trailed behind, ears twittering, a nervous state he seemed fond of. The Observer scrutinized a bench. Except for a golden medallion in the shape of a broken circle, he wore no accouterments above the waist. The Dorram's beady red eyes darted in constant scan. Excitement? Agitation? Charronna surmised the latter based on a general sense of unease that permeated the room's energy.

A telepathic probe, a luminous ball of atmosphere, formed in the continuum, and descended upon her center of gravity. *No way to start playtime, my little friend. What happened to Hello? Manners. You must be new at this.* She unleashed a sapphire trance through the probe, drowning its force until it dissolved. Her childhood instructors started with easy incursions to test defenses, trying to lull her into complacency before they savaged her mind with vicious unfeeling attacks of pure terror.

The Dorram chirped a cantankerous racket. Wings twitched. He fingered his medallion, stroking the outer edge round and round. Charronna loaded empty intensity into her expression, eyes dry, the effect (she hoped) on her adversary that of being stalked by a tenacious corpse. If fortitude counted, she would make Kor's stupid idea work.

"They are psi," Men'op said to Arn. "Why wasn't I warned?"

"Enough, little one," Charronna said. "I'm not here for playtime."

"Why are you here?"

"We've come from across the Deep Black to start a conversation."

"The Wastes beyond the Periphery?"

Charronna nodded. Unsure if the alien understood, she added, "Correct."

Men'op's wings fluttered. "How many systems does your civilization occupy?"

"The size of our Blissful Dominion changes every day."

"Five million star systems," Noi said.

"Careful, dear," Charronna said, switching to Imperial standard, the Starry Empire's common tongue. Artful lies temper their exaggeration."

"How many of you are there?" the Dorram asked.

Charronna and Noi traded devilish glances.

"One quadrillion," Noi said. "Give or take."

"Great Beyond," Men'op said, followed by undecipherable chirps.

The Dorram waddled along the other side of the force field. A foreign presence formed, a sensation reaching through Charronna's body instead of being limited to her mind's eye. Her sense of self separated into a quantum entanglement, a jagged fissure of light breaking through. Men'op attempted an empathic reading. If the Dorram succeeded, he would not possess the facts to have an intellectual understanding, but at a core emotional level, he would know the newcomers played him for a fool. In silent resolve, Charronna fought to reorder the fissure into closure. Merciless teachers failed to torture her into submission. She was not about to let some upstart alien best her. The fissure kept expanding into her resistance, into her identity.

Calling upon her invisible friends who protected her when she had no one else to cling to, she retreated inward, into her sheltered underneath. Desperate, she disassociated, her sense of being a kind of outerwear. After an indeterminable amount of time passed, flickers of outside awareness filtered through and Charronna resurfaced. The attack had dispersed.

Men'op's movement of wings and legs increased. *He's agitated. Serves him right.* The Observer's narrow eyes flattened to thin red discs and his shrunken wings moved up and down in a hypnotic fallen-angel ritual. "Why did you come here?"

"First stop. What's with the psi attack?" She put an edge of menace in her voice, should the Observer recognize such.

"You are a false echo."

An involuntary sound wheezed through his lungs. Charronna could only guess the cause of that. She smiled wicked sweet to maximize the impact of her ghastly bumps, painted head, and exotic copper-bronzed makeup. If not for the fact that her life hung in the balance, she'd never had so much fun.

The Dorram flapped and squeaked. Playtime was over. Within the continuum, a thing of prediction and dread crashed into the heart of her defenses. The intrusive force unleashed torrents of spiral energetic illuminations that diffused her strength and power. Charronna darkened the spirals in the misery of her embrace. Foreign suns, authors of many minds, burst into her realm. She retreated from the weighty onslaught to find shelter, but hostile minds invaded and violated. Steel-tipped rain pummeled Little Charro. Monsters closed in. Monsters grabbed hold. No breath, no scream, and no friends offered forth in the shattered remnant of who she was.

An angel of mercy, a cool sea-green rain shower, descended to douse the fiery globes. *Noi.* The flaming orbs faded. The foreign presence lost vitality, becoming poached and watery, yet it persisted where she defended the sum of her true self. Her mind expanded partially back into the Real. Blood trickled from the corner of her mouth.

"I'm overdone cooked, Noi."

"A circle of minds channels through the Dorram," Noi said.

Still in the form of a rain shower, Noi lifted himself out of the battle.

"Don't leave me."

Her will to fight broke down into spongy jell. She needed a friend, she needed Noi. The faded globes merged, evolving into a wraith-like image of the Dorram visage. Pale light outlined bottomless red eyes. The same moon-shadowed graveyard illumination shaped its cheeks and snout, becoming her reflection, her shadow, her everything. She and the battle were lost.

"You're E'lani," the Observer said in awful realization. "You've come for revenge, haven't you?"

CHAPTER XXII

Sala zoomed around Jeth with angel wings in a carefree flight. She grinned, a silly, lovely contour unseen since the early days of his courtship. In a sparkle of pixels, she sailed to a bed; red-painted lips called his name.

"You're being playful, my pretty sunbeam."

"I've decided to forgive you."

His nimbus cloud form condensed into himself as a young man with auburn hair, sharp teal eyes, and a clipped, groomed beard. Currents of erotic bliss drenched his thinking and lighted up the fibers of his revived body until a heated glow pulsed throughout his flesh. He threw himself on Sala, awkward and unsure. They tumbled, wrestled, and fought for more, becoming one, becoming vessels of intertwined magma. Sala moaned. He grunted. Jeth exulted in the desire, the pure *wanting*. The release built, and in the flow of the current, a buzz of insects teemed—the touch of Zaxa.

Jeth collapsed into a running wind with nowhere to flee. In a change of tactics, he shrunk into an empty place carved through utter hopelessness into the void's subquantum fabric. Faint vibrations of clemency, of ruthlessness, faded into the wash. Every thought betrayed. Bitter force crushed him into a final embrace of nonexistence, the excruciating speed of it, a fall in microgravity. The buzz of millions of tiny bugs saluted his exit—the racket of a white mother hive mind much disturbed. Fissures formed, and a shout blasted through the crushing peace. The clang of discordant strings reemerged.

"You can't evade me for long. I know you better than you do."

He wailed, opening into entropic escape. Zaxa-Sala pursued—an evil tethered to his love.

"Listen, my juicy sweet."

Never. Jeth refused to consider anything hopeful would emerge from the mouth of his destroyer. Force, overpowering, yanked him from subquantum space into the form of a spinning cloud. His supposed Sala re-materialized in a low-cut party dress dazzled with morning blossom pinks.

"There are secrets in this place to be revealed," she said, "if you keep still long enough to discover them."

"I spent lifetimes afraid of Zaxa discovering me—always here, a trap waiting to be sprung."

"My dear juicy sweet, I'm not Zaxa. I'm the real Sala."

Electric current cut through Jeth's being. Words scrambled, rushing beyond reach. Evil lied. Evil offered hope and crushed without mercy the hope given. Jeth clenched, transforming into a cube of roiling thunder. Absent escape, he would attack with every ounce of available energy.

"I sense a mood. Do you think Zaxa would spend eternity with you? I'm not your dream girl. I've always been here."

Gingerly, he tested the boundaries of his earliest memories, an incoherent landscape, disorientation, the shock of death, the loss of hope, betrayal, and abandonment . . . the visceral pain from Zaxa's brutal execution. Somewhere, Sala must not be in existence, but she always confronted. He ventured into madness, into the heart of his waking death where his consciousness shattered into shards vanishing in the dark. Terror assaulted him. The aroma of carmine wonder petals, Sala's favorite scent, wafted strong.

"I felt *her*."

"White Mothers are capable of multiple consciousnesses. Within the hive mind, Sala became Zaxa, but part of me survived, and that part went with you into the Cosmic Song. The hive mind lives in my thoughts. And oh, how I've hated you for it."

Gold-dusted lavender carmine wonder petals billowed as she twirled, a divine blessing. The petals drifted to rest. Her countenance remained pointed and confident. "But no more. You finally grasp, however imperfectly, what you did to me. The void is static, but we are not. I'm taking my old name back. I'm taking you back as well."

"Sala, my precious sunbeam."

"With truth comes responsibility. I will tear your mind to bits if I catch you using me in one of your fantasies."

"I want the real Sala. I always have."

For once, he had said the right thing at the right time. Sala's genuine, tender smile coupled with what he had longed to hear— a whispered, magical, "yes." He re-manifested as his physical self; a better, improved version, taller, stronger, and ripe for the plucking. His tongue plunged into Sala's waiting mouth—his efforts too desperate to be enjoyed. Clothes dissolved in blue fire—in wild inferno. Thunder replaced the buzz. The barriers shook. Carmine aromas condensed into solid forms. Joy, at last, pure and unadulterated. He wanted to gorge himself on it forever and ever.

"I will help you destroy Zaxa. We will be together always—the universe, our shadow."

With his entire mind, Jeth believed her. Let him be the fool, a worthwhile price to wallow in the comfort of unvarnished faith.

Kor, Zaxa, the Kimbrians, Psians, ill chance, and anything else that might threaten him, were recast to temporary obstacles. He experienced a state without fear. He was determined to stretch that moment into forever.

***

The Observer hovered within Charronna's mind's eye, a mirror to her horror. The Commonweal would finish their holocaust. Her failure, in part, to blame for the end of humankind. Denial mustered, unconvincing to her ears. She, a veteran of the Smiling Court, crumbled before the calamity of her defeat.

"You're the one who attacked us in the dreaming," the Observer said. "Discordant creature, you will pay for your crime."

"We attacked no one."

"E'lani lie and the stars shine."

"We're not your enemy. Experience our truth, unless you're afraid to see."

The Dorram's visage sharpened. Its examination deepened. Charronna unlocked doors behind where vulnerability collected, unhealed wounds festered and where shame quivered, gnawing at self-love. There was no other way except for both of them to see. In an inky rupture, the intruder vanished. Shaken, she opened her eyes.

Holding his mallet necklace, Noi stood over Men'op of Dorr. Blood, the color of mauve, dripped off the improvised weapon. The poor Psian's arms trembled. He dropped the mallet, almost striking the Dorram again. Noi shuffled back, eyes pleading for affirmation.

In between a thumping heartbeat, her off-kilter mind reordered. "Kor didn't mean for you to take the costume that literally."

"We had no hope of winning against a circle of minds trained to overcome telepathic defenses," Noi said. "Arn lowered the shield. I did the rest."

"You were a fraction too late. The Observer got what he came for, which means whoever supported him knows as well. I wish you had waited a minute longer. The Dorram and I were having a moment."

"Do you feel the continuum?"

"Yes. It sings a dark song. In sings a dark song for us all."

***

Noi clasped his hands, floundering for a calming mantra. The continuum's soul-draining cords screeched metal against metal. Sy'tallian guards pushed Noi through bright, stripped corridors, hollowed bones of the ancient dead. The clunk of his heavy costume boots, the tap of Charronna's heels, and the murmurs of the guard's flats filled the abandoned corridor in a language full of fear. Thoughts repeated, a burdensome mind loop, where he swung the mallet, an intended modest blow to the Dorram's temporal cranium. When the mauve blood spilled, his heart seized up and locked in place.

Heaving, he petered to a dead stop. Charronna joined the impromptu rest. Arn gestured to move along. The mallet kept falling, smashing into the Dorram's skull in a loop of horror. Noi unlatched Charronna's costume, which split down the middle like a perfectly cracked egg. She emerged from her outer armor in an unorthodox combination of skin-tight leather from the neck down, paired with a painted face topped by the horns.

"What a relief," she said, giving Noi an air kiss.

"No time for a costume change," Arn said.

"The costumes," Noi said, "weigh too much for us."

"No time, wait for your ship to do your reveal."

"You're letting us go," Charronna said. "Well, Arn, that deserves a kiss." She craned her neck back, catching the Sy'tallian on the cheek.

"To return the favor, you must kill me," Arn said.

Noi shed components of his costume to a simple tunic. Arn flushed deep green, his stress building. With tender remorse, Noi took Arn's hands and began a murmur of peace. Arn crouched in a nervous posture. The stream of time, slow and syrupy, shifted.

"I'm getting a bad feeling," Charronna said.

"It's the tumors sprouting on your lovely head," Noi said.

"Why, Noi, you made a joke. Bravo. But do hurry with your little chant."

"I take refuge in your kindness," Noi murmured in a mantra. "I gaze upon you with compassion. Together, we share our light."

"I won't kill you," he said to Arn in mind-speak. *"We must find another way."*

"My death or yours, a choice I grant. Make it quickly."

Arn sprang into action, pushing a relentless pace. Charronna kept up with Arn with ease, but Noi lagged. Perhaps the Psian habit of viewing the physical as an inferior manifestation was conceit. Noi's soul would be shaped in the moments to come, and how his body performed would be a part of that play. Time spent on telepathic disciplines drained the hours and the days, leaving solitary patches for the joy and the rigor of the community gardens.

"Balls to the walls, Noi!"

Down the corridor, stout broad-bodied aliens charged with arms raised. Guns built into their flesh flashed with death. Arn and Charronna rushed through an opening, disappearing from view. Breath rose in Noi's lungs. Photon shots zeroed in. He dived to the opening, his perception shifting into the quantum universe to concentrate the air density to buffer the landing. Taloned hands yanked him out of the corridor. Arn smashed a control panel next to the closing door, his green skin pale with panic.

Puffy clouds drifted across a holographic sun-drenched sky. Forests of white and pale orange bark trees with maroon flowering spikes swayed in meadows. A destination spot to share a meal or a drink with a friend—but the place hadn't seen any love in a long time. Scenic wonder tempted with distraction, but Charronna doubled down on stress. Her energy honed to a sharp edge as she hopped to the recessed floor in a fast dash to the exit on the lounge's far side.

"Wait," Noi said. "I'm sensing Yargzi, slaves to an Etamite Coercer."

"I can't read them," Charronna said.

A faint hum intruded. Charronna cocked an ear. "What's that sound? The door's hot."

"Molecular transducer," Arn said. "We have seconds, no more."

Charronna grabbed Noi by the shoulders. "We've got to mind-blast them as soon as they break through. Will you help?"

A cold wave passed through Noi. The cosmos jettisoned the virtue of justice to ask him to violate his creed to honor all life. Distressing memories crept into his thoughts. He had violated it before, and innocents died, Neewa died. Young, natural-born, she was beautiful with copper-tone skin and sunset-orange eyes. Red hair glinted with the luster of mined metal, and she wore a scent, not a perfume, but an essential oil, patchouli. A death warrant, if executed for failure to serve, meant the loss of his family. Noi betrayed her leadership role in civil disobedience. Starry Empire justice had her executed.

The door vaporized. Yargzi slaves surged into the room. Charronna whirled to confront them. Mind blasts streamed through the continuum, fracturing it into varying, shifting densities. The psi-dampener's effect shriveled under Charronna's onslaught. Several Yargzi, their minds liquefied, collapsed. The Etamite Coercer drove more slaves into battle. Charronna unbound herself, a brilliant unraveling in the continuum, spewing nova ejecta until no enemies remained.

She dropped to her haunches—a drop of blood ran from each of her eyes—her mind crackled with effort, teetering on the edge of a short circuit. Noi's heart wavered. What worthwhile creed would let a friend stand alone? Charronna's spirit shattered from the onslaught of her resistance. The continuum, beset by dense spatial anomalies, shuffled into new forms. Another wave of presences built in the corridor.

"Noi, promise you'll help," Charronna said and crumpled to the floor in a fetal ball.

Noi positioned in front of the opening in a gesture of peace, body open, arms extended. His wife Anamoreena appeared, a living presence within Noi, yet standing next to him, her loving gaze pure and willing. He chanted, cultivating his mind into a calm state of focus.

"Will you honor your creed even if you must die for its truth?" his wife asked.

"Life is sacred. I took my creed back from the Empire. It is mine to keep."

Yargzi protected a pinkish Etamite, a giant slug sliding around a latticed structure atop a floating platform. They wedged into the opening. The worm wore a bracelet about its middle; it projected fields into the quantum universe. *Psi-shield*. Noi stood firm, shaping his defensive shields to envelop the invaders, holding them fast in a network of dense quantum energy. Forward motion slowed and froze. The psi-shield's energy exploded into the continuum, a heartless reaper thrashing away in a harvest of ordered things.

The psi-shield fed on Noi's defense, hungering for expanded presence, for domination. The Yargzi whimpered, unable to retreat from the Coercer's demands, yet unable to advance. Time added weight against his effort. He delved deeper into the Yargzi and experienced them in their unvarnished torment. Hardhearted and sentient, altered, mutilated by genetic engineers to mindlessly fight, but in places untouched they danced, they jumped, they sang, and they grieved over their fate. They were beautiful. He became the Yargzi. In an instant, his shields collapsed.

The Etamite and its slaves punched into the room.

A Yargzi raised an arm twinkling death. Arn yelled and leaped into the alien. Sy'tallian guards vaulted. They sunk talons into the Yargzi's protective jackets. Combatants collided with the Coercer platform, which tipped and clipped the floor. Reinforcements joined the fray, a dozen blue-haired aliens. Noi summoned a calm center to wrap them in motionlessness. Jettison the future. Jettison the past. Exist in the ephemeral present where stillness prevailed. In effort measured by millimeters, a Yargzi pointed a weaponized hand his way. Ferocious roars swept closer. The alien formed a killing thought.

Charronna stood, disoriented—an easy target. Noi spread his energy thin to keep everyone in a slow-motion crawl. Linearity, the advance of time, consumed his essence. Soon, nothing would be left. Anamoreena held his hand. Love poured from her every nuance. Strength and longing infused, refueling, more energy, more seconds elongated, but relativity's reaper would not be denied. Time ricocheted to normal speed. Lancing death streaked. Lithe Cheemin roared into the lounge, leaping into fearsome combat.

Scorched fur piled with bloodied Yargzi. The dead outnumbered the living. Smoke covered the hologram sky in a haze. A recognizable presence emerged, the Cheemin captain, who leaned close, and sniffed. "You'll live."

Further back, Charronna tossed out a well-rehearsed glare. "No thanks to you. Consider your Prada favor cashed."

"I won't kill innocents."

"The fate of Mestjet's kin and Arn's people depends upon what we do, not to mention our lives. Find your inner barbarian, or we're today's menu special."

Mestjet growled in affirmation. "I lost five of my kin. The situation is out of control."

Arn's bloodied talons dripped blame. Anamoreena, a twinkle of easy beauty, appeared next to Charronna, drawing Noi to confront his shame. *"Will you give up your code when necessary for the sake of others?"* Anamoreena asked in direct challenge. *"Will you let them die?"*

Noi contemplated what an answer might mean to his most cherished creed.

CHAPTER XXIII

Released to *Star Horizon*, Kor cocooned on the bridge, coffee in reach, eyes on the scanner tracking Noi and Charronna. He polished off a second cup. After his comrades started to flee through the station corridors, he put Sparrow in stasis since no place on the ship would be safer. The Polarian showed up with a concrete stare fit for an enemy. In the brief distraction, his crew mates disappeared from the tracker.

"Operation Alien Costume off the rails?" Raven said.

"Score for you. Anything useful to add?"

"I'm here to help," Raven said.

"Excellent. I need a wingman to rescue our comrades." Kor headed to the ship's lower deck toward the aft docking ports. The Polarian matched pace.

Near the exit ramp, Kor put on armor and moved around to acclimate to the fit. Yargzi assembled, wielding formidable high-tech pikes that discharged energy blasts from both ends. The Polarian donned chameleon armor auto-adjusting to match his pale olive skin. Kor gripped his disrupter, loosely aiming in Raven's direction. He did need help, even back-stabbing, self-serving, liar help. After a final check, he put on battle goggles. Scans showed a cohort of armed Yargzi taking up position outside the ship. Feet planted for quick movement, he handed over a disruptor to Raven before he second-guessed.

They rushed the hangar floor in diverging directions. Burnt orange energy balls shot between them. Kor plastered the Yargzi's dense formation, striking a turbo-laser until he left a smoking wreck. The Yargzi blanketed the hangar bay with weapons discharge. Kor somersaulted to an empty fighter alcove in the mezzanine. Smoky columns spread, precious camouflage to unleash hell. Alarms of light and sound pulsed and shrilled—the station cried out its distress. Raven howled. Broadcast signals lit up the lower display on his goggles. The message was simple. "We fight E'lani."

Kor jumped to the floor and channeled a shock wave of stamina into extra bursts of quick-speed, moving ahead of the Yargzi attack, taking out a row of turbo-lasers. Feet burned. Body temperature escalated. Pressure pushed at his organs, head, and flesh—warnings of overheated blood. Faster, harder, into pain, he must push into resistance to show proof of his manhood. Quick-speed adrenals tapped out. He willed himself to fight. But overexertion force-shifted him back into normal mode. One of the enemy's burnt orange shots struck his armor, then others, in multiple converging hits.

Raven sliced the enemy with laser swords of green. Blood splattered across the hangar. He shouted a warning. A Yargzi cocked an arm, a black detonator of some kind in his hand. The detonator discharged over Kor, blinding him in brilliance.

A concussion force swept him along, shoving him into a crunch of alien battle armor. Shiny, misty white beckoned through death's doorway; the temptation to surrender mounted, flute serenades played in trouble-free existence. He reached the threshold; the door diffused and the music faded. Color intruded, sharpened into the uniforms of enemy soldiers. Many were dead; for those dazed, Kor would be the hammer of doom. In the prone position, armed with an alien pike, he fired until he tagged the last survivors. *Made to kill*.

He let the pike drop, twitched at the clang to the floor, and crawled around the slaughter, disembodied—the horror too much to be believed. Small fires crackled. Exposed wires sparked. Noxious chemical clouds spread. He propped himself up using another pike as a staff, making his way to Raven. The Polarian held his scorched, bloody leg. His goggles lay tangled on his foot. Blame poured off the Polarian. Kor helped him up, and together, they hobbled to the ship. Crimson war paint anointed them. Inside *Star Horizon*, Kor guided Raven to the floor and then slid next to him, shaking.

"They identified us," Kor said.

"Then we've lost."

Later, Noi and Charronna showed up—Noi, half-dead, and Charronna the same with a strong dose of feral. Thank the Supreme, no medical emergencies. Behind them, Arn's unsheathed talons dripped thick, orange Yargzi blood. No explanation was required. Charronna marched his way, blasting fury into a flushed face. For a second, Kor braced for a swift kick, but she stayed with a righteous glower—a fierce and welcome sight.

"Problem?" Kor asked.

"How about the top ten?"

He winced. "The ones that can't wait."

"Noi took a mallet to the Dorram's skull. Yargzi rampaged through the station. Captain Mestjet lost crew saving us because your creed-bound friend couldn't be bothered to kick ass."

She paused to give Noi a piece of her judgment. "Arn says the Etamites will destroy Mestjet's Neretu Kin, which will cripple trade routes along this stretch of the Periphery. Our hosts want us to leave before we do any more damage. Is that enough? Because I've got a personal list going, clamoring for someone's attention."

Kor concentrated, exhorting his legs to support standing weight, but he remained a puddle. Something in his eyes, or face, or the renewed shaking, caused Charronna to soften, to see him. She reached out with a soft hand to his throbbing cheek.

"You're hurt."

"A flesh wound."

"Don't make light of it. Something else, what's wrong?"

"They saw us," Kor said. "They got off a message."

Charronna squeezed a bit harder. "Same here. Game over."

"Take Raven to the med room," Kor said. "Noi, please help Charronna and check on Sparrow. I put her in stasis for safekeeping."

"You also need help," Charronna said.

"I'm fine."

"You are not fine and—"

"I'm the Amun, right? Go, please, ready the ship."

"Amun or not, you're a mere mortal like the rest of us. How many times must I say that?" With a shake of her head, she helped Noi support Raven to a med bed.

Kor waved Arn over. The Sy'tallian's skin blushed deep green, and his widened eyes strained to capture every detail. Kor wasn't a telepath, but their species shared enough common ground for him to read the signs with some confidence: Arn was under mayday-alert stress.

"I'm sorry," Kor said.

Arn clicked his talons together. "Guests should not be greeted with interrogations and guns. None of this is right for anyone, including Yargzi. We struggle in a place of hard air. Difficult to breathe, yet we must."

Blood for blood; Blessed are the Peacemakers. . . The Code and the Blood King fused in his mind to open the way into uncharted dimensions of heart-space beyond Jeth's muttered poison.

"I surrender to you. If possible, I would leave it to my comrades to choose their fate."

"Your death would be a beginning, not an ending. A better way to help takes you to Vio. Face the Permanent Council. Show them your truth and put the Long War to rest. Fail, and many will come to punish us, to act on old complaints."

Kor grasped Arn's free hand, and the Sy'tallian pulled him to standing. Was he sick with hubris to choose for the entire race? Yet the choice was clear. "Consider it done, friend."

"Whatever others may see, you are what we need, human friend. We have been waiting for your return to restore our name throughout the Commonweal. We have survived, but we do not wish to be cursed forever."

After final goodbyes, Kor trudged to the briefing room. He collapsed in a chair, knees bucking from quick-speed depleted heaviness. Charronna's presence sharpened from behind.

"This is a suicide mission for idiots." Her voice quavered as she spoke.

Watery pools spilled into gray. He tightened his eyes, unwilling to let go, unwilling to see the corpse of Jude who haunted his mindscape as a reminder of his weakness. "I won't let our new friends die because of us."

"You can't save your lost partner-to-be. Don't kill the rest of us because you can't accept what happened."

"Destiny awaits."

"That's what I'm afraid of." Charronna wanted to say more but merely rubbed his shoulders. She continued to minister in gentle strokes as Noi edged *Star Horizon* out of the station. The Dorram vessel shadowed, and the Cheemin did the same to Men'op's ship while sending coded instructions to the nav-AI.

"Once you move beyond the Periphery," warned Mestjet, "the danger increases in the uncharted routes. Raiders lurk for easy marks. Marauders powerful enough to take on cruiser-class warships attack anything of value. Assuming you prevail, the route stops well short of Vio. Monitor beacons, military installations, and Commonweal patrols, both official and trade guild, keep a tight watch. You won't go far without being challenged. Pray to whatever relics you venerate that whoever confronts you isn't from one of the many races united on killing E'lani. Happy Hunting."

Kor squeezed his charm. He bypassed the AI to feed Mestjet's list of jumps one by one into the helm. Charronna sat next to him quietly, desperate to return home, yet offering no resistance. The Red Witch, worthy of respect, scrambled his mind, throwing in doubt his condemnation of her, though it be soaked in the blood of undeniable truth.

Data feeds from the station reported fighting between Sy'tallians and Yargzi for control of Eda; local reinforcements streamed up from the planet in frantic haste. Kor took Charronna's hand, finding relief against an awful realization. The Long War was already renewed.

CHAPTER XXIV

Kor wasn't leading an army into battle, but he bore the same responsibility and it pressed into his courage. Chasing after herohood had exposed others to danger on a path mined with bad options. Faith, a pure impulse without self-deceptive camouflage, guided him to the promised land of hopeful outcomes.

After getting medical treatment, he went on a walkabout in the blue-hued corridors. The healing boost accelerated his naturally fast physical recovery. His mind, however, needed space to process the magnitude of the escalating stakes in combination with the degrading of his ability to exert control.

Charronna sauntered by, whistling, teasing with seen-it-all-but-loving-it incisive green eyes. Kor increased the pace and worked himself into a frenzy.

"Proximity alert," the AI said.

"Identify."

"A profile matching the Dorram vessel from Station Eda registers on long-range scan."

Kor raced to the command deck; Raven arrived close behind. Noi and Charronna met them as they surveyed the Dorram ship on the viewer. No longer hiding, the vessel flaunted its presence.

"They don't have the firepower to attack," Charronna said.

"But they are confident for a reason," Kor said.

"I told you this was too easy," Raven said.

Kor took a deep breath. "Then I don't need to hear it again."

"The Dorram keeps its distance," Noi said.

"It acts like a spotter," Raven said. "Hollows are transport-class, defensive hull and shields, light offensive firepower; they are built for running away."

"Provoke it," Kor said. "A warning shot to force their hand."

"Would sticking out my tongue help?" Charronna asked.

"Depends on what's close by." Kor gave Charronna the once-over the way she often did with him.

"Alert," the AI said. "Jump aperture forming fifty kilometers aft one-degree elliptic-south."

"We're about to be space-jacked." Charronna slapped Kor on the back. "Do something, wannabe hero."

Kor's mind stuck on the idea that it would be a great time for Charronna to stick out her tongue. Valiantly, he shook the image off. Fifteen minutes to the next jump. Enough time for licks around the ear, presses of the lips . . . Charronna thumped him on the head. "Bring it down, big boy."

A massive point-ship emerged from the aperture. The warship, long and sleek, came equipped with dozens of missile launchers, laser cannons, a pair of ion cannons, and other hardware the AI worked to decipher. The warship's shadow covered *Star Horizon*.

"Condition Black," Kor said.

"Condition panic," Charronna corrected.

An alien, an Asag, appeared on the view screen, imposing and muscular. Drool rolled off its fangs and put a sheen on its pointed purple-red chin. Elliptical pupils bifurcated lidless madder eyes boasted bravado. Garish lights revealed a network of scars. Leathery, dark-hued skin had the aura of a seasoned veteran. The scourge of the E'lani spread mighty wings in a flex of ripped muscle. The alien grinned devil-like. The ship's video remained off.

"Fa'Nyx," he announced. "Who do I have the pleasure of greeting?"

"Grand prize for ugly," Charronna muttered under her breath.

"Come now," Fa'Nyx said. "Don't be shy. Come to my ship. Allow me to give you a proper welcome to the Commonweal." Lips creased in a predatory smile.

"We're heading to Vio for a goodwill visit," Charronna said. "We'll take a rain check."

"Is that a *no*? But I insist. We must endeavor to preserve civilized manners."

Charronna and Fa'Nyx traded more pleasantries. Mockery dripped from his conniving lips. The middle of the marauder-class ship opened to reveal a hangar bay large enough to swallow *Star Horizon* whole. Kor cut the audio.

"Noi, give Charronna the access codes for the helm," Kor said.

"About time you started trusting me."

Kor eyed Sparrow. "Keep an eye on our red-headed princess."

"Don't sugarcoat me," Charronna quipped.

Sparrow stood straight and saluted. "Yes, sir!"

Kor went over to the girl, kneeling face to face. "They'll have to come through me to get to you. Okay?"

Sparrow beamed.

"Love your smile."

Sparrow rewarded him with a sloppy hug and a secret whisper. "Don't worry about me. Charronna's turning into a door-catcher."

Kor got up and squeezed Charronna's hand. "Keep our friend distracted. Time for Operation Trojan Horse."

"Have any of your operations actually worked?"

"I'll get back to you." He hurried out with Noi and Raven.

"Sorry for the interruption," Charronna said to the Asag.

She and Fa'Nyx continued their charming back and forth. Kor and his team raced to the armory on the lower deck. In the storage magazine, a double row of twelve warheads glistened in sheaths of metallic wonder. The seconds dropped. He kissed his choice, a shiny thirty-inch cone with a dimple near the base—a solid fifty pounds. *Save us.* "AI, recalibrate a shuttle to emit fake life signs."

Kor sent Noi to the stasis chamber. Raven, he kept in plain sight. He placed the missile inside the shuttle and headed back to the bridge.

"We are eager to greet you in person," Fa'Nyx said.

"We won't be taken captive," Kor said. "Auto-destruct sequence activated."

Fa'Nyx's pupils expanded, then narrowed into sharp, thin lines. "Polite manners must be respected."

The incoming video feed went blind. Kor rushed everyone to the stasis chamber. Phase one of the plan worked as the Asag released *Star Horizon* into open space. Phase two required them to take the offered bait.

"We know who you are." Fa'Nyx's dreadful voice echoed throughout the ship. "No worries. I won't waste a single drop of your blood."

"Oh yeah?" Charronna said under her breath. "Our goodwill mission is about to blow your brains into the next dimension."

Kor grinned. He was starting to admire the murdering monster of his people. The General would not approve.

"Attendants prep the Squeeze Vats." The Asag laughed, a rough noise nothing less than wicked. "Your species brings us such joy. You will learn some sins are never forgiven."

Flat on her regular stasis bed, Charronna tapped into her personal administrator (PA), bringing up an image of a man and woman, each about thirty years old. Heavy blue eye shadow intensified the man's gentle bright blues; fierce red hair framed the woman's stunning green eyes. She wore a chartreuse and black steel-boned corset with a satin skirt and long train. He was no less fashionable with a matching vest, brushed leather pants, and leather garters above the elbows. They exuded the determination and confidence of the upper class—Charronna's parents.

"Fifteen seconds," Kor said.

A tear streamed down Charronna's cheek. "Consequences be damned, I will see you again."

"Ten."

Charronna's mouth trembled—a plea for time none of them had.

"We can't die, Kor."

"This plan will work."

"See you on the flip side."

One last message from Fa'Nyx hissed over the comm. "Don't waste a single drop. I want them alive *and* unharmed."

The stasis chambers shut with the awful finality of coffin lids. A final fleeting prayer of deliverance flickered in Kor's dulling consciousness.

***

The stasis bed lip popped open. Kor had expected no more than a few minutes one way or the other, but the ship's clock had advanced ten hours. Emergency lighting cast a dim pallor. Without comment, he and his shipmates filed onto the bridge. The command displays spewed damage assessments in a holographic extravaganza. The ship drifted. Electronic burn mixed with sickly sweet metallic odors.

"Can we go home now?" Charronna stuttered out through a fit of coughing. "That is if we can go anywhere."

"Incoming communication," the AI said.

"Put it through," Kor said.

A scratchy, flickering visual of Mestjet appeared on the viewer alongside the remains of the Asag vessel, split in half with pockets of fire bursting on the severed hulks. "Happy to see you alive. You've done the Commonweal, and traders like me, a service. Fa'Nyx ranked high on the marauder list."

"I'm surprised his ship wasn't vaporized."

"Asags build warcraft for the ages. Lucky for us, because otherwise, we would be chasing fleet-footed shades across the fields of the dead. The Uppermost, the Dorram captain, has agreed to escort you the rest of the way, which means you jump to a safer charted route."

"You trust this Uppermost?" Kor asked.

Mestjet fingered her studded chain. "No. But odds are she'll behave. Working with a marauder is an ass-frying violation of the Trading Guild."

"Blackmail."

"Mutual backscratching."

Kor let loose with a spasm of coughs. "We need repairs to go on."

"You need a lot of repairs requiring a lot of credits. Do any of you know how to gamble? What I mean is, are any of you skilled cheaters?" A sly grin creased Mestjet's cheek.

Charronna apprised Noi. "If I give our ghost a boost, even a psi-shield won't stop him."

"Dust off your Knights of the Half-Moon garb and come over. We're going on a detour to Lucky Chances, a favorite hangout of mine that's not been so lucky."

"Aye, and thanks."

Vio, here we come.

CHAPTER XXV

Lucky Chances fulfilled its promise, and a mobile repair bay did the rest. The diversion provided a few days of needed respite. True, mixing among aliens   had an element of danger, but no one was on alert for humans. Charronna took it as a subterfuge game and as a Smiling Court survivor, she was good at such games.

Charronna sipped coffee, savoring a bit of happiness on the way to Vio. To avoid attracting too much attention, Team Knights of the Half-Moon made sure to spread the wealth. The storage hold was full. Engines were fully energized. A shopping trip for bipedal clothes boosted her spirits to no end. The one thing spoiling the good mood was that the ship headed further from home.

Some or all of us die in a heart of terror. That could mean a number of things: a citadel of doom, an emotional state, a psychopath's layer, a daredevil ride at an unsafe amusement park—endless permutations. The coffee provided fuel to expand the list.

Noi took control of the navigation at the bridge's quarter-moon console to manually set the coordinates for the last jump to the Commonweal capital. The Starfall Probability from the Psian's Oracular communion repeated in wasted warnings. The countdown reached ten. The AI intoned: "Jump commencing." For a passing split of time, mind and body separated in a changing vortex of color, and deep tones bathed the senses in harmonic resonance. Normal space snapped back to the clamor of incoming hails. The Dorram escort was gone. Red-tagged blips packed the tactical display. An orbital fortress scaled to an armored moon provided redundant backup.

"Now that's a respectful welcoming committee," Kor said. "Wait for a visual."

"I'm not the amateur here," Charronna quipped.

"The moment bursts with potentiality," Noi said.

Raven grimaced. "We're dead. It's a matter of timing."

"We're committed," Kor said. "We must secure the repeal of the Extermination Edict and gain amnesty for Arn, Mestjet, and their people against retaliation for sparing our lives."

"King's Mercy," Charronna said, "do you ever think small?"

"Plenty of men have taken that job." Kor curled his lip.

Charronna's eyes flashed with grudging respect. "No argument."

When in the presence of greater powers, one waited to be acknowledged. Charronna projected confidence, but her bowels felt like puree, and everything in between had gone to gas.

Celadon eyes enmeshed within an extended mass of skull bone evocative of a ceremonial headdress filled the viewscreen. A loose-fitting uniform in dark burgundy with gold trim emphasized the male's milky complexion. Someone worth talking to. A name tingled on the edge of her tongue—Tellerian. If the universe had a shred of balance, the Tellerians would emit a pleasant aroma or some other incidental charm. With haughty fanfare, Fleet Commodore AnaGorias of the *Flagship Protector* declared his auspicious presence. Grand, self-regarding, irreproachable, a person who counted and who knew it.

Charronna started with introductions. The routine settled haywire nerves. Polite yet firm, the Tellerian requested a visual. Kor waved a finger in a rapid gesture for *no*. Charronna resisted the urge to roll her eyes. Did her hunky shipmate think she carried a death wish? Segmented quivers ran along the Tellerian's broad cheeks. Anger? Annoyance? Charronna wasn't sure.

"Our customs forbid visual contact before a face-to-face encounter."

"A strange custom."

Just wait and see.

Aloof to begin with, the temperature of AnaGorias's voice went to icy melt. "Procedure must be followed. You may not pass without visual confirmation."

"We dispatched the Asag marauder, Fa'Nyx. I hear he wreaked havoc in the shipping lanes. Doesn't that earn us goodwill?"

"Prepare to receive orbital data. Do not deviate from your assigned vector or speed. Consider your goodwill used." The Tellerian's lips creased, a predator showing off fangs. "Welcome to Vio."

With that, the transmission ended.

"You did well," Noi said. "One way or another, a new age for humanity begins on this world, this hour, in the light of a foreign sun."

Kor's focused grays brightened as though welcoming in the dawn, a beautiful, intense, unnerving sight. A rough rider who needed a bit of taming, and she had the skills to take the edges off.

Fantasies rolled, creative and numerous and full of delight, to break in the delicious young man.

"Wake up, dreamy eyes," Kor said, thawing yet another layer in Charronna's heart as he stood, heroic, strong, vulnerable and childlike. No woman with a beating heart could resist a man like that—not hers at any rate.

"I'll lead the landing party," Kor pronounced. He confronted with his stern, don't-bother-to-argue-I'm-going stare, an uncompromising glare Charronna found difficult to overcome.

"What do you want from this?" Charronna asked.

"Peace between the Commonweal and the three civilizations."

"Liar."

Kor's intense gaze intensified. "I want to choose how I love, how I live. Rock to *Talking Heads* and the *B-52s*. Play my flute, with an audience if I want. The liberation of my sister and the breeders. Freedom from the fear of being whatever type of human we are."

"How terribly noble."

"What do you want?"

"As if you didn't know."

"You've had plenty of sex."

"With the man I love and who loves me. I want to see my parents. I want a real family."

"Ah, you're a romantic."

"Don't tell anyone. I've got a reputation to protect."

"Charronna?"

"I'm waiting."

"I want my father to be proud of me."

"You've dispatched bloodcurdling aliens and dart-shooting plants. Hell, you've stolen a war-star's drop ship. What's not to like?"

Kor averted his gaze.

"I mean it, Kor. Irritating though you can be, you impress me. But you're not invincible, and by the way, you sometimes make the worst decisions. I'm sensing something else though. You're hiding deeper emotions. There's a numb place inside of you, clinging to despair, and it devastates you when you dare to visit."

Kor threw up his arms and paced around the bridge in a wild animal stalk, grunting, grimacing, sounds of a bottled beast trying to find his voice. "Jude," he yelled. "I will never be okay until he forgives me."

"Jude is dead." Noi took a hesitant step toward Kor but was waved off.

"Dex isn't." Kor's voice escalated. "If he forgives me, so does Jude."

"You can tell the truth," Charronna said. "Wonderful. You understand you must forgive yourself."

"Easy to say to someone else. If Dex forgives me, I have permission."

Charronna poured healing energy Kor's way, a flow from a wellspring of heart-infused warmth she never knew existed. Kor's life stripped him raw; no longer confined to his Militant heritage, his exposed humanity needed a salve. She was no different. Did she want to go back to a life of wretched deeds, callous executions, back-stabbing bureaucrats, shopping, luxury, and unlimited trips to Sweet Crave? Credits to overflow a miser's keep would never fill the holes in her heart. For the first time since the thought police tore her away from her mother's arms, she liked who she was.

Sanity returned to Kor's fierce grays. He mouthed a "thank you" and refocused on the warship-choked system. "Raven, I need to know everything that might improve our chances."

"Won't be enough." In a huff, the Polarian followed Kor off the bridge.

Deflated at being left out, Sparrow wandered out.

Charronna decided to join the exodus when Noi brushed her mind. *"Stay."*

She tensed up. Whatever Noi wanted to say, she wasn't going to like it.

"On Station Eda, I also experienced a foreshadowing. One or more of us dies here."

"Do you want me to go to the planet and offer myself up?" Charronna motioned with her arm. "Over here, homicidal aliens, one sacrificial fatback ready to die for the cause."

"You, Sparrow, and I will go."

"What about Raven? I mean if anyone should greet the homicidal aliens. . ."

"He plans to sneak onboard the shuttle."

"You are the skillful one. I don't get anything out of him." Not that she tried for a second encounter with Raven's hideous mind.

"If Kor dies on Vio, the sum of his choices shall manifest as Khonsu. Everyone dies, including those back home."

"You heard him. He's got a dead almost-lover, a father, a sister, and whole worlds to save, and everyone thinks I'm the drama queen. He will never agree to stay behind."

Noi communicated his plan into Charronna's mind.

"He will never, ever, forgive you."

***

Charronna took the command seat onboard the shuttle. The AI piloted the vessel into jaw-dropping open space. In size, the *Protector* outclassed the mighty war-star. Despite believing the universe cared nothing for her survival, she took a canyon-crossing leap of faith that everything would work out. The flagship bristled with weapons beyond human technology. But she would rather face the overdone warship than Kor's anger when he woke up from Noi's telepathic slumber to discover he'd been left behind. Thank the stars, Noi didn't ask for help. She and Sparrow crowded next to Noi near the forward window.

"Five super decks," Charronna said. "One hundred-plus miles long. We're roadkill."

"They must have mind-blowing enemies," Sparrow said in a small, awed voice. "Hey, how come Kor stayed on the ship? He lives for this kind of stuff."

"Someone had to guard *Star Horizon*," Charronna replied in a smoothly delivered lie.

She squeezed Noi's shoulder. The feel of flesh was like a weight to her flighty fear. Her other hand found Sparrow, pulling her close. She was no coward, but some things, like the flagship, overloaded the circuits. Maybe this was cosmic justice for living a life that cost so many of theirs. Maybe this was her chance to make amends, to add halos to the universe's tracking list.

"Shouldn't someone be praying?" Charronna asked.

"Find the space between your heartbeats," Noi said. "Focus where inhales and exhales transition one from the other."

"Tough going there. Fairy dust? Mumbo-jumbo abracadabra?"

"Find the silence between your thoughts."

Charronna slapped Noi lightly across the back of his head. "I need an assist right now, thank you very much."

Sparrow prayed in a quiet, rhythmic voice. The AI plotted the tiny craft's course through the *Protector's* saturating glare. Charronna listened to Sparrow's strange words. *Deliver us from evil? Deliver us from madness.* Four short-range, multi-crew fighters approached in tight formation, dual fusion engines, wide-bodied, armed to show off, more overkill. The fighters escorted their shuttle to the gray-violet world full of aliens who would kill her before the first "Hello." Charronna didn't believe in Sparrow's god. She wasn't sure she believed in any god. But somewhere along the way, her pounding heart quieted.

Space transfigured into the shape of a planet engulfing the view screen at a dizzying speed. The shuttle changed too, going from star-traveler to cloud-splitter over a supersized continent packed with jungles of coral reds and pinks punctuated with electric green and blue, broken up by an inland silver sea. Prayerful words trailed off. Raven emerged from a storage locker. No one bothered to feign surprise. The shuttle landed on a platform rising above the jungle. Noi put a hand on Charronna's back. The warmth of the contact penetrated her marrow—on par with a top-of-the-line lab spawn.

Lucky Chances loot got them sensor-blocking hooded robes embedded with tech, flexible masks, and chain-link necklaces with good luck tokens. Charronna fingered hers, a thin piece of crystalline hardware that hinted at technological wizardry.

"Sacred Unity, let us know the intersection of our separate truths," Noi whispered.

"Not to quibble, but isn't that a prayer?"

"Of a sort. I speak to the faces of divinity shared within us."

An alien with a pronounced triangular face and two sets of eyes stepped off a hovering transport, a flatbed barge with no seating; the locals were not rolling out a golden carpet. Outward from a protruding nose, a three-pronged bone formation fanned over the alien's reptilian head with the sharp points curled back.

The creature wore a white vest with a prominent red circle, but the exposed hide put on a show, shifting through the primary colors before settling into cool cyan.

"Door-catcher or door-slammer?" Charronna squeezed Sparrow's arm.

"Not sure."

Charronna took the lead down the craft's ramp. Their inconsequential shuttle comprised the visible ships on the elevated landing platform. The horned, scaled cyan creature examined her with four hyper-focused eyes, one of which probably had X-ray vision. Disguised humans played dress-up with the galactic overlords.

"I am Marpun Ven Fet of the Six Hundred Terahertz, First Liaison of External Affairs." The alien spoke in Galactic Standard. "You may address me as Ven."

Charronna clasped her gloved hands and gave a short bow. "I am Charronna Ny'. With me are Noi, Raven, and Sparrow," pointing to each one.

"The choice of raiment pleases us, and you speak the tongue well," Ven said.

"Thank you and—"

"We do not have time for the ritual exchanging of compliments and pleasantries. This first contact incites discomfort."

The hover barge took them to the platform's edge where the company descended by lift to the forest floor. A silvery path wound through incandescent green vines tethered vermilion, blue, and pink globes to the ground. Small insects with pixie wings and long, pointed snouts darted. A brief exhale of gas occurred each time the insects inserted their snouts into the globes, producing a faint, sugary perfume. Sparrow giggled. To be a child again, to experience life without the shackles of responsibility and duty—who cared that they walked when there must be more efficient means available? Wonder surrounded.

They watch us. They judge us.

The Commonweal aliens had carved their capital from a massive plateau upwelling high into the sky, an abode of earthbound gods. Hundreds of towers with an ethereal pinkish aura sprouted atop the highland's flat terrain. On impish impulse, Charronna eavesdropped on Sparrow's outer consciousness to witness the sights through less jaded eyes. The young princess imagined they visited Fairyland. How quaint! Sparrow stretched her arms and relaxed into an infectious smile. Charronna matched the girl's beam.

"Second Prime," Ven said, "the summer capital. My people call her Pink Dream. I have never sensed the range of color your presence brings."

"I promise we won't be boring," Charronna said. She split her attention between Sparrow and Ven. One childish outburst could mean a quick execution.

The walkway's upward slope took them to a stone stair framed by sculpted balusters. At the top of a thousand steps, at the base of the plateau, a bank of cubicles had been carved into the rock. Each of them had a white glowing ring.

"Transmat points," explained Ven. "They have been programmed to take you near our place of parliamentary gathering."

With a shrug, Charronna proceeded as Ven directed. In a flash, she and her companions stepped off into an immense head-spinning passageway. A different Nevran, greenish-brown and with straight horns, had a gun-toting escort of four tall, yellow-bronze aliens—*Tols*. Lanky guards, almost flimsy, but the Eos Archive data rolling through her brain warned otherwise.

"I'm Lom of the Five Hundred Fifty Terahertz, Chair of the Commonweal. I bid you welcome."

Charronna bowed, eyes to the floor. The Commonweal leader guided them before a massive, paneled doorway with square panels in hues of green evolving in places to blues and yellows. Though the passageway had been cleared of others, the Tols stayed in constant motion. Charronna risked a telepath scan, but a dampening field thwarted her effort.

These were advanced beings. Surely, they had advanced morals yet somehow a mere hooded robe stood between her and a bloodthirsty mob. Tols orbited in boundary-violating closeness. None of them drew weapons. But they were military of some sort, and they moved with urgent purpose. *Who knows? Who doesn't?* Charronna's thoughts flash-froze. *Some know. Some don't.*

The Chair's hide shifted in color to beige, tan, and then darker browns. With a sweep of his reptilian arms, the enormous doors parted. "The assembled Vinculum welcomes you, strangers from afar."

The Tols herded them into the cavernous hall. The hubbub of voices, multiple languages, fought to be heard in a sea of loud energy, and it closed in with air-sucking force. Sparrow gaped at a prominent ring structure that hovered over and encircled a raised platform in the chamber's center. Among the throng, towering trees swayed, the source of whistling baritones—*Zev*. They were spectacular, and unexpected. Sparrow's essence twinkled and sang, and briefly, like the effervescence from a sparkling drink, invited Charronna to do the same.

She left Sparrow to her unspoiled childish wonder, walking into the unhinged jaws of death like she owned the place. The resonating tap of her leather-sole Prada stiletto heels reassured her that she mattered. A rolling hush moved through the Assemblers.

"The high council, I take it," Charronna said, arching her neck to cross-examine the aliens peering from the ring above.

"Vanity," Raven said.

Another round of steps encircled a raised dais—up they went. Waves of energy spanning the spectrum poured out from the Vinculum's invitees—dangerous, welcoming, calculating, assessing, strong enough to trigger ebbs and flows of nausea.

"I hereby suspend the opening rituals," the Chair said.

The Chair delivered a short speech to welcome the newcomers. The onlookers responded with polite motions, sounds, scents, colors, and other indications. Applause? When Qa, drifting in ornate mobile aquarium tanks, rolled their cephalopod eyes, was that interest, threat, or anxiety? The Dorrams stayed locked in a stasis field set to *lived*.

"Noi," Charronna said, "I'm sorry I ever thought of you as anything less than human; the same goes for Kor and the others back home."

"I once experienced you as the Red Witch," Noi said.

She motioned for a group hug—strange optics, but as compelling as a prayer between enemies. The dais's edge beckoned. Skin pricked. A room filled with monsters. Colors spun. Tacky, sticky terror clotted every thought. Giant spiders. Giant bugs. Night creatures. Things that chase you. Things that eat you. Her telepathic trainers had made frequent introductions. Here they were again, ready to devour. She fingered her crystalline talisman the way Kor did with his stone charm; how it worked, she had no idea, but the terror receded.

"*You are not alone,*" Noi said, sending a wave of reassurance.

A "thank you" floated into space. The continuum heated with the energy of many fates committed. Who was she kidding? The continuum resembled a class-one star about to go supernova.

"We have come far to address this auspicious assembly," Charronna said. "Our people want to usher in a golden age of peace and trade between our civilizations."

Five measured heartbeats thumped, the drums of war against her soul. Gingerly, she pulled back her hood while removing the mask. The others did likewise. "We come in peace," she said, her voice ringing with each syllable.

Quiescence. Abrupt flatness. Recoil and commotion. The shifts in energy occurred at a rapid pace building to shockwaves throughout the assembled Vinculum until the dams burst into screams, hisses, shrill cries, shouts, squeals, screeches, squalls, hoots, and menacing clicks, a deafening crescendo of astonishment, disbelief, threat, and ill-will. Charronna concentrated on feet to stone. She pulled Sparrow close. Noi and Raven closed ranks-- the light press of their bodies a heroic cavalry.

"Holy Covenant, they live!" many Nuxinni wailed.

"Two-legged killers," seething Z'yax hissed.

The Qa thrashed in their watery globular habitations.

"They came from Sy'tall," a host of Dorrams chirped.

Tols formed a shoulder-to-shoulder barrier around the podium. A Z'yax struck a guard with a barbed appendage. Blood splattered as his severed arm smacked the stone.

"That's us in a few seconds," Raven said.

"Say something useful or shut up," Charronna said. *One or more of us die. Probabilities be damned, Kor should be here. He deserves to face a crazed alien mob more than any of us.*

In the surge of aliens, mouths moved, and limbs swayed. Reality devolved into the surreal. Arms grabbed hold, shoving her into a cube of shimmering wet.

"Take them to the evaluation rooms," a voice said.

A thought unbidden . . . *alien shudder room.* Then nothing.

CHAPTER XXVI

Numbers—security access codes—chased Kor through a labyrinth of stairs. He sprinted, finding new ground, but no end to the maze. Exhausted, unsure where to go next, the numbers hunted him down, swirled with increasing velocity, and exploded in a photon burst.

Kor snapped upright from his bunk, smashing his head on a coffin ceiling. *Star Horizon* came with one cabin, nine rooms, and ten pods for the maintenance and noncommissioned crew. The confined space became a point of pride where the pursuit of pride had otherwise gone unfulfilled.

He wandered through the blue corridors. *Damn it, Noi, consider your neck wrung when I see you again.* Never trust a ghost. How many times must he learn that lesson? The aliens blanketed *Star Horizon* with scans. An interdiction field kept the ship on a tight leash. The sensors were blind. The locals didn't respond to his hails. He had no idea what was going on with his shipmates.

In the kitchen, coffee in hand, he hugged himself. In his entire life, he had never been so alone. The dream of numbers had deposited the library of ship's codes firmly into his memory banks, but the dream repeated every sleep cycle; Noi forgot to turn off his trigger.

To maintain sanity, he fell back to an improvised duty roster. Sleep cycles, workouts, mealtimes, mediations, therapy sessions with the AI, futile communication attempts with Vio's Defense Command (DC), and brainstorming sessions were scheduled throughout the waking hours. The periods added up, a sedating blend of sameness. More dreams, more nightmares, check that box on the daily ship-in-captivity schedule and start over in a relentless push for a stable mind.

It was day sixty since their arrival. Sooner or later, the ship's systems and equipment would fail; repairs would be inadequate; software would become less resilient; errors would creep into algorithms and analytics. Lucky Chances loot resupplied *Star Horizon*, but Mestjet warned against winning too much.

He girded himself for another wake cycle, rubbing his forehead from his requisite waking-up head bump, feeling the "All Men Are Created Equal" brand. The Supreme wasn't interested in "equal." The universe did not welcome everyone the same.

A persistent beep punctuated by a repeating mechanical voice. "You have an incoming message, priority urgent. Do you accept or decline?" The notification looped. Another time, it might have annoyed him, but the prospect of talking to someone electrified his senses.

He powered up a display built into the wall, taking pleasure in the tactile touch of the manual interface. A Vio feed scrolled across a ceiling monitor below a visual of a dour Nevran with a grayish-green hide and drooping eyes. The alien had to be a bureaucrat.

"You are to desist," the Nevran said, "from your repeated requests for communications."

"I respectfully ask to speak with my crewmates," Kor said.

"Harmony must be preserved."

"Are you implying we're disruptive?"

"We remain in our period of evaluation."

"Which means?"

"The Permanent Council conceives the possibilities."

"What might those be?"

"Not my station to say."

"We came in peace."

"The state of war between the Commonweal and the E'lani Empire continues."

"We are not E'lani."

"Blood matters here."

"Glad to hear it," he said. "You'll answer for any harm to my crew. Not the Commonweal. Not Fleet Commodore AnaGorias. You."

The Nevran dipped his horns. "I will pass along your request."

It's a start.

He waved off the open link. Unworkable plans for rescue and escape clogged mental arteries. Any one of the hundreds of blips brandished enough firepower to blow him up without breaking a sweat. Kor tapped into Defense Command's data feeds, churning his mind for heroic deeds, getting nowhere, and he had a daily sanity schedule to maintain. Do basic hygiene; drink a cup of coffee; walk the ship; listen to a song; refill the mug; hum like a madman and do a Mad Hatter dance; go to the bridge; check the ship's status; eat; work out; return to the bridge; more coffee. Heroic deeds.

Four armadas appeared beyond the limits of Vio's protective interdiction buoy network. Thousands of warships didn't show up to play nice. He and his crewmates were caught in a game without a playbook. Ensconced on the bridge, he finished off the rich, floral brew in a single gulp. The Commonweal smothered the ship's external sensors; the feed could be false.

"AI, assuming the DC data is reliable, how long before the fleets reach Vio?"

"Twenty-three hours, fourteen minutes, and twelve seconds."

"Deviate from the plotted track."

"This unit's navigational cameras, dishes, and detectors are blind," the AI said. "Risk factors for deviation are unknowable and therefore high if the course deviates from the plotted vector."

"Sounds like romance. Do it. Take it slow. Increase course divergence until we get a call."

Kor changed into his favorite bodysuit, gray with blue trim, highly elastic, with built-in sensors and deflectors, superb ventilation, and, most importantly, it breathed confidence into his skin. He headed back to the bridge, pretending he was on his way to confront the General. AnaGorias dominated the holographic viewer, as cold and distant as an airless moon.

"You violate our agreements and protocols," AnaGorias said.

"I haven't agreed to anything."

"Return to your assigned orbit parameters or our accommodation ends."

"I want to see my crewmates."

AnaGorias remained as impassive as ever, although a change for the worse might prove helpful. Sometimes the best tonic for a stuck relationship was a dose of friction.

"Harmony must be maintained. Return to your flight path or be destroyed."

Kor stared at a blank screen.

"Defense Command transmits a countdown sequence," the AI reported.

How many times had he stood before his father, the angry god, announcing punishment for his son's latest sin? Halfway across the galaxy, and still, the spirit of his father confounded. The countdown sequence reached ten. Nine, eight, seven . . . There would be other days to die.

"AI, cede to DC's order."

He had gotten the Commodore's attention—another small victory. A buzz in his head expanded, fueled by coffee, increasing frustration, or perhaps by the entity inside his head. One thing was for sure—he needed the equivalent of a win-the-Valor-match score. Attempts at meditation put his mind in overdrive. Scenarios tangled with probable defeat.

Kor paced the corridors. The ship, a holding cell in orbit, shrank with every inspection—room for twenty, yet somehow cramped for one. The AI, both male and female profiles, provided some company. One-way conversations with Jude created space for forgiveness. Replays of *Lord of the Rings, Star Wars,* and *The Wizard of Oz*, where the heroes always won, tallied higher. He danced like a crazy man to "All That Jazz," "Is That You Mo-Dean?," and "And She Was."

A one-station gym beckoned. After a few warm-ups, Kor set the bar equipped with gravity controls at two hundred and fifty pounds. "AI, I need a song. Play me 'Fire.'"

"Again?" The AI's female persona heaved a sigh. "This unit has a vast library of Earth and Starry Empire music."

"Just do it." Kor mouthed the words to tribal beats. By the tenth rep, his biceps burned. Arching his back in a cheat, he kept going. Sweat stung his eyes. The muscles screamed for relief. On the fifteenth rep, he bellowed, expelling breath with force to provide momentum for one more rep. *Gimme that burn.* The music merged with his frustration at his impotence against the Commonweal's might; he ripped out two more.

The Commonweal had swatted him to the ground.

Another rep . . . he needed . . . just . . . one . . . more. Inch by inch, he willed the bar upward until he pushed past the peak and pulled the weight in, dripping wet.

The bar floated before him in a challenge. He had won, but what about the next round? Who was the real man? Time for something stupid. Time to let his actions burn.

Kor sprinted to the briefing room. A holographic representation of proximate space appeared over the table packed with the icons of massive fleets. *Hammers of God.* Space had never seemed less infinite. The line of approaching ships, grouped into multiple task forces, stretched for millions of miles. The outer flanks, stronger than the center, advanced in an envelopment maneuver against the home force. A Commonweal civil war? Neither side rushed to battle. They positioned. What would be the trigger? When? Once the ships were in place, he might have days, hours, or minutes.

"This is either a rescue party or a hang-'em-high armada," Kor said to the AI. "Since DC permits us to track them, I'm guessing the latter."

"Conclusion is reasonable."

The huge orbiting fortress and AnaGorias's mammoth flagship anchored the defender's center. The newcomers outnumbered the defenders, but a jump gate near the planet allowed friendly reinforcements to bypass the fortress's interdiction field. Vio's fleet reorganized as new ships joined. Heaven was about to go to war.

Commander AnaGorias, the Chair, a nameless Nevran bureaucrat, or whoever, someone was going to listen. At this point, his stubborn streak went further than wherever rainbows ended.

One amazingly stupid idea coming right up.

***

The cell's hateful heartburn pink walls taxed Charronna's good humor. The opaque energy barrier, however rude, at least separated her from a planet overrun with homicidal aliens. Galactic civilization turned out to be as petty and unforgiving as anything back home. To top it off, the bastards had taken her Pradas. No manners whatsoever.

At regular intervals, food and water came through a temporary break in the barrier. After a few false starts, she picked through a piece of oblong fruit and sampled a gelatinous stew with a flavor profile of sunbaked sea slugs. The restaurants on Imperia had nothing to worry about.

Others came, Kimbrians, short, stripe-faced, stocky beings, who talked too much, and they whisked her away; their furry heads hovered in a field of shiny gadgets. The aliens diffused into hazy clouds, pressed metal objects into her, waved wands in spell casting manner, stuck her with needles, and murmured questions. "Why are you here?" "Where did you come from?" "What causes you pain?" "What causes you pleasure?" "What do you fear?" "What do you love?" "What do you want?" "What do you need?" "How are you different?" "How are you the same?" "What do our questions mean to you?" They didn't insist. They didn't demand. They simply asked over and over again. She told them anything they wanted to know.

Sleeping and waking hours blended, an obnoxious tang of sludgy dreams and memories. The monsters, once content to hide in deep mental recesses, emerged from behind closed doors; they sensed their time had come. Nails dug into fingers and arms— captivity-driven ice pick indentations on once flawless skin.

"Surrender to what is," murmured a familiar presence. *"Our armor will not save us."*

"Noi," Charronna said. *"I've never been so happy to hear a human mind."*

"I think you mean that."

"Gods, yes."

She curled into a ball—not out of character since her time in the pink closet cell. Someone, or something, likely surveilled them, and she didn't trust her practiced, mechanical Smiling Court face.

"How long?"

"Sixty-one days."

Charronna choked on Noi's answer.

"Damn Kor and his idiotic quest," Charronna said. *"Damn you for going along with it. Between you and the big bad Militant, we're roasting on an open dumpster fire."*

"We are where we are meant to be," Noi said. *"We presented the Commonweal with a riddle. Each of our genetic profiles is different. You are an exact match to the ancient E'lani. Psians were modified, so we deviate. The Earthlings' DNA is unlike any of the other humans. Polarian slaves have been bred for certain characteristics dating back to if not before the Mass Exodus, creating another divergence. To our captors, we resemble four different, albeit closely related species. If they examine Kor, they will find a fifth."*

"Pardon me if I'm not excited that I'm the one who matches the bad guys. I'll be sure to wave and put on my happy smile when the aliens let you and the others go."

Noi's presence vanished. Beating out the next thought, the energy barrier disappeared. Two Tols stood behind a Nevran in standard protocol. Stand, step outside the cell, and go blind. The

Nevran enclosed Charronna's hand in a rough, scaly hide. She remembered things she'd rather forget. Sometime later, the Nevran's hand dropped away, and her sight returned. Raven, Noi, and Sparrow sat in matching pale yellow-orange jumpsuits, perfectly tailored in the local prison wear.

"What's going on?"

"Something new," Noi said.

A couple of backless sofas in pastel hues with chairs roomy enough for sex suggested an improvement in alien–human relations. She didn't fancy that she wore the same prison wear jumpsuit from prior outings. The Chair arrived in the attire of someone who mattered, a white vest trimmed in indigo. To reiterate his importance, he wielded a white wooden staff gnarled at the top. She might have a favorable opinion but for the torture.

"The Permanent Council stayed your execution," Lom said.

"Yet the option remains," Noi said.

"Harmony must be preserved. We co-exist within diversity, a complex endeavor."

"That's it?" asked Charronna. "No apology, no explanation, no nothing?"

Four uncompromising ultra-alert eyes trained upon her, aloof and inspecting. "My purpose is to protect the Commonweal," he said in a rusty voice. "You arrived uninvited. Your presence triggered political tension. Be satisfied some are less eager to kill you than others."

Charronna took a seat next to Noi and held his hand. Whether they survived would be a cold political decision. Should they fall, the demise of human civilization would follow—it was spectacularly flawed, but home. A bit of recollection seeped into her memory. *I told them. I told the Kimbrians where we came from.*

"Today," the Chair said, "I am your tour guide."

"I accept your generous offer," Noi said. The Psian squeezed Charronna's hand and gave a sitting bow in apparent serenity. Charronna envied the man.

"I'm not going anywhere without a proper apology," Charronna said. She gestured with flare. The Tols tensed. "I've been practically dissected."

Waves of yellows and lime shifted across Lom's hide. "I apologize for the necessity of your treatment."

"Necessity? Keep your fake apology. I'm staying put."

"Let's see the aliens!" Sparrow said.

"I want a separate tour," Raven said.

Charronna second-guessed as everyone left, but taking part in a trial run for target practice didn't tickle her fancy, nor did prancing in public adorned in death-row couture. She'd rather Kor fill her ears with sugarcoated nothings.

After Raven departed with a Nevran guide, Charronna pulled Noi aside. "Don't forget we're the local roadkill. The moment of death is close. We cannot avoid it."

Noi put a hand to her cheek. "You're softening."

"Don't sweet-talk me. I mean it, Noi. I want you back in one piece."

"Will I ever see my family?"

Deeper connections to Noi beckoned, an intimacy she shunned. She cringed, recognizing a part of Noi running away from himself, finding refuge nowhere. Yet he soldiered on, stepping into his fear, willing to bear unbearable truths. She opened into a place where she never dared to venture. Noi's oil-black eyes shimmered in approval. The Chorus prevented her from seeing her parents, but she would at least make sure Noi's children fared better.

"We've become true friends," Noi said.

"I've never had a real friend." Charronna paused to marvel at both her delight and her despair. Sissy came close, but in truth, she was a Smiling Court minion. Noi, Sparrow at his side, abandoned Charronna for a sightseeing trip. Left alone, her mind rummaged for weights to hold down her wing-sprouting fear.

CHAPTER XXVII

Noi wanted to say the right thing at the right moment to steer *The Now* in the right direction. Except for Tol guards, the Chair, and Sparrow, the stone tunnels glowed for no one else. Anamoreena, shimmering in a green gown, glided next to him, content with an undemanding smile.

At the tunnel's end, a grand staircase descended into an enormous passageway. Fantastic murals soared up walls, around many levels of balconies and curved to a vaulted ceiling heavy with thick ribs as though Pink Dream had been born in the ossified carcass of a mighty beast. Columns with spiral friezes marched along in chaotic order. Towers cupped spheres, jewels on magic staffs, the source of different light spectrum realms into merging boundaries. Noi settled into an edgy stillness where the words unsaid burst with as much potential as the spoken word. Anamoreena poured love from solemn eyes, then faded away.

Dizzy, Noi reached for Sparrow. The girl's eyes widened as she took in the sight. True to her promise, she didn't say a thing, letting out no more than a faint gasp.

"The Coming Together," Lom said. "The towers you see represent the stars from member species. Here, the lights of many suns shine as one divided into the many."

Multitudinous aliens mingled within the ancient stonework over complex mosaics, a tantalizing array of meanings. Marvel gushed everywhere, the miracle of creation brandished in life, light, and stone. Beside Lom, they braved the curving staircase into the vast space.

Aliens gawked. Others averted their eyes. A few covered their ears or their noses. Some moved away. Some edged closer. Smaller contingents contented themselves with observing their fellow citizens. Clusters of floating sacs flashed in rapid color sequences. Cheemin stood proud in their showy vests and trousers, ears flattened or pointed. Sideway glances, dismissive gestures, and a smattering of respectful bows were aimed at the human intruders. The spread of wings, from the T'hyto, welcoming, from the Asags, threatening, added fanfare to their small yet weighty parade. Smiles, grimaces, lots of teeth brandished—they traversed a festival of carnivores.

A grim processional trudged with purpose; above them, bright light formed into changing messages: "Through War, Everlasting Peace!" "Defend!" "Protect Life—Kill E'lani!" "E'lani Build Warships!" "Cleanse Our Galaxy of Sinners!"

Another parade wound around the cafes, making their way to an amphitheater embedded in the enormous passage with their own attention-getting messages: "Everlasting Peace through Love!" "Discernment before Judgment!" "Compassion before Discernment!" "Sense of Humor before Compassion!" "Say No to Bigotry!" "We Are One!" The demonstrators steered clear of each other. Most aliens predominated in one group more than the other, while others were united for or against. Middle ground was a lonely place left to a tall, lanky alien standing in focused observance.

"I am surprised," Noi said, "you took us to such a public place."

"Resistance must be tested to understand the nature of flow. I see you have the attention of the Vestrians," said Lom, dipping his horns at the tall, lanky alien. "They are not Commonweal-- a troublesome, untrustworthy species."

Noi clasped his hands and checked to make sure Sparrow stayed close as they plunged into the multitudes. "I don't want our presence to be an excuse for violence."

"Your presence is violence. A Herexon Faction war fleet approaches Vio. They agitate for a favorable realignment of power. You provided them with holy cause to achieve it."

Groups of T'hyto, winged bipedal, and V'yahi, avian roost masters, followed their progress with slight eye and head rotations, neither hostile nor friendly. Scores of Nuxinni, green and blue humanoids with tendrils for hair, blocked the way. Overhead, bright lights shaped into an attack, "Kill the Vermin!" "Holy Justice, Now!" Noi didn't break stride doing his best self-assured repose. The Nuxinni melted off to the side.

Bands of bipedal Shonalli dressed in Knights of the Half-Moon-inspired garb marched through the crowds, around a fanciful sculpture, a never-ending knot of translucent links in a slow shift of color and shape. "The Knights of the Half-Moon Invasion Have Come! Run for Your Lives! Love, Laugh, Joy!" Other Shonalli hooted and cheered at their efforts. Dorrams packed into one of many cafes built into the passageway fought back in high-pitched squeals. Everyone's mood locked into serious; even the Shonalli's boisterous banter cut, a battery of knives in search of targets.

There was one exception to the sharp-edged attention. Clusters of aliens swayed back and forth with big smiles and bigger eyes plastered across white faces, striking up a conversation with a pair of carnivorous species, either of which could be eyeing up their next meal. Commonweal diversity thrived. Noi smiled, catching faint approval from Sparrow when he did.

"Bubbles," Lom said. "Sociable creatures. The four-footed felines are Farronnians—predators, though they choose their prey with care. The four-eyed upright hairies behind them are varnacks, primeval enemies to my people. Through the Covenant, we both thrive."

Bubbles. They were not in the Eos Archive. Floating sacs drifted by, pulsing with patterns of light—also, not in the database. What else did he not know that he must?

"The colors intensify," said Lom. "Division manifests throughout the Commonweal."

"I am a man of peace. I keep no weapons. Why not judge me for what I am?"

The hubbub of voices and motion intruded. Noi paused at one of the many artistic displays. Solid liquids changed shape, splitting into distinct streams, winding around in different colored bands, arching high, and curving back to the floor in a slow-motion waterfall. Aliens weighed his every move—imparted meaning to his every action. The spoken word and the perceptible action would be routed through their preconceived filters to regurgitate the narrative of their truth. He couldn't shed his human form.

"Your fate has been debated in an inclusive, living conversation," Lom said. "Some of us require more clarity before committing to your extermination. The Permanent Council authorized me to determine whether to grant a formal hearing."

"Are there magic words to say?"

Lom's hide flushed cadmium-red. "Magic won't save you. Reconciliationists favor rapprochement. Adherents demand extermination. Neither are open to compromise. Both sides fight to control the discourse, their language shrill and their manner derisive in battlegrounds where truths and facts are casualties of war."

Noi swept the crowd with a psychic net to gauge the flavors of energy that vibrated into the continuum. Impassioned impulses of fervor swelled with divergent, competing intentions. Movements of black shapes melted into the Coming Together's distant reaches. The feeling of being watched stayed with him. Remembering Sparrow, he touched the girl's thoughts; her enraptured mind was wonderstruck by the lighted towers, the variety of aliens, and the sheer scale of it.

"What can you tell me of Kor?" Noi said.

"Your companion arrives soon," Lom said. "We have become curious whether humans live united or in separation. Your genetic profiles have unusual variance."

"We have three separate civilizations-- the Earth Confederation, the Polarian League, and the Starry Empire. Our party comes from all three."

"Your intra-species intolerance is legendary," said Lom. "Your disunity hurts your cause. Even the factional, polymorphic Taag co-exist under one, albeit complex, law."

Noi gazed locked onto Lom. He wanted to say many types and levels of union exist; politics counted as but one form. Each civilization learned from the others. Humans were, in essence, going through a long process of union. But he had to be careful. Broad, faceless sweeps of humanity would win no friends.

"We only recently discovered one another," Noi said. "Give us *time*."

"We are unclear how you navigated the Wastes. The E'lani left countless traps, as did we. Natural space hazards add to a difficult journey. The Kimbrian examiners came up with no better information than, I am embarrassed to admit, a guiding ghost."

"An appropriate though imperfect answer."

Questions flowed. The Chair practiced the art of subtle interrogation. In a distant bluish haze, hundreds of black rock pinnacles stretched to the lofty ceiling and blocked the way. Proud alabaster beasts guarded the gap. Fire-red eyes glittered challenge. Noi bowed four times, in appreciation, in gratitude for the moment, to honor the creators. Sparrow's desire to say something vanished into awe. Noi bowed again to honor the girl's quiet approval.

"The Valiant Gateway," Lom said. "My tribe built the Guardians as a gift to the newly arriving government."

"Do you want us dead?"

"You are fortunate to have this walk," Lom said. "Certain parties insisted."

"As a cloak of pretended broad-mindedness?"

Lom blushed bright brown. "The edict's suspension expires today. You and your companions are to be put to death at the day's crossing."

Vitality drained from Noi. *Last meal.* Gently, Noi swept over the girl's mind to soothe bubbling feelings. They drifted along the outer realm of an orange-lighted sphere. Furtive movements, beasts from the dark, moved in and out of view.

"We are being followed," Noi said.

"Z'yax," said Lom. "They are curious. They are within flow."

Giant, armored beetles continued to appear and disappear with haunting grace. Unbidden, Eos data floated through Noi's thoughts. *Z'yax fall into many orders. Warrior drones wield heavy pincers capable of snapping bone. Unhinged jaws devour prey. Steely, stiff hairs on their legs serve as vectors for a variety of lethal poisons. The creature's appendages are built for speed. They practice ritual warfare without manufactured weapons. They prey on sentient lifeforms.*

Noi strained his telepathic senses upon the curious beasts. The continuum vibrated in discordant, brokenhearted tones.

***

Raven hungered to recover the Cosmic Song, with its equations lit in blue imperative inlaid on its egg-shaped metal gleam. The need ate into his subconscious. He needed allies to gain control of *Star Horizon*. The best options resided in the Nox, the nocturnal enclave below the city of Pink Dream. Rin, his Nevran guide, and a half dozen Tols took him on a ride aboard a mag-tube. Rin jabbered about the underground's etiquette, places to avoid— the Nox, he insisted, was dangerous.

"The Chair agreed to my request," Raven quipped in a nonnegotiable tone.

After a long silence, the lone Shadow Emperor whispered council. Raven, however, had to convince an unhappy guide to unwittingly do the Blessed Emperor's bidding. "Where are the safer places?" asked Raven.

"The Javal towers in the central district—they dominate commerce, and as long as they are fair, the others do not contest their control. Dorram hollows would be safe except for their grudge against your kind. Vorgoth taverns may take your credits, but they don't ruin, maim, or kill you unless you break one of their contracts."

"Or unless there's profit in it," added Raven. "Whatever you think—the Javals should be of interest. Take us there."

Streaks of cadmium red spread through Rin's hide. Pleased at the Nevran's annoyance, Raven pressed his interest in the Javals as they exited into a disorienting world of glare and halos. Calcite columns spiraled to the ceiling, many of them bathed in light. Aragonite chandeliers, masterpieces of water and mineral, frozen into waves of spiraling wings, reached with crystal fingers to touch treasures of gem and stone. Quartz lay abundant, in clusters, the fallen swords of giants, in translucent boulders, pink jewels and fluorite deposits in uncountable colors. The Nox's enchanted gloom prevailed.

The golden-bronze Tol guards used their height and scanners to survey the surround. The Nevran's scaly hide drained to flat, nervous lime-gray. Above, muscular, heavily armed Asags guarded the upper mag platform. Stairs, bridges, accesses, and passages connected the buildings and points of destination in three-dimensional intricacy. Raven navigated uneven stairs past the lower platform to a passage on the Nox floor.

Neon-decked establishments and luminescent quartz huddled along the byway—dens of gamblers, drinkers, addicts, and experimenters. Quiet, no souls in sight—the locals had evacuated in haste. A spilled drink pooled near Raven's feet. Spicey, cloying, pungent and sweet aromas of the departed aliens lingered. Hateful, fearful, apprehensive, and curious energies fused into the neon glow. Shadows and darkened bars vibrated with dangerous intentions. No one here liked or wanted to meet the ancient devils. Overhead, a magnetic whirr jarred his nerves. The Nox wafted ripe and heavy with tension.

A steep rise menaced the road. Atop the hill sat a maroon-stone tavern with "HOGABOAG" slapped in tilting, subdued purple Vorgoth lettering across its slanted roof. Raven repressed a smile. As he had gambled, the Nevran took him to the most viable option other than the one he had expressed an interest in seeing. Two windowless angling walls converged at a double coal-black door lettered with etchings to ward off outsiders.

"If the Vorgoths desire to meet, they will let you in," Rin said.

"They are spying on us?" Raven asked.

Rin tilted his horns lower in affirmation.

"Not what I requested, but it works for me." Raven bolted up the hill. The Tols hesitated for a moment, long enough for Raven to slip inside into a world of purple lights, smoke, and languid music. Conversations lapsed. Drinks went unfinished. Heads swiveled his way. Hopeful at his course of action, he closed the doors behind him.

Many of the lilac Vorgoths smoked thin, curly pipes, drawing slowly before exhaling aquamarine smoke. *Decadence.* A trio confronted him with swagger, their violet eyes sharp with confidence, and they each blew a ring of smoke into his face. Through the haze and shifting light, Raven spied a gathering lounging in a booth. The trio cast covert glances in that direction. Hands visible, he moved in an unhurried stride. In slow liquid draws, other Vorgoths blew smoke into his face. He sniffed the vapor—his pulse increased, the effect of a mild amphetamine. *Polluted.*

A trio of females lounged around the target table. They showed off voluptuous lilac breasts that jutted out in haughty sexual prowess, decorated with stacked gold necklaces. Beaded gems wrapped their necks. Fat gold armlets, jeweled crowns and headbands, and long, intricate earrings boasted their importance. Whispers giggles passed between them. Raven shifted his attention to the males.

Like most of the other lilacs, the men wore light-reflecting open vests, showing off their hairless pectorals and abs above billowy, swashbuckling trousers. Vorgoths appeared to be a fit race despite the smoking and drinking. Without a word, Raven took the lone empty seat. The Vorgoth males drank mauve-colored drinks in sleek glasses. Raven snapped his long fingers, gestured at the drinks, and a waiter dutifully set another before him.

"I am Mobard," one of the Vorgoths said in a clear, rich baritone that rumbled from deep canyons.

"I can't pay for the drink," Raven said.

"On the house. What brings you to the Hogaboag?"

"Adventure."

"Old tales allege the gaze of E'lan steals the soul. I'm no child. Speak your intention."

A surge of whispered murmurings broke out as patrons went about their business or pleasure. *Opportunity.*

"A deal of mutual benefit."

"Happy days. We Vorgoths appreciate factional races. Don't ever let a T'hyto corner you. They spout racial harmony until their tongues swell." Mobard laughed, no doubt enjoying a private joke. "What do you want?"

"Control of our ship," Raven said.

"An admirable goal." He exchanged smirks with the females, focusing back with the leer of a confident lover. "Fail to impress me, and you won't leave here alive."

One of the women winked. Raven gulped the mauve drink.

"Are you eager to make enemies?" Raven asked.

"For enough credits, I would kill my firstborn."

"Tols ordered to protect me surround this place."

"Credits resolve all problems, and there's a bounty on your head worth a small fleet of ships. When you passed through our doors, you left their protection. The Nevran's displeasure overflows and he argues with his superior whether he should enter."

The females giggled.

"Does trade interest you?"

"Deliciously rich trade interests me."

"The Polarian League produces food, raw materials, woods, ores, precious metals, recycled plastics, basic clothing, and linens."

Mobard banged the table. "You dare come here unprepared? The Horn Arrow, Fat Sky, Vert Stripe, or Amethyst Cut Syndicates might be interested in such conventional inducements. You deal with Red Stripe," Mobard said, glancing at a thick red band around his bicep. "We are arms traders. War helps the bottom line. If you don't understand by now, E'lani scum, you picked the wrong group of Vorgoths."

"What about drugs? We've got everything—healings, ecstatics, emotional subversives, exotic stimulants, hallucinogens, depressants, mood-enhancers."

Raven drank more of the sweet mauve concoction, wondering how shrewd Mobard was at detecting a lie in a species he had never met. The Starry Empire and the Earth Confederation produced a much wider variety of drugs than the League and with superior quality. The Polarian liked his chances.

Mobard nuzzled the nearest female, purring in sultry moans. "The competition for the drug trade is fierce. The spoils will be rich in war, whether short or long. But you've earned one more shot."

***

The Z'yax leaped and scuttled with hypnotic fluidity, poetic and supernatural, beautiful in the way of a war-star not yet committed to battle. Lom said something, an incoherent formation of sound dispersed by more compelling realities. The black creatures pulled at Noi's thoughts, leaving him with no free attention.

"Relax," Lom said. "They sustain their aggression under our governing covenant."

Telepathic talent inhibited notwithstanding, he had eyes to see. The Z'yax stalked.

Sparrow swiveled her head in a steady motion. "I don't like this," she said in comstad, the shared lingua of the three civilizations. The young princess moved closer to Noi.

Noi took Sparrow's hand. "The Chair says we are safe."

Sparrow jerked away. "The Chair locked us up. He let the aliens do bad things to us." Her breathing accelerated. With the proximity, he picked up her anxiety—it expanded, eating into her self-control, into her calm, causing her to struggle against the onset of panic.

Unnatural fog swirled and thickened to swallow the Z'yax. Birthed from foul magic, they emerged in a sweeping black wave. Tols fell in grotesque silence, crumbling statues; those standing unloaded phased plasma storm. Lom, his hide shifting in color, plunged through confused citizens. Noi froze. The beetle-like beasts moved with haunting speed. A Z'yax soared high, an arc to frame a rolling hill. A Tol fired his hand-held disruptor, striking the creature's underbelly. Sonic shards of agony screeched—it split apart in mid-air. Black bile oozed from beneath the cracked shell, mingling with the golden brown of fallen Tols. A hand-disruptor clattered across the floor, coming to rest at Noi's feet. Sparrow yanked his robe.

A floating message tilted over mangled bystanders— "E'lani Are Specie Supremacists!"

A second wave of giant beetles jumped high over the flickering sign. Powerful, grasshopper-like legs propelled the Z'yax into long, graceful leaps. They would be on him in seconds—the dead and the dying, Tols, Z'yax and bystanders between them. The hand-disruptor gleamed. Fog swirled closer. A banner drifted, "Faith in Hope!"

Sparrow's heat seeped into Noi, merging with his ache. Shaking, he reached for the weapon. Anamoreena appeared at his side in an otherworldly shimmer. "*I am with you always,*" she said.

Armed and determined, he planted his feet to confront the Z'yax.

CHAPTER XXVIII

Raven was out of his league with Mobard. The emperor's worlds were mapped into units of farm plots or production sectors. Austere days, simple meals, work and devotions, acts of service for the community—sufficient, but for most beings, unattractive. The Vorgoths would be unimpressed by the houses or possessions of Polarian servants. The Blessed One's blessing added more value than gold or fancy abodes. The League's economy flourished because the emperor's servants provided goods and materials to House-controlled worlds at slave-labor prices. He said as much as he struggled to come up with a winning story.

Mobard fingered his goatee. "You have slaves?"

"The emperor commands a vast host of humans bred to be subservient, resistant to disease, and hard working."

"Why didn't you say so? A well-supplied slave market adds spice to a potent drink." Reminded of his brew, the Vorgoth took another swallow of his mauve concoction. Raven matched him sip for sip.

"The V'yahi Masterships," continued Mobard, "seek a new supply of slaves, and they would sell their sum and substances to complete that search." He played the table with quick finger taps. "They would enjoy the irony of using E'lani. The slaves would be abused of course."

"The emperor's devoted keep no boundaries to service."

"Well, that does spice up the possibilities. Agreements and services must wait until the Assemblers make up their minds on the matter of your existence. Any fool knows your beating heart witnesses against you.”

“No stomach for risk?”

“I have nothing to lose except your carcass.”

Raven reached inside his pants pocket. Vice-like purple hands grabbed his arms, knocking an object free; it clattered to the table. “Contact communicator,” Raven said.

Mobard eyed the disc before pocketing it. “My headmaster must approve where we go with this.”

“When will I meet your headmaster?” Raven asked.

Mobard glanced at one of the females. Her playful mouth and easy eyes honed into an assertive examination.

“You intrigue the Syndicate,” the headmaster said. “Disappoint us, and we’ll take the guaranteed profit that comes with your carcass.” She gave Raven cold disdain, air kissed Mobard, and sashayed away, with her female companions in toe.

“I have a fetish,” Mobard said. He motioned for his comrades to go, checked the nearby tables, and whispered, “I like to explore the variants of pleasure. Nothing on the market, that I’m willing to touch, would be more exotic than E’lani.”

“You realize I’m male.” Not that he cared—he would do far more than have sex with an alien to achieve the Blessed One’s purpose.

"Once you cross species, such distinctions aren't important. My enjoyment comes from experimentation. I would like nothing better than to sample your females."

"I'll see to that, for a price."

Mobard fingered rings piercing through his nipples. "Spoken like a true Vorgoth."

Raven accompanied the Vorgoth to a nondescript room in the back of the tavern. Mobard pressed a button and a thick mattress unrolled across the floor. Leering, Mobard crawled onto the bed and shed his tunic.

"Tell me your pleasure points," Raven said. "I am at your service."

***

Noi had never used a gun, had never killed. Anamoreena shimmered in a questioning pose. *"Will you honor the creeds and lives of other human beings? Will you give up your code when necessary for the sake of others?"*

Noi returned his wife's challenge. *"I cannot."*

Lom halted his retreat, gesturing to the nearest white star tower. Noxious odors leaked from split Z'yax carcasses. Senses dulled. The beasts retreated into the artificial fog. They reemerged in greater numbers. Bulbous eyes fixed upon Noi. Noxious mist enveloped his mind. Voices called. *"Go into the mist, Noi. Find the peace of forever."*

Thoughts merged into alien translation. The Z'yax regressed into the Xenoxanth, the insatiable Blood Hunger that consumed their kind, driving them to agonizing madness until they devoured prey. Z'yax's thoughts circled round and round as enemies attacked them with obscene weapons. To end the madness, they must move faster in unexpected directions. They must become chaos. Floating radiance burst into his retinas. Noi coughed out his breath and broke the connection.

Listless, Sparrow swayed in a trance. Noi eased into the girl's consciousness, winding his way through complex mazes. "*We need to get moving!*" Noi shouted the telepathic command, getting flashes of Sparrow's neuron life. He poured himself into the imperative, encouraging expansion until a wave of light spread of its own accord. Terror emerged in the torpid clouds of the girl's eyes.

Fully into the Real, Noi surveyed his surroundings with speed. The orange tower's beacon flickered and buzzed. In a flash of orange, waves of leaping Z'yax descended upon the remaining Tols. Barbed legs plunged into laser melee. The last Tol standing fired at a Z'yax soaked with the golden blood of his brothers. The Z'yax's bulging backside cracked, releasing tiny scarab nymphs. The Tol backpedaled.

A blue-skinned Nuxinni spectator beheld the new threat, pulled on her short white tendrils, and shrieked, "Z'yax gives birth. Run for your lives!"

A flying horde of scarabs headed straight for the nearest food source—a Tol. Nymphs clamped themselves to wherever bronzed skin exposed itself, embedding razor-like teeth into flesh. The guard fired until he collapsed in a flurry of wild shots. The frenzied mass feasted on their kill. Noi seized up in a mute scream.

Sparrow punched his back. "We have to go."

Noi linked into a Z'yax mind. The Xenoxanth consumed it. Deep hunger enfolded pain and animal instinct in a search for safe harbor. The omnipresent psi blocker resisted, but Noi rested on patience, on perseverance, and he broke free into an ambient sea of alien thoughts. *"I'm not your enemy."*

"Whatever you are, we must kill you. Our Mother Queen commands it. Ancient sin stains your blood."

Noi recoiled, stung by his perception of the Z'yax's justified righteousness. A rush of vertigo whirled into Sparrow's pleading face.

"Noi!" she screamed; her face flushed with desperation.

He was a father, and a good father would get Sparrow to safety. Death's acerbic nearness coated his tongue. Part of him wished the cup would pass to Charronna, but she wielded the authority to set his family free. A headache pounded and his flesh rebelled, but he could think, and he could run. They sprinted beyond the flickering orange tower's domain. A sign's brilliant green symbols lost its moorings, drifting away. Cafes had been evacuated, with food and drinks unfinished. Confusion, shouting, noise—yet with every footfall, the Z'yax's fumes receded.

No breath to shout. No moments to stop. Safety loomed, a white tower, an ascending Angel of Mercy sheathed in the power of terrible light. Cries saturated in the savage whiteness. A stampede of beings broke his handhold with Sparrow. Noi yelled her name, a tiny call fading to a quick death in the clamorous commotion. Howling force dug into his cells, leaving his hopes for the future thin and raw.

"Tols come," voices cried. "We're saved."

He cast his mind out for the girl—too many minds, too much terror. Hints of her presence tossed in a wild, energetic hurricane. A behemoth screeched above. Frightful shapes descended in the harsh white blur—where to go, to run, to escape, others doing the same, unsure where to turn, to slow or dodge. It sliced into a Cheemin's back. The Z'yax's antennae gyrated, legs thrashed, and ripped through another mangled victim. The Z'yax hopped backward, shaking off its latest kill. Memory flashes of Noi's children throbbed with the afterimages of the chaotic scene. More than anything, he wanted to see his son and two daughters.

A small form appeared outside the safety of the white light. *Sparrow*. Digging deep, he crafted a psi-blast to shatter through the dampening field. The focused intention crumbled in his mental grasp. Deeper to the root of his creation, he shaped an energetic force mighty enough to slay giants, when another presence surged into the continuum.

Kor!

"Sparrow, get down," Noi yelled, and motioned to the floor.

She flopped to the stone.

Anamoreena appeared at his side. *"Will you give up your code when necessary for the sake of others?"*

Noi, his soul weeping, his heart betrayed, squeezed the gun's discharge mechanism. No beam fired. Z'yax charged toward the girl. As did Kor. As did Noi.

CHAPTER XXIX

Raven closed the tavern door with controlled ease, satisfied with his venture. A potential ally was cultivated in a most pleasurable way, and he earned bonus points by irritating his guide. Angry black streaks metastasized across the Nevran's scaly hide.

"I estimated an infinitesimal possibility that you would come out alive," Rin said. "What did you promise them?"

"We enjoyed a pleasant exploration of each other's positions."

Four Nevran eyes tapered in bloodthirsty appraisal. Rin snapped orders at the Tols, who took to the road. The Nox ceiling shined in surreal glory, a captive heaven that inspired wonder where none should be. High cliffs crowned with muted-glowing Dorram hollows penned the canyon-like passage. The Nevran's streaks expanded with every footfall.

"This isn't the way we came," Raven said, staying alert for sudden trouble.

Rin marched on without comment. Raven replayed the encounter with Mobard. Give him credit, the Vorgoth didn't know the meaning of shy. Mobard uncovered pleasure centers Raven had been unaware of. Service to the emperor had left him incomplete. *I am whole. I am devoted.* The words spun into an endless loop, submerging sacrilegious thought. His new ally promised to help. Nothing else mattered.

A ghost-pale androgynous alien in a satin gown approached. Small pinkish eyes exuded sharp intelligence.

"You stray far afield, Nearcherlus," Rin said.

"Unexpected variables revive stale equations," the Vestrian said.

"Do not interfere."

"You cling to old solutions when new expressions present themselves to be computed."

"I'm in no mood for troublemakers."

"You will understand when you lose confidence in old math."

Rin charged ahead. The pale alien skirted out of the way. As Raven passed, Nearcherlus brushed up against him. Rin's hide shifted to murderous inky blacks. Structures loomed, lit in wild varieties of garish colors, gothic and fanciful, the abodes of Mo'sari, Javal, Me'luh, and others in the gloomy hues of Asag strongholds. Goosebump-inducing, eardrum-vibrating chirps and clicks, escalated, a sinister humming and buzzing. *Z'yax singing*—a symphony to steal his breath. The Nevran's pace quickened. Ramps, stairs, paths, and roads offered many options but no safety from a Z'yax hunting pack.

Light flashed in his mind; the Blessed One's presence stirred. *"Take the next ramp,"* Ashtore said.

Raven zagged onto an alley-sized incline with a street sign post etched in a secret symbol, a slanted inverted **Y** inside a triangle. The Tols kept going. The incline curved around a two-hundred-foot rock wall, smack into a dead end of solid stone. Ropes dangled. The Z'yax hummed, an itchy call for blood. Raven climbed, the lifeline sticky and easy to grip, fifty feet, a hundred, he focused on the next hold. At the top, he found himself in a macabre park. Statues littered the landscape—slashed human forms, some tilting, others missing limbs or heads. A distortion field occupied the center.

Whatever waited on the other side had to be better than Z'yax. He was wrong.

"E'lani." The whisper repeated, hissing wind across summer fields, an overlapping chant to evaporate vital blood. The distortion field acted as a portal, taking him inside a macabre space of grayish murk. Cyani abided everywhere, standing tall, clinging to walls, hanging from thick webs anchored to the ceiling. Nerves tingled. Fusty hides enveloped, a breath-smothering pile of wet blankets. The creatures parted, opening a path with no escape.

"Go," the whispered chant encircled.

At the head of the chamber, a silk-shrouded altar formed a half arc around a mummy suspended over a round stone table. He dropped to his knees and bowed his head to honor the spent carcass of a shadow emperor. Ashtore remembered that one of the discarded vessels had disappeared, an ancient mystery solved, and a new one created. Why would the Cyani possess the corpse? Fetid air crowded his breath.

From impenetrable webs in every corner, large and small Cyani watched, a galaxy of vermilion, flame, and yellow chrome orbs. A big-girthed spider-beast scuttled close, red cords on its hide twined—the symbol of status for a female Dominant.

"I am Ungoth," she said. "Guardian of the Cradle of Defiance."

"Z'yax come," another hissed. "The vibrations of many."

"Send our sisters to greet them," Ungoth said. "Ready the traps in case our guests provoke disrespect."

"Who are you?" Raven asked.

Ungoth waved fuzzy arms. "Worshipers of malefic relics."

At either end of the chamber, human skulls pitted sinewy double columns, some of them jeweled. Reliefs in panel sections altered between hands and pelvic bones connected by networks of intricate silk webs. Diamond, ruby, sapphire, topaz, emerald, aquamarine, tourmaline, and opal embedded silk and bone, a magnificent mosaic of spent life and precious stone.

"Keeps the tourists away," Ungoth said, a hissing wind.

The altar's shrouds covered sacred objects; the Amber Crown, the emperor's divinity; the Watcher Eye, his wisdom; the Crooked Staff, his authority over good and evil; the Diamond Mask, his invincibility.

"You do more than ward off. You venerate."

"Silly man-thing. We mock the ancient enemy; our worship is a practice of disgust."

"You are of the Select. You follow the Master of the Cosmic Song."

Ungoth's abdomen bloated. "No one speaks of it. What name do you claim?"

"The Blessed One's chosen."

Ungoth didn't react in a way Raven perceived. But most of the Cyani watchers melted away. "Does the Blessed One hold the Vibrating Crucible?"

"I am here to retrieve it."

Ungoth remained in a moment of suspense where paths diverged.

"I recognized the secret sign you placed by the road," Raven said.

"I am accepting. We will pay respect to the unexpected."

The silk strings vibrated, a call to war. Ungoth scooped him up. They emerged from the temple into a yellow fog. Acrid ozone, the stink of too many Z'yax, scoured his lungs. "Stay your breath."

Scores of Cyani and Z'yax lay poisoned, gutted, smothered in web, decapitated, while others battled among the dead. Streams of cobwebby material, a rain of silky arrows, poured against a surging charge of black shells. Ungoth jumped around the haphazard human statues in quick strikes. A host of Z'yax trained their eyes on them, hopping and leaping over and under flying silk strands. Z'yax mandibles sliced into thick bellies, and barbed legs finished the job. Cyani emptied their sacks of poison. Vapors leaked through split black shells, feeding the eerie yellow fog over poisonous pools. No pleading, no negotiation, the grotesque fought with honor.

The silken defense diminished. A Z'yax lunged—screeched to numb one's heart. Ungoth bolted through a distortion portal. Though it promptly locked, she didn't slow until she reached the central district's outer boundary, far from the battle.

"You must go," the mammoth spider whispered. "Do you hear the humming? More Z'yax come. The Javal Trading Complex has many transmats. Do not waste our sacrifice. Do not forget your promise."

"You will be redeemed in paradise from the curse of your birth to the shape of your choosing. The Blessed One remembers his promise."

Ungoth brought four limbs together in a brief prayer and scampered off. Raven savored an effervescent sensation of pleasure from the emperor within. A remnant of the secret faithful persisted. More than anyone else, they would be rewarded. Encouraged, he ran at full speed to one of the Javal's blue-sheathed buildings, and the hope of a future preserved.

***

The Tols were fast. But the Z'yax were too close to their human prey.

Leaving his Nevran guide behind, Kor dodged the dazzle-glare of a daunting theatrical-styled Qa aquarium, speeding through the zigzagging crowd without jumping into quick-speed. Signs drifted overhead . . . *"E'lani Seek Anti-Life Weapons!"* *"E'lani Are Anti-Life!"* T'hyto evacuated in hurried winged flight between them. A Cheemin cub, separated from her mother, snagged an electric-yellow plush toy within a mass of panicked adults. A fancy-dressed lioness came to the rescue. In the mad rush, getting trampled had become a constant threat.

Kor entered the outer rim of the white tower's light—his internal lens darkened automatically to filter the intense luminosity. Aliens scrambled, some visually impaired by the harsh white, others were stone-blind.

Noi ran toward Sparrow, but too slow. Flashes of reddish laser and incandescent pulses teased his peripheral vision. Tol reinforcements charged into the fray. In a brief burst of quick-speed, Kor bolted to the other side of the luminous camouflage. Black silhouettes soared high. Red streaks burned through the light, slicing shapes before breaking the shadows. Kor dove at the princess, sweeping her up to avoid a falling chunk of Z'yax reeking of a pungent scorched shell stench. A neon-colored idea tested Kor's sensibilities— *"The Source Created All Life."*

Fumes from dead Z'yax snaked into his lungs; enhanced bio-agent defenses warded off the fog. But the girl wasn't equipped to deal with the foul air, and he held her tight. Noi joined them, shaking with unbounded emotion, unlike any ghost Kor had encountered.

Tol troops dispatched the last few Z'yax. The colossal tunnel's energies calmed. Relief and horror, joy and grief, co-mingled. Kor gathered in Noi with his free arm. Voices cried out their despair. A fresh wave of Z'yax swept toward the white tower. These Z'yax wore goggles, their shells glimmered with protective sheen, and they had small cannons mounted on their shoulders, spitting explosive goo.

Aliens evacuated the white tower zone in a panic of arm waving, tendril swaying, wing flapping, and fur flying rampage to safer destinations. Tol foot soldiers rushed through the mob. Single-man fliers converged. Kor loosened his hold on Noi and the girl and shook them into a semblance of awareness. Noi's liquid black eyes and Sparrow's blues firmed into hopeful recognition.

"Can you run?" Kor asked Noi.

"I will manage," Noi said.

Tol's weapon fire deflected off the armored shells. The Z'yax blistered the Tol fliers with goo that split into explosive blobs. On the ground, lines of troops advanced, temple columns to hold back the onrushing evil. The dreadful wave crashed into the Tol defenders in a ruthless clash of laser, photon, and plasma. Bronze temple columns crumbled. Z'yax broke through, painted in the golden blood of their victims.

Sparrow woke from the chemical-induced haze. Kor kissed Noi on the cheek, and with a firm grip on Sparrow's hand, he bolted. Noi fell further behind. Terror flowed from the girl. Tol reinforcements headed into the fray, bolstered by anti-grav gunships and mobile artillery. Calculations rolled through Kor's head with quick checks on Noi's progress—the Z'yax too fast—Noi too slow. The attackers didn't bother with evasive maneuvers. Kor slowed, looking down at Sparrow.

"Meagan Alessandra Hayleigh Baxter the Second, you must be brave. Go. Now!"

Sparrow straightened her back. Kor gave her a light push to jumpstart her momentum. He risked a burst of quick-speed to return to Noi. The universe was good, the universe was just, and, by damn, the universe better show its true colors.

The Psian waved Kor off—a slew of Z'yax a leap away. Noi stopped running. Disruptor fire from oncoming guards failed to penetrate the fortified armored black shells. The Tols concentrated their attack. They felled leaping giants in mid-leap. Z'yax jumped over their smoldering dead and blasted the gunships and mobile artillery. Kor angled in Noi's direction, ready to sweep him up in a tight arc. A detonation cracked the stone, shoving him away.

Z'yax riddled with lancing burns leaped straight for Noi. Kor pivoted and accelerated to the limits of quick-speed. Multiple Tols hammered the armored beasts; heavy hover units joined the defense. The Z'yax propelled through a hail of crossing light swords. Kor launched into a flying tackle with concussion-force impact. Vision shimmered, a momentary shroud covered the world, and Kor crashed to the great tunnel's floor. Flat on his back in a stunned haze, barbed legs stabbed into his body, shredding muscle. Blood gushed between them. Sparrow screamed their names in tortured refrain.

***

Joy should be less fleeting. Dejected at the turn of events, Jeth sulked within one of his viewscapes. No one wanted him to be happy. Sala coalesced into the minimalist bedroom wearing black lipstick, matching accents, and a white powder lead base, which united into a callous visage ready to torment. Jeth collapsed the vision and retreated into a wind. Sala flew after him with obstinate determination. Lightning flashes cut through Jeth's cloud form. Sala drifted above, a ghoul moving in for the kill.

"As bad as this prison is," Sala said, "worse outcomes are possible. Sever your connection with Kor."

"You said you wanted freedom at any cost."

Throwing daggers appeared in Sala's hands. "Don't pretend you understand me. Zaxa will destroy you. Count yourself as lucky. She will digest me over time."

"I won't give up this chance."

Sala threw the daggers. Bloody excruciating trails sliced through Jeth. Tormented, hurt, he compacted his presence and imagined ointment to soothe the wound.

"Toughen up," Sala said.

"Kor and I were one—to be safe, he would have to die and he's a worthy man. He deserves more than an empty, meaningless end."

Sala faded into a pastel sky. "As in a sacrifice for our salvation? Sentimental. On another day, I would approve. But if Zaxa detects us, that cold, hard place you tried to disappear into better have room for two."

Sudden agony seared Kor's mind. Jeth recoiled into splintering bits at ripping pain from his savior.

***

Mortal wounds—poison spreads—fingers of death—nails into the heart—claws into the soul. Noi and I are dying. I am dying.

Kor woke from a haze of comingled thoughts.

"Why did you leave me behind?"

"I don't want my children forced into doing terrible things for the love of their children. You are the Amun."

Noi's voice faded . . . Noi had the mortal wounds.

Kor's friend coughed up blood. Dozens of floating sacs congregated around them, pulsing hues of greens. Shouts of profanity, perhaps, but Kor sensed solidarity.

"What if I fail?"

"*Then you fail,*" Noi said into Kor's mind. "*Destinies do not happen without intention. The universe grants nothing but allows for everything.*"

Kor stroked Noi's hair with hands dripping red. Blood flowed from a wound near Kor's rib cage—minor compared to the unfolding loss. The urge to cry battered at the gates of his self-control built from the emotional ruin of the General's lash.

"I forgive you, Noi."

"*I and my family follow the Harmonist Way. Our faith is unsanctioned and no one outside of our brotherhood and sisterhood knows of our existence. Do not concern yourself with Psian burial rituals. Use my death for the cause of good.*"

Kor held Noi and his carnage. The universe must be insane. A final gesture, futile and meaningful, a lesson to the uncaring cosmos—Noi would depart with love.

An odd Earth tune called. Without thinking, he let the words of "Strange Fruit" tumble forth.

The Chair approached, shifting into thoughtful green grays. "What does this poem mean?"

"Not my place to say, but I hear unnecessary loss—brutality by genteel people. Beauty and death, wonder and grief, abound in this place, enough to shatter the purest heart. I sing for Noi. I sing for the human race you plan to kill."

The floating sacs multiplied, tinging the air with cooling green; they hummed sweet hissing heart-lightening sounds. Sparrow hovered nearby, doing her best to keep her strained eyes on Noi. A lament cut through the noise—a musical voice carving a drop of peace in a sea of despair. The rich, sad tones amplified Kor's sorrow but also gave rise to hope. Someone else understood.

"This is a mockery of the Coming Together," Lom said.

Noi blossomed in Kor's mind, a clear presence. Water streamed from Noi's eyes—the heartbeats, thready and thin. The Chair summoned help. The Psian relaxed into a tranquil transition. Lom, the galactic leader of over a trillion beings, had no power to change the moment.

They shared that final bit of irony. Kor loved Noi; he poured whatever love might be, whatever joy might be, over and through his comrade, his friend, a shower of morning-dew petals.

Beyond the communion of their minds, a vortex appeared. In the halo of a white-yellow glow, Anamoreena, a radiant goddess, beamed with quiet strength. Taking Noi's hand, she led him into the light. They turned to each other. Noi glowed within an aura of his wife's warmth and love. Deep joy passed between them, but Kor wanted to demand, to throw a tantrum—to insist Noi fight harder for life. Instead, he opened himself more to the rain shower of pinks, yellows, reds, lavenders, and oranges that cascaded upon his friend.

Noi raised a finger. "The floating sacs, the LaLa, bid you their sympathy. You will find many friends among them. Righteous wrath boils in your heart. Against your instincts, against your genetic coding, forgive my killers as you forgave me for leaving you behind."

"You think way too much of me."

"You harbor the faith of a true believer. Embrace yourself, Independence Man."

Protest denial rattled at Noi's impossible request, dispersing into grief.

"No goodbyes between us," Kor said. Undeniable sadness filled his underneath, the part of him he kept hidden. In his eyes, he filtered for joy.

Noi floated into perfection. His wife observed with heartbroken love. With enough faith, there were no goodbyes . . . Kor woke from the light-dream. Cupping his friend's head, amazed at lifeless lips parted in wonder, Kor ululated, spreading his grief into the passageway. In the breaking of old damns, at last, the tears came.

CHAPTER XXX

Charronna paced. The aliens' replacement sandals were polite, quiet, death walking on the stone floor. Walls distracted her with evolving geometric shapes of ever-changing colors in pastel hues. Crescent couches and luscious chairs teased with comfort. Fresh fruit in wooden bowls enticed. Water collected on ornate glass jars with panels of gold scrolls featuring a script of some kind—tasteful, a gesture of goodwill.

She wished upon a star for her Prada shoes, for leather, skin-hugging and skin-titillating, neck to ankles and diva-approved, a massage from hands blessed by the sex gods, and an emergency makeover from her hairstylist and makeup artist to wipe away the days since the Chorus ordered her to Zorn. The excruciating waiting . . . she played a safe game, exchanging adventure for room service. Not her style, but the imprisonment had left her shellshocked.

The doors parted, and words carved into a weapon readied at the tip of her tongue. Shattered eyes stopped her cold. Bloodied hands and clothes, the ghastly art of a cartoonist, awakened primal fear. Misery howled from Kor's entire being. Trembling, she took his hands.

"He stopped running," Kor said, a hoarse whisper to crack a calloused heart. Steel grays threatened to splinter into an unbridled craze—eyes roamed in a frantic search for a nonexistent escape from grief.

"That sweet man sacrificed himself," Charronna said, "and the god-damned universe obliged. I promise to set his family free." Nothing felt right anymore, except the promise, and Kor.

"You honor Noi in the best way possible. Be true to your word, and I will anoint you with a new name—Red Angel."

She squeezed his hand, wondering if her eyes teared up in return.

A reedy woman with silky white-blond hair glided in, holding Sparrow's hand with the ease of longtime friends. The woman had the appearance of an elevated human, with lustrous pearl skin, flawless pink painted nails, stunning in presence, a star among the common folk. She measured the room, taking notes, her eyes gentle, yet set in mystery-laden layers of stained glass. Sparrow clung to the woman's iridescent green gown. No matter—she would take any allies, even those prettier than herself.

I saved your life, little Sparrow, everyone's life, on the twilight death world. Don't I accrue bonus points for that to exchange for shows of affection?

At least the girl survived, buried in the fair woman's gown, sobbing in quiet affliction. *Doesn't she want to squeeze my hand as well? I should stand next to her, pretend that she does, much like the joggers I shared the morning trails with.* She managed not to move. *Never, ever show need-- ammunition to those who would hurt you.*

The Chair, in a rough raspy voice, told the awful tale. The reek of death defiled him, but she reigned in her stomach filling with an anxious atmosphere. The aliens tricked her with the comfortable room. They lured her into quasi-relaxation through a spell of pastel geometric patterns—a tactic to throw her off.

The Chair tilted his horns back. "Countermeasures are underway. The Z'yax who orchestrated the attack will be punished in accordance with the law."

"Before or after you execute us?" asked Charronna.

"The Permanent Council authorized a formal hearing. Do not take the procedural change as anything more."

Kor ran a finger through the blood on his ripped bodysuit— Noi's, Kor's, impossible to tell. Charronna shuddered.

"I take it as a reason to hope," Kor said.

Sparrow tugged at the fair lady. "Why does everyone hate us?"

The Avue, C-Glenmarra, bent down to meet Sparrow at eye level. "Those who seem to hate you—it's pretend. No one here knows you well enough to hate you in truth."

"What happened to Noi wasn't pretend," Sparrow said.

"No," said the fair woman, her face creased. "People sometimes do real things out of pretend thoughts."

"Hear, hear," Charronna said.

"Every mind conjures stories," C-Glenmarra said. "Most stories feed suffering because most beings nurture burdens that demand no less. Let them go."

The Avue reached into her cloak and pulled out a bud vase. It glittered in translucent gold no doubt spun from the golden rays of a youthful star. "This vase shows the holder's truth. Stories, no matter how well told, have no influence. Please accept this as a gift of conscience from the Avue people."

Charronna accepted the vase, giving the Chair an eye roll, though the message likely didn't translate. *May leaders everywhere rot in eternity.* Action, consequences, reparations, safety—tangled aspirations lost in vague statements of regret. The vase turned more than half opaque. Multiple cracks spread. As if she didn't know. Quickly, she handed it to Kor, ready to take a swipe at C-Glenmarra as the vase recovered much of its transparent clarity. But not all by far. Her hunky barbarian visited the dark side. Thank the stars.

Holding Sparrow's hand, C-Glenmarra circled in a slow walk, her gown flowing behind in an entrancing wave. "A war fleet comes to Vio, demanding your executions," she said, pointing to Charronna and her companions. "If the Vinculum refuses, the ruling SARASIN faction must make unpleasant concessions."

"You speak out of turn," Lom warned.

C-Glenmarra's smile darkened. *The lovely bright Avue also visits the underside of life. Nice.* Charronna brushed C-Glenmarra with a warm psychic embrace.

"Many among us," G-Glenmarra said, "cannot abide a campaign of extermination for political convenience or to right the sins of the ancient dead. Our voices grow stronger."

"Consequences have a way of keeping the balance," the Chair said, "except with C-Glenmarra."

C-Glenmarra tapped her closed mouth; she completed another circle, not saying a word.

"I have another matter to discuss," the Chair said. "The disposition of your friend."

"Psians scatter the ashes of their dead to the winds," Charronna said, "preferably over a sea or desert, where they merge with Anonymity."

"I'll bury him in a public ceremony," Kor said. He dipped his head at the Chair. "If you agree."

Lom dipped his horns in return. "The ritual must be today. I'll dispatch Ven to make preparations and to contact you for instructions."

The fair woman fingered an amulet dangling on her chest, a golden spiral suspended in amber. A bit of Eos data revealed itself to memory; this Avue was a queen, an arbiter of sacred rites, and a friend worth having.

"Our moral high ground is at best aspirational," C-Glenmarra said. "Make sure I'm on the guest list and include Tau Ring."

"Who?" Charronna asked.

"The T'hyto Permanent Councilor."

Charronna endured the Smiling Court long enough to know she wasted breath with the Chair. Fortunately, murmuring into Kor's delectable ear required none. "Time for you to take charge, fearless leader."

She reclined on a couch, hoping for a fabulous show. The Militant's seething grief needed a target—hot, glowing emotion, child's play compared to the guilt that boiled underneath. Kor blamed himself for not saving Noi, for Jude, for his selfish need to see himself as human. What was she supposed to do with that? Best to move out of the way and find cover.

"Laws cage the unconscious," Kor said. "Blood drips from your hide. Where is the justice? The sacred comes from an open heart. Laws are a choice someone makes. You and your Commonweal killed my friend. You and your Commonweal threaten to kill every human. Your choice. Your oppression. Your crime."

Charronna marveled. Kor talked like he had fused with Noi . . . more passed between them than she realized. Unable to resist, she strained against the psi-shield to pilfer through his mind. Even when he railed with righteous resentment at the norms of his world, a part of him clung to the guiding principles of Militant culture etched into his DNA. Separated from the priests, and the boundaries of his home, his faith in the Code's relevance slipped into the denizens of lost dreams. He was no longer sure of who he was or his proper place in the universe. Charronna empathized.

She recoiled back into solitary confinement. Saps fell in love. Saps deluded themselves into thinking anyone cared. Bitter aftertastes coated her tongue. Smiling Court lies designed to keep everyone mistrustful and miserable.

Tellerian medics came and sealed Kor's wounds—the ones they could see. Civilized peoples did such things to shield themselves from the reality of their hardened hearts. We take from you, oppress and kill you because we can, as we must in the cause to protect civilization from the evils of outsiders. Charronna had done much the same thing in the name of the Smiling Court— the cost of her service nothing less than her inherent goodness. Did any of it remain? Kor believed so—he saw a light in her that no one else had except Noi.

The Chair, the Avue, and the rest of the aliens withdrew from the lounge. Kor sagged. Sparrow crumpled into his arms. Charronna joined them, pressing into Kor's back. Unexpectedly, she had found a family—one she wanted to get to know better.

***

After much internal debate, Kor opted for a burial. Scattering the ashes would have done Noi honor, but a permanent reminder of his death would be a powerful memorial to injustice. Somehow, some way, Noi's death would matter. At Sparrow's request, everyone wore black to the funeral. Charronna and C-Glenmarra, who provided the clothes, ushered the young princess to the service. The young princess, shaken and traumatized, held their hands white knuckle tight. They and Kor donned a sun visor to protect against Bluefire's brightness.

Rainfalls of visible tassel-shaped prisms undulated, curtains of the cosmos, beauty before the dark. Waves crashed on the crystalline beach, wordless reassurance from the world. Lom and Ven came for the Nevrans. Nearcherlus, a Vestrian observer, joined a venerable crowd of Commonweal representatives. The sea flamed with light captured from the descending star in an awesome conflagration. The onlookers diminished in the spectacle of creation, yet they wielded authority to decide the fate of every human. The future balanced on a sphere. It could fall anywhere, at the slightest provocation.

Kor approached Lom and gave a modest bow. The combination of Noi's assassination and Raven's harrowing escape from the Nox swayed the Commonweal into improved treatment. Everyone got upgraded quarters for the night. The Commonweal cherished adherence to their principles even when that meant protecting their ancient enemies before the scheduled execution. "Thank you for coming," Kor said.

Lime green flushed with grays throughout Lom's chameleon hide. "The Law binds the Commonweal in an enduring yet fragile union where we must be vigilant and ever respectful."

"The Commonweal wants to do the killing instead of vigilantes. I get it. Where is Raven?"

"In your shuttle guarded by Tols."

Tension locked into Kor's muscles, but he fought for calm in his voice with focused concentration. "Did he tell you why he's there and not here?"

"He told the guards nothing." Lom's four eyes blinked in sync. "I have matters more pressing on my mind than your companion's itinerary."

Kor gave another bow, fighting off waves of anger. Growing up on Zorn meant he had a lot of practice.

Nevran workers had carved a neat rectangular hole into the sunbaked soil a full six feet deep. Wearing green garments similar to cassocks, they lowered Noi into place in a transparent capsule. At the head of the grave, a pinkish-gold glow illuminated a thick granite slab. Kor provided the words inscribed around a looping infinity symbol. *Be thy Soul in joy at the union with The All, Noi Zekra, of Humankind.*

The shower of prisms dimmed. The guests formed two broken crescents flanking Noi's grave. Kor took his spot by the monument and activated a holographic image of Noi, serene, with a touch of a smile, hovering over the grave, much like the ghost he had been. Stiff winds blew off the sea—the waves peaked higher and crashed with vigor on the beach.

Noi's people dispersed their ashes. But ashes didn't have the visual impact of brutalized flesh. Noi rested on a flat piece of wood, his vicious wounds visible, a strange fruit from a harvest of ancient condemnation. How could anyone not tremble at such a sight even if hate overflowed their souls? In time, Noi would merge into nature, in keeping with the Psian way.

Z'yax arrived but kept their distance, hiding behind goggles, their shells gleaming under a protective coating. The aliens were inscrutable, yet his emotional sense conveyed neither challenge nor reproach. They were simply present. Noi would have appreciated that.

Kor chanted words he didn't understand, a poem of passing, dating from the Starry Empire's earliest records. Ribbons of grief infused his exhalations. Heated filaments flared in Kor's head. The old god's presence surfaced.

"Not now, Jeth-ka."

"You sing in the language of the gods."

Translation flowed into Kor's thoughts.

Weep not, Fair Child, for the falling stars

That brought us nightly beauty from afar.

We each move on, we each make way

For new creation to birth and hold sway.

Let go of the beauty from your tight heart

And know that to live is always to part

To change, to let go, to be something other

As ordained from the beginning by the Great Mother.

Rejoice in stars to come and beauty that never clings

We see the falling stars and we celebrate and sing.

The poem swirled, reshaping hope from angry sorrow.

"Have you heard the song before?" he asked Jeth.

Pindrop silence. *"Yes."*

"The gods are not so different. Is there no way we can work together?"

Kor asked again, but Jeth-ka retreated from conscious view.

Charronna spoke kind words, naming Noi a friend, an unexpected softening from the once Red Witch. Sparrow proclaimed Noi a prime-class door-catcher. Among the alien guests, circumspection prevailed. Farther away, the Z'yax just *were*. Grief stole Kor's joy, and his knees gave way, sending him to the ground. With cupped hands, he gathered loamy dirt, and sprinkled clumps over Noi's body, the last goodbye.

"Let Noi, who sleeps the endless sleep, be in peace eternal. Let no creature, no being, disturb the vessel that housed his soul. We give thanks for the life, the kindness, the beauty of Noi Zekra."

Pile by pile, Kor filled the grave. Noi's corpse transformed into Jude—the dirt into the blood-soaked mud from the war game on the far side of Zorn. Walls shattered. Thoughts shouted. *Blood for blood. Honor your father. A soldier of virtue protects. Do our clan honor wherever you go.* Loam slipped through quaking fingers. The ground disappeared in a liquid blur. *Love your enemies. Bless them who curse you. Do good to those who despise you and persecute you.*

Imperatives dueled, flashing in an echo of the Coming Together's lighted signs. He put his hands to his ears and let loose a muted war cry. Kor clutched his black stone charm, his private remembrance of Jude, of their time together. On a boulder-strewn beach, on the day they agreed to their union, Jude had leaned into him. Surf surged and wrapped around them. Within reach lay a smooth black rock with a crossed notch. Kor plucked it from the water to imbue in timeless stone the happy occasion.

Legs quivering, Kor walked to the water's edge and scooped up a handful of wet salt—in the scoop, a pale rock. Hands opened, releasing the new and old stones, which came alive in the setting star's fading dazzle.

He used a knife-edged stone that he found near the grave to slice a bloody line across his palm. "When does the cycle of retribution end? Why can't we see each other's divine?"

Blood dripped to the dirt in a liquid crimson reverie. A drop splashed on his charm—it splashed into his mind. No matter what, he would always be a Militant. The realization, the necessity of acceptance, stirred relief in a cooling wave. He would always be a Militant, but he was the sum of many parts. No need to run from any of them; he could never escape from who he was, and why would he try?

After the blood clotted, he rubbed salt into the wound, numbing the pain. "Blood for blood. I offer mine over this grave. Let it be enough for Noi and for the Commonweal."

He took Charronna's hand. The aliens had returned her fashion-statement shoes. She wore them with delight. Yet within her sense of personal power, vulnerability cracked into her fully alive self. "I forgive you."

She squeezed Kor's hand. "Thank you. I can't make honest promises about future behavior. The Chorus owns me as much as any subset."

"There is always a choice," Kor said, "even when you can't imagine otherwise." He picked up the bloodstained charm and its new pale brother. "We have finished."

Words such as "noble," "civilized," "interesting," "strange," and "honorable" flavored the Vio breeze with hope.

Kor put a light hand on Sparrow's shoulder. "I am here for you." The young princess didn't respond; Kor dropped to his haunches. The girl's eyes twinkled with the adult pain of knowing lost dreams. No answers came to the rescue; his spirit swam in the same muddied sea.

"My dad says every crime must be punished," Sparrow said. "He says some enemies can be converted, some can be co-opted, some can be contained, some can be ruined, some can be isolated, some can be stalemated. But some have to be killed. I think the Z'yax are that kind of enemy."

"That's what Noi's killers think about us. We must be better."

Sparrow bit her lip. "Being better didn't save Noi."

Charronna pulled Sparrow away in a soft hug. The girl stiffened at first but melted into touch, breaking into heartrending sobs.

The uninvited Z'yax, in their sightseeing pose, intruded. In a stiff stride, Kor closed the distance between them.

CHAPTER XXXI

The Z'yax huddled near one of the scattered wide-bodied trunks, a boneyard tree casting an ethereal pall as the sky dimmed to blood blue. Teeth locked, Kor halted a few feet away. One of the beetle-shell beasts dropped to its hind legs and scuttled closer to challenge Kor's self-restraint. A sharp, biting odor fired up his brain with signals to retreat or to fight. He put feelings aside, pretended he spoke to his father, and with deadpan calm, asked his burning question. "Why are you here?"

"I am Irhhasa of the Red Leaf Hive. Our Queen Gunaseak sent us to present an offering."

"What possible offering atones for atrocity?"

The Z'yax's antennae quivered. Kor got the distinct impression that he amused the Z'yax. "Well?" He welcomed the rushing seethe of quick-speed loaded yet locked. "Must I fight you at my friend's last rite?"

"Your kind overflows with passion. Our lakes are dry. We are sometimes envious. Other times, we are content."

Kor cut off his prepared retort. A cursory examination of Irhhasa made clear that physical diversity existed among the Z'yax: smaller, thinner armor, dark green, a different breed and perhaps a different mindset. "You appear less suited to battle than the ones who attacked us."

Irhhasa bobbed her head. "We are green shell. We arrived late because Bluefire harms us. Adequate protections are cumbersome."

"Are you here to apologize for your brethren's atrocity?"

Irhhasa's antennae gyrated. The movement repeated in a set pattern. Z'yax laughter?

"Z'yax do not manage guilt with forceless words," Irhhasa said. "We deal in covenants."

"We have no covenant."

"We did not come here as enemies. But if you insist, we will leave that way."

Kor checked himself. The Earthers had a saying, "Walk the talk." He picked up a limb and threw it against the tree, causing a nick that oozed brown-red sap—a thoughtless act of violence unworthy of the Amun he hoped to be.

"Say your peace."

"Rogue drones of an allied nest took part in the attack. Z'yax killed at an improper place and time. We, therefore, present you with a promise."

Irhhasa tilted her weight to her back legs and extended one of her arms. A square shell dangled from an alloy chain.

"This comes from our Mother Queen's Mother Queen," Irhhasa said. "We offer a sacred gift. Where law-abiding Z'yax tread or fly, you will be respected."

Kor rubbed the smooth ultra-dark green shell. In his other hand, he clutched his stones, the old and the new. Maybe the universe heard his prayers. Maybe the charm summoned a wizard's magic. He held out his hand, palm open. "Charms. Choose one."

Choose what I need to give up. My memory of love or my hope in a new way.

The Z'yax extended a limb, using delicate pincers to grab the black stone.

"Your blood stains the rock."

"Aye," Kor said.

"You give of yourself as the mother gave to you. Remarkable."

Irhhasa waved its limbs in a slow sensuous motion. The other greens joined in. They weaved around one another—their bulky forms surprisingly lithe. Appendages went up and out, over and under in overlapping fluidity. The movements picked up speed, the motions more complex, a voiceless symphony to catch one's purest spirit.

As the creatures danced, one of the T'hyto attendees, Permanent Councilor Tau Ring, approached with a lantern held high. The distinguished guest spread blue gem-tinted wings—a fanciful, fantastic being at once noble in bearing and resolute in purpose.

"I am over four hundred years old," Tau Ring said. "Yet I have never seen one of their ballets. No other species except the Sy'tallians dared to honor you as much. The irony swirls to my soul. You and these Z'yax created a beautiful moment. I hope it's not the last."

"You and me both."

The T'hyto's fire-bright tourmaline eyes flashed; his pale green skin gave way to golden scales blushing with passion. The ballet shrunk the universe to an intimate space under the wide-bodied tree. In a fluid unwinding of movement, the Z'yax slowed to a stillness in the gathering dark. Ache knotted deep in Kor's throat. The aliens chirped in interweaving notes, a mesmerizing harmony, repeating in voice what they had accomplished in movement. In the following silence, their hush thundered. *Among these green shells, the Supreme reveals its presence.*

"Honorable Z'yax will respect our covenant," Irhhasa said.

In a flash, they hopped away toward an air transport, outlined in a murky malachite shimmer, parked near a tree with multiple, intertwining sinewy trunks. "Goodbye, my new, unexpected alien friends." *Goodbye, my sweet Jude, until we meet again over the event horizon.*

He fingered the square talisman. On death's ground, good magic abounded.

***

Raven sat lotus style on the floor in the shuttle's rear passenger section, singing murmured praises to the Blessed One. Prayers once filled his days. Devotion, however, was no longer enough. A circle of heat from the contact communicator seeped into his upper thigh. Surging expectation channeled into an undeniable intention.

"The sentiments are against you, E'lani," Mobard said.

"I thought your people had balls."

"Use that tone with the headmaster, and she would cut yours off. Lucky for you, she rates you a cup's worth of trouble. The V'yahi Masterships are eager for a source of slaves. We offer a deal."

"Go on."

"The headmaster agreed to provide you an incapacitating agent favored by Qa and a stealth-field generator powerful enough to conceal your ship—restricted technology and a prize by itself. You must use it to disappear."

"Power supply requirements?"

"Ten exajoules."

"Our ship—"

"Has been scanned more times than my purple ass. Which is a lot, in case you're wondering. Another interested party provided an off-market energy supply to initialize the generator."

"How does the agent work?"

"It's set to release ten minutes after your shuttle passes through your ship's containment field. The gas remains active for twenty minutes before it breaks down."

"Perfect. How does that help you?"

"Your shipmate's assassination generated gold-proof sympathy. Alliances shift and opinions diverge, but the majority hold to enforcing the extermination edict. Your vanishing act, and assumed destruction, may tip the balance of sentiment further in your favor—a plus for the V'yahi securing their product."

"Vio DC monitors the ship."

"Anyone with at least a telescope monitors your ship. Figure out a distraction. Fly into the glow of a cruiser. Blow something up. Two armadas face off throughout the Bluefire System. Improvise. Whatever you do, everyone must believe your ship was destroyed. You will receive rendezvous coordinates far from here."

"You intend to send one of your ships with me?"

"The headmaster wants to collect a sample shipment to test the waters of a trade deal."

"I accept your terms."

"Wait for our contact. Expect delivery soon."

The communicator cooled. The plan of action incurred risk, but without control of *Star Horizon*, failure was assured. Preparation for duplicitous helpfulness included telling lies in front of a mirror with warmth and friendliness. Kor had *Star Horizon's* access codes—cooperation would be required. One way or another, he would get back to the ship, another area where Kor might be needed, and finish the mission of retrieving the sacred endless.

Raven emerged from the shuttle under the watchful eyes of his Tol handlers. Raven flexed his hands. A light sweat glistened on his flesh. The mighty star rose to reveal thousands of ships, merchant galleons, yachts, shuttles, transports, freighters, and more, a grounded armada on the immense landing platform. More dropped from the sky. Refugees pushed to safe harbors by the coming sweep of battle.

The realization stirred primordial foreboding. The Living God had seen too much of war, its devastation, suffering, and uncertain outcomes. Yet more must come. A phalanx of Tols escorted Kor around the long, graceful tip of a Tellerian Skybird Skiff—his mood as black as his bodysuit.

Kor's nostrils flared. Jaw muscles rippled. Anger rippled across his brow, terrifying, emotional, undisciplined, un-militant, a puppet on a string. "Noi saved your life on Eos," he said.

"I'm grateful for Noi. A life debt remains between us—the Blessed Emperor honors such debts as Militants honor the Code." *Unless the debt interferes with the mission to gain the sacred endless.* Raven held his arms wide in welcome and blinked an eye to signal Kor to play along. They embraced, and Raven whispered into Kor's ear. "I've made friends. They provided us a means to escape if we can get back to the ship."

Kor relaxed, squeezed genuine warmth into the hug, and added a kiss on the cheek. The Tols watched, letting the barbarians love on each other. The emperor's satisfaction flowed.

They headed back to the rock-hewn city. The Tols shadowed. Once on *Star Horizon*, assuming the plan got that far, Raven only needed to slip into a stasis bed while the incapacitating agent did its work. With Kor knocked out, and then waking up in an airlock, Raven would gain the upper hand. The promise of Paradise for his people was within reach.

CHAPTER XXXII

"The conversation around your fate concludes."

The Nevran's finality flooded Charronna's insides with dirty meltwater. Sparrow gripped Charronna's hand extra tight. *Misery loves company*—a saying unique to the Earthers, yet universal.

She witnessed her reflection for too long. Mirror queen was a common dig from Smiling Court white-eyes who had nothing better to do than malign and disparage. What harm manifested in positive self-reinforcement? C-Glenmarra's generous gift of a stunning green gown, light years ahead of prison wear, helped. Standing tall, a goddess, Sparrow presented in a multi-hued flow of rich purples.

"We will survive this," Charronna said.

"Father says real hope comes from strength, from having power."

"Look in the mirror. Don't you see? We command both."

Ven led his charges through one of Pink Dream's endless hallways with an unbroken wall of guards, a constant reminder of her captive status. Sparrow's chatter filled the void; the little princess had regained her smile and threw off bright mental emissions Charronna did her best to soak up.

At the entrance to the Vinculum, a tall, serpentine being with aquatic slits along the torso, blocked the way-- *Sus*. Protuberant fisheyes opened and closed in languid blinks. The Sus swept scanners over every inch of Charronna. Arms went up when told, and she kept them there until directed otherwise. Hot vapors expanded in her mind. She should request a vid for all those she had wronged back home who would throw a party to see her humiliated.

Ven waved off the Sus. "No need for more examination."

The Sus's face pulsed with iridescence. "Of course."

Aliens packed the Assembled Vinculum. A bevy of Tols escorted Charronna and Sparrow to the center podium. The configuration had changed. The stage sat below the assemblers, a giant sinkhole that would mercifully collapse into a much more pleasant reality if the gods paid any attention. Wide-eyed Sparrow hovered close by, riveted to the spectacle, but she no longer spun fairy tale dreams.

One odd creature, pale, wispy hair, standing far away in the balcony's first row, generated enough laser-focused awareness to draw her interest despite the psi blockers. *Vestrian.* Charronna shivered. Her admirer wanted something—or was he planning to do something? She applied gentle pressure to her lobes. Anxiety and telepathy didn't mix.

The chamber's paneled door shut; throughout the perimeter, the others closed, the shutting of coffin lids. The thickening atmosphere doused the buzzing Assemblers into an abrupt hush. Charronna set her gaze to a full-on challenge. The little girl forged by psi-instructors into a weapon would not wilt. Those instructors pushed little Charro to the precipice of the abyss, but she never fell then and wouldn't now.

The hall reopened to the outside world, no more than a sliver, an air hole to release the tension. Two silhouetted figures stood in a flood of light. Perhaps it was the proud way he carried himself, or maybe she had memorized his masculine shape, the sharp V riding to delicious curves. But she knew. Kor had arrived.

Charronna threw aside a lifetime of decorum and jumped with the zeal of a girl fresh into puberty. Never mind what anyone else thought. Kor gave a thumbs up and grinned like someone who was genuinely glad to see her. And she thought she might fall at last into a place she never expected.

***

The Z'yax talisman, fastened to a chain, dangled against Kor's chest. A vast civilization assembled in the great hall ready to pass judgment, but for a spine-tingling moment, he saw only Charronna. With a free hand, he clutched his new stone, squeezing for a fairy-tale ending.

The exhilaration diffused into tension. Guards tucked Kor, Raven, and his Nevran escort, Ven, in a tight sandwich, keeping him siloed from the aliens. His clothing, a gift from C-Glenmarra, caressed his skin, luxurious and titillating. The pale green and taupe colors were cool and safe. No need to fear him.

"They wait for you to begin," Ven said.

"You want them to execute us," Kor said.

"I've come to like you. Why did you disfigure your brand with two vertical lines?"

"To broaden the meaning. All Are Created Equal."

"The slashes are identical and straight and at the proper width, a holy mark among many that has provoked much conversation. You have citizenship potential. But rules are rules."

Kor leaned into Ven. "You would make an excellent priest should you ever make it to Zorn." He held out his hand.

Ven's bottom pair of eyes fixed on Kor's outstretched arm.

"A handshake. It's a thing friends do."

Ven didn't move, though he oscillated through a series of color changes. Confused? Insulted? "You have to start somewhere," he added.

Kor grabbed the scaly hide, shaking the clawed hand. "Rules are important. Don't let them masquerade as your conscience."

"Your death will be a loss. Be vibrant."

Encouraged, Kor stepped further into the cavernous hall ahead of Raven. Scents competed, voices strived, the wild ends of the spectrum, motions on the ground, in the air, in watery habitats, a diversified legion assailing his senses. The walls pulsed with living-stone portraits who gazed with dispassionate appraisal, with the power of the Red Beast.

Charronna, not to be denied, delivered a simple message before the connection vanished into the muddle of psi-dampeners. *Thanks for coming.*

Kor shouldered his way past blue and green Nuxinni and keen-eyed Cheemin dressed in flamboyant color draped in bejeweled gold chains. He squeezed between Tynthions with waving, light-emitting scalp-anchored tendrils, walking around the Qa in extravagant aquariums; the crimson and burnt orange aquatics, a few of them inky blacks, moved delicate limbs in a symphony of motion. Anger? Applause? He settled on the latter as he passed under Zev canopies blowing baritone notes to the sway of branches. The chamber combined spectacle, beauty, and the weight of authority to unleash horror and terror for the cause of civilization.

Kor ducted and veered right into a bisecting aisle. Raven continued to the stage of judgment.

"Halt," barked a Tol guard.

In response, he quickened his pace. An Asag, topless except for suspenders and glistening with peppery scented lubricant, blocked the way, leather wings spread. The aisle behind him filled with spectators. Kor pulled out a pocketknife, a composite blade made to be undetectable, and pricked his thumb. The Asag remained an immovable object. Kor pricked each of his digits in turn. "*With eyes to see,*" he sang, "*your soul to burning quick, with mind closed in, your heart to frigid sick, beware true sin. Seek out the true balance in always search, never stop, your body becomes the sought-after church.*" He repeated the verse. Red lifeforce painted his palms and arms. The mantra rolled off his tongue.

Mountains moved. Oceans spilled onto dry land. Glaciers slipped lower. Mantle grated against itself. Blood thundered in his ears. To life or death, there was no stopping a bloodletting until another shared the ritual. His eyes fluttered. The Asag enclosed Kor's hand and plucked the knife away. Kor opened his bleeding hands, palms up, unsure what would happen next.

The alien licked the blade. Onyx wings vibrated layers of wind sounds. Thin, oval pupils expanded to triple the diameter. In quick succession, the Asag nipped his five-digit hands. "I am Fa' Klinza." He grabbed Kor's hands. Black and red blood combined; they held the position with the ease of lovers enjoying a long embrace.

The Asag flicked his split tongue. "You may pass, warrior to warrior, poet to poet; we are one, we are two, the two are one."

Kor pulled his hands away and walked past Fa' Klinza. The Asag's comrades vibrated their wings in salute; they also blocked the Tol guards. No one else challenged him; the path was clear to the Z'yax delegation. He reached for Noi's spirit. Militants didn't offer reconciliation to a remorseless enemy.

The nearest Z'yax clicked its mandibles and twirled its front legs in a menacing posture. Kor ordered his arm to rise to no avail. His heart seized. His forehead brand itched. Do something!

Jeth's voice detonated into Kor's mind with the explosive force of a singularity bomb. *"She is among them."*

Kor staggered. *"Not a good time."*

"These Z'yax stink of Zaxa's aroma."

"I've got bigger issues."

"There are no bigger issues. She would burn the galaxy to see me gone."

"One problem at a time."

Blue firestorm whipped through Kor's thoughts. Jeth confronted, howling the torment of a burning forest. *You will do as you're told, boy.* Kor wanted to be a good son, to be loved by his father, and the impulse to obey ate into his resistance.

Neither arm budged. The giant armored beetle made tiny hops and lunges, an agitated dance. He also wanted to be forgiven for killing Jude. How could he in truth desire forgiveness and not be generous toward others? The flat of his palm pressed into a cool shell. The Z'yax shifted weight to its hind legs, head reared. Antennae gyrated. Comingled crimson and black blood coated the shell. The Z'yax let out a high squeak that the translator failed to decipher. In a horror-vid movement, the beast sprang at Kor.

Cohesive light struck the creature. It vaporized in an instant. Fa' Klinza pointed a hefty gun at other Z'yax assemblers.

"The human will not die yet."

The rest of the giant beetles boiled. Kor backed away; others did the same. Acrid, ozone odors burned into his lungs. Tol guards appeared with weapons aimed at everyone, including Kor and the Asag. One of the Permanent Councilors, a Z'yax, descended in a mobile podium, long limbs spiraled in animated performance.

"The Fa', despite violating our law by smuggling a weapon into our assembly, an egregious violation which *will* be investigated," the Z'yax Councilor said, "speaks for us all. Let us finish our deliberations and execute our wisdom."

The immense Z'yax Councilor swooped to Kor. He stood his ground. An exchange of one for billions. . . The Councilor stopped a finger-width short; upper limbs slicing and cutting in a menacing weave. Kor got the distinct impression that she weighed whether to say anything more. The T'hyto Councilor Tau Ring descended to a counterpoint position.

"The T'hyto Way," Tau Ring said, "has declared a beautiful moment with the humans. They have souls worth saving. We commit a crime against life if we proceed with genocide."

A bird-faced Assembler with puffy white hair spoke into the quiet in ringing tones. Eos archive memories came to the fore . . . *Rumen. Many Rumen cooperated with the E'lani Empire during its occupation of part of the Commonweal. Vengeful hunter ships destroyed the Rumen home world and colonies after the Kimbrian anti-life weapons drove the E'lani back.*

"We say 'We are One,'" the Rumen said. "Is that our truth or our pretension?"

For long seconds, the Vinculum remained suspended in a breathless bubble.

A lone voice yelled, "Truth!" Ovations erupted from every corner. The hall rumbled with shouts of truth. Energies of joy, hatred, excitement and rage crackled in the great hall with the tension of unresolved conflict. The Z'yax Permanent Councilor ascended on high, demanding a recess. Many assemblers exited the chamber with non-stop angry buzz. Others continued to shout.

Kor stared at his hands, covered in sticky red and black blood. What decisions would be made among the aliens and what results would manifest? He searched deep inside himself but had no idea what he perceived, a stranger, a new person coming into being. Would he love this self-becoming, this changed Kor? The throng cleared. Energy leeched and loneliness intruded in the form of a monster from his conscious nether regions. It had grown strong during his isolation. The arrival of his comrades, the glow of Charronna, Sparrow, and even Raven, banished, at least for a time, the hurtful devourer.

"That took guts," Charronna said, "and not the Militant kind. I believe you."

Kor lifted his brows in query.

"I believe you are one hundred percent, full-blooded human. I hope there's room for one more in the club."

Charronna's emerald eyes watered. Kor wished for clean hands to pull her, Sparrow, and Raven into a hug as gun-toting Tols closed ranks around them.

***

In a tight ball of smoldering ash, Jeth hovered and churned until whitish-gray particles broke off, the detritus drifting in fading life force. Nearby, as if there was anything else in the forsaken void, Sala flayed. Her fiery red gown intensified into frightening saturation. Yet Jeth's engagement ring faithfully glittered.

"You should have listened to me," Sala said.

"We don't know she felt us."

Sala rolled her seductive, entrancing eyes. "We felt *her.* You spent far too much time in your labs. Somewhere along the way, you lost track of how the human condition works."

"She may not have detected us," insisted Jeth. "She wasn't expecting me."

"She wasn't expecting any humans. I promise you she reevaluates her assumptions. I would."

Uncertainty and vacillation poured through Jeth, unstoppable acid flows eating at his self-resolve and illusion of control. Odd how error compounded onto itself, increasing in magnitude as it recycled over and over through time into ever-worsening consequences. Another mistake would be fatal. Possible decision paths spread into unfollowable permutations.

Sala drifted closer. "Kill the Militant. Do whatever it takes. I'd sooner face another million years with you than face Zaxa."

***

Zaxa arched her intellect into artistic probabilities. Anticipation electrified the connections between the sum of her uulli—millions of milky white scarabs. *Uulli come, uulli go, but the mind goes on forever.* Biological minds were not meant to endure *forever.* She shifted the weight of her hive mind onto caretaker HoZo, a host of giant millipedes. They carried her to the salt chamber, an expansive cathedral space glowing in pinks, yellows, reds, and oranges. The caretakers deposited her in a warm shallow basin. Ions bombarded, fueling the pleasurable connectivity of her uulli.

Godhood and immortality—those were Jeth's obsessions. No, she simply wanted revenge. What normal woman wouldn't want payback for being dumped into a hive mind monstrosity because her husband-to-be didn't grasp the concept of *letting go*? But her opinion on godhood had changed.

The war on Avad ravaged the home world and every colony in The Unity. The White Mothers allied with the E'lani against the Avas, who dominated the human political structures, and the Irrosan, the weakest of the three major powers. In the final days, with civilization on the verge of collapse, the E'lani, those able, fled to a distant star. The war turned. The Avas-Irrosan alliance neared victory. To avoid defeat, Zaxa launched a scorched-world campaign, nuclear bombardments, and asteroid strikes—a holocaust to all life. Deep underground, she and a few White Mothers survived. Recovery took thousands of years.

In the interim, the Commonweal burst across the Milky Way. Self-determination was more out of reach than ever. The Cosmic Song provided the ultimate solution to meddlesome governments, narcissistic husbands, and anyone else in creation unable to mind their own business.

The memory of the Cosmic Song's egg-shaped alloy tantalized in a shimmer of blue, every inch of it etched in musical notes structured as string equations. To touch the artifact was to feel a cool surface, to luxuriate in waves of harmonics and in tones constructing mathematical structure, to experience in meter the voice of God—a paradox of infinity. In a twist of fate, she had a chance to recover it, to shed her hive mind form, and to achieve her rightful destiny—Mother of the Universe. The stars would sing *Alleluia!* until the end of days.

Kor reeked of Jeth. Either the human possessed the Cosmic Song or he had been in contact. No other explanation satisfied. Through her ambassador, she observed. The hall emptied. Those who remained celebrated with victorious noise. Tols started to move the humans into a protective bubble. Kor stood next to Fa' Klinza, who kept the guards at bay with a menacing wing spread. E'lani and Asag meeting without an exchange of life-shedding blood? How unexpected! The latest version of the accursed E'lani was more dangerous than ever.

Closer. Zaxa exerted her desire upon the Ambassador. Lacey wings fluttered. One of the Tols pointed his weapon and ordered the Ambassador to stay clear. She pushed past in haughty bluff. The male extended a hand, a friendly gesture. A slight improvement in the race? Zaxa would delight in testing them out. The human's heated skin penetrated. Torrents of sensation scalded. It soaked into the sum of her uulli network, an unleashing of unsatiated anger. *Jeth-ka lived.*

"I'm Kor of Steel Rose. I come in peace."

"We all come in peace," the Ambassador said, "until peace no longer suits us."

Gray eyes pierced the veils of deceit. Involuntary shivers rustled through millions of her milky white uulli. A quick move, a spit of an alkylating toxin, and she removed the threat. *Stay rational.* The Ambassador would be arrested. Authorities would come for her. Jeth's rottenness incited. His foulness offended. The Ambassador's poison sacs filled. The E'lani-human carried Jeth's consciousness. The prison was unescapable, but no other explanation accounted for his insufferable presence.

"I hope," Kor said, "we get the opportunity to know one another."

"Opportunities are treasures easily lost."

"Then we should do everything possible not to lose them."

"Ability and desire, such attributes must be managed. It is beyond you."

"Shouldn't we start with a cup of coffee together before the rejection?"

"You hold the Commonweal hostage to something as small as a single act. I never waste my time."

A physical reflex surged, an orgasm of passion and need, and an alkylating mist covered its victim in sweet, fragrant justice. There, it was done. The offending male would soon die. The Ambassador headed to the nearest transmat. Best to be elsewhere when Kor collapsed.

CHAPTER XXXIII

Kor had been poisoned. No one else seemed to notice the brief spray of mist.

Any of his companions would be dying or dead—nothing his bio-filters couldn't handle. He spotted the green cicada-like assailant, but Tols cut him off. Raven made eye contact in a pointed reminder that he had a way to escape. Kor raised his shoulders, a minimal gesture of *"What do you expect me to do?"* One of the soldiers motioned at him to get moving.

The Polarian's agitation escalated, and in an odd move, he spat on the nearest trooper. The Tol hammered Raven to the ground. Blood trickled from a gash in Raven's arm. The guards, who before rarely spoke, argued with one other in melodic, bass-timbre tones.

They were under strict orders to prevent further injury to the human prisoners. The disagreement ended with a consensus to send Raven back to *Star Horizon* to conceal the injury along with Kor and feign misunderstanding if anyone questioned the mix-up. Several of the High Councilors had already requested that Kor be sent back to his ship; another E'lani should not cause trouble. Either way, whether planet-side or in orbit, they would soon be dead.

The decision made, the Tols whisked Kor and his comrade back to the landing platform in a windowless transport. Kor strapped in on a bench; Raven did the same across a narrow aisle. Four Tols kept a studied watch. Blood trickled down Raven's arm until natural clotting staunched the flow. Eyes down, he seemed subdued, but he sweated, and his nervous breathing stayed high in the lungs. Anticipation? Stress? A faint sulfurous odor emanated from the Polarian, which in turn heightened Kor's already on-alert senses. No one spoke the entire trip.

The guards hustled them into the shuttlecraft and ordered them back to *Star Horizon*. Reinforcements winked in around the planet as the incoming armadas organized into dozens of attack groups. Charronna and Sparrow remained on Vio, impossibly out of reach. The shuttle passed through *Star Horizon's* containment field. Kor left the bay doors open to space crawling with warships, satellites, armed platforms, probes, and mobile fortresses. The awesome assembly of forces arrayed with enough might to storm the gates of heaven. Kor, a step ahead of Raven, exited the shuttle.

"Spitting on the Tol?" Kor said.

"Got us back to the ship. Unlike yours, my plans work." Raven gave his bloody gash a light touch. "I'll be in the med-lab."

Kor nodded, fixed his gaze beyond the containment field where Vio's northern hemisphere threatened from afar. The Vinculum's decision would soon come, a shock wave primed to devour possibility. His offer of forgiveness swayed hearts, but not enough. A multitude of species coexisted in the discovered galaxy, and yet the same patterns persisted on both sides of the Deep Black—proof of the Supreme if one nurtured a drop of faith.

Kor poured himself a glass of water; wet coolness coated his throat with the sublime pleasure of a gourmet meal. The incoming fleet continued to deploy. Vio's terminator, a blur of gray between night and day, advanced, an unstoppable marker of time. A beep flashed on his armband-- ten Imperial standard hours before the Vinculum's judgment.

"Foreign object detected on the shuttle," the AI reported.

Kor's mind jumped. The means to escape that Raven had mentioned?

"AI, patch me into the med-lab."

"Your shipmate is unavailable."

"What do you mean?"

"He's in stasis."

"How long?"

"Seven point five minutes."

Sweat streamed onto Kor's cheeks and pooled around his lips. The Polarian had sprung a trap.

***

With the specter of death practically licking her ears, Charronna wanted to gorge on hot, muscular men. Sex would keep the terror at bay. She wanted it until the thought of more left her dry. She wanted Kor. But she hadn't seen him or the Polarian since the altercation in the Vinculum. No one had come to explain what happened.

Walls sucked the oxygen from the waiting-room cage. Beyond the walls was an enclosed city overrun with bloodlust aliens. Sparrow babbled on about seven brothers competing for favor with an emotionally frozen father and about a mother better at throwing galas than raising children. Paradise pills called her name, promising relief, but she wasn't ready to give up.

The Hermesian princess lost steam and sulked into a corner. *Be hard, little Charro. Be a diamond, admired, desired by many, indestructible. People die, little Charro. Diamonds are forever.* Of course, the aliens possessed a variety of ways to pulverize or otherwise vaporize any level of resistance. She couldn't be hard enough.

Their waiting-to-be-executed closet of a room came with a slab bench and cheerless Tol guards, always in abundant supply. Denied the elixir of coffee, she settled for rutti, a cold and bitter local brew to rival the half-machine hearts of the ruling Chorus. She ran her fingers through hair, no longer silken-soft with the loss of civilized basics such as a decent hair conditioner. Her heart pounded faster. Maybe the alien brew contained a stimulant. Maybe she caught a second wind. Overtaxed brain cells popped in vain hope.

Frustrated, she pushed against the psi-dampener, getting a throbbing headache in return. By damn, she wanted to know something, anything that might be useful. She redoubled her efforts, diving into rapids of hot wires. Bit by bit, through curated spite, she lodged her awareness into the continuum.

She wasn't alone.

A wooden tetrahedron engulfed in a bonfire blazed without being consumed. It drew closer with purpose . . . *improbable.* Whoever it was, they were not linked, and quantum space had rules like everything else. She attempted to pull back. The force of the intruder's desire wrapped burning chains around her will.

"Death becomes you," the consciousness intoned.

Pressure stripped Charronna of substance. The link of energy binding her into the continuum remained strong. She concentrated on severing the connection. The malformed mind resisted letting go. In a heartbeat, she would splinter into nothingness. She directed streams of Eos data into the bonfire to keep the presence filled, earning a few extra beats to devise an escape.

The consciousness pulled—familiar sensation expanded—it resonated in the nether regions of her worst impulses. "You voyaged to E'lan," the consciousness said.

"Never made it," Charronna quipped.

"Did you find the Cosmic Song?"

"We haven't found any such thing."

"Your trick won't last long."

"Why are you attacking me?"

"Survival is the way of life."

"You were once a woman, weren't you?"

The harsh siphon suspended. Charronna metaphorically curled into a ball. The wooden form shattered. Psychic shock waves severed the link to the continuum.

Back in the Real, she fell off the bench with a thud. So much for soft landings.

Sparrow squealed. "What's wrong?" she said.

Charronna struggled to speak. The door to their quarters opened with a whispered sigh. Ven stood there in a tunic, stretching thinner the line between life and death; the room's oxygen hot-flashed away. The tunic's prominent solid red circle within a greater circle, the Commonweal symbol of unity and harmony, mocked—a lie, a conceit, a homage to the capacity of thinking beings to self-deceive.

"The Assembly votes tomorrow morning," Ven said. "The Chair requires you to bear witness."

Charronna pushed buttery legs to Ven, doing her best to lock on the Nevran's four eyes. "Why haven't I been able to see Kor?"

"We are still sorting that out, but Tol guards sent him back to your ship."

"You mean he's off the planet? Is your shame that much that you can't stomach his presence?"

Ven's deep forest-green hide washed out as if struck by acid tears. Distress. No need to overcome psi-dampeners for that insight. *A little more time and the locals might see us. Time they won't concede.*

A wall panel opened to reveal a glass cylinder with an ornate cap of golden horns. A ball, shifting through the color spectrum, floated in a clear liquid near the top.

"Expect my return," Ven said, "when the ball reaches the bottom."

He exited. Charronna paced around the room, eyes glued to the cylinder. Swell, on top of everything else, a deathwatch. The presence in the continuum had been a human female, yet alien. She needed quiet time, a lot, to process. The pretty ball dropped in poisonous increments.

"I wish Kor was here," Charronna said.

"You love him, don't you?" Sparrow asked.

"Love is a fairy tale."

"You mean it isn't real?"

Charronna clasped Sparrow's hand. "Love is a miracle, never to be turned away."

"You and Kor will live happily ever after."

"Forever and ever. The way any good story ends."

The ball gleamed. She hated to look at it. She obsessively did nothing else. In quiet torment, they passed the slipping seconds. If fairy tales existed, the author either left her out or cast her with the villains. To violet, indigo, purple, blue, lethal green, the slow-falling ball rejoiced in its condemnation. The end was near, and she had only her sorry Red Witch ass to thank.

***

Kor dashed inside the shuttle where the AI directed, a sealed storage compartment. The unlock code failed. His hands shook. The numbers jumbled together—they danced, they swapped, they did the dosado. Eject the shuttle? The compartment opened on its own, revealing a bronzed tube with a timer using alien symbols on a countdown sequence.

He snagged the canister and switched to quick-speed in a Flash-Gordon zip out of the bay and to the airlock. In quick-speed time, he punched in the access code. A message flashed across a display over the door: "Error 3 failure." In punch-faced panic mode, he set the canister down and opened a panel with a manual turn-wheel. The handle wouldn't release on the infernal, uncooperative airlock. Full-on muscle, savage effort, yielded not a budge. The countdown reduced to a single symbol. He raced back to the bay and tossed the tube toward the containment field.

"AI, decompress bay."

"Safety protocols require—"

A golden mist expanded, dispersing into the airflow. The ventilation system would spread the poison throughout the vessel within seconds.

"Emergency override. Authorization Code If-I-Could-Fly-Alpha-Six."

"Decompression commencing."

With a final push of quick-speed adrenals, he lunged into the adjoining corridor. A windstorm sucked the oxygen out of the bay. The exit didn't close. He body-blocked the opening to avoid flying into the vacuum. With a death grip on a handhold, he used his free arm to muscle the door. In the rushing roar, Kor summoned every ounce of augmented strength to wrench the blasted door closed.

The Code advised that he kill Raven for his betrayal. The Blood King called for mercy. He bowed his head. Raven was a shadow of his emperor. Would he ever be anything more?

"Priority alert," the AI announced. "Fleet Two deploys infantry."

Command Defense had lifted the jamming. No more second-hand data. A nearby interface confirmed one of the incoming armadas spewed millions of one-person units. *Insect maneuver.* He skipped the lift and used the ladders to climb to the bridge. On-screen, half a dozen globes with enough firepower to split a planet rolled in from the enveloping flanks. Mobile fortress hives from Z'yax and White Mothers, lantern battle cruisers from the Qa, and Bludgeon-class marauders from the Asags—the Terrible Four mentioned in the Eos Archive flaunted their strength.

Though the data feeds contained no embedded commentary, Kor guessed the size of the force caught the Commonweal flatfooted. The Vio fleet scrambled to match the oncoming armada in part with armed merchant ships, mobile platforms, minefields, and converted support vessels. Given the patchwork of defending forces, Fleet Two held the advantage.

"AI, why would an enemy with an advantage delay an attack?" Kor asked.

"To wait for a bigger advantage."

"Send the shuttle back to Vio." *Before the fighting starts.*

If the Blood King gave signs, perhaps Kor had received his. He had more critical enemies to confront. Raven would remain in stasis instead of getting thrown into space.

CHAPTER XXXIV

The deathwatch ball neared the bottom in a dance of color. Charronna hugged Sparrow. They watched. They breathed. They made friends with terror. The ball went transparent, ejecting rainbows into the cylinder—into their holding room. Sparrow tightened her hold, or was it the other way around? Such a pretty ball.

Ven appeared, a gray-draped sentinel of doom. "The vote commences," he said. "Are you ready?"

The words "for your execution," though unspoken, reverberated in the silence.

Encircled by Tol guards and energy fields, they passed through glowing tunnels and into the overflowing Assembled Vinculum. Castle-thick walls trapped electric energies, dark and fearful, expectant and roused, full of nervous expectation. Resolve slipped into child-like desperation in the enemy crush. She forced oxygen into her lungs, expelled carbon dioxide, and imagined Kor with his body wrapped around hers in a reassuring cuddle.

Was this weakness? She didn't care.

Torrid audio torments crackled. Various odors, a blend of emotions and communications, distilled into stomach-turning perfume. Nevrans put on a show of color in ever-shifting skin pigments as too-many-to-count species of Taag bounded about the hall, creating alarm and havoc in their wake before the apish aliens "calmed" into hand clapping and feet stomping. The Shonalli's boisterous laughter carried to the far reaches, but their harsh mirth failed to warm the big chill digging into her misspent life.

Cheemin bandied small talk with their four-footed cousins, the Farronnians whose dark striping on their legs and chest flushed brighter with excitement. Other-worldly, exotic-beautiful solemn Avue flowed toward their seats with the ease of a people detached from their troubles. The LaLa drifted in a cloud of pulsing pink and aqua. Bubbles, as always, smiled; in another time and place, Charronna might have returned the favor, but not with death licking her cheeks, sucking after her breath, a triumphant in-your-face reminder of her tenuous hold on life.

Councilors took their haughty thrones on a tribunal bench that curved around a sunken dais. The ceiling transformed into an ocean of stars, the mighty, the stupendous, the unbreakable Commonweal expanse. Each step became a forced slog through waist-high molasses. Cold acid crawled up Charronna's throat. In fantasy land, Kor held her hand. Why should she do this alone? Desperate, in love, or old-fashioned crazy? *All of the above.* Charronna pulled Sparrow close and sat in a chair with her back straight.

"Sentiments are in flux," Ven said. "Mine as well."

"Kor grows on you."

"Grows, yes. I believe I understand. You all grow upon me. You become more than E'lani." Ven hesitated. "Except for the one called Raven. He distresses us."

"Welcome to the party. And thank you."

The hall's energy condensed into an overload big enough to lay waste to half the galaxy. The Nevran dipped his horns, a signal of support. The scaly reptile deserved a kiss, but he withdrew to a transmat and winked out. The Chair banged a white staff three times, sending stiff reverberation to the far recesses of the hall. Hubbub subsided, voices stilled, motion suspended, and the wheel turned to fates unknown. For several heartbeats, the peace persisted, the prayer before the storm.

"We gather to celebrate the telling of our truth," Lom said. "Each of us discerns a piece of the ultimate truth. Sixty-six delegations, including ten comprised of multiple species, have gathered here to issue their judgment. To overturn an Edict, a minimum of two-thirds of voting assemblers must consent."

"What are you thinking?" Charronna whispered to Sparrow.

The young princess gazed at the assemblage with messianic eyes. The intensity in such a young face didn't seem right. "The universe is amazing." Sparrow beamed.

I'm glad someone is in a party mood. She couldn't quite plug into the idea that her life depended upon winning a popularity contest.

A holographic display materialized over the Permanent Council. One by one, delegations rose to vote their condemnation, their mercy, their guilt, and their greed: Tynthion Associations, Asag Domains, Kimbrian Community, Vorgoth Syndicates, V'yahi Masterships, Nuxinni Metropolitans. The votes tallied. Her mind crunched tighter. The display tormented—another kind of deathwatch ball. Death by slow-motion electrocution.

Why couldn't they vote all at once?

"Protocol," Ven had said.

Waterboarding.

She fell off a cliff and there was no one, not Kor, not an angel, to catch her. The T'hyto, co-creators of the Commonweal, had their turn, and they were not content with a mere tally of sentiment.

"The T'hyto Way favors reconciliation. We declare our intent to withdraw from the Commonweal if the measure for repeal fails. We will not be a party to a crime against life."

Sustained outbursts flared up from the assemblers and the public galleries, a mini war of disbelief and consternation. Lom banged his staff.

"Outrageous blackmail," declared a Qa.

"Where the T'hyto go, we go," countered a Rumen.

"Reevaluate, my friends," a Kimbrian admonished.

"Our harmony must be preserved," a V'yahi squawked. "We must repeal!"

The uproar ebbed into a resentful stalemate. The psi-dampeners made reading the competing emotional energies difficult; a narrow band of potent anger overrode everything else. Several more races cast their positions, united for reconciliation. *Thank you, Mr. T'hyto.* The Janzorian Suzerainties voted for repeal. They had been in the opposing camp. Charronna wanted to clap but was unsure how that would be received.

"We've got a chance," Sparrow said. "Some of the door-slammers notice themselves."

"Optimism is a set-up for disappointment," Charronna quipped.

Joy stretched across Sparrow's face. Cynical rebukes would not dim her natural enthusiasm. The sore spot in Sparrow's heart caused by Noi's murder did not snuff out her belief in the aliens and their justice. Spectators in the public balconies celebrated. The fall would come.

"I call upon the Qa to speak their truth," Lom said.

A Qa assembler thrashed in her watery home. Fellow delegates did the same in smaller habitats. Agitation—no dictionary required.

"The Dominions speak with different voices—twenty-three votes to retain and two to repeal," the Qa announced. The other Qa convulsed. In shock? Charronna had no clue. Pro-repeal balcony celebrations erupted.

"We win if the Tellerians vote for us," Sparrow said.

"You calculated the number?"

"Many times."

"Good girl."

Lom banged his staff. He called on the last delegation.

The Tellerians supported repeal . . . *we are going to live . . . we are . . .*

Charronna trembled. Betrayal amplified in the glow of something astonishing.

***

With the jamming lifted, Kor headed to the bridge for Operation Rescue. To Tau Ring, he sent a simple message—*You have seen us. Have mercy*. Idea two, try a crazy rescue attempt. He tapped into navigation and steadily increased the ship's orbital velocity; in tandem, his pulse raced. Once *Star Horizon* gained enough velocity, he'd planet-side jump right over the Vinculum where he'd blast his way in and hope that he didn't kill his companions. Idea three, pray for divine intervention. Given the dire straits, he would try them all simultaneously.

"I'm not leaving you," he transmitted to Charronna with intense mental focus, hoping the message would find a way through quantum entanglement and into her mind. *Star Horizon* eased toward jump speed. No warnings yet from DC; after all, the interdiction field prevented escape. But that didn't preclude a jump within the field itself.

Eyes closed, he chanted "Fair Child." The spirits he carried came to pay their respects. Noi radiated calm. Broc's sharp approval encouraged. His sister offered hope with a candy-sticky kiss. Wolf reminded him of his promise to live. Garrison saluted, eyes brimming with admiration. His father showed up, surrendering a begrudged smile full of sour pride.

"Encrypted communication continues between the four armadas and Vio's forces," the AI said. "Defense grids are active."

"Any complaints about our increasing velocity?"

"Receiving now."

Kor strapped himself to the command chair. "Play me 'Fire' and increase to jump velocity."

"The Commonweal DC has not authorized a change in our plotted vector."

"Maneuver into the fortress's shadow," Kor interrupted. The massive construction, showing off its might in the shape of two opposing mountains joined at the base, bristled with thousands of pinnacles, turrets, and spires. Redoubts, each one an armed-to-the-teeth fortification, dotted the surface to whither challengers to dust. Watchtowers, twisting columns loaded with sensors, saturated proximate space with surveillance. Light bathed the superstructure's awesome magnificence. Dreams of heroic deeds saturated his accelerating mind.

"Emissions from the fortress will blind ship sensors," the AI said.

"Who put you in charge?"

"Starry Empire safety procedures must be observed."

In a flourish, Kor's fingers tapped over an inset display on the chair's arm, flipped a compartment open, and pressed a button inside.

"Are you there?" Kor asked. Silence confirmed success. The AI was offline. The effectiveness of the simulator sessions at the Academy was about to be tested live.

Safe living is a slow death. To the driving beat of "Fire," the ship angled below the fortress. On approach, a group of nearby fighters fired warning shots across the bow. The fortress's scans disabled sensors. He was blind and reckless, and he had never been more alive. Painted Garden prayers had been answered in a way he had never expected. Belting out "Burn's" last line, he dipped the ship deeper into forbidden lanes. Near Pink Dream, the shuttle approached the landing platform.

Defense Command boomed ire over the intercom. "Return to your charted path or be destroyed."

In reply, Kor blasted the comm with music from the group Rush, "One Little Victory". He rocked the ship leeward toward a nearby war cruiser, spinning over the cruiser's topside, and arced back in free-fall descent, reaching jump velocity. Pressure rushed to his ears. Sensors cleared, showing a spray of missiles zeroing in for the kill.

He short-jumped blind. In a twist of time, *Star Horizon* hurtled away from the upper atmosphere on the other side of Vio. Alarms rang and buzzed. Switching channels, he found bandwidth broadcasting the proceedings in Vinculum. A Tellerian announced his delegation's vote. Wild commotion, cheering in any language, exploded. Victory? The ship vectored back toward the planet in a brutal arc.

***

An impenetrable lump hardened in Charronna's throat, stretching to her lungs with running amok anxiety. Stars whirled in the Vinculum's holographic sky. The agony of life and death was reduced to a political vote . . . her captors pulled her through a draw plate and would leave her a smear. Heated conversations swept through the hall like fire through the chaff. Lom's colors fragmented into broken kaleidoscopes. Uncertainty spread in airborne contagion, leaving few untouched.

A Tellerian rose. Quiet zones spread to the farthest reaches of the immense chamber. Iron bands wrapped around Charronna's strained lungs. She seized Sparrow's hand in a vice-like grip. Would they die? Would they live? Would it matter what the Tellerian said? Rulers, kings, premiers, presidents, high councils, the Chorus, the Commonweal Chair . . . they marketed the same drink with different flavored poisons. *I'll never survive the debriefing if I get home.*

After the tortured interlude, the male Tellerian spoke. The voting display adjusted its tally. Lom banged the staff three times. "The final vote reads two hundred and fifty-two for repeal, one hundred and six to retain, with thirty abstentions. The edict. . ." The Chair paused for several long seconds. Did he not believe his senses? Did he toy with her? Charronna's lungs stretched thin... Sparrow, nifty with numbers, grinned in triumph.

"The edict has been repealed."

We won? Celebrations accelerated into hyperdrive to challenge common sense. Sparrow vaulted, becoming part of the commotion. Something was *wrong*. Pro-edict delegations hurried in testy departures. On the floor, departing Qa assemblers rolled their habitats into boisterous Tynthions, forcing chaotic scrambles. So much for the Commonweal's vaunted harmony.

Sparrow, in cheerleader mode, jumped and whooped the excitement of victory. "Let's see my brothers top this. Never ever!"

A grove of towering Zev approached the dais; they blew bright, exultant notes. Underneath their swaying canopies, Taag leaped among dancing Shonalli, radiant Avue, and proud Cheemin in their swashbuckling couture. Some T'hyto spread their wings, taking flight. Celebrants dispersed throughout the Vinculum in the wake of the losing side's evacuation.

Charronna brushed away troubled feelings. Smiling Court machinations held no sway in the Commonweal assembly. They had won. Old patterns had a way of clinging to one's ego in needy desperation. Today was a day for something different. Sparrow wrapped her with a joyful hug. Charronna unclenched her toes and started to tap her heels.

"You need to stay like this," Sparrow said.

Charronna lifted Sparrow into a gleeful spin. With the princess at her side, they greeted streams of supporters. There must be gods. How else to explain such a magnificent ending? She weaved her way to Lom, who talked with a group of icy-faced Tellerians.

"Does this mean we're free to go?" Charronna asked.

Lopholea, female Tellerian Permanent Councilor, wore a superior expression with the ease of a pro. "By all means and good riddance. Thousands of enemy ships are eager to make your acquaintance."

Lopholea arched her neck. "Damn those Qa. Millennia of planning tossed away. The Qa orchestrated their defections to appease those T'hyto do-gooders. I'm sure of it."

"Are you telling me," Charronna said, "this place could be obliterated any second?"

"They wouldn't dare. Your ship is another matter."

The impenetrable lump in Charronna's throat returned with a vengeance.

***

Flying on instinct, Kor arced *Star Horizon* around in a trajectory to the planet. A gunboat-class vessel patrolling Vio's rear lines picked up the ship. It closed the gap. He didn't have velocity for another jump. The weight of human survival turned his blood into lead—or maybe that was the fear. The gunboat achieved weapons lock. *Star Horizon* burned into the atmosphere. The gunboat peeled away. Scans showed the all-clear. Communication networks unleashed heady electronic output, saturating the arrays. Snatches of a message said that they had won the peace. He rode a joyous, intoxicating flow, belting out Rush lyrics into the exosphere.

"Zaxa won't accept the outcome," Jeth-ka said.

"We won, old god. Do us both a favor and keep quiet. I've got a tune going."

From one of the Z'yax cruisers, a beam of plasma shot through the dark. The bolt stabbed into a converted merchant ship, splitting it in half. The galaxy rearranged itself into an altered reality. Blood rushed to his head to help him comprehend. *The Commonweal is hostage to something as small as a single act.* A scattered barrage of retaliatory turbo-blasts peppered the four armadas. The exchange of weapons spread. The heavens opened to war.

Microwave, laser, tachyon, and other wavelengths overloaded *Star Horizon's* externals in an invisible storm. When the static cleared, blips flashed onto the tactical display. Like an outgoing solar flare, the blips raced toward both the Vio defense fleet and the planet in layered waves stretched across oceans. Kor returned the ship to a steep decline.

He couldn't save the Blood King's followers. He couldn't save his comrades in a muddy war game trench. He couldn't save Noi. A virtuous soldier protects. More than cold, mechanical duty imprinted into his DNA by the Transgeneticists stoked his resolve. A woman and child, people he cared for, needed his help. Primitive urge, primitive need, electrified his every cell, his every neuron, to the pinpoints of his untamed maleness.

The blips were quantum singularity missiles. One hit would be devastating. A few dozen hits would doom life on the planet. The war between the gods had begun.

CHAPTER XXXV

A rotating image of Commander AnaGorias hovered in the Vinculum. Nothing about that reassured Charronna, and he lived up to her expectations.

"The Herexon Fleet has broken covenant. Long-range quantum singularity missiles and mass drivers target Vio. Level five and above personnel report to designated security zones."

Translation—planetary annihilation was imminent. Charronna checked to make sure Sparrow remained within reach. Stay close to the authorities, the influencers, the movers, and the shakers, and hope for an extraction. Sirens wailed. A gods-thumping concussion plastered Charronna to the floor. Teeth clenching, she swept away panic wild enough to slay giants. *Being a victim isn't in the playbook.*

AnaGorias' image started to pixelate. "Missile strikes sustained by Vio Prime defense shield. Planetary evacuation advised."

The Permanent Councilors winked out. The hall rumbled to its bones. Lom's skin color shouted. Fissures formed in the ceiling. Parts of the holographic sky broke off—a plummet of stars, of dark futures that smote many beings. Mobs jammed the exits. Others winked out in banks of transmats not visible before.

Charronna grabbed the Chair's arm, unfazed by its sandpaper roughness. "Do something."

Muffled booms preceded convulsion. The world wavered. Sparrow lost balance, pulling Charronna away from the Chair, away from hope for escape. The Nevran leader scrambled toward a cluster of transmats on the far side of the raised dais. More of the Vinculum sky fell, changing to chunks of metal as whatever illusory alchemy the aliens employed failed. Screams, blaring horns, angry bellows impaled. A crush of foreign scents pressed with the force of clamps.

Electric grid patterns flashed across the crumbling roof. A bungalow-sized hunk of infrastructure plummeted. Sizzling ruin crushed the Chair. A hysterical fit lurched up Charronna's throat. Greenish-red fluid leaked from the edges of the debris. She wiped the corpse splatter from her cheek.

Pointing for Sparrow's benefit, Charronna scrambled toward the highest-ranked person around—Councilor Lopholea. Every able-bodied lifeform headed to the glowing transmat circles. The princess showed spunk, leaping onto a transmat between Charronna and the Tellerian.

"Vio's defense shield weakens. Gaps form. Citizens unable to leave Vio should report to underground shelters." AnaGorias's image vanished.

Yellow light vaporized the ceiling and engulfed the hall. In a transfigured moment, Charronna was a golden ghost moving between dimensions. Hundreds of aliens, mirrors to her terror, struggled to evacuate. She reappeared on another transmat and fought back sobs. Muffled cries overtook Sparrow—a cry with the sound restrained by fear. Sometime later, Sparrow rubbed Charronna's hand—the small dose of human touch was an anchor to her sanity more satisfying than any P-Hyper had ever managed.

"The Tellerian went somewhere else," Sparrow said.

"Probably straight to a spaceship." The narrow tunnel could be anywhere on the planet under threat of imminent annihilation by unsympathetic alien war fleets. Sparrow, a conflicted optimism in her expectant gaze, squashed any thought of giving up.

"Let's get moving," Charronna said, "and see where that gets us."

***

Kor pushed awareness to its maximum. Debris clogged proximate space—an instant asteroid field with no more than intermittent sensor feeds from externals unable to cope with the barrage of dueling signals. The Vio fortress, guardian of civilization, gleamed. He steered into its technological shadow as a shield against the enemy. Blips representing missiles, warships, fighters, orbiting platforms, and other satellites crammed the flickering tactical display with too many ways to die. A *Rush* encore saluted his reckless endeavor.

Life was beyond crazy.

His attention split to mirror the fragments of his heart. Survive the battlefield, rescue his crewmates, and find a way back home— did the universe care? What about those he left behind, Wolf, his father, family and friends? What about sparkling visions of Chi side-by-side with the confident demand of Tara? His father, his clan, and his people required a new kind of leader. Sparrow depended upon him; Charronna wanted him. Were his thoughts nothing more than hubris to satisfy an unmet need? He would battle the gods, if necessary, to spread the wealth of happy endings.

Mountain-based arrays swept the heavens with giant lances to smite the incoming missiles. Civilian ships roared into the ocean sky in scrambled evacuation. Kor accelerated *Star Horizon* into a steep dive in the cracks of Vio's defenses. A wise man would accept his losses and survive. Switching to holographic controls, he ululated, his blood sang in tandem with *Rush*, and the planet rushed closer.

***

The tunnel pulsated in nerve-taxing electric pink. Charronna picked a direction and ran. Mists of pulverized stone swirled. Dust thickened into dense clouds. Rock particles enveloped, penetrating, irritating, micro-quartz blades cutting into lungs. She needed an oral hygienist to tackle the grit in her mouth. Sparrow dashed ahead, disappearing into the abrasive cloud. Blades flashed in nighttime heat, and the tunnel filled with debris. Instincts howled for retreat, but Charronna plunged into the morass. Blinded, her senses were useless. Except one. No longer disrupted, the continuum opened into an unhindered flow where the girl shined, a diamond on black velvet.

But Sparrow's inner fire diminished. The princess was dying.

Falling bits of rock battered. The planet thumped in opposition to her heartbeat. Acrid particles scraped soft tissues. Powdery sweat stung her eyes. Close, a flicker of energetic light—Charronna extended her arm to the half-buried princess. Grab hold, tug, pull, not too hard, try not to injure, be gradual, and remember to breathe.

With uncharacteristic patience, Charronna freed the girl. A sob burst into the open, but she swept away the emotion. Where to go? No power would deny her credit for a selfless act. Rubble piled high. Bloody hell.

On her knees, with Sparrow's head resting on her legs, she rolled into the princess's mind to coax her into consciousness. The tips of her fingers tingled upon the girl's dust-coated cheeks. Empathy, raw emotion, foreign and dangerous, descended. Desire for family, for love, blossomed, but she didn't sweep away its onslaught. Tunnel sediments clogged her throat, coming back out in hacks of dusty spittle. Sparrow coughed, spitting out slush. A few seconds of heaving and crying broke through Charronna's determined stoic armor. Death by planetary obliteration, falling rocks, by asphyxiation—let the wheel spin where it may.

Charronna stroked Sparrow's forehead. The planet thumping from whatever battle raged above receded into the distance. Rubble blocked the tunnel. There might be an open path behind them, or there might be angels. She'd settle for a map and a shower. Sparrow hacked with full body upheaval.

In front of the rockslide, a reddish whirlpool formed like the mouth of some nether pit. The Angel of Death emerged. Despite a lifetime of rejecting religious myths, she couldn't quite suppress the terror that her eternity was about to be decided by someone unsympathetic. The dust repelled from the figure, creating a horror-sim halo. Ensconced in the glow, a tall, pale alien dressed in a simple rosy gown bowed awkwardly.

"I am Nearcherlus, Intellectivus for the Vestrian Information Bureau."

"My stalker by another name."

"I have come to offer assistance in the coming war."

"Happy days. Can you get us out of here?"

"Theoretically."

"How about in reality?"

"Unfortunately, my vortex is illegal technology. Even now, with the world falling, monitors scan for its use. I must be mindful. Punishments are severe."

Nearcherlus stepped closer, bringing the dust-free zone with him. The superior-sounding alien deserved to be put down. The Vestrian held a field medical scanner, or something similar, and pressed it against Sparrow's temple. Charronna brushed the device away.

"Not without my say-so."

"The device won't always work on telepaths as intended," he explained.

"Work how?"

"A download of data your governments will find useful. Once certain conditions are met, the data becomes available."

Charronna ignored an expanding queasiness. "What conditions?"

"The right conditions. Consider this a tangible gesture of the Vestrian people's desire to see your species survive."

"Do you propose an alliance?"

Nearcherlus twirled his arms. "We must first learn simple arithmetic. You're a variable with potential."

"Go ahead, but so help me, I'll fry your mind if you hurt her."

Nearcherlus completed the download. Charronna second-guessed herself the entire time—a habit for the common folk.

"I advise leaving the planet." The Vestrian stepped back into the whirlpool. "It's about to be destroyed. Safe travels." He twirled his gangly arms and vanished.

A scream of "bloody hell" transitioned into a cough from her dust-coated throat.

Sparrow's eyes fluttered open.

"Good girl. Time to play a let's-get-the-hell-out-here game."

Breathable air collected near the tunnel's floor. Crawl and keep moving. Sparrow, ever the trooper, followed on her heels. One hand forward and repeat. Water splashed. With each crawl, the water rose higher. The cursed lottery decided it would be death by drowning.

"Sparrow, we need to run for it."

The young princess flashed a thumbs up.

Charronna spat muddy paste. They waded through a watery mess. The dust thinned; whoever built the ventilation system deserved a gold medal. The water level surged, reaching her waist and Sparrow's chest. The infernal tunnel sloped in the wrong direction. The girl stretched out her arms in swimming strokes. Smart move. Taking off her Pradas, Charronna joined her. The white glow of a transmat illuminated the water half a pool length away. By the time they got there, the water level topped her head. She paddled, clutching her shoes, trying to think as they floated up to the ceiling. Terror swelled, a monster with teeth and demented eyes eating her away from the inside. Something brushed her leg. She thrashed, knocking away the girl's foot.

Don't panic!

"Swim to the floor and grab something heavy like a rock," Charronna said. "Take it to the transmat and lock your feet on the rock." *And hope we go to a better place.* "One breath. Ready?"

"Roger Wilco."

Charronna gulped a lung full of air, let go of her beloved Pradas, and dove into the murky water. Feet planted on the shimmering underwater white circle with a foot and hand death grip on a chunk of tunnel rock, she counted on the transmat builders being as competent as the ones who did the ventilation.

Warm wind massaged her face. She coughed fumes. Not only were they somewhere else, but they also landed outside the half-ruined city. Sparrow gave her a soggy embrace. She could get addicted to hugs—wet, dry, hard, soft, the whole bit.

Lights flashed and fire painted the night sky. Plume flowers rooted in the planetary surface, smoky tombstones, multiplied. The transmats were on the edge of Pink Dream's landing platform, thank the stars. Aliens winked in, and they ran, galloped, scuttled, and flew to their craft, their fear brushfires in the continuum. Small ones fell, trampled in the stampede—some stopped to help, others kept going.

A gray, troll-like alien, *Me'luh*, brushed by, knocking her to the ground. Sparrow held out her hand. Denotations blossomed in effervescent bouquets. Scores of vessels lifted into the firing-squad war zone. No choice except to roll the same dice. Several dozen aliens of various species sprawled dead on the platform, a few of them clutching disruptors or blasters. With clinical determination, she wrenched a pair from the still-warm grasp of blue, alien fingers.

"Here you go." Charronna gave one to Sparrow. "Don't shoot unless you're sure."

Charronna hit full stride, on the lookout for sharp objects. Something slick threw off her balance. She slid along the smooth surface and plowed into a marvelous surprise—*Star Horizon's* shuttle. Sparrow skidded to a stop next to her. Huge fires floated through the sky. Short-lived mini-novae punctuated the night. Lasers swept the land. Pink Dream transformed into a smoking apocalypse. She and Sparrow scrambled into their only hope of ever returning home.

"Strap in," Charronna said. She added a quick prayer that Kor waited for them in the burning sky.

"He won't leave us," Sparrow said.

Charronna unlocked the command display and waved a hand over the power control. The energy readings didn't move.

"What's wrong?" Sparrow said.

"Bad Karma."

"Why aren't we moving?"

"The AI pilot is down and I don't know how to get this bird flying. I'm sending a distress signal to Kor. How about one of your prayers?"

The rain of fire moved closer in a full mind-blowing view from the shuttle's forward window. *Damn it, Kor, you better come.*

***

Kor landed *Star Horizon* on Pink Dream's landing port near a transport engulfed in flame. The platform burned and smoldered with the broken remnants of once space-worthy ships. Smoke and fire inundated the jungle. The feet of giants had smashed Pink Dream. Fighters swarmed in dogfights. Energy balls crisscrossed the heavens in a technicolored death blizzard.

Near the base of *Horizon's* ramp, a pair of charred bodies stopped him cold—an adult and a child. Kor sank to his knees, into ready-to-cook heat. Smoke dispersed in the wind, opening the night to diffused glare. Novae great and small bloomed across the sky, washing out the stars. *To live is to fight is to die.* Death stalked. Hope faded into recriminating shouts of too late . . .

"Get up herd-puncher, we're not dead yet," Charronna yelled.

Kor leaped to his feet. Charronna charged between burning hulks in a heroic, battle-tested war-survivor stride. She jumped on Kor, smacking the hunky barbarian with a wet, gritty kiss. "Hello, sweetie pie."

The most stunning green eyes in the galaxy sparkled; wisps of soaked red hair matted over cheeks were more beautiful than sunset after a storm. "Hello, my soggy dust-bunny."

Charronna kissed him again before falling off. "I think you like me."

Sparrow, carrying a disruptor, waved it at Kor, who challenged Charronna with raised eyebrows.

"She practiced. Remember?"

He smiled at Sparrow, lifting her high. "Another soggy dust-bunny."

The girl squealed with delight. Kor relieved her of the gun and swung her to the ground in the direction of the ship. With Charronna at his side, he dashed inside and took *Star Horizon* up. Other vessels did the same, preferring the hell above to the hell below.

"You're piloting," Charronna said. "Why are you piloting?"

"The AI and I had a disagreement." Kor put on his battle visor. "Strap in."

Liftoff took them straight into heavy turbulence. Sensor bombardments continued to blot out *Star Horizon's* modest capabilities. Kor locked his hands onto the nav system's neural interface; his sense of self magnified to include the ship. In his mind's eye, he rode bareback on the hull. Most humans couldn't handle it without drugs for nausea and anxiety. But Militants weren't like most people.

"Rough ride," Charronna said, her voice slightly flirtatious. "Not that I'm complaining."

Kor concentrated. Weapons discharge around the ship intensified— space transmuted into an exploding minefield. Debris fields expanded. Calculate. Navigate. Respond faster. He needed the AI; he needed bigger guns. *Star Horizon* broke free of the atmosphere underneath an orbital platform firing sprays of missiles. Fighters multiplied in quantum physics gone mad. Swarms of fighters headed toward a distant orb, a small moon, which attracted ships with the pull of a giant magnet. Geometry in motion. By luck, he flew into a less congested zone. External sensors popped back online. Nine blips surrounding a larger one showed up on short-range. Grimacing, he dropped out of the neural link. The switch from the heady force of unfiltered creation to *Star Horizon's* alloyed innards left him muddled.

Cool, strong hands massaged his shoulders.

"We're hot," Kor said. "I told you to strap in."

"Too nervous. Enjoy the massage."

Star Horizon lifted above the planet's ecliptic plane. The other ships matched, closing. The girl inhaled in rapid tempo—scary music. Fuel ceased to be a resource to conserve. Kor maximized thrust in a sustained burst. Fifteen degrees off the bow, a burning warship plowed into another. "Shock wave," he warned.

Star Horizon spun. Internal lighting flickered. The ship groaned. Hyper-fiber reinforcements buckled but didn't break. Kor stabilized the vessel. An enemy squadron zeroed in. None of the plotted escape vectors showed green. Charronna kept her hands on his shoulders, a pure blessing—every slight adjustment, every nuance, a sensation to savor.

"I *do* like you," Kor said.

Bursts of static overpowered her response.

A friendly furry face filled the viewscreen.

"Captain Mestjet!" Kor beamed. "Glad to see you, but this isn't a fight for merchants."

"Kin Neretu has been tamed for too long." The feline bared her fangs.

"Merchant transports won't win the day. We've got warships on our tail."

"I've brought friends. Ten to one, my friend, and DC outfitted us with upgrades. In this fight, no one worthwhile cowers."

"I've enough blood to account for."

"Learn to count higher. We're coming in."

The Cheemin's ragtag flotilla parted to allow *Star Horizon* through. The mass of converging blips scrambled into a dueling bloodbath. One by one, dots of light winked off the short-range scan. Kor raised Mestjet's ship. Runny violet streamed from a gash across the captain's forehead.

"Break off," urged Kor.

"Remember the pride of the Neretu."

An explosion threw Mestjet off her chair. The screen went blank.

An active blip on the tactical view wheeled toward Mestjet's drifting ship. Kor changed course to intercept the attacking vessel. *Honor before life*. Voices burst into his head, shouting the names of people he would not save if he didn't survive this fight.

"Are you insane?" Charronna said.

"Aye. Who isn't?"

Kor launched a round of boson torpedoes at the enemy ship's backside and veered away. The enhanced weapons impacted near the other vessel's engines, blowing through weakened shields. A mighty bird with a muscular double wing-back hull eclipsed the glare of battle. It glided in and headed straight for Mestjet's transport. *Star Horizon* measured no more than a gnat against its immensity. Data overloaded his retinal higher function display.

"Mestjet," he barked. "Do you read? Badass hostile approaching."

C-Glenmarra appeared on the screen, no longer gentle, her face and eyes forged from molten steel resolve. Kor was in love.

"I am taking the Neretu into our protection."

C-Glenmarra's commanding presence rendered Kor speechless. Mighty ships didn't jibe with his image of the peace-loving Avue. As if reading his mind, C-Glenmarra continued.

"Our ship has limited offensive capabilities. But our shields are superior and our speed is fast. Do not worry about us or Neretu. What is a bad ass?"

"Another time, and thank you, friend."

A spread of vortices opened. Several dozen warships winked in. Kor maneuvered behind them. Other ships joined the convoy headed to reinforce the fortress.

"I'm not a tactician," Charronna said, "but shouldn't we head away from the battle?"

"Something's happening to the fortress," Sparrow said.

"Scans intermittent," Kor said. A spreading shadow blotted the Vio's mighty protector. "Infantry—tens of millions."

"Along with as many mini probes keeping track of contested space," Charronna added, "and every particle in it."

Laser beams and photon fire spewed from the fortress. Power waves from weapons that sensors failed to identify swept through the attackers, clearing huge swaths of space. Newcomers filled in the gaps. Some of them latched onto the fortress's exterior. Protected by super cruisers, enemy carriers advanced, dumping their troops closer to their target.

"Break away," Charronna said.

"On the itinerary."

"We're still headed toward the fortress."

"Working on it."

"How long does it take to change course?"

"Do you want to drive?"

Kor piloted to the edge of the fleet. The incoming armada collapsed its flanks to envelop the fortress. The fortress ejected a torrent of energy discharges that ravaged the attackers. Committed, unable to escape, they pressed ahead in a suicide mission against their primary target.

A flotilla of flowing, intricate vessels appeared near one of Vio's small moons. No two were alike. One was like a stretched snowflake, another like a floating abstract tree, another like a series of waves in motion, and every one of them sprouted solar sails. Artistic. They came to the wrong party.

Kor split the screen into dual views. The fortress rotated off-center. Liquid and atmosphere spewed from the wounded beast. It drifted toward the planet, a falling star of doomsday.

"The gods play rough," Kor said.

"Normally a good thing." Charronna blushed.

The artistic ships retracted their sails, picking up speed.

Arn, green and beautiful, appeared onscreen with twitching ears and wild eyes.

"Happy to see you," Kor said. "But you're flying art pieces."

"We're not here to fight but to warn that another Herexon fleet is coming," Arn said. "The interdiction network is offline. The fortress—"

"Controlled it," finished Kor.

He split the viewer to show the forward view. Jump apertures formed, gateways of light too many to count. The heavens opened to vomit forth calamity. Enemy warships, from immense to mini drone-fighters, came through in a titanic surge. His mind divided into modules as he analyzed the situation. A vision of the Crimson Circus wolf passed through; its determined dark eyes heated with the desire to survive.

Arn twittered, oscillating from high pitch to low, a choppy, nervous range of octaves. "Herexon ships, powerful, Z'yax and Qa,

Mo'sari, Me'luh—some Vorgoth, Buri and Etamites join them, more than expected."

"Do something," Charronna said.

"On it," Kor said. "Arn, are you able to form a jump point? We don't have the speed."

"Yes, but you must enter the front of the wormhole. Your trajectory takes you beyond the gravity well."

"Adjust course thirty degrees. We'll meet at an angle. Agreed?"

"I think, yes," Arn said.

"Turn the AI on," Charronna said.

"It would have to recalibrate," Kor said.

"What? Five whole seconds?"

The fresh onslaught of warships advanced. Charronna threw up her arms and wrapped them around his waist from behind. Tactical fields shrunk. Another pair of hands wrapped around Kor's torso. Charronna hugged Kor, and Sparrow did the same. The titanic wave of enemy ships charged closer—his attention strained in pursuit of a strategy. The fierce wolf eyes nestled in his heart gleamed, attempting to give a message he didn't understand. A flat-topped battleship with giant pincers running underneath took aim at *Star Horizon*.

"Death is coming straight at us," Charronna said.

"That's it." Kor addressed Arn, "Come straight at us."

"Please say again."

"Lock tractor beams and drag us along. Copy?"

Space noise crackled.

"We're being jammed," Kor said.

"Did he understand?" Charronna asked.

"Best you strap in. A rough ride ahead."

The Sy'tallians maintained their heading; Kor altered his vector to cross paths with the flotilla. Dozens of incoming war cruisers and scores of fighters converged. Not one to cower, Charronna secured herself and gave an air kiss.

"Tractor beam in thirty seconds."

Charronna squeezed Kor's arm.

"In four, three, two, one. . ."

Star Horizon passed under the belly of Arn's how-did-it-fly stretched snowflake. The oncoming enemy fleet, immense and beautiful, dominated space beyond. Arn's ship emitted a tractor beam. *Star Horizon's* stressed structure shuddered, synth-metal ground on hyper-fiber. The engines' output wavered in a fit of hiccups.

The beam slipped off. Arn's vessel continued to open a jump point. Super-heavy red lasers sliced Sy'tallian ships into pieces. With every blink, another one disappeared. Escape pods jettisoned, shooting toward *Star Horizon*. Single-engine fighters zoomed in with a pair of small-scale fusion cannons at the ready on either side of the cockpit and four laser modules on wicked-angled wings. Kor reduced velocity and opened the hangar to any who might survive the massacre. In rapid succession, hundreds of pods vaporized.

"One made it onboard," Charronna said.

A black and silver attack cruiser backlit in dark green, a titanic winged insect, locked weapons. Kor's heart pounded into his head, rattling the shell on his chest. *Where law-abiding Z'yax tread or fly, you will be protected.* He ripped the talisman off and put it on a console panel. The wolf-dream howled approval. A shaft of light engulfed the artifact.

"What are you doing?" Charronna asked.

"Scanning for codes, numbers, geometries, the ass-saving magic word."

Star Horizon bounced; muscle strained against the straining straps. Kor glimpsed why Baps felt fully alive on his Brigade rotation. Militants were made to fight, to be complete in blood and battle; to die for duty was sweet, to gain victory sweeter.

A tractor beam grabbed hold and dragged them toward the maw of the Z'yax warship. In *Horizon's* structural core, gravity-compressed synth-metal shifted into a deep undulation of despair. He willed the piece of green shell on the table to yield its secrets. The light on the artifact vanished. Biological representations flashed.

"Signal away."

"What signal?" asked Charronna. "Dammit, Kor..."

He checked tactical. The tractor beam continued to pull them in.

"Start the self-destruct," Charronna said.

"Believe," Kor said.

"Believe what?"

Another Z'yax attack cruiser unleashed a laser lightning storm on the vessel pulling them in. Other warships added to the counterattack. *Star Horizon* broke free. A cohort of Z'yax behemoths slugged it out. Kor turned the ship back on track toward a lone Sy'tallian survivor. "Sy'tallians have entered the aperture. Jump point in ten seconds. Vortex unstable."

An explosion rocked *Star Horizon*, blowing out the instrument panels.

"Five."

Another blast hit the ship.

"Entering aperture. Vortex collapsing."

Wild current crisscrossed the holographic displays. Kor passed into bright light . . . Zornian Paradise, Heaven . . . or something he'd never imagined. He prayed. If nothing else, he had done his best.

CHAPTER XXXVI

The warmongers will dominate the peacemakers. Those who have will take from those who have not. The fear of death will outweigh the love of life. These and other signs will light the last days.

Sacred Teachings, Harmonist Way

"I'd forgotten what it was like to be alive." Sala hovered in a reflective pose over a bed of blue flowers in a modest dress colored of gray hair and smelling of morning rain.

"I don't understand," Jeth said.

"Frailty. Hope. Desperation. I've seen your unstable emotions battle for supremacy. For the first time since my separation from Zaxa, I experienced them in me."

Jeth gathered his awareness to soak in her glory. "I need you to be strong," Jeth said.

"*You* need?" Sala asked. "What about what I need?"

Sala's pale cheeks trembled. Was she about to cry? Astonished, Jeth shifted into his human form and gave her a gentle head massage. After a while, he spoke in his most studious tone. "I've got an idea."

"Don't tease."

"Sparrow's mental instability increased after Noi's death. She's vulnerable to a transference."

"Kor grows stronger. Your spark diminishes. This Cosmic Song supports your distant connections; limitations block any hope for success."

"Precisely why I need to take the opportunity."

Sala brushed her lips across Jeth's. "Choose your time with care, a moment without too much turbulence. We have no more second chances."

***

Aromatic color swirled. Kor inhaled. Blush-berry blossoms, the start of spring, intermingled with heady rose. He chased after a stream of yellow. The ground hardened. Hands and feet tingled, growing cold. Leafless trees took on the shape of Halloween frights.

A bright vortex churned. Kor straightened his shoulders and walked toward the light. *We all must answer for our lives.* At the vortex's rim, the roaring surf of ocean washed into his senses . . . the banging of drums . . . the whistle of helium . . . magnetized gas screeched. Electric fingers reached for him, wrapped around him, pulling him back. His heart raced. Dying should be calmer.

He stepped into the spinning light.

The vortex spilled into a red pall. Shapes emerged. Quarter-moon console, chairs, motionless bodies . . . the bridge. Metallic-laced smoke burned his lungs. Weakness pursued his resolve. Spats of coughing drained his strength as he carried Sparrow and then Charronna off the bridge. Colors and images rushed through his head, whirling blades. Kor needed something. What did he need?

He reactivated the AI. "Report."

"System rebooted," the AI said. "Emergency protocols in place. Proceed to stasis. Environmental conditions fall below minimum parameters."

Kor carried his companions to the stasis beds. At the last minute, he remembered the escape pod where he found two survivors, Arn and Ly', unconscious but alive. Tears welled. Renewed energy infused his legs as he carried the Sy'tallians. He closed the lids over his new friends; subdued green illumination indicated that they and his shipmates lived. Another hacking fit proved he too survived. Wisps of toxic smoke trailed into the room. He climbed into one of the beds. There was no choice but to surrender his fate to the cold calculations of the AI.

The lid shut. The descent began into suspended animation. Far-off whispers, the moans of the old god, crowded the edge of thought. He brushed the distractions aside and gave himself over to total surrender.

***

She almost had the Cosmic Song. When the E'lani-humans, on the brink of capture, broadcast Queen Gunaseak's protection signet, "almost" had left her emptyhanded.

The thought repeated in remorseless self-torture, burrowing into reservoirs of anger Zaxa believed long ago depleted. In a wild craze, she summoned dozens of HoZo, butchering them until the heavy death haze bothered her more than the anger. Meaningless violence, yet for a moment it soothed the rage of her mind, and her uulli shifted to haunting shades of dark cyan, purples and royal blues.

HoZo initiators gathered. They danced, sang, painted the rocks, and performed meaningful movements of memory and possibility. Inspired by the performance art, she visited a place of ancient history, the Pantheon of Days. The temple's circle of human observers heaped scorn, judged, mocked, pleaded—likely prayed for their final death. The men and women took on the shape of wood, metal, stone, and more, but in truth, crystal inhabited the forms and housed millions of inert Avue consciousnesses. Existence continued at the boundary between life and death where they suffered in limbo—delightful justice for their many crimes.

History's flow changed because of the Pantheon—the place that inspired Jeth to create his precious Cosmic Song. Here she would ascend with the remnant of the Lords and Ladies watching on until she was tired of them and obliterated the crystal circuitry holding their inert minds and digitized DNA.

The E'lani ship was a speck in blowing wind with no more than her Battle of Vio battered fleet to find them. Death's perfume spread—a pestilence in search of life to consume. The Forum, the gathering of White Mothers, demanded ships to protect their worlds. Zaxa, though the oldest of all White Mothers, had to obey or risk their combined wrath. The later generations, those not born human, harbored distrust for those who were.

Throughout the Commonweal, terror took root in the soil, in the sky, in space, and in the minds of many, and it grew in ways impossible to predict. Most living beings would do anything to alleviate fear. Zaxa hummed. There was a way... a path where terror attracted weakness of mind ripened for a bitter harvest.

Sensing the uplift of emotion, some of her children sang. Others danced, unwinding energy shaped into heat. The woman, Charronna Ny', *knew* her. They shared an understanding about men, about life. Something awakened within Zaxa, cracking into untrodden domains. *I want her. I want to share my destiny. She must come to me willingly. And she will.*

The encounter with Charronna was enough to encapsulate her vital essence. A cruel creature, absorbed with her fate, lonely, nurturing soft centers, clinging to toughness, wanting to be loved in the darkest corners of her being. They were both monsters. They both knew it.

Zaxa opened into an unexpected flow. According to Charronna, they sought E'lan, a world the Kimbrians destroyed during the Virtuous War. The dancers glided over the floor. Some of them took flight, adding dimension, their cries louder, their ecstasy higher. *We will love each other, Charronna Ny'. We will capture the joy hoarded by the heavens. We will rule the cosmos together through the end of time.*

Zaxa's intention exploded through her HoZo. Servants lay sprawled across the floor, scores of them dead and others unconscious. Zaxa pondered the beauty of transitory art. She had many plans to balance and to consider—creation, revenge, satisfaction, essential elements, and the supposedly destroyed capital world of the E'lani Empire.

***

Kor opened his eyes, taking stock of the status of his existence.

The reassuring voice of the AI filled the stasis chamber. "*Star Horizon* approaches New Britannia of the Earth Confederation."

"What happened to E'lan?"

"The ship suffered material damage during the Battle of Vio. Safety protocols required returning to the nearest Confederation colony with a suitable shipyard for repairs. Life-sustaining environmental conditions are maintainable for a maximum of ten hours."

After injecting a dose of stim, Kor rolled out of the stasis bed; his head throbbed into multiple dimensions, his breath stale, but small complaints. *We're home.* Startled, he realized how much more expansive his definition of home had become. He grazed his fingers over the ship's interior hyper-fiber skin.

"You served us well." He kissed the hard surface.

To the whir of machines and the blinking bright of electronics, Charronna's and Sparrow's beds slid out from the wall. The lids popped open with a whoosh and a puff of greenish cloud. Kor injected his companions with a recovery serum and hustled them to the bridge, giving an update along the way. They smelled of Vio dust and their hair was tangled from the swim to the transmat. He presented a full pot of coffee.

"Thank the shining stars," Charronna said.

Kor sat a cup in front of her, brushing his scruffy chin over her shoulder, making contact with her hypnotizing emerald spell-casters. "Becoming religious, are we?" Kor said in her ear. He slid into the next chair—and savored the black brew sweetened with victory, with accomplishment, with life yet to live.

Charronna's lips puckered in an air kiss. "I'll show you the real meaning of life anytime."

"It's a date."

"Do you plan on waking our Sy'tallian guests?"

"Under consideration. Raven stays put for as long as possible."

"Let's take an inventory first, shall we?" Charronna held up a finger. "We've started a galactic war." She held up another. "About a third of the Milky Way races want us exterminated." Another. "We lost Noi. You knocked out a war-star. You started a civil war on Zorn." She closed the other hand into a fist with the index finger raised. "You have one of the Polarian Emperor's Chosen locked up in stasis. You kidnapped a Starry Empire agent (that would be me). You stole this drop ship. And you wrecked it. Did I miss anything? I've got one finger left."

"I've got the perfect place to put it," Kor said. "I also have a list." He raised a finger. "You helped murder millions of my people. You killed my father's partner. You held Noi's family hostage to force him to act against his creed. You—"

"Stop it," Sparrow said. "You both know you love each other. Ya'll make bedroom eyes more than my parents ever did, and I've got seven brothers."

Kor's face reddened. Charronna flushed seductive rose, a bloom of innocence that somehow survived years of mindless sex. He leaned over and kissed a bit of her Vio grime. "Busted."

Traffic control hailed them. A local warship swung into view, firm yet polite; the captain demanded the passenger list, cargo, and itinerary.

"I am Kor of Steel Rose. We carry no cargo." He went on to list the passengers.

"Baxter as in the Baxters of Hermes?" the captain asked.

"Aye."

"She's been missing for eight years."

"I assure you, she's right by my side."

"State origination point and destination."

"We came from across the Deep Black," Kor said. "Our destination is home."

"No one has crossed the DB and returned."

"Until now."

"You better be straight. I'm allowing your ship to dock at the Flying Drake."

"Roger that," said a com-tech from the Flying Drake. "Prepare to surrender navigation to traffic control."

"It's good to be back," Kor said.

***

Kor took a sponge bath, used the leftovers for a clean shave, and finished off with a haircut, showing up at the exit ramp ready to face whatever awaited them. In the best mood of his life, he reconsidered his decision to leave Raven in stasis. He woke up the Polarian and gave him a shot of stim.

"We're back home," Kor said. What kind of home, given the passage of years, remained to be discovered.

Raven perked up. "Surprised you woke me up."

"So am I," Kor said. "You tried to murder me and, by extension, Sparrow and Charronna."

Raven nodded. "You surprise me, Militant."

"Sometimes forgiveness can't be earned but should be given. A gesture for all of us that can't earn our forgiveness no matter how hard we try."

"I can't believe we made it back. I underestimated you. The emperor remains in your debt."

Conviction of a better future infused Kor with relaxed energy, a boost to his good mood. "Get yourself presentable. We are due for a meet and greet with Confed locals."

Kor hightailed it back to the docking port exit. Charronna had transformed into her self-assured beautiful persona with every red hair in place, looking smart in a fresh imperial-blue uniform. Sparrow, sporting an eager grin, wore C-Glenmarra's gift, a flowing outfit. Shoulders less slouchy, jawline more determined, Sparrow bubbled with confidence. Arn and Ly' presented themselves in official attire, brown cloaks clasped by silver pendants, green pants, and long-sleeved shirts.

Kor grabbed his crewmates in a group hug. The press of warmth upon his fingers worked its way through him. Soon, Charronna would return to the Chorus and Sparrow to her duties as a princess to one of the Confederation's most powerful families. Everyone would want a piece of the Sy'tallians. Kor pressed harder, wanting to brand the moment into memory.

"Let's go away to one of the Confederation's settled worlds," Charronna said, "New Eden's virgin forests, abundant game, and plentiful waterways make for a perfect place for a remote log cabin. After a suitable time, if that ever comes, we move into one of New Eden's metropolises."

Charronna nuzzled his neck. Was she what he wanted in his future forever? Whatever the degenerative state of the bioengineering in his genetic line, he was still a Militant, and he had not lost any of his desire for the men of Zorn.

"I have no problems sharing," Charronna said. "You are more than capable."

Kor quieted his mind, shifting into a meditation open to possibility. Sparrow held his hand. The world blurred. Voices shouted through the neural network depths. Blue tornadoes spun in his mind. He broke away, gulping hard. Charronna's eyes shimmered with concern. Kor pulled out the Avue talisman. The measure of its shadow diminished. Whatever had happened, it was agreeable, at least to the Avue's magic.

"Jeth's presence no longer burns."

Charronna swept Kor with a psychic probe. "You're right. Of course, to officially pronounce you free of possession, I would need to conduct a thorough scan."

"Another time. Our hosts may be getting impatient."

"I'm waiting for my answer."

"I must stand before the clans and be held to account for my actions. Ask me about the house in the woods another time."

"I love you. Remember that."

Kor brushed his lips against hers, letting go, driving his tongue into her mouth, their bodies one. She opened wider, and he stretched his darting member to the experiential infinite. "Remember *that*," he said in response.

Sparrow's eyes searched the floor. "Make sure whoever you talk to realizes most of the aliens are totally awesome like Arn and Ly'. Tell them about Bubbles, the Coming Together, and Green Shells. Tell them about the amazing talking trees."

"Do you think your people will harm us?" Arn asked.

"Unsure. Two rules—smile a lot and make no sudden moves."

Raven arrived, a bit bedraggled, but with a weary grin. Kor took a deep breath and opened the outer door. In the pit of his gut, he feared he had taken the Khonsu's path. With the threat of a galactic war waged against human civilization, the Red Beast must be salivating.

Kor's eyes shifted to his impossible love. A Militant truism echoed. *Safe living is a slow death*. Charronna would be anything but safe.

Dressed in his skin-tight black outfit, Kor descended the ramp with Charronna and Sparrow on one side, Arn and Ly' on the other, with Raven trailing behind. A station security detail closed around them. *To see is death.* Death was the price to truly see. And Kor wanted to see . . . wanted everyone to see. Arn and Ly's very presence would help.

"The Flying Drake erupts with pandemonium," the guard in charge said. "I'm Donald. Love the forehead brand."

"You're an unusual group," Donald said. "Never seen aliens. Never seen anyone from the League. Never seen a Militant."

"Strength through diversity."

"On this world, it's through common cause." Donald winked. "You're a big hit and the hour's headline. Your green friends are driving people nuts. Hell, you might last a full cycle. The stationmaster wants me to take you through the promenade to satisfy the crowds."

"Let's celebrate," Charronna said. "You like Earth music. Anything come to mind?"

A ballad of victory to commemorate their quest, but also sad to acknowledge the cost. "Donald, I have a song request."

"You name it."

"*Paths of Victory*, the Cat Power version."

"Never heard of it," Donald said, but as they boarded a mag-tube, the soulful lyrics filled the cabin in a bursting union of joy and sorrow.

In a long park with trees flanking a manicured carpet of green, the ground vibrated. Men, women, and children dressed in shocks of wild colors waved their arms and cheered. Some were physically present—others were holographic avatars. Vampires, Nymphs, Elves, Romulans, and Goblins cheered alongside standard human fare, some with fanciful skin hues. The crazy mix was as alien as the Vinculum throngs.

Station security created a people-free zone down the center. Kor, Sparrow, and Charronna waved, and the crowd roared. Hundreds of light-crackers exploded throughout the park in thunderclaps of color. Dizzying numbers of recording devices captured every detail. In some strange custom, many onlookers were themselves the object of adoration.

Wonder saturated the senses. Gas balls bounced from one side of the park to the other. A glittering magical confetti rain blended into a hail of shooting Roman light candles where he imagined Noi's spirit roamed to celebrate Charronna's promise to free his wife and children. The scent of roses thickened. Excitement electrified the saliva in his mouth. Sparrow grinned the biggest delighted grin he'd ever seen. Raven waved with delight.

"What will you do once the party ends?" Charronna asked. "Many on Zorn won't welcome you back despite our epic adventure."

"Play a flute to honor Jude. Dive off Suicide Ledge to honor a bargain—jump into a freaking-cold ice hole."

"Sure we can't run away together?" Charronna said. "Touch the sky, visit heaven, swing by hell, and swim the stars? I promise you, I'm anything but boring."

Fragile hope glimmered in her emerald eyes, a siren song draining Kor's resolve. He rubbed his new stone charm plucked from the waters of Vio.

"Another day. I swear. Older promises call my name."

"I don't even warrant a flip of your Vio charm?"

"My heart knows." Kor squeezed Charronna's hand. "Besides, it's smooth on both sides. The Vio stone must be for some other use."

"You're not the militant you were created to be, but you are a warrior. Trust in your inner power. The Starfall Probability is in motion. There will be consequences."

"I'm ready to claim them."

"Not just you."

Kor sank into the dark space where Jude and the other trainees lurked in a gray, bloody mess. They stared, flickers of hope, but they wanted more to forgive. He had not yet earned their forgiveness. Did he still need to?

"Aye. What about you? You are no longer a creature of the Smiling Court."

"First, a good detox. Second, make my report. I'm working on the you-have-done-your-damage spin. My role as savior of the Starry Empire kicks off. We'll see how that goes. Remove the death warrant, if I'm able, on Noi's family. With luck, we'll find each other again."

"And fly off into the sunset."

Charronna smiled. "Let's do it now. Just in case."

She slid into his thoughts much like he envisioned sliding into her. Together, holding hands, they soared with feathered wings over a white beach, racing after orange blaze sinking into the horizon. The sun's warmth caressed. The wind's flow uplifted. He tightened his grip, both in the Real and in the dream, and wondered if they ever caught the sun, would they burn or would they capture the love of life?

Arn and Ly' waved to the cheering crowds. Raven held his arms high in victory. Exotic colors from lights and gas balls continued to burst throughout the promenade to mesmerize the most jaded soul. Sparrow beamed with glee. The song of *Human* played in his head where he hugged his lost friends, Jude, Creo, and Noi foremost among them, where no price had to be paid for wanting to be one's true self. No moment in his life had satisfied him as much.

"We're glad to be home!" Sparrow shouted at the top of her lungs.

Kor grinned, staring into the sunset dream, and waved to the crowd's resounding roar. For better or for worse, they had indeed come home.

When the Maker came to behold Her work, She saw all living things standing against one another in conflict unending. And She turned away in shame, for it was of Her Image. Sacred Teachings, Harmonist Way

—THE END—

AUTHOR'S NOTE

I started writing within a crucible of emotional darkness. I was wounded but had no understanding of how to heal. I was gay but had to reject myself to be loved by God, family, and friends. Trapped within my mind, I prayed with all that I could grasp, and an answer came: go, get up, and write. And so, I did. Lacking any knowledge of the craft, I handwrote an absolute travesty in world-building, characters, and plot. Faith in the journey kept me going. The years rolled by, and I attended workshops, read books on writing, partnered with editors to understand my weaknesses, and embarked on a discovery of who I was apart from the shadows.

Eventually, I figured out what I was trying to write about. The story in my heart that wanted voice is that *I am okay*. Human imperatives seem driven to break us apart, and in our divisions, the judgments flow. But whatever I am, I am ok, you are ok, but for those of us who forget that truth, or have it taken from us, it becomes a journey, a quest to reclaim it.

I chose to create a non-Earth culture as I wanted to tell the story without the burden of too many familiar labels. I'm happy with the result, and I hope you, the reader, are as well.

Special thanks to my departed husband, Tony Pryor, who sat with me on too-many-to-count nights to provide his honest, often difficult to hear, reactions and comments. The AutoCrit platform has been a crucial editing tool. AutoCrit editors have been part of the team in my learning process. As I struggled to get a grasp on the craft of writing, Donald Maass was my primary teacher, and it was at one of his workshops that the first light bulb ignited. My writing journey had begun in earnest.

The shadow of attachment, of wanting a specific outcome in releasing this to the world, the fear of rejection, and the shame of misspent time, worked against the risk of self-publishing. But in the end, we are not our outcomes--- we are the sum of our journeys. Why else are we here but to dream and to try?

If you enjoyed this book, or even if you didn't, please take a few moments to write a review of it. Thank you!